MW01094729

This novel is a work of fiction based on ancient fact.

For Mam and Dad

In front of the truth hangs a curtain of lies.

Will you dare lift it, and put back the ties?

The Nephilim, The Knights Templar,

And The Secrets They Held Together.

The

Wisdom

of

Secrets

A.M.I. Noone

Chapter 1

Marcus fell to his knees and gazed at the archangel and the hourglass carved into the face of the gravestone. Symbols of his brotherhood were all around him – the archangel, their symbol for immortality and the hourglass, their symbol for the passing of time. But for Marcus right now, immortality was far beyond his grasp and his time was running out. He knew he would die within minutes and that no one could reach him in time to save him.

He looked down at his blood-drenched white cotton shirt. There was a relentless throbbing sensation where a dagger had been thrust into his abdomen. He pushed hard against the wound to stem the bleeding. The increased pressure caused a sharp pain to sear his body and warm blood seeped through his fingers.

He exhaled deeply and looked in the direction of the thirteenth-century stone church that stood beyond the graveyard. He knew his enemy lurked within the devastated remnants of the arched stone walls, preparing for his final assault on him. Instinctively Marcus wanted to run for cover, but a fear more profound than facing his demise embraced him. A fear that the sacred ancient artefact his family had kept safe for almost one thousand years would be lost or fall into the wrong hands.

He paused and gathered his thoughts. He held the top of the gravestone to support his shattered body and bent forward. He moved a small section of the frost-covered grass at the base of the gravestone and uncovered a space in its centre. He took a small, black cylindrical object, three inches in length and one inch in diameter, from his inside jacket pocket and placed it in the hole he had just created. He replaced the grass neatly over the cylinder to hide it from prying eyes. Once it was hidden he stood and glanced at his hands. The light from the full moon turned the blood on his hands a black colour. It reminded him of the sacrifices that he and his predecessors had made before they'd come to this sacred place. And of the sacrifices his successors would need to make.

Stay focused, Marcus, and send the message, he thought.

He glanced from side to side, scanning the area around the church.

The coast was clear.

He swayed through the grass, making his way to a tree at the edge of the graveyard. He faced the church once again where his attacker had inflicted the fatal wound. There was nothing only the sound of his heartbeat intertwined with each breath he took. He stood still for a moment, then reached into his jacket pocket once again. This time he removed his mobile. He placed his thumb on the bottom right-hand corner and the small screen came to life. He opened the message he had prepared earlier and read it one last time.

The time has come.

Marcus scanned the area around him. His tormentor was still nowhere to be seen. He pressed the send icon. His thoughts changed for a moment to his family – his son, Peter, his daughter, Ava, and his wife, Sophia. He knew he'd never see them again.

Marcus was a wealthy, successful geneticist who had dedicated most of his adult life to teaching and research.

Nevertheless, his family's ancient legacy provided him with a greater purpose in life. On the day he'd become, like his father before him, an affiliate of an Order that had for centuries intentionally banished its existence into the pages of history and legend, he'd also inherited his family's enormous wealth. But it had come at a price. Secrecy was pertinent to the Order's survival and he had made an oath to protect those secrets with his life. Yet even at sixty-five years old, the reality of breathing his last breath was something he could never have been prepared for.

It is fitting though, he thought, *that my life should come to an end in the very place in which my ancestors had originally sought refuge in* AD *1308.*

Balantrodoch, as it was originally known, is located fifteen miles south of Edinburgh. It was his secret meeting place. A place he'd been familiar with since a child. A place of peace and tranquillity that had not yet received the level of Templar notoriety that places such as Rosslyn Chapel had gained. A place unknown to many.

Yet, they knew where and when to attack, but I'm prepared, he thought.

His phone chimed, once.

Message sent and encoded

2 recipients

He smashed the phone against the stone wall beside him and dropped the shattered pieces to the ground. He had destroyed any evidence that may help his attacker identify those who would help protect his legacy. Marcus breathed a sigh of relief. He had set in motion a chain of events that would make accessible to those he had chosen the ancient secrets his brotherhood had protected for almost a thousand years.

He leaned heavily against the tree. His hands shook and a cold feeling ebbed through him. Suddenly, from behind, a sharp cracking noise travelled through the cold frosty air.

He looked in the direction of the noise.

He was no longer alone.

The hunter had found his prey.

A surge of adrenaline soared through Marcus' body.

He looked up at the startling silhouette of the man who stood before him. His ample shoulder-length grey hair was tied at the back of his head. His skin was ashen and his dark clothing enhanced his sharp Icelandic features. The gaze of his bright, icy blue eyes penetrated beyond his high cheekbones and radiated straight through Marcus. His black coat draped his entire length, the front opening tucked behind a dagger at one hip. His fingers gripped its ornately decorated handle, anticipating his next move.

Marcus' heart thumped hard against his ribcage, like a thoroughbred racehorse running within his chest. His enemy's appearance enhanced every feeling of fear Marcus had already been experiencing.

'Where is it?' Nergal roared. His neck stretched forward and down. The heat of his words could be seen in the cold Scottish air, as his foreign accent resonated through Marcus' head.

Marcus stared in silence at his enemy.

Nergal's broad, eight-foot-tall physique radiated a physical strength Marcus knew he could never overcome with his slender frame. The sheer stature of the man left Marcus motionless. A sudden serenity overcame him. He had sent the message and now he could do nothing more than pray that his legacy would be secure. Like those who had gone before him, Marcus was prepared to die. He dropped to his knees and closed his eyes.

The shadow of his attacker loomed over him. Unexpectedly, Marcus felt his shirt and jacket being pulled upward. He was lifted into the air by the scruff of his neck. At just over six feet tall he could feel the weight of his body transfer to under his arms. He was brought eye to eye with his attacker, hanging in his outstretched arm like a lost, frightened puppy. His tormentor's patience was growing thin as he glared at his victim.

'The Knights have had in their possession for centuries a powerful ancient artefact that is not rightfully theirs. On this night it will be returned to its rightful place. You will make amends for the sins of your brotherhood. So tell me, where have you hidden it?'

Marcus stared into his assailant's eyes. He knew what his attacker was looking for: the artefact his brotherhood had used to gain the knowledge of Zep Tepi, the knowledge of the first time. It had made them rich and powerful, but it also gained them many dangerous enemies.

'I've no idea what you're looking for,' Marcus said in a low, sombre voice.

In a fit of rage at Marcus' persistent refusal to give him what he wanted, Nergal tossed him to the ground. Pain radiated from Marcus' abdomen through every part of him. Nergal bent to his knees and held his victim's head up by grasping his thick, greying hair. Enraged at Marcus' unrelenting silence, he grimaced as he spoke.

'I know that you will pass the secrets you have been protecting on to someone. She has told us whom you have chosen. I had hoped you would join us and spare him the torment that I will rain upon him, but alas here you lie, defeated and broken. Now that you are exposed and drawing your last breath, it will be just a matter of time before I find him,' Nergal said with confidence, glaring at his victim.

Marcus stared back at him. He could tell by his inability to concentrate and focus that it wouldn't be long before he lost consciousness. His life was drawing to a close. He held on to Nergal's coat and pulled himself toward his tormentor. Marcus looked into his eyes, heaving to catch his breath to utter his last words.

'You have your brother's eyes.' His voice was reduced to a breathless whisper.

Nergal's entire being tingled with anticipation. His joy was followed by a brief outburst of rage.

'My brother is a coward!' Nergal thundered back at his victim, pushing him onto his back. He opened Marcus' navy jacket and analysed his wounds. Satisfied that Marcus would not survive, Nergal stood tall and proud. He paused for a moment to savour his deeds, staring back into Marcus' eyes. 'Thank you for recognising me.'

Chapter 2

The candles on the mahogany floor sent a soft iridescent light flickering across the room. Raziel's broad silhouette appeared then disappeared with each flicker. His feet were crossed in front of him. His hands rested on his knees, palms facing the ceiling, revealing the underside of his left wrist branded with the ancient symbols of his brotherhood. A golden-winged disc sat atop a golden double-barred cross. Each symbol embodied the depth and secrecy of their respective ancient origins. That for which Raziel lived and was created.

He sat motionless on the floor in the centre of his one-room apartment. The bare magnolia-coloured walls were a modest backdrop to a small pine table and a tall dresser that sat in one corner, a bed, bedside table and a lamp in the other.

He required no earthly possessions.

Raziel's purpose in life nourished his soul.

In the distance he could hear a faint, familiar sound: his phone had chimed once, indicating he'd received a message. The only piece of modern technology he possessed sat on the bedside table at the farthest end of the room. Raziel opened his eyes. Awakening from the meditative state that helped him to focus on his sole purpose in life, he stared out the window in front of him and prepared to stand. He turned his hands and placed one palm on each knee. He then transferred the entire weight of his body to the sides of his feet. He lifted himself off the ground and raised his body to a standing position. Like a phoenix reborn, he stretched his arms above his head. His fingertips almost touched the ceiling before he lowered his arms to his sides.

As his immense eight-foot muscular frame glided across the room with ease, his bright blue eyes were focused on the small mobile phone on his bedside table. He touched the screen and retrieved the message.

The time has come

He sat onto his bed and looked at the black cylinder on the table in the far corner. He rubbed his hands along his smooth bald head. Memories of his first time came flooding through his mind. The day he had been awoken and his life filled with purpose. The day he had begun to uphold a sacred ancient agreement to protect and keep secret what the Templars had unearthed from beneath King Solomon's Temple in Jerusalem in AD 1120. Raziel glanced for a moment at the symbols on his wrist. He knew all too well that the burdens they represented were his to carry alone.

Crossing to the dresser, he opened the top drawer and removed the neatly folded clothes he had prepared. He dressed himself, then stood after he had secured the black cylinder in his inside jacket pocket and meditated in silence ahead of beginning his mission. His mentor had been murdered and his promise to him and his brotherhood would be fulfilled at any cost. His failure this night was unthinkable. The ancient secrets could not be lost, nor could they be relinquished to their enemies.

They needed to be protected.

Raziel was not born of this Earth. He was a warrior created by the gods themselves and would give his life to protect the sacred agreement between the Nephilim and the Templars. His enemies had once again arisen from their secret hiding places. This night would bring on the ultimate struggle. A struggle that would decide the fate of the human race for millennia to come.

Chapter 3

The grey and silver hangar roofs glimmered through the darkness as the G550 turned to align with the runway ahead. The jet glided through the wet South African air and prepared to land on the runway at Klerksdorp Airport.

Abaddon's thoughts were consumed with the unfolding events. He had watched the glimmer of twilight some hours ago on another continent. And was celebrating the fact that by the time the sun set again, he would be able to walk the Earth once more as a Nephilim. No more hiding in shadows and waiting for the right moment to attack.

His hour was nigh.

The hum of the landing gear stretching out from the undercarriage resonated beneath Abaddon's feet as he moved his attention to his reflection in the small aircraft window. He rubbed his head of tightly shaven blond hair. His azure blue eyes and his ruggedly handsome features veiled the mind of a meticulous, ruthless killer who would fulfil his own desires at any cost. He thought of how this moment would not have been conceivable a few months earlier. He had almost given up hope. But now his master had a new ally. And she was going to get them what they needed. Although his journey was just beginning, Abaddon could feel success was within his grasp.

This time we will be victorious, he thought.

He placed his hands on the arms of his cream-coloured seat, feeling the vibrations from the jet's wheels as they came in contact with the tarmac and taxied to the black Range Rover awaiting his arrival. Although the Gulfstream jet was luxurious by human standards, Abaddon thought of how good it would feel to be out of its confines and back on solid ground. He'd found it difficult to accommodate his eight-foot broad frame with any comfort within his miniscule surroundings.

Abaddon's ringing phone drew his attention. He retrieved it from the inside pocket of his grey jacket. Seeing the caller ID, he smiled: he had been anticipating this call. He held the phone to his ear.

The voice on the other end immediately began to relate the details of his activities and the success of his recent undertaking.

'Abaddon,' he said, 'as we anticipated, he would not join us. My brother chose his ally well. He was willing to die to keep the artefact out of our control.'

Years of experience had taught Abaddon never to underestimate anyone. He had not expected the Grand Master to give up his secrets too easily. It was always his plan to attack at a time when his enemy least expected it. Disturb the hornet's nest just enough to ensure its secrets would come leaking out one by one. He paused before asking.

'Did he give you anything?'

'Yes.' Nergal said. 'Madeloy was indeed a Templar Grand Master and one of my brother's closest friends, a fact he confirmed himself when he commented on how much I look like Marduk. It proves he has indeed met my brother and is in possession of the artefact.'

There was silence as Abaddon savoured every moment. The sense of fulfilment he gained from the information lingered.

'Then the young woman has been telling us the truth. He *is* the Templar Grand Master and he has been working with your brother Marduk. We are most certainly on the right track. You have done a great service for our people, Nergal.'

'Indeed. Our plans are unfolding well. Our ally has told

me that Madeloy's son will be the heir to his legacy. Only he now remains. The last descendant of our old enemy. It is just a matter of time before Madeloy's son leads us to victory.' Nergal's thoughts were consumed with each meticulous aspect of his plan.

'Yet we must not be hasty, my young prince. The humans are resilient. He may resist just like his father. And if he does, our plans will turn to dust before our eyes,' Abaddon said, not willing to lose the power he could feel just within his grasp.

'If he does not take us to the artefact willingly, I have an incentive for him to comply.'

'Yes. Madeloy's wife. The young man's mother.' There was a hint of a cunning laugh in Abaddon's reply. 'Then our plans will forge ahead. This time we *will* succeed,' Abaddon said as their call came to an end.

~

Over six thousand miles away, Sophia sat twisting uncomfortably in the back of a vehicle, staring at Nergal. Her hands and feet were bound and her mouth was covered with a band of grey tape. She looked out of the back window, toward Balantrodoch, where her husband's body was left lifeless beneath a tree. Tears rolled down her cheeks.

From the seat opposite her, Nergal glared at Sophia then smiled as his phone conversation came to an end. Her pain was bringing him one step closer to realising his dreams. His pawns were starting to take their place on his intricately designed chessboard, their every movement guided by his actions.

Soon it will all be mine, he thought. He tapped the glass partition behind him. 'Take us to Simpson Loan,' Nergal instructed the driver. 'I need to see a young man about an ancient secret.'

Chapter 4

'Did you hear that? There's someone at the door.' Emily reached for the bedside lamp and turned it on. She looked at the clock on the bedside locker.

It was 10.31 p.m.

She nudged her husband, Peter, gently in the ribs. He turned over and moaned. She nudged him again, this time much harder.

He sat up, glanced around the dimly lit bedroom and looked at Emily. He'd been looking forward to getting some much needed sleep after their long flight from Australia, where they'd spent the past three weeks on honeymoon. But Peter was brought back to reality by the incessant thumping on their apartment door.

'What time is it? I feel like I've only been asleep for a couple of minutes.' Peter yawned as he spoke. He ran his hands through his head of thick, curly blond hair. His green eyes were hazy. A light stubble covered his tanned rounded jaw and chin.

'It's ten thirty. And you've only been asleep for a couple of minutes. Can't you hear the banging? There's someone at the door,' Emily said in a delicate, soft English and Irish mixed accent. Peter gave her an affectionate smile and turned his head in the direction of the noise. He listened to what sounded like a large heavy fist thumping hard against the door. He slid out of bed, rubbing his ribs.

'My ribs hurt,' he joked, as he strolled out of the bedroom, his toes sinking into the thick cream carpet.

'You'll waken up quicker next time, dear. Just send them away.' Emily yawned and curled back underneath the duvet.

Peter rubbed his eyes in an effort to focus. 'I'm coming. There's no need to knock the door down. I'll open it!' Peter responded to the incessant heavy banging.

He yawned as he looked through the peephole.

The man standing outside was dressed from top to toe in black.

Peter stepped backward and frowned. He rubbed his eyes. *He's enormous,* he thought, looking at the immense silhouette of the man standing in the corridor, waiting impatiently for Peter to open the door.

For some reason the man seemed familiar. Peter's stomach sank as the realisation hit him.

He fumbled to place the security chain on the door and opened it a few inches. The bald steely blue-eyed giant moved forward toward the small opening and placed his hand on the doorframe. Straight away Peter recognised the symbols on the underside of the stranger's wrist.

His mind ushered him back to the day, fourteen years earlier, when he was with his father in his study at their Dunbar home in Scotland. Peter had been sixteen years old, but the memory of being introduced to Raziel and his father's warning afterwards were never far from Peter's thoughts.

He felt as if he'd just been hit in the chest with a baseball bat. A feeling of utter helplessness engulfed him.

'Raziel,' Peter said.

Raziel tilted his head to one side and stared down at Peter.

'Peter. Your father is dead.'

Peter shook his head. He heard the words Raziel said, yet they didn't mean anything to him. All he could think about was how Raziel hadn't aged one single day in the fourteen years since they'd met. Even his deep foreign accent remained the same. Peter was numb as he peered vacantly through the four-inch gap.

Then Raziel's words hit him.

My father is dead.

He had died before telling Peter everything. Everything he had one day promised to tell him.

Raziel stared down at Peter. 'Perhaps you should let me in?' His voice was quiet. 'We do not have much time.'

Peter's hand trembled as he removed the chain and opened the door. He stared at Raziel as he entered the apartment, shutting the door behind him. Peter could feel his ability to stand was leaving him; the room spun around him. He leaned against the wall, bent forward and placed his hands on his knees.

Raziel allowed Peter a moment to take it all in. He looked around the large apartment space. He could smell a hint of cherry in the air. The luxurious furnishings and artwork that adorned the walls looked appealing, but to him they served no useful purpose.

Raziel turned as he heard Emily's approaching footsteps.

She hurried to Peter. 'What's happened?' She glanced in Raziel's direction. 'Who's he?' she said, looking at Peter for an answer.

There was silence.

Raziel moved closer to Emily. She grasped Peter's arm and held him tight.

'I am Raziel. I have come as agreed to let Peter know his father is dead,' he said, and looked at Peter. 'Have you not told her about your obligations, Peter?' He was assuming that the legacy he was about to hand over to Peter was also Peter's sole purpose in life.

Emily stared at Raziel. *This guy is nuts. I should call the police*, she thought. To her amazement, her husband replied to the stranger.

'No, Raziel, I didn't. My father had told me not so long ago that perhaps there'd be no need for me to carry his burdens,' Peter said.

Emily's heart skipped a beat.

'You know him?' she said, pointing at Raziel. Her voice trembled. She took a step back from her husband.

Peter remained silent.

'We have undeniably enjoyed many years of peace. But right now our enemies have arisen. And they are stronger than ever. Your father, my master, sent me a message tonight. A message we had agreed he would send if his death was inevitable, now it is up to you to protect his secrets. The pact the Grand Master held with the Nephilim must be upheld at all costs. Whoever murdered your father will come for you next, Peter. You must get dressed and leave here before they kill you both.'

Peter had often heard his father speak about the Nephilim. They were a powerful ancient brotherhood, shrouded in secrecy. Secrets that Marcus had one day promised to tell Peter. But Marcus had also warned his son that not all the Nephilim could be trusted.

'Marcus is dead? What obligations?' Emily said, her head filled with questions, and her voice raised with fear. She stared at Peter, wondering if she really knew the man she'd fallen in love with and married.

'Emily, I'm sorry. I am so sorry. I really never thought this day would come.'

'What day would come? Peter, what's going on?' she said.

Moving toward her, he said to Raziel, 'You need to take her somewhere safe. I'm not getting her mixed up in all of this.'

'Like hell you're shipping me off somewhere, Peter Madeloy.' Her voice had deepened. 'I'm not going anywhere. And as for you!' She turned to Raziel to ask him to leave, but suddenly the apartment was plunged into darkness.

Peter could just about make out her slender outline in front of him.

'Get dressed. As fast as you can! We do not have much time. They are here,' Raziel said.

Peter held Emily's arm. His eyes had fully adjusted to the soft light that filtered through the balcony window from the street light outside. Her brown, shoulder-length hair was tied in a ponytail at the back of her neck and her large brown eyes were filled with doubt and confusion. There was little he could do to make amends for keeping secrets from her. He hoped that once he explained to her what was at stake, she would understand.

'Emily, darling, I need you to trust me. I promise I'll explain everything. But right now we need to get out of here,' Peter said, his green eyes pleading with her.

Emily could see the agony etched in his face. She hoped there was a logical explanation as to why he'd kept these secrets from her, but she was willing to wait for when he was ready to give it.

'Fine, I'm with you on this, but you'd better tell me everything,' she said, her voice firm.

'I promise,' Peter said. He looked at Raziel. 'How much

time do you think we have?'

'Not long. They have cut the power and have most likely removed anyone standing in their way of getting in here. You must hurry.'

Peter and Emily hurried back into the bedroom to get dressed.

Raziel scanned the apartment. 'Is there another way out of here?' He raised his voice just enough so that Peter and Emily could hear him.

'There's a fire escape just below the balcony. It can be accessed from the glass gate on the left-hand side,' Peter said.

Raziel pushed hard on the balcony door's black handle and stepped outside. He leaned over the glass railing and looked from left to right along the entire length of the alleyway below. It was quiet and empty. The perfect place for Peter and Emily to escape into.

If Raziel was right, then the renegade Nephilim Nergal, their greatest enemy, and his band of loyal followers were behind Marcus' death. Raziel presumed the Nephilim would enter through the front of the building. They'd try to use the element of surprise to their advantage and attack Peter while he slept. They'd torture and kill Emily to make Peter tell them what they wanted to know. But Raziel was one step ahead: Peter would be gone and the Nephilim would find him waiting instead. If he could slow them down enough for Peter to get a head start, then his purpose would be fulfilled and Peter would be on the path his father had intended him to follow.

He re-entered the room and extended his arm in Peter's direction. 'This is for you. Your father asked me to give this to you,' Raziel said. He held out the shiny black cylinder from his apartment.

Peter looked up at him. At six feet four inches tall he rarely encountered anyone taller than himself. Yet here he stood. Raziel grasped Peter's hand and placed the black cylinder into it.

Peter felt an enormous weight had been pressed against his chest. He'd known from the first day he'd met Raziel that if they met again, his father would be dead and his death set in motion a chain of events that'd allow Peter to uncover his secrets. 'This cylinder will lead you to whatever your father was protecting. I am passing it on to you as agreed.'

'He didn't get to tell me—,' Peter said.

'And he will not be able to help you now. Peter, this is your destiny. Your father will have ensured that you, and only you, will be able to figure out what is in this cylinder. But you need to act now. And remember, some of the Nephilim cannot be trusted. They will kill you if they find you.'

Emily held tight to Peter's arm. 'I think we should go to the police.'

'We can't. What my father was protecting is much too valuable to be entrusted to just anyone. He died to protect what's in this cylinder,' he said.

Raziel looked to his right. Whispered voices echoed along the corridor on the other side of the apartment door. A clicking noise filtered through the keyhole as the lock opened.

Raziel whispered as he reached for the gun at his waist. 'You need to leave. The secrets of our brotherhood need to be protected and you are now its only guardian. The Nephilim and many others will kill you for what your father has left you. You must leave here now.' He positioned himself in front of Emily and Peter and gestured to them to move toward the fire escape. 'I will hold them back for as long as I can. Now leave!' Raziel raised his weapon and pointed it at the apartment door that was opening slowly.

Peter secured the cylinder in his jacket pocket and hurried down the fire escape. Emily was close behind him. The sound of gunshots filtered out through the balcony door and into the alleyway below, as they manoeuvred each step with hurried precision. Peter jumped off the final step and held on tight to Emily's waist, helping her down into the alleyway.

'My car's just down there,' he said, pointing in the direction of Nightingale Way.

'I think they've stopped shooting,' Emily said, as they ran toward the car.

They came to a standstill for a moment and looked back at the balcony. They could see Raziel faltering backward, a man inches taller than him loomed over him. Raziel pressed hard against the balcony railing. Emily watched in horror as the stranger held an ornately decorated dagger above Raziel, then thrust it deep into his chest. Raziel fell onto the balcony, motionless.

His killer bent over the body and cleaned his dagger on Raziel's jacket, then changed his attention to Peter and Emily. They could see, even from a distance, that his eyes were bathed in vengeance as he held onto the balcony railing, vaulted over it and descended down to the alleyway, landing just feet from where they stood. They were transfixed: he'd jumped down three floors from their apartment balcony and had landed without a scratch.

Nergal walked toward them.

What the hell is he! Peter thought, grabbing Emily's arm. 'Let's go!'

They ran down the alley to where Peter's red Audi A6 was parked.

He pulled the keys from his jacket pocket, flicked the button to unlock the doors and sat into the driver's seat, as Emily got into the passenger seat.

His hands were shaking. A ripple of panic cascaded through him as he sensed Nergal gaining on them.

'Start the car, Peter. Start the car!' Emily shouted. She could see the distance between them and Nergal grow smaller in the wing mirror. Nergal pulled his gun from his belt and moved quicker, heading right for them.

Peter turned the key and the engine roared to life. He put the car into first gear, jammed his foot on the accelerator and sped down the remainder of the alleyway toward Nightingale Way. He glanced in the rear-view mirror. Nergal was close behind, pointing the gun at them. The piercing sound of a gunshot followed by the sound of glass shattering echoed behind them. Emily glanced into the back. The rear window was shattered.

Peter's grip on the steering wheel tightened as he tried to maintain control of the vehicle. He jammed on the brakes as they approached the junction at the end of the alleyway. The tyres screeched in protest as he swerved onto Nightingale Way. He looked to his left in the direction of their apartment. Nergal was almost at the passenger side of the car. Emily pushed the car's central locking button.

Peter was now in a panic. Emily could see straight down the barrel of Nergal's handgun. He was feet from her head as he pressed the trigger. At the same instant Peter jammed on the accelerator and the car sped off down Nightingale Way. The windows behind them shattered as the bullet sped from one side to the other. In the rear-view mirror, he could see Nergal standing in the middle of the road, his icy blue eyes fixed on Peter as he sped away.

Where do we go from here? Peter thought, and tried to

picture the layout of the city from his early morning jogs with Emily, which they'd started when they moved into their new apartment a year ago.

At this time of night Peter knew Edinburgh would be easy to navigate by car. The multitude of tourists who came to visit the cultural city would have dispersed, and the bustling street activities and traffic congestion would have all but disappeared. Peter turned the car to the right and glanced in the rear-view mirror. He relaxed his grip on the steering wheel. Nergal was nowhere to be seen, but Peter was taking no chances as he accelerated along Lady Lawson Street.

'Who the hell is he?' Emily said. 'Please don't tell me you know him too!'

'I have no idea who he is. I've never seen him before! And I'm not staying around to make his acquaintance.'

Chapter 5

Seven thousand one hundred and fifty-five feet above sea level exists the most unforgiving, isolated, cold and extreme environment on Earth: the east Antarctic ice sheet.

Maggie stood at the furthest end of the conference room and stared out of the enormous, semicircular window that framed the Antarctic landscape like a beautiful artistic masterpiece. She watched the green flags that outlined the path to the observatory sway from side to side, as the circumpolar wind brushed against them.

Her actions over the past two years, since she'd first started working at the observatory, brought a tempest of thoughts rushing through her mind. She recalled the first day she'd set foot in this very room, when she'd met Marduk. Maggie could still at once recall every word, feeling and nuance of their conversation that day.

'Good evening, Dr O'Connell. I am pleased to finally make your acquaintance.' She had heard the familiar foreign male accent just over her left shoulder, and had recognised it without hesitation from their many telephone conversations.

Maggie faced her guest.

She had imagined Marduk's appearance on several occasions, but it had not done him justice. At well over eight feet tall, Marduk was taller than any other Nephilim she'd encountered, and he exuded an air of confidence with every word he spoke and every move he made. He was the Nephilim leader, the one who had intricately connected with, and had ensured that the Nephilim's existence was kept secret by, the most powerful people and governments on Earth. And all of this was controlled from a base deep within the east Antarctic ice sheet, right beneath where she stood.

A mixture of fate and intricate planning had led her to this very moment, and she felt an uneasy trepidation. She was about to become entrenched deep within the very fabric of a brotherhood that had been in existence since long before the time of Christ.

Maggie took a couple of steps toward the Nephilim leader. Her hands clenched by her sides.

'Good evening, your Majesty. This is an unexpected pleasure,' Maggie said, extending her hand to greet him.

'Likewise,' Marduk said. He shook her hand firmly.

'I see you have wasted no time in familiarising yourself with the facility and you have resolved the problems with the infrared equipment.' Marduk's steely blue eyes radiated through Maggie as his broad muscular frame towered above her.

'Yes. It's working well. The detail we're getting is astounding. We're to begin relaying information today.' Maggie shifted her gaze upward at Marduk.

'Good.' Marduk walked to the enormous window and stared out across the Antarctic landscape. 'I cannot stress the confidentiality required to carry out what I am asking of you. Nor can I emphasise the gravity of the consequences that will arise should the information you are providing us with, or our existence here, become public knowledge. The base beneath you remains a secret to the rest of humanity. Although some have tried to uncover it, they have not been successful. And I am sure you would concur that what you are tracking for me beyond our solar system and what we are doing here necessitates a certain level of … concealment that needs to be maintained at all times.' Marduk tilted his head a little to the right as he spoke. He looked down at Maggie. She knew he was analysing even the smallest change in her demeanour.

Looking for any signs that she may betray him.

'I understand. Not another soul will know what we're doing here. As far as the scientific community is concerned, I'm an astrophysicist observing and cataloguing supernovae.'

Maggie knew Marduk had chosen the South Pole as the location of his base as it provided him with the safe haven he needed to keep his secrets hidden. It was the one place on Earth that belonged to everyone on the planet, yet no one owned any one piece of it.

'Then I will take my leave of you,' Marduk said, and walked toward the conference room door, where a well-built, bearded Nephilim, Marduk's security chief, Chasid, stood waiting for his departure. There was silence as they both exited the room and closed the door behind them.

Maggie moved back to the large window and gazed at the giant men as they walked across the ice outside and entered the enormous aircraft waiting to transport Marduk away. Its large oval shape, with a wingspan of about three hundred feet was awe-inspiring against the Antarctic landscape. The aircraft's landing gear comprised of four enormous feet that replaced the usual wheels on conventional aircraft. Its undercarriage was covered in silver reflective tiles, and the outer hull was painted in a silvery metallic coating that reflected the light off the aircraft's surface and made it impossible for the many satellites monitoring the surface of the Earth to see it. For all intents and purposes this was not a conventional aircraft, then again neither were its passengers.

'I've updated the program.'

Maggie was transported back to the present by the familiar sound of her research assistant Andrew's voice. The tall, dark-haired thirty-three year old was standing at the conference room door.

She walked toward him, stopping to glance at a framed map on the wall. The map, a copy of an original drawn by the famous Turkish admiral Piri Reis in AD 1513, depicted the coastline of West Africa, the east coast of South America and an ice-free coastline of North Antarctica. Reis had left details of how he'd drawn the map, admitting that the original cartography was not his own, but copies of maps he'd gained access to during his time as admiral. Some of the original maps dated back as far as the fourth century BC or perhaps even further. An amazing fact considering that Antarctica had not been discovered until the eighteenth century AD, and that the ice on Antarctica was thousands of years old. Someone in ancient times had mapped an ice-free Antarctica long before humans had ever explored its shores. When Maggie had first seen the map, she'd thought it a fake. But events over the past five years – since she'd first met Nergal – left no doubt in her mind that an ice-free Antarctica had been mapped by someone millennia ago.

'When should we begin to scramble the signals?' Andrew said, shifting Maggie's attention back to him.

'When Micah is ready, he'll let us know.'

Chapter 6

The familiar shriek of the Police Scotland siren faded into the distance as the squad car sped down George IV Bridge in the direction of their apartment on Simpson Loan. Peter had found a quiet place on Victoria Street to park the car and regroup, but he knew that their respite would be short-lived.

This can't be real, he thought. But the news images on the television in the shop window beside them confirmed his worst fears. A man had been found murdered in Balantrodoch, his father's secret meeting place, just outside Edinburgh. The police were looking for eyewitnesses.

Peter knew the gunshots at his apartment would've been reported by neighbours and Raziel's body found on their balcony. Peter would have a lot of questions to answer about these events and how they related to his father's death. But without knowing what his father had been protecting, Peter would have no plausible solutions to offer anyone. He was being hunted for something his father hadn't had the chance to tell him about. And all he could do was stare at his distorted reflection in the black shiny cylinder in his hands. He noticed a very fine seam that stretched along the length of the cylinder on both sides. He examined it in detail. It felt sleek, measuring about seven inches long and two in diameter. Peter moved it around slowly; it felt heavier than it looked.

This has to open somehow. He ran his index finger along one of the seams.

Emily sat in silence in the passenger seat, her eyes red from crying. Wiping away her tears, she tried to compose herself. She'd known Marcus for more than four years. After she'd graduated with a PhD in genetics, he'd given her the opportunity to participate in one of his research projects. From that day he'd been like a father to her. He'd seen her potential straight away and encouraged her to use it. She knew from the many years she'd worked alongside Marcus that he was meticulous and rather secretive. Everything he did had a purpose, so she knew he'd left the cylinder to Peter for a reason and they owed it to him to find out why.

Peter shifted his gaze to Emily. He knew he'd placed her in great danger, but his father had always said Emily was tougher than she looked. And somehow he knew his father was glad she was with him.

The cold winter air passed through the broken windows in the back. Emily rubbed her hands in an effort to warm herself. 'What do you think your father was protecting?' she said, looking at Peter.

Peter had known for years that his father was a Templar Grand Master. His brotherhood was his second family. His father's secrets had secrets and that's exactly how he'd liked it. Marcus had always told Peter that one day he'd have to entrust him with the knowledge he was protecting. But he hadn't wanted it to be anytime soon. He had wanted Peter to enjoy life first. To get married and have a family, just as he had done. But in an instant that had all changed and Peter was fighting to protect a deadly ancient artefact he knew little about.

He placed the cylinder back into his jacket pocket. 'Have you ever heard of Jacques DeMolay?'

'Yes. He was one of the Knights Templar. He was a Grand Master. Wasn't he burned at the stake for heresy?'

'Not exactly.' Peter's voice was firm. 'He was burned for his secrets and the power they could bring to whoever has control over them.' He gazed out the window and watched a group of people as they passed. Their lives seemed uncomplicated as they chatted and strolled along. He faced Emily once again.

'My surname. Madeloy, is an anagram of DeMolay. That's my real surname.' Peter was unable to look his wife in the eyes.

I don't even know his real name, she thought.

'My father told me that what he was protecting has been in his family for generations, and it could give its possessor the power to create and to destroy. He'd often told me that proof of its existence would alter the history and future of humanity simultaneously. He also told me he'd find a way for me access his secrets and begin where he left off, should anything unexpected happen to him. That was when he introduced me to Raziel.' Peter went silent for a moment. 'I always felt that when the time was right, he'd tell me what I needed to know. Now, I guess I'll have to find out the hard way,' he said.

'So what's in that cylinder could lead us anywhere?'

'Well, yes. My father said that when I realised what he was protecting, I too would give my life to safeguard it. He never told me what it was. He always kept it secret. The only thing he did say was that what I didn't know would keep me alive.' Peter looked at his wife and took her hand. 'I never asked for any of this. I'd always presumed this day would never come. My father had even hinted in the past few weeks at the fact that I may not have to shoulder his burdens. I—'

'I understand.' Emily held his hand tight.

Peter smiled with relief. He knew he was asking her to take a leap of faith. Even he had no idea where his father's secrets would lead them.

He scanned the street ahead and checked the rear-view mirror. *We should get moving again.*

'We'll leave the car here. If they could find out where I live, then I'm sure they know what car I drive. Staying here'll just make it easier for them to track us,' Peter said, looking over his shoulder. 'And the broken windows will just draw unwanted attention.' His voice was quiet.

'Let's go find somewhere to sit and think things through. We need to see what's inside that cylinder. A public place might be best. What about that coffee shop on George IV Bridge – it's not far from here. The one you always promised to take me to. I hear they serve great coffee,' Emily said, trying to lighten the mood.

There was no answer from Peter. He stared out of the windscreen. He couldn't take his mind off the fact that his father was dead.

'Peter? We need to decide what to do. And there's a lot more you still have to tell me. Like who exactly are the Nephilim?' Emily said, and gave him a firm, chastising look.

Peter nodded. 'Let's go then.' He was about to step out of the car when he felt his mobile phone vibrate in his jacket pocket. He pulled out the phone and held it in front of him.

It was his mother.

Amidst the panic, fear and confusion he'd just been thrown into, he'd forgotten about his mother and sister. He knew his mother would be at their home in Dunbar and his sister in London. Yet he felt as if a giant weight had been thrust into his stomach pushing it downward.

How am I going to tell either of them Dad is dead? Maybe she already knows. Maybe she's seen the news, Peter thought, staring at his phone.

'It's Mum,' he whispered. 'I'd better answer this.'

He touched the screen and lifted the phone to his ear.

'Hey Mum,' Peter's voice was quiet.

'Hello Peter!' said a deep foreign male voice.

'Who is this?' A sense of nervous hesitation was evident in Peter's raised voice.

'You should not have run away from me, Peter,' the voice said. 'I am only here to help you.'

'Help me!' Peter raged. 'Help me to do what?' A sudden realisation hit him. 'What are you doing with my mother's phone?'

'Peter, I need you to listen to me very carefully.' There was an uncomfortable silence before the stranger continued. 'I want you to look at the photo I am sending to your phone,' the voice instructed.

Peter moved the phone in front of him and looked at the image displayed on the screen. He felt as if the space he was sitting in was closing around him and he was trapped. He felt it getting harder to catch his breath. There, in the image, was his mother. Dressed in her dark-green cashmere jumper and blue jeans and sitting in what looked like the back of a large vehicle. Her hands were tied behind her back and her mouth was covered with grey tape. Her eyes were red, there was a cut on her head and Peter could tell by her shoulder-length blonde hair, which had come untied from the bun at the back of her head, she had put up some resistance to her kidnappers. Peter was filled with a sense of disbelief. He returned the phone to his ear.

'Who the hell are you?' His hands were shaking.

'Have you seen the picture?' the voice said.

'What do you think you're playing at? Who are you?' Peter replied in a confident tone, but inside he was beginning to fall apart. First his father, now his mother.

Where is this going to end? Who are these people? he thought.

'I need you to listen to me, Peter. If you do exactly as I say, then your mother will come to no more harm. Are you listening?'

I guess I have no choice, but to listen. He took a deep breath. 'Yes, I'm listening.'

'Among other things, your father was guarding the location of an ancient artefact. A location he promised to pass on to you in the event of his demise. The black cylinder that was given to you this evening will lead you to the secrets and the artefact your father and his ancestors have been hiding for centuries. This is what I want in return for your mother.'

How does he know I have the cylinder? And even if I could access my father's secrets, how do I know I can trust him?

'Why should I trust you?' Peter said.

'Because any delays on your part would be a mistake that will result in my returning your mother to you in a much less fortunate condition than she is in right now.'

Peter glanced at Emily, any hint of colour had drained from his face.

'You don't need to hurt anyone else. I'll get you what you're looking for. I just need some time to figure this out,' Peter said.

'Then we have an agreement. As long as you keep your side of the bargain and get me access to the artefact, I will abide by my promise to return your mother to you unharmed. You have twenty-four hours from now,' the voice said.

There was a brief silence as Peter stared at his watch.

It was 11.38 p.m.

The clock was ticking.

~

Outside Peter's apartment Nergal stood on the pavement and watched a black Range Rover pull up in front of him. The passenger door opened and he sat inside holding his mobile phone to his ear. The flashing blue lights of the police cars that had pulled up to investigate the reports of gunshots cascaded down Nergal's face. He shut the door and continued his conversation.

'And Peter, the svelte brunette accompanying you on your journey?' Nergal paused. 'If you fail, I will find her. And I will make you watch while I wrest the life from her body.'

Chapter 7

Peter placed his hand over his jacket pocket ensuring that the cylinder was secure. He walked behind Emily who was weaving her way through the late night revellers that consumed the uplifting night-time atmosphere Edinburgh had to offer. She stopped outside a small coffee shop and looked back at Peter.

'Here it is. They stay open until 1.00 a.m., so we'll have some time to talk and figure things out,' Emily said. Peter nodded and followed her in.

Inside the coffee shop was warm with the smell of freshly brewed coffee seeping through the air. It was bustling with activity downstairs. People were sitting and laughing. Life as it should be was happening all around them. Emily pointed toward the stairs indicating to Peter to follow her up. *It'll be quieter up there and we'll have space to think,* she thought, as they navigated through the crowded tables and chairs.

Peter glanced to his left. Behind the refrigerated counter a tall, slender, dark-haired waiter gave him a smile as they passed. Peter continued to focus on the dark wooden floor beneath his feet until he reached the bottom of the stairs where he caught a glimpse of his own reflection in a small mirror. His eyes were hazy and his complexion pallid. He looked tired and weary, and felt as if he'd aged an eternity since Raziel had come to his apartment.

Upstairs they sat in the relaxing Victorian chairs arranged alongside a dark-brown table nestled into a corner near a large, tall, rectangular window. A group of students laughed and chatted at the tables opposite them.

Peter held his phone to his ear as he glanced around the room. This was the third time he'd called his sister, Ava, and again there was no reply. He listened to her short, but effective mailbox message – 'Leave a message after the beep' – then waited for the beep before he spoke.

'Ava, it's Peter. As soon as you get this message, call me back,' he said, and ended the call.

A tall, athletic young man with jet black hair and tanned skin approached their table. His black trousers were covered by a short black apron tied around his trim waist. 'Can I take your order?' he said.

Peter gazed at his crisp white shirt while he spoke.

'Two black coffees, please,' Emily said in a low voice.

The waiter nodded and smiled, and went downstairs.

Peter took the cylinder from his pocket and placed it on the table in front of them, resting it against the sugar bowl.

The dim light and smell of coffee were comforting, and for a moment it made them feel at ease. Peter relaxed back into the chair and stared at the medieval view from the window. He could see one of Edinburgh's most famous historical landmarks, Edinburgh Castle, an imposing stone fortress that sat silently on the hilltop.

Emily lifted the cylinder to get a closer look. Turning it around in her hands, she examined every millimetre of it. 'So, start from the beginning. Tell me everything you know,' she said. 'Even the smallest detail could be important.'

Peter continued to stare out of the window for a moment, gathering his thoughts. He shrugged his shoulders and shook his head. He tried to recall as many memories of his father as he could. Memories from his childhood mixed with more recent ones flooded his mind. *Which ones are most important?* A swell of frustration built up inside him.

He leaned forward.

'The history of the Templars is quite well known. They started off as a group of nine men who protected the pilgrims during the crusades. Hughes de Payens and Godfrey de Saint-Omer were the Order's original founders who set up their headquarters in the Al-Aqsa Mosque in Jerusalem. A gift given to them by King Baldwin of Jerusalem. Unbeknown to many, this gift was of particular importance because it is believed that the mosque was built on the Temple Mount, which is also known as the Mount of Zion, and is purported to be the exact location where King Solomon's Temple was built, around the tenth century before Christ. Legend states that the Templars spent several years excavating and searching beneath the mosque, looking for treasures the Bible says were contained in the Temple of Solomon. They're believed to have found several ancient treasures within Solomon's Temple.' Peter paused for a moment. 'You see, the Templar Order after only a couple of years had increased to a great extent in numbers and wealth. They became even more prominent with an official endorsement by the Catholic Church in AD 1129. Ten years later Pope Innocent II issued a papal bull *Omne Datum Optimum*, Latin for 'every perfect gift', and exempted the Order from local laws and made them answerable to the Church alone. No other order in history, founded by so few, had become so powerful and influential so quickly,' he said.

'So whatever they found beneath the Temple Mount was obviously something very ancient and very significant?'

'Yes. And I guess in some ways many people began to fear the Knights' sudden rise to power.'

'Is that why the Catholic Church had the Templars imprisoned and murdered?'

'It's part of the reason. At first King Philip of France accused the Templars of heresy and had them arrested. The

Templar's secret initiation ceremonies, their increasing hold on power and the wealth they had accumulated made some people very nervous. On Friday the 13th of October AD 1307 the Templars were rounded up and the Order was thrown into chaos. To many, the Order appeared to have been destroyed, especially after the pope at that time, Pope Clement, was pressurised by King Philip to issue a papal bull *Pastoralis Praeeminentiae*, after which Christian monarchs across Europe arrested the Templars and seized their assets. Some of them found refuge in places like England, Ireland and here in Scotland. They even brought some of their treasures and some of the Order's ancient secrets with them.'

'So your ancestors were murdered for their secrets.' She was thinking of Peter's ancestor Jacques DeMolay who was executed in AD 1314.

'Yes. However, ironically a document was found of late in the papal archives – I think in 2001. It states that Pope Clement had absolved the Templars of all heresies in AD 1308. But King Philip feared the Knights and even threatened military action against the Church. So Clement gave in and disbanded the Order in AD 1312 at the council of Vienne with the papal bull *Vox in Excelsior*. You know, it's beyond belief what some people will do to justify their own misdeeds. Anyway both Clement and Philip died quite soon afterward.'

'I'm sure I read it somewhere that your ancestor Jacques DeMolay foresaw the deaths of both Clement and Philip.' Emily was completely engrossed in what Peter was telling her.

'Moments before his death Jacques is reported to have said that both Pope Clement and King Philip would soon meet him before God. Clement died a month later, and before the year was over, Philip died in a hunting accident.' Peter's train of thought was interrupted by the waiter who'd returned with their coffee. He placed a tall, white coffee mug in front of each of them, along with some serviettes.

'Enjoy,' the waiter said.

Emily held the coffee cup with both her hands. She took one small sip.

'So, if whatever they found beneath the Temple Mount gave them this power and wealth, then it was without doubt something the Catholic Church and King of France were afraid the Templars could use against them. It's obvious – why else would the Church give them so much power in the first place and then be so easily influenced to take it away?' Emily said.

'Exactly! And this will lead us to it.' Peter turned the cylinder in his hands. 'Many researchers and scholars over the centuries have speculated as to what treasures King Solomon's Temple contained. In the Hebrew Bible, the Old Testament states that the original Temple of Solomon was dedicated to Yahweh and was built to house the Ark of the Covenant.' Peter took a sip of coffee. 'I guess my Dad would be able to tell us … if he were still alive.'

There was silence as Peter's words lingered in the air.

'The Ark of the Covenant. Can you be sure that's what your father was protecting?' Emily said.

'Not really. Solomon was believed to have had in his possession far more treasures than just the Ark. And I never really pushed my father to tell me what his secrets were. I always felt he'd tell me what I needed to know, when I needed to know it.' A sense of regret shrouded Peter's response.

'And the Nephilim, the ones at our apartment, and Raziel, where do they fit in to all this?'

'After seeing them tonight I'm not sure what they are,'

Peter said. 'My father was involved with a brotherhood he referred to as the Nephilim. I did overhear some conversations in which he mentioned them, but I always got the impression from his tone that he preferred to keep some of them at arm's length. All I know is that their Brotherhood was founded thousands of years ago. I think they existed even before the time of Christ.'

Emily felt the hairs rise on her arms and a chill run down her spine. 'Since before the time of Christ.' *An organisation that has survived into the third millennium AD is without question a very powerful one,* she thought.

Chapter 8

The striking Victorian sandstone building, known as the Klerksdorp Museum, was situated beyond the black wrought-iron gates that had the words 'Stock Exchange' arched above them. The building, a former prison intermingled with the more modern remnants of a stock exchange, alluded to an interesting concept in the contemporary world: an integrated stock exchange and prison. An easy transition for the lawless predators that shrewdly frequent both spheres of modern life.

Lochemel scanned the small office at the back of the museum, beyond the covered central courtyard. He held a small torch between his teeth and stooped to his knees behind the curator's desk. He opened the cabinet door, revealing the safe. He entered the code into its white keypad. It was followed by a click then a high-pitched beep. Lochemel pushed the handle downward and pulled the large heavy door open.

Its black interior was divided into two halves. The bottom half contained some of the curator's personal documents and a sack of money – the museum's revenue from the previous day. Above it sat a square metallic case measuring about twenty-two inches in length and fifteen in width. Lochemel lifted the case off the top shelf. Holding it in both hands he placed it on the stone floor beside him. He opened the lid and shone the torch inside to examine the box's contents.

Its inside was covered in a black velvet material with six circular indentations carved into its lid and base. Inside each indentation sat a small sphere that measured exactly six inches in diameter.

Lochemel knew that each of these spherical devices had

been flawlessly crafted by the Nephilim in a zero gravity environment to ensure they were balanced to absolute perfection. He also knew that the Nephilim had used the spheres on Earth before. Destruction and disease followed for decades after their use. Men, women and children died and their homelands became uninhabitable for generations. For centuries the spheres had been hidden by the Nephilim leader, Marduk, at various locations on Earth. The Klerksdorp Museum was their most recent hiding place. They were kept here under the watchful eye of the museum's curator until this evening when their enemies had once again arisen and threatened the peace that Lochemel's leader had fought so hard to maintain for centuries.

Lochemel lifted one of the spheres; it had a brassy appearance with three parallel grooves carved across its equator. He examined each of the six spheres in turn, then returned them to the security of the case. He closed the safe door and stood up as he lifted a dark-green backpack from the stone floor beside him and secured the case inside. He paused for a moment to wipe his forehead beneath his long, grey hair. Beads of sweat rolled down his back. The dense South African heat was hitting thirty-seven degrees centigrade during the day and only cooling to twenty-two degrees at night. The heat made the former prison cell seem increasingly miniscule and even more difficult for his eight-foot frame to navigate and breathe in. His deep blue eyes gazed across the courtyard. He arched his neck a little to the left to get a better view beyond the vehicles that formed part of the museum display. Behind them he could see rays of light shining along a corridor at the front of the museum.

He had company. His enemy had arrived sooner than he'd anticipated.

His instincts prompted him to turn off his torch and he hoped that it hadn't given his location away.

He stood still for a moment. Assessing his options.

He knew the old prison well. He'd worked here as a night security guard for the past two years. Strategically placed there by his commander to guard the spheres. He thought to use this to his advantage. He moved to the office door, holding tight to the backpack. There was an exit at the back of the museum that not many people used, and not far from his current location. It would lead him in the opposite direction to his unexpected guests. He crept out of the curator's office and down the corridor, ensuring he didn't make a sound. He could see the exit straight in front of him. He glanced behind as he moved toward the exit, trying to gauge how far away his enemies were. He immediately recognised the distant silhouette of his adversary. The Nephilim known as Abaddon was fast approaching down the corridor behind him.

Lochemel knew he'd been seen and now had no further reason to be covert.

The stone walls of the prison surrounded him on either side. He had nowhere to hide. He ran toward the exit with his enemy closing in behind him.

Suddenly he felt a sharp pain in his right-hand side, in the middle of his ribcage. The silencer on his enemy's gun had muffled the noise as the bullet shot from the barrel. Lochemel held tight to his side and stumbled toward the exit door, which braced his fall and kept him on his feet. He pushed heavily on the long bar across the middle of the door, turning once more to look back as he exited the building. Another gunshot blasted the stone wall beside him. Pieces of sandstone shot out in all directions. Lochemel closed the door behind him. He foraged through a pile of large branches by the exit, the remnants of the landscapers' work for the day due for shredding the next morning, for something he could use to wedge the door handle to stop his enemy from following him. He pulled the strongest branch he could find and wedged it under the fire exit door's metal bar to prevent it from being pushed down and releasing the lock.

Lochemel took a deep breath. He felt a warm trickling sensation beneath where the bullet had lodged; blood was running from his wound. He scanned the outside of the building. In the distance he could see two black Range Rovers parked beyond the wrought-iron gates outside the museum's main entrance on Lombard Street. He heard the muffled sound of his adversary on the other side of the exit door. Unable to force the door open, Lochemel could hear Abaddon instruct his men to go back to the main entrance and seize the enemy.

Lochemel ran toward the black iron railing on his right, and crouched out of sight behind the bushes. Two well-built guards protected the vehicles beyond the fence. Lochemel moved along the shrubs and out onto the road behind the vehicle nearest the exit. He approached one of the guards from behind and placed his hand on his shoulder. As the guard faced him, Lochemel punched him in the throat to ensure he couldn't call out. Lochemel grabbed the man's weapon and hit him hard on the back of the head. The guard fell to the ground unconscious. Lochemel leaned forward, removed the vehicle's keys from his belt. He opened its door without a sound and sat onto the front seat. He placed the backpack and weapon on the passenger seat and evaluated his options.

He would be unable to rendezvous with the aircraft waiting for him in Klerksdorp Airport. He now had no other choice but to activate the transponder signal on his phone. The signal would alert his commander, Chasid, to the fact that he'd been compromised and that the spheres were in danger of being taken from him. Chasid would then monitor his every move.

Lochemel watched the front of the museum. The other guard lifted a walkie-talkie to his ear. He faced Lochemel and raised his gun in his direction, shooting at the vehicle that Lochemel had taken charge of. The sounds of bullets discharging and hitting the Range Rover echoed around him. He bent down behind the steering wheel. Glass shattered around him and scattered in every direction onto the vehicle floor, as the passenger door window was hit with the bullets from his enemy's weapon.

Lochemel turned the key in the ignition, put the vehicle in reverse and pressed hard on the accelerator. The Range Rover sped backward and then screeched forward. Lochemel grabbed the weapon on the passenger seat, extended his hand out of the window and fired at Abaddon's accomplice, who cowered in response. Lochemel discharged a further two bullets with unparalleled precision, hitting the front and back tyres of the remaining Range Rover. He sped down Lombard Street glancing in the rear-view mirror as he escaped. He could see Abaddon standing motionless in the centre of the road, his rage brimming within him like an overburdened teacup waiting to be emptied.

Lochemel breathed a sigh of relief. He had paralysed his adversary for now. But his mission was far from over.

Chapter 9

A hazy reflection of the light that hung above the table in the café reflected off the cylinder like a beacon.

'I have no idea what this is,' Peter said. He could feel the sense of panic that had overcome him earlier begin to resurface. He couldn't think straight. In his head, he could hear his mother's voice pleading with him to help her. He knew he couldn't go to the police, and he couldn't help but wonder what his enemy's next move would be. Deep down inside he didn't want to know what was in the cylinder. But his mother's life depended on it.

He looked at Emily.

She was examining every detail of the cylinder. Running her fingers along its length. For some reason it seemed familiar to her. Then, suddenly, it dawned on her. She had seen one of these cylinders before. She looked at Peter and smiled.

'I think I know what this is. No, in fact I'm sure. It's a specimen tube. It uses a retinal scan to ensure the contents can only be opened by the intended recipient. I saw your father with one of these once before. He was using it to carry DNA samples.'

She examined the cylinder from every angle. 'The cylinder Marcus had was dark-blue in colour. But otherwise it was exactly the same as this.' She lifted the cylinder to her ear and tilted it gently from side to side. 'There's liquid inside here. I can hear it move.' She handed the cylinder to Peter. 'Move it from side to side and listen.'

Peter took the cylinder and listened for the quiet swishing sound as he rolled it. He could definitely hear liquid

51

moving inside. 'Do you know how to open it?'

'Like this, I think.' With the cylinder held in front of her face, Emily placed her palms on either end of it. A green light emitted from the slit in its front and scanned both her eyes. It vibrated for a moment. Then the light vanished and the cylinder remained closed. Peter scanned the café to make sure no one had noticed the strange light.

'I'm guessing it will only open for the person whom your father intended it to. That's what Raziel said – at our apartment. I bet if you try, it'll open for you. Whatever's inside here is meant for you, Peter. We could learn something more about what your father was protecting, maybe even find his killer.' She moved the cylinder across the table toward him.

Peter knew he needed to open the cylinder. Time was running out and the answers to everything sat beneath its shiny black surface. He delayed for a second before taking it in his right hand. Now that he was about to open the door into his father's world, he hoped he'd be able to control whatever came through it.

'There's no going back!' he whispered to Emily. He placed his palms on either end and pushed them toward each other. The green light once again appeared and scanned his eyes. The cylinder vibrated. Then after a moment they could hear a hiss and the cylinder opened along the seam.

Peter pushed the lid back fully, before the cylinder had a chance to lock again, and placed it on the table in front of them.

The first thing he noticed was that the inside of the cylinder was cold.

Emily was right, he thought.

It was an airtight refrigerated unit for storing biological samples.

Peter examined the inside. He could see three small indentations in both the top and the bottom, inside which three small vials of liquid had been stored. And on the left-hand side, a larger more elongated indentation held what looked like a small scroll. No writing, no symbols and no other markings were visible anywhere on the shiny polished gold interior.

This cylinder was purposely designed to hold these, Peter thought.

He and Emily sat in silence and examined the contents in every detail before disturbing anything.

'There's the liquid we could hear,' Emily whispered, pointing to the neatly nestled vials.

'And this?' Peter pointed to what looked like a piece of parchment paper rolled up next to them.

'Perhaps it's a map! Go on. Roll it out.' Emily was eager to see what was inside. She had often pretended to search for treasure as a child with friends during her summer holidays. They would draw out maps of the area. And X always marked the spot.

But not today.

Peter lifted the tiny scroll in his hand and opened it with care. On the top, in the centre, a golden-winged disc sat atop a golden double-barred cross. The symbol his father had used to seal his secret documents. The same symbol that Raziel bore on his left wrist.

'Do you know what that symbol represents?' Emily said.

'My father used this symbol to seal his ...' Peter paused. 'Well, his clandestine correspondences.'

Emily managed a smile and a quiet laugh. 'What do you mean "his clandestine correspondences"?'

'Encoded messages that he would send to the other members of his Brotherhood.' Peter looked at the parchment once more. 'The winged disc that's drawn here is an ancient symbol of royalty, divinity and power. It was used not only in ancient Egypt, but also in Mesopotamia, Persia and Anatolia,' Peter said. He pointed to the cross beneath the disc. 'This symbol here, the double-barred cross, is the Cross of Lorraine. It's the original cross that the Templar founding members used as their symbol during the crusades. It was granted to them for use by the then Patriarch of Jerusalem.'

'A winged disc. Does it represent some other organisation? Like the Illuminati?' Emily said.

'Yes. It's also the symbol of the Nephilim Brotherhood. The ancient royal brotherhood that is far more powerful than the Templars.'

'This doesn't make sense. If this symbol represents the Nephilim and your father was working with them, then why are they trying to kill you? Remember what Raziel said at the apartment? The Nephilim will kill us if they find us. Why would your father be working with these people? And why have they now turned against him?'

'I guess that's what we need to figure out.'

Peter placed the scroll on the table in front of them and rolled it out fully. It measured about four inches wide and six inches long and contained two passages written in his father's handwriting. Peter read the two verses aloud.

'For the thing that I fear comes upon me,
And what I dread befalls me.'

Inanna lies immortalised within her stony wall,

54

A pilgrim takes a journey 'aft the giants standing tall.

Seek The Track Not Of Heaven where it lies in wait,

Neath its starry globe lies the key to your fate.'

Peter and Emily read the two verses over and over again hoping the repetition might invoke some hidden memory, or spark some idea of what they needed to do. But the words meant nothing.

'The first verse sounds very familiar. I'm sure it's a quote from the Bible,' Peter said, at last. Emily lifted her phone from her pocket and entered the quote into the search engine.

The search results appeared.

'You're right, it is a quote from the Bible. "Job laments his birth." There are several references to it. This verse is about fear. Job is talking about his fears for himself and his family.'

'I can empathise with that.' Fear was the emotion that he was experiencing right now.

He shook his head and handed the scroll to Emily. There was nothing about the verse or the quote from the Bible that made any sense to him.

She continued to examine the scroll hoping to find something, anything, etched into the paper itself. She rubbed her thumbs along it, feeling its texture. It was cream coloured and stiff. Then unexpectedly she noticed the back of the scroll separated from the front.

She was now holding two scrolls: a second had been hidden behind the first.

It was blank.

'There's a second scroll,' she said. She ran her fingers over it. The uneven texture of the first scroll was only apparent on one side of the second.

Peter held the first scroll as Emily examined the second. *Why two?* Peter thought. He couldn't comprehend the reasoning behind the blank scroll. However, he knew it must serve some purpose.

Emily sat without making a sound, deep in thought. She held the blank sheet in both hands, rubbing her thumbs and index fingers along its surface.

Peter removed one of the vials from the cylinder.

'All of these are somehow connected. We just have to figure out how,' he said. He turned the vial upside down and moved it under the light. Noticing something glistening on the bottom of the vial, he took a closer look, then raised his head and looked at Emily.

'Look! Can you see them?' Peter turned the bottom of the vial to Emily. She tilted her head to get a better look. A series of letters and numbers were imprinted in a circle onto the bottom of the vial. 'Numbers and letters. Etched in gold,' Peter said.

Emily took out another vial. Turned it upside down. More letters and numbers. Then Peter removed the final vial. Again, another set of letters and numbers. They all looked the same, but the letter and number sequences on the bottom of each were different.

Three vials. Three different combinations.

What could they be? Peter thought.

He stood up and went to the table across from where they were sitting. Two young students were deep in conversation. He spoke to them quietly as they ruffled through their bags. Emily could hear him say 'Thank you' before he arrived back at the table equipped with paper and a pencil. He wrote on the paper. Emily watched as he wrote each number and letter combination down.

N2 O4 S C16 H18

O4 S C16 H19 N3

O13 C38 H69 N

'Is it some sort of code?' Emily said, examining the sequences again.

'I'm not sure. There's nothing obvious, yet they have to mean something. Perhaps these sequences of letters and numbers describe in some way what each of the vials contains,' Peter said.

Emily read each sequence. The letters and numbers appeared to be random, yet something about them and the texture of the second scroll seemed familiar to her.

She looked at Peter and smiled. 'That's it! You're right. I know what this is. I know what the vials are for. This is perfect! A perfect way to hide a message. There *is* a connection between all these.' Emily placed the vials and the blank scroll on the table. She paused for a moment before she explained to Peter what she'd just figured out. She moved the paper in front of her and started to write, re-arranging the letters and numbers.

$$C_{16} H_{18} N_2 O_4 S$$

$$C_{16} H_{19} N_3 O_4 S$$

$$C_{38} H_{69} N O_{13}$$

She rotated the piece of paper on the table so that Peter could see what she'd just written.

'These are molecular formulae. Look here.' Emily pointed to the number and letter sequences she had re-written. 'When you write them out as they should be, you can identify what's in the vials. They're different types of antibiotics. Penicillin, ampicillin and …' Emily checked the molecular combination once again just to be sure. 'Yes I'm certain it's clarithromycin.'

Peter frowned; he couldn't see the logic in his father leaving him a piece of paper and some antibiotics. Especially since he was allergic to penicillin. 'For what? What am I expected to do with antibiotics? This doesn't make any sense.'

'But there's more. This sheet has a nitrocellulose membrane on this side here.' Emily pointed to the blank scroll she was holding. 'Feel it. You can tell by the even, silky texture and the yellowish white colour.' She handed the scroll to Peter.

He rubbed his thumbs along its surface. It was smooth and even, unlike the scroll with the verses written on it.

'Your father had been working on a way to use biological systems to encrypt information. He was working on a system to genetically manipulate E. coli to fluoresce in response to a certain type of antibiotic.' Peter stared at her. He was beginning to realise how little he know about the work his father had done. 'He was developing the technique so that he could send encoded messages. Only the receiver would know the correct key. I'm betting that on this sheet there's E. coli that your father would've genetically modified to respond to a specific type of antibiotic that's in one of these vials. If we use the correct antibiotic, we'll get whatever message he left you.'

'How do we know which antibiotic to use?'

'*You* must know. It has to be something that's significant to you. You have to figure out which one to use. Otherwise this is meaningless. The first verse – does it mean anything at all to you?'

Peter looked once again at the vials. Then at the scroll. He read the verse aloud. 'For the thing that I fear comes upon me, and what I dread befalls me.' He repeated the words over and over.

What do I fear? What do I dread? he thought.

Then it dawned on him. He was transported reluctantly back to his fourth birthday. He had spent the previous two weeks in hospital. Unbeknown to his parents at that time, Peter had been allergic to penicillin and a dose of the drug for a chest infection had almost killed him. One week in ICU, a further week recovering in hospital and careful rehabilitation at home had seen him back on his feet, but only just. The memories of this event had stayed with Peter, as did the fear of ever receiving penicillin again. He held the vial of penicillin and smiled at Emily.

Both of them spoke in unison.

'Penicillin!'

'That has to be it. My allergy to penicillin. That's what I fear most. This is what the passage from the Bible is telling me.'

'Then we need to get to a lab. Whatever's on that sheet can be unlocked with this vial. I'll call in a favour from an old friend.' Emily took her phone out of her pocket and made the call.

Peter looked at his watch.

It was 12.56 a.m.

Chapter 10

Abaddon stood motionless in the centre of Lombard Street outside the museum entrance. He could still see the outline of the black Range Rover as it sped into the distance and turned left onto Coetzee Street. He knew, all too well, how things could accelerate out of his control. He couldn't help but feel his plans were hurtling into disarray. His enemies had once again escaped with something he needed. The sounds of his henchmen calling for backup transportation rang in his ears as his mind churned with thoughts of the spheres leaving South Africa and never appearing again, rendering Nergal's plans useless. A silent rage built inside him.

'Father, judging by the amount of blood that has accumulated at the museum exit, he will not survive without medical attention. We should follow him now while he is wounded and ensure we capture him before he can get the spheres to safety. The vehicle is low jacked. We're tracking him,' Meregel said, and pointed toward the black van that had just screeched to a halt behind them.

Abaddon faced his son. He remained still for a moment – weighing up his options. He recalled the earlier conversation he'd had with Nergal before he arrived at the museum. Nergal's plans were unfolding just as he had expected. Madeloy was the Templar Grand Master they had been looking for. The spheres were where she'd said they'd be. Nergal's contact had served him well and had stayed true to her promises. They were now closer than ever to realising their dreams. The consequences of his failure to secure the spheres were immeasurable. He could not fail Nergal. Lochemel must be stopped.

Abaddon walked toward the vehicle. He could hear his

son, Meregel, instruct the remaining guards to get the Range Rover back in action before he sat into the back of the van beside his father. Two of their henchmen were close behind him and shut the door. One of them was focused on a blue dot moving across a map of Klerksdorp. Lochemel's every move was being tracked.

Meregel looked at his father. 'My sources sent me the location of the aircraft he was going to use to leave South Africa and return to their base. We have taken control of it. He will not be leaving South Africa anytime soon.'

Abaddon remained silent, staring out the back window of the van.

'Do you know who he is?' Meregel asked tentatively, he was expecting to get an icy glance or no reply at all.

Abaddon looked at his son. 'His name is Lochemel. He is a Nephilim loyal to our enemy. He cares nothing of our plight. He only cares about serving his leader, Marduk. He will not falter from his task, nor will his emotions for anyone, or anything, get in his way. We should not hesitate to remove him from our path should he come between us and our ultimate goals. He will not be turned against Marduk,' Abaddon said.

'And the spheres. What are they for?'

'You will see soon enough. They are part of an ancient device created by the Nephilim a long time ago. They are the means by which we will bring the humans and those Nephilim who resist us to their knees.' Abaddon thought of the last time the spheres were unleashed on Earth and the devastation they had caused. He stared straight ahead. 'There are very few who know what truly lies beneath the surface of the Earth. Or what you can uncover beneath the ancient soil on which we exist. All you need to do is seek and you shall find.'

Chapter 11

The metallic red roof of the Mini Cooper could be seen from the doors of the scientific research centre off Marine Esplanade in Edinburgh as it meandered through the car park and came to a stop outside the main entrance. The research centre director, Eugene Reid, had been a good friend of Emily's since they had graduated from Trinity College in Dublin over four years ago.

'Hey Emily. Hey Peter.' Eugene said as he approached where they stood. His large smile that framed his veneered teeth was further accentuated by his thick black-framed glasses and his shoulder-length brown wavy hair.

'Hi,' Emily said, beginning to feel a little tired.

'Thanks for doing this,' Peter said, noticing that Eugene was a little more unnerved and clumsy than usual, as he watched him fiddle with a large set of keys.

'Not a problem,' Eugene said, in his deep, strong Irish accent before finding the correct key. He glanced behind him, then placed the key in the lock and unlocked the door. He pushed the door forward and ushered them both inside. 'Give me one second,' he said, as he rushed toward the reception desk.

Peter frowned and whispered to Emily, 'Is it just me or is he very jittery?'

'Yeah. He does look more unnerved that usual.' She watched Eugene turn off the alarm before returning to where they were standing.

'Are you sure you're okay with this?' Emily said. She knew Eugene was never one to break the rules and that she was asking a lot of him. To sneak them into a state-owned lab at 1.33 a.m. and use the equipment for personal reasons was without question breaking the rules. But Emily had no doubt that the nitrocellulose sheet contained a strain of E. coli, which under the right conditions could be cultivated in around twenty minutes. Eugene would be back home in no time and she and Peter would be one step closer to figuring out his father's secrets.

Eugene let out a brief sigh. 'Your father's murder is all over the TV.'

'I know,' Peter said. 'That's why we're here. We're trying to find out why he was killed and perhaps who's responsible for his death.'

Eugene pushed his glasses up the bridge of his nose. 'There are policemen and women who could do that for you,' he said.

'It's a sensitive matter. There's no one we can trust at the moment,' Peter said, in a firm voice.

'Well then, anything I can do to help.' Eugene looked at Emily. 'You said you need to cultivate and transfer something from a nitrocellulose sheet. The lab is this way.' Eugene pointed to a door straight across from the reception desk. She and Peter followed close behind him.

Eugene opened the lab door and reached for the lights on the wall to his right. He flicked the switch and the extensive laboratory lit up. The light bounced off the white walls momentarily blinding an unsuspecting Peter, who could barely make out the myriad of equipment neatly arranged across the worktops nearest the walls on either side and down the centre of the lab. Eugene led Peter and Emily to the farthest end of the room, where the equipment he needed to cultivate the bacteria was located.

He stopped and faced Emily. 'Do you have the membrane?'

'It's in here,' Peter said, taking the black cylinder from

his pocket and holding it carefully between his palms.

Eugene watched with interest as the green beam of light flashed across Peter's face and the cylinder hissed open. Peter placed the open cylinder on the countertop beside them. Emily removed the scrolls from the cylinder. She rolled them out and glanced at Peter.

There was only one scroll: the sheet of nitrocellulose.

Peter patted his chest, indicating to her that he'd kept the other scroll in his jacket. Relieved it hadn't been lost, Emily explained to Eugene what they needed to do.

'Peter's father had been working on a way to genetically modify E. coli to fluoresce in response to the introduction of a certain medium. He was developing the technique so that he could encode messages within bacteria. Marcus would have seeded the E. coli in a coded pattern onto an agar plate and then transferred it to this sheet. What we need to do is cultivate the E. coli that's on this membrane and introduce the antibiotic medium so we can access Marcus' message.'

Eugene nodded, listening to her every word. 'You do know that you need the correct medium to decode the message. Which I'm presuming is in one of these vials.' He held one of the small vials up to the light.

'We know,' Peter said. 'We think it's penicillin that will decode the correct message.'

'And you know that how?'

Peter stalled before answering. He was reluctant to give Eugene too much information. Firstly, because he didn't know who, to trust, and secondly, too much information could get him killed. 'My father left me a clue. And I'm sure the correct vial is the one with penicillin in it. Telling you any more than that could put you in grave danger.'

Eugene raised his eyebrows in response to Peter's covert

yet effective warning.

'Penicillin it is then,' Eugene said.

Emily handed him the vial of penicillin from the cylinder. Eugene paused, lost in thought.

'Eugene?' Emily placed her hand on his arm. 'We kind of have a tight deadline.' She handed him the nitrocellulose sheet.

'Of course,' he said, taking the sheet. 'You know if you introduce the wrong medium, you'll get the wrong message,' Eugene said, shuffling toward a refrigerator against the wall behind him.

'We know,' Emily said, and moved closer to Peter. He was staring at his mobile phone, waiting for any sign of contact from his mother's kidnappers or his sister returning his call. 'You look exhausted,' she said.

'I'm fine,' Peter whispered, to reassure her.

She smiled at him and looked around the lab. 'I'll help Eugene to get this done as soon as possible. We can speed up the cultivation process, so it shouldn't take longer than half an hour. Why don't you take a seat in there?' She pointed to a nearby office enclosed behind a glass partition. 'Maybe it'll help clear your head to sit alone for a while. You never know, something might just trigger a memory that will help. Soon as we've cultivated what's on the nitrocellulose sheet, I'll come and get you.'

Peter nodded and strolled to the office. He slumped into a comfortable black padded leather chair behind a large pine desk. It could swivel around a full three hundred and sixty degrees. He had a bird's eye view of the entire lab; Emily and Eugene were moving between pieces of lab equipment. His head felt heavy and his thoughts drifted to his sister. He'd still had no reply to the messages he'd left her. If she had been kidnapped, Peter was sure the stranger on the phone would have mentioned that fact.

Peter thought of the scroll. He lifted it from his jacket pocket and reread the passage. He felt overwhelmed. Even if they did decode the message on the blank scroll, was he going to be able to see this through to the end? Would he even be able to understand it? Peter knew he needed more help. He lifted his mobile phone and shuffled through his recent contact list. He touched the screen and made a call.

'Calling Daniel' displayed in the centre of the screen. He was very close to his uncle and despite the late hour he knew he could call his uncle at any time, but there was no response. Daniel in all likelihood had his phone on silent, so he left a message for him to call him back.

He looked at the time on the top left-hand corner of his phone. It was 2.13 a.m.

Outside the office Peter could hear soft footsteps coming toward him. It was Emily. She looked at the mobile phone in Peter's hand.

'Did you get another call from him?' Emily said, her voice beginning to tremble.

'No.' Peter stared at his phone. 'I think we should get some help.'

'Can we trust the police?'

'I wasn't thinking of the police. I've called Daniel.' He looked at Emily for any hint of hesitation; he knew his uncle, a professor of philology and mythology at Trinity College Dublin, was eccentric in an Indiana Jones type of way, with an innate ability to cause a storm in a teacup. His motto 'Don't knock it till you've tried it' epitomised his existence. But Peter knew he could trust him, and given the nature of what they were looking for, he needed the knowledge Daniel had gathered as an avid researcher of veiled organisations and ancient secrets. He was perhaps one of the best in his field. Deep down, Peter knew that Emily realised this. She had often commented on how great his mind was. However, she always followed that statement with the words: 'There's a chance that someday his mind might just get us all killed.'

'He does know a lot about ancient artefacts, and he is mum's brother. We need to let him know she's in danger.'

'Okay,' Emily said in a quiet tone. She knew Peter was right. Although Daniel had a daughter of his own, he and Peter were very close and no matter what happened she knew Daniel would give his life to protect Peter.

'I hope he'll call me back soon.' Peter stood up. 'So what have you found? Is it a map?'

'I'm not sure what it is. I don't think it's a map. It's just a series of bright dots.'

'Bright dots!' Peter had been hoping for something more meaningful and concrete.

'Come and take a look. Maybe they'll mean something to you.'

He followed her back to Eugene, who was looking at an agar plate he'd placed beneath an ultraviolet light to increase the fluorescence the bacteria were producing.

'Their luminescence is fading. You'd better come and look at this quick.' Eugene's deep Irish accent was tinted with a sense of urgency.

Peter stared at the agar plate. He counted the dots. 'Thirteen fluorescent blue dots,' he said. They were scattered around the agar plate. Then he noticed, at the very top, a group of bacteria had formed another shape in a red fluorescent pattern. 'And the Cross of Lorraine. None of this makes any sense,' he said.

Chapter 12

Positioned deep within a subglacial lake, two miles beneath the astronomical observatory, surrounded by an electromagnetic field that distorted any image of its structure and prevented anyone from finding its exact location, the Nephilim base was an ancient impenetrable fortress. From the outside the windowless edifice was designed like an enormous torpedo, supported at its base by six giant columns embedded well below the lakebed to secure it in place.

Within the cylindrical structure its intricate functions were maintained by three hundred and fifteen members of the Nephilim Brotherhood who lived and worked on the base. On the first floor, the level closest to the lakebed, an ancient power source sat in a vault forty foot in diameter. It was only accessible through a long, vertical, cylindrical shaft that stretched upward through the centre of each of the six levels within the base, toward a circular door that opened into the centre of the immense hangar bay on level six.

One level above the first floor the secure control room was bustling with activity. The vast circular space was divided across its diameter into two sections. On one side, analysts were sitting at their workstations tracking and analysing information from the Nephilim's many satellites in low-earth and geostationary orbits around the Earth. Others, known as special operations supervisors, were organising, tracking, and analysing all Nephilim operations, including the information being relayed to the base from the observatory atop the ice sheet, two miles above. On the other side of the room, technicians were encoding and decoding all communications into and out of the base. Security personnel were continually scrutinising the base's advanced security features, including drones, force fields, electromagnetic fields and the polar satellites that monitored the area around the east Antarctic ice sheet beneath which the base was located.

Chasid sat at a desk watching data filter onto the enormous screen surrounding the section of the vault shaft that passed through the centre of the control room. He was dressed in the standard uniform worn by the base's security personnel and other operatives when on duty – thick heavy black boots, navy slacks and a navy sweatshirt with a golden-winged disc embellished into the top left-hand side. Moments earlier Lochemel's transponder signal had been activated, and as he was unable to contact the operatives that had accompanied Lochemel on his mission to bring the spheres back to the Antarctic base, Chasid was following his movements across Klerksdorp in South Africa knowing that their enemy would be hot on Lochemel's tail. Chasid glanced once more at the message on his phone.

The time has come.

The message that had prompted him to instruct Lochemel to move the spheres. The message that had signalled they were under attack and that his trusted friend Marcus DeMolay was dead.

Chasid stretched his head backward and stared at the ceiling high above him. *If I can get to Lochemel in time, I may be able to salvage the situation without having to let Marduk know,* he thought. He would only inform Marduk, the Nephilim leader, if the situation warranted his involvement. And right now he was not prepared to accept defeat.

Chasid pushed an icon on the screen in front of him.

'Speak!' he commanded.

'The LEO and an operations team are ready. You will be in South Africa within the next half hour.' The young male voice echoed out from the screen in front of Chasid. 'Sir, there is something else you need to see before you leave,' he said before Chasid had a chance to end the call.

'What is it?' Chasid said.

'I have just received the satellite footage from the front of the museum at Klerksdorp, sir. You might want to take a look at it before you leave the base.' The young man's deep accent was wrought with urgency. Chasid frowned and ended the call. He didn't want to be delayed any further, but he knew that Ulpan would not delay him without good reason.

Chasid touched another icon on the screen and watched the recording of the satellite footage of the Klerksdorp Museum. He watched Lochemel leave in one of their enemy's vehicles. Chasid breathed a sigh of relief, then leaned in closer to get a better look at his adversaries – Meregel and Abaddon entering a vehicle in front of the museum. Chasid felt a growing ominous apprehension build inside him. Abaddon was a ruthless, meticulous killer and would stop at nothing to get what he wanted. Lochemel needed Chasid's help sooner rather than later.

Chasid stood up. He knew that Marduk's fleet of Low Earth Orbiters, referred to as LEOs and capable of flying at over seventeen thousand miles per hour in a low-earth orbit, would get him to Lochemel in just under half an hour. Once in orbit, the aircraft could reach staggering speeds within seconds and transport its passengers to anywhere on Earth in a fraction of the time that even the fastest aircraft known to humans could achieve. Chasid could rendezvous with Lochemel in a matter of minutes and rescue the spheres. The situation was still salvageable.

The climate-controlled air inside the base felt heavy as Chasid walked toward the lift on the western side of the control room. He navigated his way past the twenty-six Nephilim operatives sitting at their desks carrying out various tasks, one of whom was organising random special operations teams to respond to threats to Marduk and his corporation, LINEL Aerospace.

Chasid came to a stop behind Ulpan. The striking blond-haired, blue-eyed young man looked up at him.

'Section twelve, sir. They're waiting for you,' he said.

'Continue to relay the transponder signal to me. I do not want to lose his location,' Chasid said. Ulpan nodded and watched as he placed a small communications device in his right ear and entered the lift.

Inside, Chasid watched the display move through each level of the base as it brought him to the aircraft hangar bay on the sixth floor. The lift came to a stop and the doors opened, and he walked in a north-westerly direction toward section twelve, crossing the entrance to the vault in the centre of the golden-winged disc etched in the middle of the hangar bay floor. A team of four operatives were waiting beside the LEO that would take them to South Africa. They were dressed in black uniforms and were busy talking and readying their weapons for use. Chasid pushed the small button on the outside of his earpiece and made a call as he hurried toward the aircraft. He heard a beep in his ear.

'Rossi,' Chasid said the instant the call was answered. He waited a moment for a reply; a cough and a muffled voice came through from the other end.

'Hello,' the male voice answered.

'Rossi, it is Chasid. I am sending you someone who is being pursued by Abaddon, one of our deadliest enemies. Lochemel will be at your door any moment now. You need to keep him safe until I arrive. I am approximately thirty minutes out,' Chasid said as he walked up the gangway and into the back of the aircraft.

'I … I understand,' Rossi said.

Chasid ended the call. 'I want you to take a team to Gibil in the Transvaal Mountains and Make sure he is secure. If Abaddon gets the spheres, that is where he will go to next.' He said to the soldier next to him.

Chapter 13

Peter held his mobile phone above the transparent agar plate and took a picture. There was silence in the lab as he stared at the maze of dots on the screen. The only pattern that was recognisable without hesitation was the Cross of Lorraine, the symbol the original Knights Templar used during the crusades.

He moved his phone from side to side, looking at the dots from different angles. He walked to the other end of the lab. There had to be some sort of pattern amidst the collection of dots. Something he would recognise. Something he knew his father would have thought was familiar to him. He just couldn't figure out what.

He stood for a moment and repeated the verse in his head. His thoughts were interrupted by the sound of Emily's voice.

'The cross has to be there for a reason. It has to mean something other than just a symbol your father or the Templars used.'

'The Cross of Lorraine when drawn symmetrically, as it is here, is a hermetic maxim translated as "As above so below",' Eugene said out of the blue.

'Really!' Emily said.

Eugene nodded.

Peter looked at him, then gazed at the blank wall in front of him. He could see an imprint of the dots on the white wall as random pieces from his father's clue, and Eugene's words flowed through his mind. *As above so below. As above, Heaven, track not of Heaven; these are connected, somehow,* he thought. In an instant everything became clear. The series of dots on the agar plate – he'd seen this pattern hundreds of times before. Just not like this. And the cross was a message telling him what the dots represented.

He faced Emily and Eugene. 'Eugene, that's it! You're a genius. The dots are arranged in the same configuration as—' Peter stopped mid-sentence.

'Carry on,' Eugene said. He was holding a gun to Emily's head. 'We've been watching you for some time now, Peter. All they want is the location of the artefact. To give it to the Nephilim who attacked you tonight would be a mistake. Your father's secrets need to be buried, so humankind can never find out about their true heritage. Knowledge like that would only make us harder to control.' Eugene's head twitched to the side. 'I have been instructed to kill you both, but if you cooperate, I'll lock you in the lab until morning. It'll all be over by then.' Eugene's face was pallid and taut.

Peter's thoughts turned straight away to his mother. *She'll be dead by then.*

Peter held his hands in the air, level with his shoulders. His fingers held tight across his phone. He was about to try to convince Eugene to put the gun down, and think about what he was doing, when all of a sudden his phone started to vibrate.

Eugene's concentration lapsed for a moment. Just enough for Emily to elbow him hard in the gut, forcing him to heave forward in an effort to catch his breath, while a reflex action caused him to pull the trigger before he dropped the gun to the floor. One bullet fired from the gun, aimed in Peter's direction. It skimmed past him missing his left hip by millimetres. Emily lunged forward and grabbed the gun. She held it tight with both hands and pointed it at Eugene.

'If you move, I'll shoot. I mean it!' she said.

Eugene hunched over, nursing his wounded stomach.

Emily glanced at Peter. 'Are you okay?' she said.

'I'm fine.' Peter checked his waist for any sign of injury. 'That bullet just missed me!' He eyed the spot where the bullet had lodged in the laboratory wall, then realised his phone was still vibrating.

'I'd better answer this. It's Daniel. If he moves, shoot him,' Peter said, tapping the screen on his phone to answer the call. He could just about hear the voice on the other end. The half yawning, half talking male sounded like a disgruntled Irish bear. Peter was relieved to hear his uncle's voice.

'Hey shorty. Has she thrown you out already?' Daniel said.

'Daniel, I need your help.'

There was seriousness in Peter's voice that unsettled Daniel a little. 'Have you been arrested?'

'No. Not yet. It's much worse than that. Dad is dead.'

'What do you mean, Marcus is dead?'

'He was murdered this evening. At Balantrodoch. Haven't you been watching the news?' A lump formed in Peter's throat at the thought of his father lying dead.

'No. All my recent late nights on the town caught up with me, so I went to bed early.'

Peter could hear his uncle move in the background.

'I'm getting dressed. Stay right where you are. I'll be on the next flight up to you.'

'Wait. There's more.'

'More!'

'The people who killed Dad have kidnapped Mum. And Ava's not safe either. I've tried to call her but there was no answer.' Peter paused to catch his breath. 'Mum will be dead in twenty-one hours if I don't give her kidnappers the location of what Dad was protecting. And Raziel came to my apartment tonight. You remember the guy I told you about – the one Dad had introduced me to?'

'Yeah, I remember.'

'He gave me a cylinder Dad had left for me. He said that the Nephilim could not be trusted and I should try to protect Dad's secrets at all costs.'

'Did you open the cylinder?' Daniel felt his pulse begin to race.

'Yes. But it's a long story. He's left me what looks like a map of the constellation of Virgo laid out beneath the Cross of Lorraine, and a cryptic verse, some of which we've already figured out.' Peter stalled for a moment. 'Daniel, I just can't focus. Everything is happening too fast.'

There was silence on the other end.

'Peter, take a deep breath. Are you hurt?' his uncle said in an even tone.

'No. I'm fine.'

'Where's Emily? Is she there with you? Is she okay?'

'Yes, and yes she's fine. She's just a little busy at the moment.' Peter glanced at his wife holding Eugene at gunpoint.

'Are you sure it's the constellation of Virgo and the Cross of Lorraine? The Cross of Lorraine has two bars on it.'

'Yes, I'm positive. The dots are in the exact formation of the constellation, and I'm sure the cross is the original double-barred one the Templars used during the crusades.

I've seen them both hundreds of times before.'

'The verse – read it to me.'

Peter took the scroll from his pocket and read the verse to his uncle. '"Inanna lies immortalised within her stony wall, a pilgrim takes a journey 'aft the giants standing tall. Seek the track not of Heaven where it lies in wait, neath its starry globe lies the key to your fate."'

Daniel remained silent as he digested the words. 'Son, you know you can't trust anyone.'

'I know,' Peter said in a low voice.

'Where are you now?'

'We're in a lab near Seafield. Eugene, a friend of Emily's, was helping us to decode the message Dad left. She's holding a gun to his head at the moment. He kind of ... turned on us.'

'You know there are several organisations that would like to get their hands on what you have.'

'At the moment I have nothing.'

'On the contrary, Peter, at the moment you have everything.' Daniel said in a confident tone. 'Listen to me. Can you send me a photo of the dots and the verse?'

'I'll send it to you now.'

'Good. I reckon it'll be safer if you get out of Edinburgh. You can fly down to London yourself; just make sure you leave no trail behind. That should give you a head start. You'll also need to lock your friend Eugene up somewhere and make sure he can't get out. Take his phone and don't let him contact anyone. He already knows too much. When you get to London, come to the meeting statue. I'll get your sister and we'll meet you there. You understand where I'm talking about, don't you?' Daniel said.

'Yes, I understand. I'll see you there.' Peter ended the call. He walked over to Emily and Eugene.

'You've no idea whom your father was working with and what he was hiding for him, do you?' Eugene said.

'And you do?' Peter said sarcastically.

'The Nephilim are everywhere – different factions of them scattered throughout the globe. Nergal is not your only enemy.'

'Nergal?'

'Yes. The Nephilim that was at your apartment this evening. The one who almost captured you.'

'Why would you do something like this? Why would you betray your friends?' Emily said, and tightened her grip on the gun.

'When Nergal murdered your father this evening, it sent a shockwave throughout a secret world that only a select few know exist. An ancient war has been re-ignited with each side vying to get control over your father's secrets. Imagine! Secrets that would change everything. Tell me, Peter and Emily, what if we were suddenly thrust into a world where we were certain that only one version of God exists, where everything we know, everything we believed in, had been a lie? Our entire existence would be thrown into chaos,' Eugene said.

'So you know the man who murdered my father?' Peter said scowling at him.

'Peter DeMolay, you ignorant fool! Oh yes, I know all about you. You'll follow in your father's footsteps for sure. Right to a grave beside him.'

Peter extended his fist at Eugene's face with as much force as he could muster. It made contact with Eugene's nose sending him faltering backward, flat on his back. Blood streamed down his face as he looked at Peter.

'Do what you want. I'll tell you nothing. When they realise I have failed, they'll kill me anyway,' Eugene said, nursing his broken nose.

Peter looked at Emily who remained steadfast pointing the gun at Eugene.

'There's a storage room at the back of the lab. We can lock him in there. No one will find him until Monday morning,' she said.

Peter pulled Eugene to his feet and pointed him toward the storage room. 'Move,' he said and shoved Eugene forward.

'They'll get you no matter where you go,' Eugene said as Peter locked the storage room door.

He then placed his hand on Emily's arm. 'I've arranged to meet Daniel. We need to get to London.' Peter looked at the time on his phone. 'We most likely won't get a flight there at this time of night. So, honey, I know you're not going to like this, but I'm going to have to fly us there.'

Chapter 14

Daniel O'Brien was feeling a small sense of relief as he ended the phone call he had just made. At last he had been able to contact his niece, Ava. He had advised her to stay at home and keep her doors locked, but Ava was headstrong and had insisted on coming with him to meet Peter. By now she was traversing the short distance between their two apartments in London so she could be with her uncle and brother until her mother was found unharmed.

He waited patiently to hear his phone chime, as visions of what Peter was about to uncover were suspended before his eyes. For years he had been shunned by the academic community as a conspiracy theorist with a PhD. But tonight, perhaps this was all about to change. For some time, Daniel had been aware that his brother-in-law, Marcus DeMolay, was a descendant of the legendary Jacques DeMolay, and a Templar Grand Master. It was a family secret kept as deeply hidden as the ancient treasures the Templars had uncovered all those centuries ago beneath the Temple Mount.

For years the existence of Solomon's Temple was debated with heated enthusiasm in academic circles. The Bible had credited its construction to Solomon, King of the Israelites, during the tenth century before Christ and its destruction some time later, after the siege of Jerusalem in 587 BC, by Nebuchadnezzar II. But because of the tumultuous history of the area, no direct archaeological evidence to prove the Temple's existence had survived. And with no surviving evidence, outside of that in the Bible, the existence of Solomon's Temple was deemed a myth, just like the Templars who remained to this day. Yet rumours and legends and even ancient writings preserved their fabled existences.

Daniel's phone chimed. He lifted it, slid off his bed and strolled toward his bedroom door. He ran his finger across the mobile's screen and opened the message from Peter. He stared at the first image it contained. A shot of adrenaline surged through him. The genetically modified bacteria were indeed showing the constellation of Virgo beneath the Cross of Lorraine. A clue that Peter, as an astrophysicist, would no doubt recognise.

Daniel flicked to the second image that showed a small scroll. He read the verses written on it with care.

'For the thing that I fear comes upon me,
And what I dread befalls me.'

Inanna lies immortalised within her stony wall,
A pilgrim takes a journey 'aft the giants standing tall.
Seek The Track Not Of Heaven where it lies in wait,
Neath its starry globe lies the key to your fate.

Daniel now had a complete understanding of why Peter had figured out the first part of the clue – facing one's fears was always a good motivator.

He glanced at the clock on his bedside table.

2.57 a.m.

He knew it would take Peter at least three hours to prepare a flight plan and fly from Scotland to London in his own light aircraft. This would provide Daniel with just enough time to try to figure out where Marcus intended them to go.

He grabbed his black dressing gown from the back of his bedroom door, put it on and walked barefoot to the kitchen at the furthest end of his London apartment. A warm cup of tea was just what he needed. It would help him focus on what Peter had just sent him.

Daniel cleared his mind and focused on the second verse. He read it over and over again, looking for the hidden meanings in each line. The sound of the kettle boiling beside him faded away as his mind wandered through the verse.

Inanna, he thought. *The queen of Heaven and Earth. She is immortalised in this place.*

He rubbed his hand across his stubble-covered chin and poured the boiling water into the cup on the worktop. He looked at his reflection in the glass door of the cabinet. His light-brown, ginger-tinted hair was greying at the sides, yet his youthful face veiled his fifty-two years. Daniel had always credited his youthful appearance in part to his Irish heritage, but above all to his beautiful daughter, Rachel, whom he always said kept him young in heart, mind, body and soul.

He sipped on the freshly brewed cup of green tea. The aroma filled his lungs. He strolled out of the kitchen and into the sitting room. Again, repeating the verse over and over in his mind.

'A pilgrim takes a journey,' he said aloud.

Somewhere that pilgrims journey to. To a holy place. A grotto. A church.

Daniel sat on the brown couch near the large bay window.

The constellation of Virgo. The Cross of Lorraine. These two have to be connected somehow.

He stared at the bookcase across from where he was

sitting. He placed his cup on the small table beside him and stood upright. He walked to the bookcase and removed his computer tablet from the top shelf. He switched it on and ran an internet search of the words 'The constellation of Virgo'.

Various results flooded the screen: pictures of the constellation, the translation of the Latin word 'Virgo' – the virgin. Another result revealed that the constellation had twenty-six known exoplanets, and another that Virgo was the only female member of the Zodiac.

Daniel looked at his bookcase once again. The moonlight shone on his collection of replicas of ancient artefacts, showing each in a different light. His gaze was drawn to the goddess replica on top of the oak bookshelf and he took it down to examine it. He had often used the statue to prove a point. The original statue, known as the goddess with the vase, measured almost five feet in height and had been found in Mari, an ancient city on the western bank of the Euphrates, in what is known today as Syria. What Daniel had found most intriguing about the statue was the exotic headdress and clothing carved out by a civilisation that was over four thousand years old.

He moved the four-inch high white replica around in his hand. From behind, the headdress looked like a helmet, with what seemed like a pair of objects covering her ears. Two parallel straps ran across her chest and around her back and seemed to hold in place an unusual rectangular box secured to the helmet with a horizontal strap. All of this was supported by two large shoulder pads which seemed to take the weight of the rectangular box. To Daniel it looked more like an ancient astronaut suit than an ornate headdress and clothing. But this idea had been dismissed in an instant by the enlightened academics who had insisted she wore an ancient irrigation system, which would allow the statue be used as a fountain. She was not an astronaut. After all, astronauts and space flight didn't exist at the time she was carved, over four thousand years ago.

Daniel laughed to himself and allowed his mind to ponder the search results he'd read through.

The constellation of Virgo. The lady in the sky. A map showing the specific locations of stars in the sky. He looked again at the image Peter had sent him.

The Cross of Lorraine.

The symbol used by the Templars during the crusades when they helped pilgrims to travel in safety to the Holy Land. He knew the symbol was an aphorism translated as 'As above so below'. Daniel studied the image on his phone.

As above so below, could that really be it? he thought.

He typed the words 'Virgo, France, map' into the search engine on his tablet and watched the results display on the screen. In an instant he was sure. Marcus was telling them to go to a place where Inanna, the queen of Heaven and Earth, was indeed immortalised by the Templars almost nine hundred years ago. What Marcus had been trying to tell all of a sudden became very clear. The stars in the constellation corresponded to particular places on Earth.

Daniel was sure it was a map and there was no doubt in his mind.

Marcus was telling them to go to Northern France.

Chapter 15

Lochemel parked on Brenda Avenue. He was relieved to hear his mobile phone ring. His plans to rendezvous with the Nephilim operations team at Klerksdorp Airport and to get out of South Africa with the spheres had come undone, and he knew his wounds would overcome him before he could get the spheres to safety. He lifted the backpack onto his lap, removed his phone from inside a small pocket at the front and replaced the backpack on the passenger seat. He answered the call and used his shoulder to hold the phone against his ear.

'Chasid, I have secured the spheres, but I am being followed.' An air of disappointment lingered in Lochemel's voice. He had been hoping to retrieve the spheres without being noticed, but his adversary was hot on his heels. He grabbed the backpack and got out of the vehicle. He walked as fast as he could along Brenda Avenue in the direction of Benroy Street, pressing his wound in an effort to stall the bleeding.

'I know. It is Abaddon,' Chasid said.

There was a momentary silence as both Chasid and Lochemel calculated their next move.

'I am walking east toward Elysia Avenue. I have abandoned the vehicle I stole from him. I am sure they have a tracking device on all their vehicles just like we have on ours, so they will have an approximation of my current location. Chasid, I am injured and I fear I cannot protect the spheres for much longer. I am now on foot and need to reach one of our allies soon.' Lochemel's breathing had become quicker and deeper.

'Lochemel, my friend, there is a cathedral on Poppy Avenue, not far from where you are now. We have many allies in the Catholic Church. I have already spoken to Cardinal Rossi – he will meet you at the cathedral and he has agreed to keep you safe until I arrive.'

'Understood,' Lochemel said, and ended the call.

He held firmly onto his backpack . He placed his phone into his jacket pocket and leaned against the wall on his left. A searing pain ran through his abdomen. The tree-lined avenue before him was wavering as if he were staring at a mirage. His only hope now was that he would stay conscious long enough to reach the cathedral.

~

Chasid's eyes focused on the transponder beacon. It came to a standstill, then it started to move again down Krisant Street toward Poppy Avenue.

'What is taking so long?' Chasid asked the pilot.

'We are ten minutes out, sir. And we are travelling at top speed. There is nothing more I can do,' the pilot said, speaking into the microphone arched across his face from his helmet.

Chasid thumped the hull of the aircraft.

I never should have let him go alone. He will be dead by the time we get there.

Chapter 16

Sophia looked out of the vehicle window to her left. She was looking for a sign of anything familiar that would tell her where Nergal was taking her next, but the surrounding landscape was difficult to identify in the darkness. She looked as far ahead as she could see. In the distance a familiar white sign became visible, as the light from the vehicle brushed against its reflective surface. She could see the words 'Edinburgh Airport' displayed across the top.

She looked at Nergal sitting opposite her and wondered whom he would torment this time. He was searching through the contact list on his phone. She'd been both horrified and relieved the last time Nergal had made a call, and even though she regretted that her son, Peter, was left to bear his father's burdens, she was glad to hear his voice. Her thoughts drifted to her daughter, Ava. She had wondered if she too had become a victim of Nergal's lust for power. Ava lived close to her brother, Daniel, in London and she knew that Peter would tell her to go to him at the first sign of any trouble. *Daniel will keep her safe*, Sophia thought, and once again watched the road ahead. She noticed that the vehicle had passed the airport and continued in a westerly direction, as Nergal lifted his phone to his ear and spoke.

'I am sorry. I was unable to sway him. He would not reveal his secret location to me, so I had to kill him and make him reveal his secrets to his son,' Nergal said.

There was a momentary silence on the other end before the female voice replied. 'His life was in his own hands and now his son must bear the same fate. Either he gives you what you are looking for or you will take it from him.'

Sophia could just about hear the quiet female voice

respond to Nergal, but something about it seemed familiar. She focused on Nergal's phone call and sat forward hoping to hear the muffled voice on the other end a little better.

Nergal's smile widened. 'How are things progressing on your end?' He said.

'I should have a location for you soon.'

A lump formed in Sophia's throat and a nauseating sensation settled in the pit of her stomach. The voice was familiar. In fact she knew it very well.

'You will be rewarded for what you have done. Without you we would have never been able to find my brother's allies. Soon they will be defeated and everything will be ours.'

'Yes. Soon we will get what is rightfully ours.'

Nergal's excitement at the prospect of his plans becoming reality rose as he ended the call. Visions of his destiny being fulfilled flashed before him.

Sophia could feel a knot in her stomach as the vehicle came to a stop and the driver opened the partition behind his seat.

'We have arrived, your Majesty. The aircraft is ready to leave,' the driver said, and closed the partition again.

Nergal looked at Sophia. He could tell by the vacant, troubled look on her face that she had recognised his accomplice's voice.

He leaned in close to her.

'There is nothing you can do for your son now. His father has sealed his fate for him. The wheels of destiny have been set in motion. Soon I will triumph and the Earth will tremble beneath my feet,' Nergal said, and exited the vehicle.

Sophia watched him walk to the jet. Then all of a sudden, the door beside her swung open. A strong hand grabbed her arm and pulled her out of the vehicle toward the jet. She had neither the strength nor the will to fight him off. She followed her kidnappers onto the aircraft awaiting them in the hangar bay. She now knew how profoundly deceived her husband had been and hoped that her son, Peter, would figure out who his enemies were before it was too late.

Chapter 17

'Bring my car to the rear entrance of the church and wait for me. Keep the engine running. I'll meet you there in a moment,' Rossi said, and watched his aide, Father Gustavus, leave the room to carry out his request.

Rossi stood up. His red vestments flowed out in front of his six-foot frame. He removed the red cardinal's cap from his head revealing his thinning hairline and grasped the gold crucifix that was draped around his neck and squeezed it tight. He stood in the sitting room of his private residence at the back of the cathedral, an air of unease surrounded him. He had heard Chasid mention Abaddon's name before. He was the one who'd always left a trail of death and torture in his wake, and had eluded the Nephilim leader, Marduk, for many years.

Rossi closed his eyes and prayed silently for a moment.

Before he had taken up the position as cardinal and moved to Klerksdorp in South Africa, Rossi had been chair to the Pontifical Academy of Science and had spent over a decade working at the Vatican helping to fight the battle to maintain the well-constructed veil of truth his religion had helped to place between mankind and the reality of their existence. He worked tirelessly to ensure that the darkest secrets of the human race remained in the shadows where his superiors deemed they belonged.

The Catholic Church, like many of the world's governments and other influential individuals and organisations, had known of the Nephilim's existence for centuries. They had worked together to help the Nephilim conceal their true identity, fearing that the mutually beneficial relationship they'd built, based on the secret origins of humankind, would come crumbling down around them if the human race was ever to find out the secrets kept hidden for centuries. But tonight their greatest secrets were about to be unleashed and Rossi knew that he and many others would have to sacrifice everything to ensure this Pandora's box remained shut.

Rossi gathered his thoughts and hurried out of his living quarters to the cathedral's smaller side entrance. He navigated the pathway with a hurried precision, looking in every direction to make sure the area was safe. When he reached the entrance he reached into the pocket beneath his vestments and removed a set of keys. He placed a long brass key into the lock and unlocked the small wooden door.

Inside the cathedral was dimly lit, with the large electronic candle stand at the rear of the Church providing what little illumination there was. Rossi walked down the aisle toward the main entrance. The sound of his footsteps shadowed him, as the silence inside the empty cathedral enhanced the unsettling feelings he was already experiencing.

He hurried into the narthex of the cathedral, stopping abruptly for a moment to listen to the sounds around him. He could hear hurried footsteps outside, then the main entrance doors started to shake. Rossi rushed forward and unlocked the doors. They burst open, ushering Rossi back into the cathedral. Lochemel had arrived sooner than anticipated. When he regained his balance, Rossi looked to where Lochemel had fallen to his knees clutching a metallic case. He hurried to him, his gaze turning to Lochemel's blood-drenched shirt.

Lochemel gasped for air as he pushed the case at Rossi.

'Take the spheres. Get them to safety,' he said.

'You need medical treatment for that wound,' Rossi said.

'The spheres are now secure in your hands. You must leave me and protect them at all costs.' Lochemel slumped forward, loosening his grip on the handle of the case.

Rossi lowered himself to his knees and held Lochemel's wrist hoping to find a pulse, but there was none.

Lochemel was dead.

Rossi leaned on his knee to support his weight, and got back up to go to Gustavus.

But Gustavus had already entered the cathedral and was standing motionless behind the cardinal, waiting for him to turn around.

Rossi saw him and took a couple of tentative steps backward. 'What are you doing?' he demanded, at the sight of the barrel of Gustavus' gun pointing at the centre of his forehead.

There was a dead look in Gustavus' eyes as he moved closer to the cardinal.

'I couldn't believe how fortune had turned in my favour when I heard you speak to the Nephilim, Chasid, on the phone earlier. I have been waiting for years to serve my master. We have known for some time that you have been involved in helping his brother maintain his covert existence on Earth. Soon that will all change.' Gustavus smiled at Rossi. 'You know, there were many spheres found at Ottosdal in the ancient mines, but only the ones in that metal case were created by the Nephilim. The Templars helped our enemy to hide them in the museum, hoping we could never find them and use the awesome power those tiny objects can unleash to our advantage,' Gustavus said.

'The *destructive* power they can unleash,' Rossi said.

'Our ally, the one who will help Nergal take control of the Earth once again – she told him everything. How the Grand Master had arranged to hide these in the museum. All the Brotherhood's secrets are now Nergal's,' Gustavus said, and lifted his phone to his ear. He could hear the call being answered on the other end. 'Your Majesty, I am in the cathedral. I have secured the spheres,' he said.

'You will be rewarded for your deeds, Father Gustavus. Abaddon will be with you before long,' Nergal said in a sharp tone, before ending the call.

Gustavus stared in pity at Cardinal Rossi. 'You didn't think the Nephilim would trust someone like me with their secrets, did you? And that will be your downfall. You see, I know everything. All the intricate details about the Nephilim and the Templars and their sacred agreement to protect the secrets they hold together. I know all about their secret existence on Earth and how they have hidden the truth about the origins of humankind,' Gustavus said.

Rossi looked at him. 'They'll kill you. Once you've served your purpose.'

'Worry about your own fate, Cardinal. You and your legions have been shuffling around the Vatican for centuries trying to stop some of the Nephilim from revealing their true identity and crushing you and your religion forever.' Gustavus leaned toward the cardinal. 'The end is nigh. Neither you nor any other religion or government on Earth will be able to fill us humans with your lies any longer. We will know soon enough the fantasy we have been led to believe.' Gustavus held the gun to Rossi's head. 'We've been watching DeMolay and the rest of his Brotherhood for months. We know everything. His enemies were close to his heart. Deep within his own family. No one will ever suspect her.'

Gustavus' phone rang. He answered the call and lifted it

to his ear.

'Yes, I have secured them. Where are you?' Cardinal Rossi could hear Gustavus' accomplice's muffled reply on the other end. 'Yes. I'll deal with it,' Gustavus said, and hung up the phone. He held the gun at Rossi's head.

'You have served your purpose. It's time to meet your maker.' Gustavus grinned, and started to squeeze the trigger.

'I've met him already,' Rossi said, and held tight to the double-barred gold cross that hung around his neck, and prayed.

The gunshot echoed into every corner of the cathedral as Rossi fell to the floor.

Chapter 18

Abaddon exited the black van and walked toward Father Gustavus who was watching him from the cathedral entrance. Gustavus' smug appearance reflected his recent accomplishments. Abaddon greeted him with a reluctant grin. Nergal's contact in the Catholic Church had proven useful after he had relayed his superior's activities to Nergal and informed him of the location of the spheres. But the fact that Nergal had to rescue the spheres after Abaddon had let them slip from his hands was unacceptable. Failure was not an option for him and not a feeling he was accustomed to.

'Let me see them,' Abaddon said. Gustavus beamed with self-satisfaction as he turned and walked back into the church. Abaddon followed behind him, glancing over his shoulder to signal to Meregel to remain outside until his return. Gustavus was to be rewarded for his efforts and Abaddon would take advantage of the empty cathedral to do so.

Each footstep Father Gustavus took on the hardwood floor echoed around the church. He stepped over the bodies of Rossi and Lochemel to retrieve the metal case from the ground. Abaddon focused his attention on Gustavus as he placed it on the old wooden seat nearest him and lifted the lid to reveal the spheres. He turned the case toward Abaddon.

Abaddon's eyes widened. At last, he had them. His destiny was back on track. He looked down at Gustavus.

'You have done well.' There was a momentary silence. 'For a human,' Abaddon added.

'Thank you,' Gustavus said, eager to serve the Nephilim.

'His Majesty has asked me to reward you for your efforts.' Abaddon smiled. He slid his gun from his waist, gripped it in his hand and pointed it at Gustavus' head.

Gustavus took a step backward, but there was nowhere for him to go. He could feel the silencer push against him before Abaddon pulled the trigger.

Abaddon kneeled down beside Gustavus and checked for a pulse. There was none. He returned to the case, closed the lid, grabbed it by the handle and hurried toward the door. He closed his eyes and rolled his head from side to side, flexing the muscles in his neck and shoulders.

Outside the orange sunrise enhanced Abaddon's sense of triumph. Meregel stood steadfastly beside the van, scanning the area around the cathedral as his father approached.

'We are back on track,' Abaddon said, but Meregel did not reply. His eyes were focused on the bushes opposite the cathedral. He could see them moving in the early dawn light. He recognised the dark silhouette of a rifle pointed at his father. He lunged forward, grabbed his father's arm and pulled him toward the van waiting to take them to the airport.

'Take cover,' Meregel yelled as the window of the vehicle door shattered beside him. Meregel placed his hand on his father's back pushing him into the vehicle, then pulled a gun from his waist and returned fire. Meregel slammed the door shut and thumped hard on it, shouting to the driver to 'Move!'

Chasid moved toward Meregel, ordering two of his soldiers to fire at the escaping vehicle. But they were too late. Under heavy fire, Chasid and his men could only watch as Abaddon sped away on Poppy Avenue.

'Cover me,' Meregel shouted to the four remaining guards at the Range Rover behind him, then he lowered himself onto the dusty car park.

Out of gunshot range he made his way along the side of the vehicle and around to the back. He opened the rear door, removed a portable missile launcher and placed it on his shoulder. He scanned the car park. In the distance he could hear Chasid shout to his three accomplices to 'Run, take cover.' But Meregel was not aiming for his enemy. He didn't want to waste any more time exchanging bullets. Instead he had evaluated his enemy's weak point and decided to disable their transportation. He knew Chasid would have arrived in one of Marduk's aircraft, so he scanned the area around the cathedral for any sign of the LEO. The photoreceptive cells on its hull would have hidden it from view, but Meregel guessed from the direction Chasid's soldiers were coming from that the LEO was right in front of his current position. He pointed the launcher and targeted the area in the weapon's sight. He pulled hard on the firing mechanism. A loud shriek came from the weapon as it traversed the car park, followed by a giant explosion as the aircraft burst into flames. The blast radiated outward across the car park, knocking Chasid and his men flat on their backs.

Meregel felt a swell of accomplishment as he placed the weapon back into the vehicle and sat into the front seat, instructing the driver to leave.

The tyres grinded on the tarmac as Meregel and his men made their escape. Chasid jumped to his feet and ran forward shooting at the vehicle. But his efforts were wasted. Meregel and his henchmen continued to drive to safety and onto Poppy Avenue in the direction of his father's vehicle.

They had the spheres.

The first part of their plan was complete.

~

A sharp pain radiated along Abaddon's right arm down to the

tips of his fingers. He sat for a moment and examined the deep wound on his left shoulder through the tear in his jacket and shirt. *Just a scratch*, he thought.

'Did you give the coordinates to the pilot?' Abaddon said to one of his young accomplices seated across from him.

'Yes,' the young man said, and handed the computer tablet to Abaddon who glanced at the set of coordinates displayed on the screen.

25° 37' 54.36" South

30° 45' 36.00" East

'Good. Then we are almost ready to proceed. My son is five minutes out as soon as he arrives instruct the pilot to leave. We need to stick to the plan. Adam's Calendar is next.'

Chapter 19

Beneath the sky blue, wrought-iron supports that held the impressive building in place, Daniel stood beyond the meeting statue and scanned the station below. Above him, the arched vaulted roof of London's Saint Pancras International railway station spanned an impressive two hundred and forty-three feet and rose one hundred feet high. It had been the largest enclosed space in the world when it was first completed in 1863, and was one of the most celebrated Victorian Gothic architecturally designed structures ever built in Britain.

He glanced back at the twenty tonne, twenty-seven feet high bronze statue of a man and a woman embracing each other, erected in the train station to symbolise the romance of travel. A sentiment that Daniel was unable to appreciate at this moment as he held on tight to the brown strap of his old leather satchel, which sat over his shoulder and stretched across his chest. It was his constant companion and contained everything he could envision needing at any one point in time.

He scanned the station once more, then stared at his watch.

It was 6.30 a.m.

He walked over to his niece, Ava, who stood at the glass railing overlooking the entranceway below. She was three years older than her brother, Peter, but just as tall. They were alike in many ways: green eyes, dark blonde hair and sallow complexion, yet their personalities were very different. Peter was laid back, settled, compassionate and affectionate. Ava was headstrong, determined and meticulous. Everyone had always commented on how much like her father she was. But she had always felt they were worlds apart.

Perhaps that's why she'd taken the news of his death so well, Daniel thought, as he approached her. She had never been as close to her father as her brother was, and had always envied him this. Living in Peter's shadow was a burden she'd never wanted to bear. But it was a burden she'd inflicted on herself. No one had ever tried to make her feel that way.

'The train to Paris leaves at seven. I thought they'd be here by now,' Daniel said.

Ava faced him and placed her hand on his shoulder. 'They'll be here,' she whispered, and continued to scan the entrance hall in harmony with her uncle.

'There they are!' Ava said suddenly.

'Where? I don't see them.'

'Over there, walking toward the escalators.' Ava pointed in the direction of the main doors that led from the street outside into the main concourse below where they stood.

Amidst the crowds of busy travellers Daniel could see the tall athletic silhouette of his nephew approach in black jeans, a blue-grey sweatshirt and a warm, black jacket. Followed by a very pale-looking Emily wrapped in a puffy sea green jacket, blue jeans and flat, black ankle boots. Peter looked up from the main concourse toward the statue. His unshaven tired-looking appearance showed that the night's events were foremost on his mind. He glanced back at Emily as they took the escalator to the upper level. She gave him a weary, affectionate smile as they walked off the escalator toward where Daniel and Ava were waiting for them.

'You look dreadful,' Daniel said, and hugged Emily.

She put her arms around him and hugged him tight. She

was relieved to see him. 'Really bad flight from Edinburgh. I'll fill you in some other time,' Emily said, which made Daniel laugh.

'You do realise that anyone who gets into that tiny metal can with wings he calls a light aircraft is just a guinea pig?' Daniel said.

'I know that now,' she said.

The one and a half hour flight from Edinburgh to London had made Emily a little queasy. Even though Peter was an experienced pilot and had been flying since he was thirteen years old, she was still stricken with the same nauseating feeling every time she thought of him flying a plane and always preferred where possible to keep her feet on solid ground. She watched as Peter embraced his sister.

Peter knew his father's death and his mother's kidnapping would impact greatly on Ava. He had been preparing for this moment since they'd left Edinburgh. He held her tight as they embraced..

'We don't have much time. The train is leaving for Paris at seven so we need to get to the departure gate,' Daniel said. He knew they needed time to come to terms with everything that had happened, but he didn't want to have to wait for another train. They needed to leave now.

Daniel's friend, who worked for the Eurostar, was going to let them onto the train without their passports, as a returned favour to Daniel. Daniel had used Peter's and Emily's passport details he'd saved from their recent trip to Ireland to book the tickets, but the window to avoid the remaining security check was closing soon.

'Paris?' Peter said.

'I'll explain when we're on the train,' Daniel said as he handed each of them a ticket and pointed toward the departure gate one level down, just off the main lower level concourse. They had ten minutes left to get to the boarding area.

'A friend of mine will let you and Emily onto the train without an ID security check, but we must hurry. She finishes her shift after this train departs,' Daniel said, and hurried toward the escalator to the lower concourse. Emily, Ava and Peter followed hot on his heels. They navigated the crowd as fast as they could and arrived at the automatic gates. The queue, much to Daniel's relief, had dwindled. Only a handful of passengers was left.

Young and old, business and pleasure. Everyone's journey had a purpose and Peter's was weighing heavily on his mind as they hurried past the automatic gates and journeyed onto the security checkpoints. Daniel gestured to Emily and Peter to join the queue with him. His friend was waiting for them to arrive.

Emily stood beside Peter and glanced over at Ava who had joined a separate queue to their right. She'd been expecting a rather different reaction from Ava to her father's death, as she knew what it was like to lose a parent. Her mother had died soon after she was born; her father had raised her but had been killed in a car crash when she was fourteen years old. She had been brought up in England until his death, after which she'd moved to Ireland to live with her grandmother.

Probably shock, Emily thought.

'Madame, can I have your boarding pass, please,' the ticket attendant asked Emily, in a quiet French accent.

Emily pivoted around to face her. 'Sorry I was ...'

'You're late,' the attendant said, and smiled. 'You'll need to hurry. Boarding has almost closed.'

Emily handed her ticket to the attendant who glanced at it.

'The boarding gate is that way. Have a nice trip.' The tall, athletic-looking brunette in her early thirties pointed toward where Daniel was waiting with Peter and Ava, just beyond the security checkpoint. Daniel waved to Emily in an effort to hurry her up. As she approached them, she was still deep in thought.

'Are you okay?' Peter asked her as they hurried onto the platform where the train was about to leave.

'Yeah, I'm fine,' she said, and glanced at Daniel and then Ava.

'I'll just be glad when this is all over.'

Chapter 20

Peter sat opposite his sister in the large, comfortable, beige seat and stared at the picture of the fluorescent dots on his phone. The flotsam of accumulated memories of the events over the past eight hours had completely occupied his thoughts. *What and who really are the Nephilim, and why did they turn against my father? What exactly did my father give his life to protect?*

The business class cabin was empty, and the time to think and the space to talk freely were a luxury everyone appreciated. Daniel placed four cups of freshly brewed coffee and some croissants on the cream table nestled between Peter and Ava. The steady rhythmic sway of the Eurostar had an almost tranquilising effect as it sped gently along the track toward the entrance to the Channel Tunnel – the undersea double rail track that links the south-east of England with Calais in the north of France. Its twenty-three miles of high-speed railway is the longest undersea portion of any tunnel in the world and allows passengers to access Paris from England within two hours and fifteen minutes.

Ava sat silently and looked out of the window as far ahead as she could see. She knew they'd soon be nearing the entrance to the Eurotunnel. She checked the signal bars on her phone; they were all full. Then she checked the status of her last message. Message delivered at 6.29 a.m. She watched the tunnel entrance come closer and closer. She could feel the habitual vibration of the train slow as it decelerated from one hundred and eighty-six miles per hour, to the required one hundred for travel through the tunnel.

Inside the carriage the light became fainter as the outside morning light vanished at the tunnel entrance and was replaced by the fluorescent lighting on the ceiling in the centre of the carriage. Finally they had begun their journey underneath the sea and would not see daylight again for another twenty-five minutes. Ava glanced at her phone once more then quietly placed it back in her pocket. She was relieved that advances in technology, allowing mobile communication signals to penetrate underground, permitted them continuous mobile coverage even at an average distance of one hundred and forty-eight feet below the seabed.

'How much time do we have left?' Daniel said, bringing everyone firmly back to reality. Emily closed her eyes and inhaled the smell of freshly brewed coffee that lingered in the air. Peter placed his phone gently on the table in front of him, taking note of the time.

It was 7.39 a.m.

'We have until 11.40 this evening. Just sixteen hours from now,' Peter said, as he took the coffee cup from Daniel's outstretched hand.

Daniel was making sure his companions were well caffeinated and nourished. He knew the next sixteen hours would take their toll.

'So. Why Paris? How did you figure it out?' Peter said, and looked over at his uncle who was busy rummaging in his satchel.

'Ah, here it is,' Daniel said, and smiled as he pulled a white computer tablet from his bag.

Peter had introduced his uncle to the wonders of the latest computer tablet technology some time ago. Immediately afterward Daniel was hooked. Before the invention of the tablet and its user-friendly apps, Daniel had been a complete technophobe. Technology consistently malfunctioned around him. It was always his equipment that failed him: never the fact that he had an impulsive nature and a tendency to lose interest quickly. But his new gadget provided him with an extensive library of digitally formatted books and at times was akin to an extension to his mind, allowing him to construct a mobile repository of almost every book he'd ever owned through the wonders of digital imaging. Although it would never replace the look and smell of a physical book, having such a large collection at his fingertips did have its advantages.

Daniel organised his thoughts as he prepared to tell Emily, Peter and Ava about the Nephilim and the Templars and how their story, immersed in betrayal, deception and fear, spanned hundreds of years.

He lifted Peter's phone from the table and rose to his feet. He stood straight and composed himself, as if about to make a speech at a state dinner. However, his attire was not befitting such an occasion. His blue jeans, cream shirt and navy V-neck jumper were more suited to a relaxing night on the town.

Daniel pointed to the group of E. coli bacteria that formed a double-barred cross above the series of dots in the picture of the agar plate on Peter's phone.

'This symbol here is known as the Cross of Lorraine,' Daniel said. 'I presume you've all seen or heard of it before?'

'Yes,' Emily said. 'The Cross of Lorraine. When drawn symmetrically, as it is there, it's a hermetic maxim translated as "As above so below",' she said, modestly.

'Correct! A steadfast motto used by the Knights to identify their involvement in the order,' Daniel said, and gave Emily a surprised look.

'Eugene told us before he tried to kill us at the lab,' she said, sheepishly.

'Who's Eugene?' Ava said, wondering whom else Emily and Peter had told about her father's secrets.

'He's a friend of Emily's who helped us to decode the message. It was his description of the Cross of Lorraine that made me realise the dots were in the exact same positions as the stars in the constellation of Virgo. We hadn't realised he had an ulterior motive until he produced a gun,' Peter said.

Daniel cleared his throat, returning their attention to what he was telling them.

'And he was correct; its *meaning* in this instance is what's important.' There was silence as Daniel explained further. 'Peter, you too were correct to assume that this is indeed the constellation of Virgo. If we look at the two of these together and take the translation we've just used for the Cross of Lorraine, we get "As above" – the constellation of Virgo. "So below" – the Earth. Essentially each star in the constellation provides us with an approximate location for a corresponding place on Earth. What Marcus left you is a map that relates to coordinates right here on Earth. Northern France, to be precise,' Daniel said.

'That sounds familiar,' Peter said, slightly annoyed with himself that he hadn't thought of this before.

'Yes, it does. It brings to mind a very convincing argument that dates the Giza pyramid complex to before 10000 BC.' Daniel raised his eyebrows as he spoke. 'But that's a story for another day.'

Peter smiled, recalling their conversation at his wedding. Daniel had often had discussions with Peter and his father regarding the mounting evidence, using computer technology and other dating techniques, which could possibly prove that the pyramids in Egypt were built earlier than Egyptologists were willing to accept. Computer simulations showed that at a date in the distant past, around 10000 BC, the pyramids were in alignment with the three stars in Orion's belt and the Nile in alignment with the Milky Way. This had led to the belief that the Giza complex was a reconstruction of the skies at a specific point in time, when the Sphinx was looking at the sun as it rose in the constellation of Leo. Hence, Daniel believed that the sphinx should have the face of a lion and not that of a human, as it had been reconstructed to resemble.

'So you're saying that the constellation of Virgo is a map of places on Earth rather than in the heavens?' Ava said.

'Precisely. A map that was created by the Knights Templar at a time when they constructed their cathedrals and set up their Order in various places in Northern France,' Daniel said.

'But we need a specific location. It could take us years to find an ancient artefact with a map this vague.'

'Yes, it would. But the constellation of Virgo is no ordinary map: it specifically points to a number of cathedrals and cities in Northern France. In particular, cathedrals built by the Templars and dedicated to *Notre Dame de Lumière* – Our Lady of Light.' Daniel lifted his coffee cup and took a sip before continuing. 'You see, the Templars held Mary – and no, I'm not getting into whether it's Mary Magdalene or Mary the mother of Jesus; it could be either – in special reverence. They built many of their cathedrals to commemorate her – building them in particular places across Northern France, in effect mapping out the constellation of Virgo on the ground and immortalising her importance for generations to come. The virgin of the skies immortalised here on Earth. "As above so below".'

Daniel held his tablet toward his eager audience. A picture of the stars in the constellation of Virgo was transposed onto a map of Northern France. Everyone could see how the stars in the constellation matched the locations of cathedrals and cities in Northern France. Emily, Ava and Peter took a closer look. Chartres Notre Dame, Amiens Notre Dame, Reims Notre Dame, Laval Notre Dame. The list looked endless.

'And here's where we need to go,' Daniel said, pointing to one of the stars displayed on the screen.

'Spica?' Peter said, and frowned at his uncle.

'Chartres Cathedral in Northern France to be exact. A masterpiece in Templar architecture,' Daniel said.

'How can you be sure that's the right place? There're twelve other dots to choose from,' Peter said, realising he had visited Chartres Cathedral with his father while they were on holiday in Paris. Marcus had never once mentioned that it held any significance for him.

'The second verse Marcus left tells us it's Chartres Cathedral we need to go to. The first verse, the quote from the Bible, related to the key that would unlock the map. Thus it follows that the second verse would unlock our intended destination. Marcus had plenty of time to plan how his secrets would be revealed. I would say that each clue you are presented with will follow a similar pattern, revealing a location or an action that you need to take to reach your final destination,' Daniel said, and began to read aloud the verse on the small scroll. '"Inanna lies immortalised within her stony wall." Inanna, mentioned here in the first line, is the Sumerian word for "Queen of Heaven and Earth". Throughout the ages she's also had other names. In Egypt she's known as Isis, Akkadians called her Ishtar and the Greeks referred to her as Persephone or Demeter. I would say that your father chose the constellation of Virgo as it has often been associated with the mother goddess by many civilisations,' Daniel said.

'So the first line of the verse refers to a place where Inanna, the mother of Heaven and Earth, has been immortalised?' Peter was following Daniel's train of thought.

'Precisely. And Chartres Cathedral epitomises this in

many ways. Even since before the time of Christ, pilgrims journeyed there in their thousands. You see, the mound of earth on which Chartres rests was at first a pagan site dedicated to the traditional mother goddess, and has held special significance for pilgrims throughout the ages. It's also a well-known fact that the *Sancta Camisia*, the tunic the Blessed Virgin Mary wore during the birth of Christ, is housed in the cathedral. The tunic miraculously survived two fires, one of which destroyed much of the town of Chartres.'

'So are you saying that the Templars worshiped Inanna, the Queen of Heaven and Earth as opposed to Christ?' Emily said.

'Yes. Very much so. And she has most certainly been immortalised within their architecture,' Daniel said.

'But didn't you say earlier that there's more than one cathedral in Northern France dedicated to Mary?' Ava said.

'Yes, indeed I did. And this is where the rest of your father's clue shows us exactly where to go,' Daniel said. '"A pilgrim takes a journey" is the next crucial link to Chartres Cathedral, as it is referring to a labyrinth. Labyrinths occur in different cultures, at different points in time and in different places across the globe, such as Peru, Arizona, Iceland, Crete and Egypt, yet the origin of the labyrinth still remains a mystery today.

'In the Middle Ages it became more and more popular to include labyrinths in the architecture of cathedrals and churches. Initially the seven-circuit labyrinth or Cretan labyrinth, where the seven circuits referred to seven paths that led the pilgrim on a spiritual quest to the centre, was the most popular. But in Chartres, set into the stone floor in its nave, we have the more elaborate eleven-circuit labyrinth divided into four quadrants that came about in the middle ages. The labyrinth was said to bring a pilgrim closer to God as they walked and meditated through the winding paths on their journey to reach the centre. It was often travelled by pilgrims as a substitute for the actual pilgrimage to Jerusalem.

'However, most of the labyrinths were destroyed or removed on purpose. Mainly by the Catholic Church, as usual fearing what they didn't understand.' Daniel flicked his finger across his tablet before handing it to Ava. A picture of a labyrinth was displayed on the screen with the caption 'The Labyrinth at Chartres Cathedral'. 'The Labyrinth in Chartres Cathedral is one of the most famous labyrinths in the world.'

'Yes, but there's more than one Cathedral of Notre Dame with a labyrinth in it,' Ava said. She recalled reading this fact somewhere.

'Yes, yes, you're correct. There are others. One in Amiens and one in Reims; however, can you tell me do any of those other cathedrals have giants depicted in their art or architecture?' Daniel said.

'Not that I know of and I don't think there's any in Chartres either,' she said, recalling the fact that she'd visited the cathedral with her parents and Peter, and she was sure that never once had her father mentioned giants.

'That's where you're wrong, my dear. There are giants depicted in the architecture in Chartres Cathedral and I'll prove it to you when we get there. But there's more.' Daniel gave his niece an affectionate smile. 'Your father left one final clue that leads us to Chartres.' Daniel shifted the scroll from beside Emily and moved it to the centre of the table. He bent forward and pointed to one particular sentence. 'The words here – in the clue.'

'"The track not of Heaven",' everyone said.

'This one sentence contains two vital clues. First, to reiterate that the scattered dots in the first clue are not a map of Heaven. "The track not of Heaven." And secondly, I

111

believe it's an anagram. And it translates as—' Daniel began.

'The Ark of the Covenant,' Peter said.

'Well done, Peter. Top marks! Chartres Cathedral is one of the presumed final resting places for the Ark. Supposedly brought there by the Templars after they excavated it from beneath King Solomon's Temple in Jerusalem. We all know that the Templar movement became so rich and powerful over a very short period of time, after they had set up their headquarters on the Temple Mount. I believe that they found King Solomon's treasures there and that this is what made them so rich and powerful in such a short space of time. I also believe it's one of these treasures that your ancestor Jacques DeMolay and your father died to protect. Unfortunately, it's also what the Nephilim are looking to have returned to them. The ancient artefact the Nephilim instructed Moses to build on Mount Sinai all those thousands of years ago. The Ark of the Covenant.'

Chapter 21

'What do you mean the Nephilim instructed Moses to build the Ark? *God* instructed Moses to build the Ark to hold the Ten Commandments. The Nephilim are not God. They're just an ancient brotherhood like the Templars. Aren't they?' Emily said. She had been hesitant to ask. The Nephilim were like the elephant in the room. They had been mentioned several times throughout the past number of hours, yet she still had no conclusive idea of who or what they really were. Emily stared at Peter who was looking at Daniel.

Peter knew what was coming next. His uncle was about to unleash his thoughts on the real origins of humankind.

'Oh my dear Emily, the Nephilim are much, much more than just an ancient brotherhood. They are far more secretive and far more powerful than any other organisation known to man. Although to refer to them as an organisation or a brotherhood is a grave misconception.'

Daniel recalled when he'd first become intrigued by the Nephilim, after he had been invited by a friend to accompany him on a trip to Egypt. It was during that trip that Daniel had visited, for the first time, the Temple of Seti I in Abydos, located almost seven miles west of the Nile. The purpose of the trip was to see some ancient hieroglyphs that were carved into a roof beam of the temple built around1300 BC. What was so unusual about these hieroglyphs, his friend had told him, was that they depicted what modern day humans would refer to as a helicopter and a submarine. The combination of rotor blade, tailpiece and rotor shaft, as well as a cockpit and fuselage, which could be clearly seen in the image, was astounding, given that the temple is over three and a half thousand years old. At that time Daniel also concurred that

113

beneath the helicopter was an image of an object that, to him, resembled a submarine with a quite distinct fin emerging from the back of it.

To prove his theory correct, Adam had shown a picture of the hieroglyphs in Abydos to a group of children and asked them what they could see drawn on the beam. Every child that looked at the picture concurred with his views. They saw a helicopter and a submarine. From that day forward Daniel had entered a world in which academics and conspiracy theorists were agreeing to differ, that evidence of advanced modern technology existed within the vast realms of ancient history.

Daniel glanced at the scanned copy of his 150-year-old King James Bible on his tablet screen.

'The word "Nephilim" itself,' he said, 'can sometimes be translated as the "fallen ones" or "those whom from Heaven to Earth came". But the most generally accepted translation is "giants".' He flicked his finger across his tablet before handing it to Emily. 'Click on the search icon and enter the word "giant". You'll see for yourselves they're mentioned several times throughout the Bible.'

Emily clicked on the magnifying glass and entered "giant". The search results filled the screen. She read aloud. 'Genesis, chapter six, verse four: "Now giants were upon the earth in those days for after the sons of God went in to the daughters of men and they brought forth children. These are the mighty men of old, men of renown".' Emily looked further down and began to read again. 'Numbers, chapter thirteen, verse thirty-four: "There we saw certain monsters of the sons of Enac, of the giant kind: in comparison of whom, we seemed like locusts".'

Daniel looked toward Peter. 'The Nephilim. God or gods. The Watchers. Take your pick. They have been called many names throughout the ages of humanity and are the race of giants who existed on Earth long before we did. The first reference to them is in the Old Testament in the Book of Genesis and relates to a time before the flood. Over twelve thousand years ago.'

Peter smiled and looked at Emily and Ava. 'Daniel thinks the Nephilim, or the giants, in the Bible are actually an advanced ancient civilisation who once roamed throughout our solar system and lived here on Earth.'

'Think, Peter? I know!' Daniel said, mockingly.

'Based on what? To say that the Nephilim are ancient spacefaring race is circumstantial at best. Have you ever met a Nephilim? Have you ever seen one of them?' Peter couldn't believe they were sitting talking about the giants in the Bible while his mother's life hung in the balance. He had always believed the Nephilim were an ancient brotherhood that existed long before the Templars. His father had told him so. They were more secretive, human and far more powerful than any other organisation on Earth, not an advanced alien species or the giants from the Bible.

'Well, yes, we have,' Emily said out of the blue, her voice frayed with emotion. She was recalling the night's events as Daniel spoke and an extract from the Bible was foremost in her thoughts. '*In comparison of whom, we seemed like locusts.*' 'We saw them tonight. Raziel and Nergal, the man who killed Raziel. The one who kidnapped your mother. Couldn't they be Nephilim?' Although this was an irrational thought that had entered Emily's mind, she had allowed herself to express it aloud, knowing deep down that the events of the past hours were anything but rational.

Peter stared at his wife as the realisation of what she'd just said settled in.

There was a momentary silence before Daniel spoke again. 'Peter, there is an unspoken truth about humanity's existence that has been thrust into the pages of myth and fantasy by those who would like to keep control on humankind. The evidence does exist to prove that the Nephilim, the watchers, and even God himself are, in reality, members of an advanced alien species who have had many names and have lived here on Earth in ancient times.' He ruffled through the pages of a small book he'd taken from his satchel. 'If these people – aliens, Gods, call them whatever you like – didn't exist in ancient times, then why are traces of them scattered throughout the world?' Daniel's voice was firm yet sincere.

Peter took a deep breath. He knew deep down the only evidence his uncle was lacking in his theory was an actual Nephilim. And even though he was terrified to admit it, he feared his wife had provided the final piece of the puzzle for him.

'Are you saying that evidence exists here on Earth that proves that these Nephilim once really lived here?' Emily turned to Peter. Then stared at Daniel.

'Well, yes,' Peter said softly, 'there are ancient ruins, the Sumerian Tablets of Creation, petroglyphs, hieroglyphs in ancient Egypt and mentions of an advanced civilisation in ancient manuscripts, that do essentially point to the existence of some other race of beings that lived on Earth in ancient times. A lot of which has been written off or just treated as mere myths or fairy tales.' Peter raised his head and looked at Daniel. 'But I must concede that, given the events of the past couple of hours, perhaps Daniel is right after all.'

Daniel's shoulders slumped as he sighed with relief. At last his nephew was beginning to see the world through his eyes. Daniel looked once again at his tablet and opened a stored document. He placed the device on the table in front of everyone and flicked through the images on screen. A picture of the pyramids and the Sphinx in Egypt appeared.

'The pyramids in Egypt.' Daniel said. 'The precision with which the stones were cut and the distances they were carried were impossible for humans given the level of technology they possessed at the time the pyramids were believed to have been built. You do know that some of the largest stones at the base of the great pyramid weigh a staggering two and a half tonne each, yet we're supposed to believe that the ancient Egyptians hauled these across Egypt without any technological assistance whatsoever.' Daniel raised his eyebrows. 'There are also many debates in academic circles as to how old the pyramids really are. The erosion patterns around the Sphinx show indications of prolonged water erosion which could lead to a far different story regarding the actual date it was built, in comparison to the accepted date of 2550 to 2490 BC. The extensive precipitation required to cause this degree of erosion couldn't have happened during the third millennium before Christ, but most likely happened much, much earlier.'

Daniel ran his finger across the screen again. The pyramids were replaced by pictures of large, neatly carved grey square stones with perfect circles and other complex shapes carved into them. 'This is Puma Punku, in the Tiwanaku complex in Bolivia. Its age is debated with vigour in academic circles, with some accepted dates for its construction as old as fourteen thousand years before Christ, yet the stones that were used to build this complex were crafted to a precision that is only possible using the laser technology we have today, most certainly not the tools they had access to at the time of its construction. The crafting of the metal used in the joints to keep each of these interlocking stones in place was way beyond the technology of the time in which they were built. The precision-cut holes in the stone, the blind holes created to link the blocks together and the precision with which these blocks fitted together to form the final structure were so precise in some instances that you couldn't even fit a razor blade through the joints. An advanced and sophisticated knowledge of stone cutting and descriptive geometry is required to get this level of accuracy, yet here they stand.'

Daniel swiped the screen again. This time a large stone structure carved into the side of a mountain appeared. 'Lake Titicaca, over six miles away from Puma Punku, is well known to the indigenous people of the area as a gateway to the gods. Legend states that a golden disc was placed into the indentation here.' Daniel pointed to a small circular hollow in the centre of the T-shaped doorway. 'Tradition holds that a blue light appeared once the disc was inserted into the circle. Once the blue light appeared, the gateway of the gods opened and literally swallowed the people up – in short they disappeared.'

He swiped the screen again. This time a familiar picture of an ancient geoglyph on Earth appeared. 'The Nazca Lines in Peru. Why can they only be seen from above? How were they drawn? What purpose do they serve?'

Daniel flicked the screen once again. 'Stonehenge in England. Newgrange in Ireland, which is even older that Stonehenge as it was built around 3200 BC. The "cavemen" who built these structures would have required advanced astronomical knowledge to align these passageways with the sun at the summer and winter solstices. They were geniuses!' Daniel was like a man possessed; his arms raised as he recounted the evidence that ancient aliens had left behind on Earth. 'And God only knows what's hidden underneath the mounds of earth that we haven't uncovered yet! Take the moai statues on Easter Island as an example. They were bodiless until very recently.' Daniel stopped only to catch his breath. 'You can't deny that this all points toward an advanced civilisation being here on Earth in the past.' Daniel looked at Peter.

'No, I can't. I know the Earth is billions of years old and

the thousands of years that humans have existed here is only a flash in the pan in comparison. I concede that these structures are here by design rather than by evolution or accident. But, what I can't get my head around is that my father had always known that this advanced ancient civilisation existed,' Peter said.

Daniel relaxed back into his seat and smiled at Peter. 'I've spent many years studying, translating, deciphering, analysing and reconstructing ancient documents, artefacts and symbols. And for me they all point toward the same conclusion, shocking as it may seem: an advanced civilisation existed here on Earth long before you and me. Their existence here in ancient times has been documented many times.

'Take the Sumerians, for example; they called them the Annunaki, those who from Heaven to Earth came. They even documented how some of them guided and educated humanity for centuries. In return we treated them as gods. Referred to them as the enlightened ones. The angels in the Bible who from Heaven to Earth came. They are the ones who told Noah to build the ark that saved humanity during the flood. You do know that the ark Noah built was almost the size of the *Titanic*. Think about it!' Daniel prodded the table with his index finger. 'Noah knew the principle of buoyancy almost ten thousand years before Archimedes discovered it. Yet another out-of-time feat of engineering. In truth, Archimedes had only rediscovered an ancient scientific principle that the Nephilim had given to humanity thousands of years before he was even born.

'The Nephilim are also the ones who instructed Moses to build the Ark of the Covenant. The proof of such knowledge was what Marcus gave his life to protect. I suppose you could consider it as the greatest story never told.' Daniel paused and organised his thoughts. 'The proof is all around us. All we have to do is consider the facts and they will lead us to the truth: that an advance species existed on Earth long before we did,' Daniel said.

'Do you have any idea what would happen if we could prove that this advanced race existed?' Peter's eyes widened at the thought.

'Yes. I do. And so did your father and all the Grand Masters in your family before him. This is what he died for, Peter. I believe that generations of your family have known about and have worked with the Nephilim for centuries. This is what they were protecting. Proof of the existence of one true God. A version of God that no religion on this planet would ever acknowledge exists,' Daniel said.

'It would destroy us,' Emily said, and exchanged a nervous glance with Peter. 'Every religion on Earth has its own version of God. Their own version of events. If we were without warning thrust into a world where God was an actual physical alien being—'

'Or group of beings,' Daniel said.

'—or group of beings,' Emily said, 'the entire planet would be thrust into chaos.'

'Yes, it would. And some of the Nephilim want that to happen,' Daniel said.

'You're talking as if there are a lot of them and that they're all still here,' Emily said, her voice tinted with astonishment. 'Are they?' she asked.

'Yes,' Daniel said, 'some of them have been here for millennia and still remain.'

'But that would make them,' Emily hesitated for a moment, 'immortal by our standards – if they were still alive today.'

'By our standards, yes, it would,' Daniel said. 'You see, God gave humans a limited life span. According to the Bible, one hundred and twenty years to be exact. The Nephilim, however, live for thousands of years. And their direct offspring with humans also live for much longer than the average human lifespan we experience today. Take Noah, for example. He was almost six hundred years old when he started to build the ark. And Methuselah, Noah's grandfather, lived to the ripe old age of nine hundred and sixty-nine. It's all here in the Bible.'

Daniel looked at each one of them in turn. 'I know we could sit here for decades and discuss all the ancient structures built on Earth for which we have no plausible explanation as to how they got here. I could continue to paraphrase those words written in ancient texts and books to try to get you to understand how the history of the world around you has been manipulated to control you,' Daniel paused, 'but I need you *all* to understand one important fact: some of the Nephilim are akin to a group of renegade absentee landlords. If they get what they're looking for from you, it will provide them with the tools necessary to carry out their deeds, and our lease on planet Earth will soon expire. So for your mother's sake, Peter, and the sake of humanity, I need you to take a leap of faith and trust me. Don't immediately dismiss the possibility that in the past our planet was visited by extraterrestrials   just because existing scientific knowledge we've access to today says it's not possible.' Daniel paused again, and looked at his nephew. 'We cannot ignore the conclusion that all this evidence presents us with: the human race was never alone.'

Chapter 22

Paris is our destination.

Nergal eased himself into the large, cream leather seat and contemplated his next move. He could feel a gentle vibration in the cabin in response to the increased G-force it experienced during take-off. He stared at the phone message from his ally and smiled as he pondered his recent successes. Abaddon had the spheres, and Peter DeMolay was without his knowledge going to lead him to the one place on Earth that his brother Marduk would never allow him access to. His plans to destroy his brother and take control of his Nephilim Empire were unfolding as expected.

Suddenly his thoughts were interrupted by the approach of his aide, Micah.

'Our contact at your brother's base has infiltrated their computer systems. The transponder signals on Marduk's LEO aircraft are now under our control,' Micah said. He leaned forward and touched the glass screen embedded into the mahogany desk in front of Nergal. Instantly the surface of the desk was transformed into a computer screen that displayed a map showing the locations of his brother's advanced aircraft. Nergal beamed in response.

The aircraft he was travelling in was a gift from his brother Marduk, a gift that was always monitored by him, as he assessed and watched every move Nergal made. But soon his brother's ability to dissect and interfere in his activities would end.

'As you requested, I have switched the signal of our aircraft with that of another of Marduk's Low Earth Orbiting aircraft. If your brother looks to his tracking systems to confirm your location, it will show him that you are off the west coast of Ireland and not on your way to Paris. We have ensured that he has no way of telling where you really are. If the need arises, we can change the signals again,' Micah said, then glanced at the computer tablet in his hand. 'We will arrive in Paris in approximately one hour,' he said, walking toward the stairs to the lower deck.

Nergal immediately examined the screen. He could now see everything that Marduk could see. His brother's efforts to track him would prove useless. The tables had been turned and Nergal was now in control. He could watch Marduk's every move and anticipate Marduk's response to his plans as they unfolded. Micah's contact from the Antarctic base had proven to be a valuable asset. Inside, Nergal was beaming; aside from having to rescue the spheres, everything was going just as he'd planned.

He glanced at Sophia who sat bound on the opposite side of the lavish aircraft. She was wriggling in a futile effort to free herself. Nergal lifted a glass of water from the table beside him, stood up and walked over to her. He leaned down, pulled the grey tape from her mouth and placed the glass of water on the dark-brown table in front of her.

'I will remove your restraints if you agree to behave. No more kicking and screaming. Agreed?' Nergal said softly.

Sophia nodded. Nergal removed the dagger from his waist and reached down to Sophia's hands, bound behind her back. He slipped the dagger between her wrists and cut the restraints. Sophia pulled her arms out in front of her and removed the remaining grey tape from her wrists. She reached for the glass and began to sip. Nergal returned the dagger to his waist and sat down on the large cream sofa opposite her.

'He'll never give you what you're looking for. You do know that, don't you?' Sophia said, and stared at Nergal.

'And what is it that I seek? Tell me.'

'The Ark of the Covenant. The one your father instructed Moses to build. That's what my husband was protecting.'

Nergal laughed and stood up. He glared down at Sophia.

'Yes, the Ark is one of the things I seek and I will get it. Unfortunately, the Ark I am looking for is not what your husband was protecting.'

Chapter 23

'The human race was never alone.'

The words kept running through Emily's mind, like a song you hear and can't stop singing. She looked at Daniel. 'You said that the Nephilim are basically God.'

Daniel's expression was unusually serious. 'Yes.'

Emily threw Peter and Ava an astonished look, then she looked back at Daniel. A frightening realisation of truth rippled through her. 'Then if they created us? The Garden of Eden, Adam, Eve? That was all the Nephilim?' she said.

'Yes,' Daniel said, 'only the Garden of Eden is not where humans were created. It's where they lived and worked for the Nephilim. But our creation stories and records of what these ancient aliens have told humanity throughout the ages, about how the universe was created, go back much further than the Garden of Eden and Adam and Eve. There are many early stories from all around the world that detail how we, and the universe, came into being. Some of them aren't too much of a stretch from what science teaches us today. The Aztecs believed the universe started with a void and that we were created from nothing. It's the same with the Greek creation myth, which says that in the beginning there was a void and then chaos ensued and Gaia, the Earth, was created. These are quite similar to our own most recent observations of the universe and the current big bang theory, which suggests the universe started over thirteen billion years ago from a small singularity, otherwise known as a void. Scientific observations of radiation in the universe have corroborated this theory thus far. It's also universally acceptable that an omnipresent being or God created the heavens, the Earth and all its inhabitants – both human and

1 – out of this void. One of the oldest creation stories, known as the *Enuma Elish*, is a collection of seven tablets onto which the Sumerians inscribed what they believed to be the history of their creation. The Egyptians called it the knowledge of Zep Tepi, the knowledge of their first time.' Daniel shuffled through the pages of the tiny book he had taken from his satchel. He opened it almost in the centre and handed it to Emily. Pictures of ancient stone tablets were printed on each page. The writing on the tablets was almost childlike, and illegible to her.

'Here are pictures of the Sumerian tablets of creation. They were written over six thousand years ago by the ancient Sumerians, and have some of the most controversial knowledge of our existence contained on them. The writing you see on the tablets is known as cuneiform and it tells us about the Nephilim, or as the Sumerians called them, the Annunaki, and how they journeyed from their home planet to Earth thousands of years ago on gold-mining expeditions. At first they mined the gold themselves but after a while they tired of that and became restless. The Nephilim working in the mines disputed the fact they had to work so hard to keep their leaders happy. So about two hundred and fifty thousand years ago the Nephilim decided to create a race of primitive workers by mixing some of their own DNA with an indigenous species already evolving on the planet.'

Daniel paused.

'Scientists today still can't agree on how humans made the evolutionary jump from Australopithecus to the genus Homo, which includes Homo sapiens. That's because we didn't evolve: we were created. The Nephilim created us. At first they gave us some of their DNA and created a primitive human and as the years passed, they gave us other DNA upgrades as they deemed necessary. Just as the Bible tells us, God made man in his own image. In his own likeness. Then once we were created, they used us as slaves to mine their gold and as soldiers to take sides and fight in their wars with one another. They liked us and then they tired of us. After a while they tried to destroy us by flooding the Earth. But some of the gods were sympathetic to humans and warned us of the impending flood and helped Noah to build the ark so that we could survive. They also used nuclear weapons on Earth and we were almost destroyed in the process. But again, we survived.'

'Nuclear weapons? How do you know they had nuclear weapons,' Ava said.

'You've heard of Sodom and Gomorrah, where Lot's wife turned into a pillar of salt?' Daniel said.

'Well, yes,' Ava said.

'The Nephilim had the technology to create a new species. Doesn't it go without saying that if they had the ability to do this, nuclear fusion was also within their capabilities. The *Erra* epic, written in the first century before Christ, describes in detail what happened in Sodom and Gomorrah and how the Nephilim Nergal, the one you saw tonight, was responsible for the nuclear fallout. Sodom and Gomorrah was literally an act of God and not a natural disaster. An act of the gods who were at war with one another, and who had a nuclear arsenal at their disposal,' Daniel said, and smiled.

'So, you're saying that there was a genetics lab here on Earth where we were created by an advanced species. To work as slaves?' Emily said, eager to hear more of what Daniel had to say about the creation of humanity.

'Yes. I mean look at us – over six million years ago, the hominid and the chimpanzee lines diverged and we started on our evolutionary path. Then, boom, all of a sudden between fifty to one hundred thousand years ago culture started and we developed the ability to speak and communicate with one another. Six million years of evolution and then overnight we went from grunting, hooting and crying out to expressing thoughts, giving commands and conveying information to one another using speech. It sounds more like a DNA upgrade as opposed to evolution to me, and all we have to do to prove this is look at the Sumerian tablets of creation to see the advanced knowledge our ancestors had access to. They describe in detail how two planets collided millions of years ago when our solar system was being formed. From this collision, the Earth, its moon, the asteroid belt and the Nephilim home planet Nibiru were all formed. And as a result, Earth orbits the sun once every three hundred and sixty-five and one quarter days, once every four years that quarter gives us one day we call a leap year. And one orbit of Nibiru, the Nephilim home world, takes approximately three thousand six hundred years and takes their planet in a more eccentric orbit to the coldest, outermost part of our solar system which makes it very difficult for us to see,' Daniel said.

'But there's no such planet within our solar system,' Emily said, and looked at Peter. 'Is there?'

Peter shrugged before answering. 'To be honest we don't know for sure. Astronomy and physics has advanced to a staggering extent over the past number of years, but we're still finding things in the universe that astound and mystify us. Astronomers have been looking for a fabled planet X for years, but no one has ever definitively confirmed or denied its existence. Some scientists and astronomers believe it's possible that there's quite a large object in the outer regions of our solar system. Which could be four times as large as Earth. Scientists know this because they've observed a gravitational pull on Uranus and Neptune that as yet remains unexplained. There's an ancient Sumerian tablet that shows the sun as the centre of our solar system. How they knew this six thousand years ago is open to interpretation. So, it's possible the ancient Sumerians had advanced astronomical knowledge and perhaps knew more about the solar system than we give them credit for.' Peter smiled at Daniel. 'It could be knowledge that was passed down to them from a more superior race.'

Daniel reached across the table and handed his tablet to Emily. Displayed on the screen was an ancient drawing on a clay tablet. Emily counted three people in the drawing. They were all dressed in ornate clothing with some kind of elaborate headdress on their heads. Two of the people were standing and one was sitting on a chair. Behind the first person was a drawing: a star in the centre of eleven dots of different sizes. The caption at the top of the image was 'Sumerian Cylinder Seal VA243'.

Emily was suddenly distracted by a vibrating sound. She placed the tablet on the table and removed her phone from her jacket pocket.

'It's Linda from work. Maybe she's heard about Marcus' death. I'd better take this call – I'll be back in a moment,' Emily said, and stood up. She walked toward the end of the carriage, watching her faint reflection in the windows as she passed each one. When she reached the bathroom, she answered the call, placing the phone to her ear as she locked the bathroom door.

At the other end of the carriage, Daniel, Peter and Ava were still deep in conversation.

'This cylinder seal was created by the Sumerians and is over six thousand years old. See the sun in the centre of the eleven dots, and do you notice anything else that's odd about the three people?' Daniel asked Ava, who was examining the picture of the cylinder seal.

She frowned and looked closer, then at Peter. 'Do *you* notice anything?' she asked him.

'The guy who's sitting down,' Peter said.

'Yeah, I see him. But he doesn't look much different from the other two except for the fact that he's seated and has more ornate clothing,' she said.

'Are you sure?' Daniel said.

Ava looked at the drawing again. She smiled when she realised. *Of course*, she thought. *How could I miss it?*

She looked up from the tablet screen. 'The guy who's sitting down is one of the Nephilim. He's the same height as the other two even though he's sitting,' she said.

'Precisely,' said Daniel. 'The Sumerians had intimate knowledge of the Nephilim. They lived among them and taught them how to cultivate crops. They taught them astronomy and mathematics and how to form effective social structures. The Nephilim remained on Earth, teaching and visiting humans in spaceships for thousands of years.' Daniel flicked through his tablet and handed it to Peter. 'Remember this?'

Peter nodded and smiled.

'What is it?' Ava said, contorting her neck to get a better look.

'It's Ezekiel's spaceship,' Daniel said. 'The Book of Ezekiel gives one of the most detailed accounts in existence today of an ancient spaceship. The writings confirm that Ezekiel had at least four encounters with spacecrafts over a period of about twenty years. This drawing is by a former NASA engineer and is based on the descriptions, in the writings of Ezekiel, of the crafts he saw and journeyed in. His first encounter took place in about 592 BC.'

'So this picture was drawn from descriptions in the Bible?' Ava said.

'Yes. By a former NASA engineer who'd spent his life

designing and working on aircraft for NASA. He'd found Ezekiel's descriptions very convincing back in 1974 when he did his research,' Daniel said.

'592 BC,' Ava said, 'and neither a military aircraft nor a weather balloon in sight!'

Daniel laughed. 'No. Ezekiel's sightings cannot be put down to the usual suspects. Neither can this painting,' he said, and handed the tablet back to Ava.

'What's this?' Ava said.

'It's a fresco of the Crucifixion. It's on the wall in the Visoki Dečani Monastery in Kosovo. It was painted around AD 1350. You can clearly see two objects on either side of the cross in the painting. Now why would someone put a UFO into a painting in the thirteen hundreds unless they knew they existed? How could something like this be drawn by an artist unless they'd either seen or been told about such objects. Human flight had not been possible during that time,' Daniel said.

Ava held the tablet and examined the painting up close. Two small crafts were painted on either side of the crucified Christ. Each of the crafts depicted someone inside at the helm.

'How can we just ignore all this? Why has no one tried to definitively prove their existence based on everything we've seen and talked about here?' she said.

'I guess they won't allow us to,' Peter said, 'considering what's happened to our father and mother this evening. Can you imagine what they're capable of doing to someone who'd try to undermine and expose them? They'll stop at nothing to hide their existence. Not even murder.'

The carriage fell silent.

Peter glanced at the time on his mobile phone. It was

9.03 a.m. They had just over fourteen hours to get the Nephilim what they were looking for in return for his mother. And although they had a better idea of where they were going, Peter was still unsure as to what they were looking for. He gazed out of the window and watched the French countryside idle by.

'Do you think the Ark is what Marcus was protecting? And is it really in Chartres Cathedral?' Emily said, as she returned to her seat.

'We can't be sure,' Daniel said. 'There are some ancient sources such as the Dead Sea scrolls and the Treatise of the Vessels that alludes to the treasures Solomon may have had in his Temple. One of them being the Ark of the Covenant, another being the seventy-seven tablets of gold from the walls in the Garden of Eden. The last time the Ark was mentioned in the Bible was when King Josiah of Judah instructed that the Ark be returned to Solomon's Temple for safekeeping. It was claimed to have been hidden beneath Solomon's Temple before King Nebuchadnezzar of Babylon captured Jerusalem. Apparently, he never gained control of the Ark and it remained hidden until the Templars were given permission from King Baldwin II of Jerusalem to set up their headquarters in the Temple Mount, which was believed to have been built atop the ruins of the Temple of Solomon. Underneath which the Ark of the Covenant was buried for safe keeping.'

'Is there any evidence that the Templars had the Ark?' Ava said.

'There's one extra-biblical written reference to the Ark that was made by the Templars themselves. It's on a pillar in the northern entrance of Chartres Cathedral.' Daniel paused for a moment. 'The Templars' sudden rise to power came after they'd been excavating at the site of Solomon's Temple. They definitely found something very powerful beneath those ruins.'

'But why now? And how did they find out that my father knew the location of the Ark?' Peter said, staring at the scroll deep in thought. 'Someone who knew my father well has betrayed him. Someone who knew what he was guarding,' Peter added.

A silence fell across the carriage.

'Yes,' Daniel said, 'and because of that, we need to be careful whom we trust.' Daniel looked at Peter. 'At least no one else knows where we're going. No one else has the map or the clues.' Daniel's words were only a small consolation to Peter. But any consolation was better than none.

Chapter 24

Gibil sprinted through the dense South African forest of the Waterval Boven Valley. The heavy undergrowth pounded against his body, tearing at his arms and legs through his light linen clothing. Beads of sweat rolled down his face and trickled along his spine as he navigated his way toward the underground shelter that had become his home.

Straight ahead of him he could see the outline of the concealed entrance. A tunnel hidden by the rocks and trees that surrounded it. Only he and his allies knew it was there.

He glanced behind him. One of his attackers had placed a rifle to his shoulder and was following Gibil's movements through the weapon's eyepiece. Like a roar of thunder, a gunshot echoed through the forest. Gibil lunged to the ground in an effort to avoid being shot. He landed heavily on his side then raised his head to evaluate his enemy's approach. He could see the black outline of three of his adversaries approaching fast, ducking and diving through the vast undergrowth.

Gibil scrambled to his feet and started to run again. He could see the two large boulders that concealed the entrance to the tunnel just feet away. He continued to run straight ahead. When he reached the boulders, he vaulted high into the entrance above them. He landed flat on his back in a long, low-lit tunnel that led deep inside the mountain.

Gibil jumped up. He could hear the voices of his adversaries planning their attack outside the tunnel entrance. He paused and looked along the limestone corridor, at the end of which was a large limestone door. The door's dimensions were the same as the corridor's – ten feet tall and eight wide.

Once he was inside the room beyond the door, he knew he would be safe from his enemies. He would contact his brother Marduk who would bring his wrath down on those who dared hunt him. He bent forward holding his hands on his knees. A sharp pain surged through his left thigh. He looked down. There was a bullet hole in his cream linen trousers, covered with his blood. He tore a strip of cloth from the bottom of his beige linen shirt and tied it around his thigh in an effort to stem the bleeding, and moved as fast as he could toward the doorway up ahead.

Suddenly he heard the voices of his adversaries behind him as they made their way into the tunnel entrance. 'Stop where you are or I'll shoot.' The voice travelled down the corridor, followed by a bullet that tore past Gibil's head. Gibil placed his right hand over the scanner on the wall beside him and turned to his enemy. The limestone door lifted behind him.

'Not today, I am afraid,' he yelled back at his pursuers. He took a step backward and to his right, behind the protection of the room wall. Gibil's enemies fired a barrage of gunshots in his direction. The bullets embedded in the wall beside him. He placed his hand on the sensor inside the room and a loud thud echoed down the tunnel toward his enemy as the limestone door shut in front of them.

Gibil's breathing was fast and heavy as he leaned against the wall to his right. *That was close*, he thought rubbing his hands over his face.

Suddenly the room went pitch black.

It took a few moments for Gibil's vision to adjust to the darkness. He felt along the limestone wall, edging his way around the room to his work area.

He fumbled through the contents of his workbench until he found a large torch. He switched it on and focused the beam on the two white cylinders on the other side of the room.

They measured nine feet in height and four in diameter and had been brought to Earth by his ancestors. For over two thousand years they had remained a secret, but now his enemy was closing in. They'd cut the power to the weapons storage room and had driven a wedge between Gibil and the outside world. He was trapped and had no way of calling for help.

Chapter 25

Marduk's flying goliath maintained a low-Earth orbit at two hundred and eighty miles above the surface of the Earth. The enormous two-storey aircraft was built to his exact specifications and was the flying mobile administration centre from which he maintained constant contact with his Antarctic base, from where his vast organisation, known to the world as LINEL Aerospace, was controlled. All the technologies that LINEL Aerospace developed and invested in were a legacy of his advanced ancestry and provided him with the vast wealth required to maintain the Nephilim's covert existence on Earth.

The aerodynamically designed fuselage measured two hundred and ten feet in length, with a three hundred feet wingspan. It was coated in a reflective silver-coloured radar-absorption material that covered all wavelengths including infrared, allowing the aircraft to sail undetected through the skies above the Earth at all times. The fuselage also included an integrated thermal protection system to ensure a smooth journey from and to the Earth's surface, where Marduk could interact with the most powerful people and governments, anywhere, any time. A dedicated communications room and on-board satellite system allowed encrypted communications via Marduk's Antarctic base to anywhere on Earth, while the lower deck was fully equipped with all the latest aerospace technologies. A staff of thirty-five Nephilim worked around the clock to maintain and manage all Marduk's activities outside his main operations centre in the Antarctic, including an advanced medical facility to see to his every need.

Marduk rested his head against the back of the large cream leather chair and stared across the vast cabin space at the map displayed on the giant screen embedded into the cabin wall. The words from Chasid's last message were still emblazoned before his eyes.

`Abaddon has taken the spheres.`

`Lochemel is dead.`

He shifted his gaze toward the view of Earth through the small oval window to his right. It spun below him at just over one thousand miles per hour. He thought of how over one hundred and eight billion humans had graced the Earth over the past one hundred thousand years, most of them blissfully unaware of their true heritage, ignorant to the true beauty and fragility of the planet they called home. All of which could change in an instant if his brother was to reveal to humanity that the Nephilim still existed on Earth.

Marduk glanced at the message on the computer control panel in front of him.

`Connection failed - Nergal unavailable`

He reread Chasid's message, then looked at the large screen where his brother's aircraft transponder signal was displaying his location, just off the coast of Ireland.

What is he up to? he thought.

His attention was drawn to the new icon that appeared on the control screen in front of him.

`Incoming call - Nergal`

Marduk's blue eyes stared at the icon for a moment as he ran his hands through his thick, layered, shoulder-length blond hair and composed his thoughts. Then he reached forward and answered the call. An image of his brother displayed on the giant screen on the cabin wall.

'What are the reasons for your delay in responding to me?' Marduk said.

Nergal restrained the urge to display his infuriation. His

brother insisted on treating him like a child and having every move he made monitored by Marduk was a constant thorn in Nergal's side. After all, he too was the grandson of a king.

'Brother, you look more human every day,' Nergal said snidely. He was referring to Marduk's expensive well-tailored navy pinstripe suit, white shirt with a thin light-blue stripe and a cobalt-blue tie that framed his neat appearance. An appearance he preferred when meeting with the human leaders. An appearance he felt made them more at ease in his company. 'You know I had some loose ends to tie up off the coast of Ireland. Remember the crash the day before yesterday? You said it yourself: we do not want to have to cover up another Roswell incident, now do we, brother?' Nergal said calmly.

He was referring to one of Marduk's advanced aircrafts which had crashed on an island off the Irish coast, sparking UFO speculations on an unprecedented scale. Marduk's team of analysts at the Antarctic base were monitoring internet and other media traffic, ensuring that pictures of the aircraft and the renegade Nephilim, who was found with the wreckage, were removed or where possible destroyed. Instead of reporting the truth, Marduk ensured that the ensuing media circus reported it as nothing more than a fireball that had come streaking across the skies and landed on the island.

'And what about your old friend Abaddon? Do you know where he is?' Marduk said.

'You know that I have had no contact with Abaddon. Not since—'

'Not since he assisted you and your cousin Ninurta to deploy nuclear weapons on Earth. You almost obliterated the entire human and Nephilim races in the process.' Marduk paused to stand up. His imposing physique and direct manner made most of the Nephilim uneasy in his presence, but not Nergal. 'Abaddon has been sighted in South Africa looking for ancient artefacts that should not be in his control. If I find out that you are in any way plotting with him again, there will not be a crack or crevice in the entire universe that will shelter you from my wrath. We have had over two thousand years of peace in this solar system. So take note, brother. I will obliterate anything that threatens this peace. Including you. Do you understand?' Marduk said in a firm voice. His bright, blue eyes glared at Nergal from behind sharp, high cheekbones.

Nergal sat back in his chair. He knew his plan relied on a predetermined course of events that he had already initiated by his actions. There was no way he could lose, so he composed his thoughts and replied to his brother in a calm and quiet tone.

'You wound me, brother. Why would you presume that I am always plotting and planning your demise? I have enjoyed the peace we have cultivated over the past centuries as much as anyone. Why would I want to spoil that now?'

'Indeed.' A snide overtone enveloped his reply. *Why would you do anything to cause disruption now? Why now?* Marduk thought.

'Then I will take my leave of you, brother. I have things to do.' Nergal leaned forward and ended the call.

Marduk stared at the blank screen. He could still see the silhouette of his brother's face in front of him. He knew Nergal's hatred of him was deep within him, swathed by his profound lust for power. A combination that made him a dangerous and powerful adversary if he chose to rise against him.

Marduk sat back down and touched the screen on his desk to begin another call. This time Chasid's image displayed before him.

'How are you progressing?' Marduk said when the call

was answered.

'Our backup transportation arrived moments ago. We have removed Lochemel's body, but the bodies of the cardinal and his assistant are still in the cathedral. The Klerksdorp emergency services and the police arrived before we had a chance to move them. We had to leave,' Chasid said.

'I will arrange to have this matter left under the jurisdiction of the Vatican. My allies there will take care of it.'

'Your Majesty, the team I sent to the weapons storage in the Transvaal Mountains beneath Adam's Calendar—'

'Yes,' Marduk said abruptly.

'I fear that we have been too late. I should have had an update from them by now.'

'Then go to South Africa yourself and see that they are secure. My brother Gibil will most likely bow under pressure and arm the weapons if he is forced to. As Abaddon possesses the detonators, this will be his next step.' Marduk paused. 'Take no prisoners, Chasid. Abaddon must be stopped.'

Chapter 26

The two contrasting towers of the gothic Chartres Cathedral soared high into the skyline either side of its western façade, as they guarded over the royal portal that enshrined the late Romanesque-style figures of the Old Testament's queens and kings. Even from a distance, Daniel could make out the shape of the arched, heavy flying buttresses on either side that pressed imposingly against the cathedral walls. The buttresses had been designed by the architects to take the weight of the enormous roof away from the walls of the cathedral and allow the builders to increase the window size by a considerable amount.

Peter, Daniel, Ava and Emily weaved their way toward the cathedral through the many tourists who had come to experience the magnificent architecture and divine ambience the cathedral had to offer. Their second train ride – from Paris to Chartres – had taken just under an hour and their discussion on the Eurostar regarding what his father might be protecting was foremost in Peter's mind. Yet despite the fact that he felt they'd solved the clue his father had left for him, Peter still had no idea what he was looking for, or where he would eventually find it. The ancient legend that suggested the Knights Templar had unearthed the Ark of the Covenant from King Solomon's Temple and moved it to Chartres Cathedral seemed too obvious to Peter. *If it was that straightforward, the Nephilim would have found the Ark by now*, Peter thought, looking toward the main entrance on the western façade, the sight of which transported him back to the last time he and his father had visited the cathedral together. Marcus had told Peter of its history, how it had been used as a school by the Templars and how it had almost been destroyed by two fires. But never once had he mentioned that its deepest secret could be one so ancient.

The rows of twelfth-century statues that protruded from their columns became clearer as Peter and Daniel approached the triple door entranceway to the west. Peter glanced behind at Emily and Ava. Their heads were raised, looking upward taking in the vastness of the cathedral.

At first its sheer stature, towering above the city of Chartres, had left Emily speechless. But the intricate designs and complexity of the architecture that surrounded her as she entered the cathedral through its oldest part, the western façade, made its towering imposition on the surrounding landscape pale in comparison.

The space inside was both intimidating and serene. It was softly lit by the faint light coming through the windows and the many candles that adorned the nave and aisles. For a moment everyone stood silent in the narthex and allowed their eyes adjust to the change in light.

Daniel looked around to get his bearings. He could get a faint smell of incense as he looked toward the altar, just beyond the transepts that jutted out each side of the nave giving the cathedral its cruciform shape. He turned first in the direction of the southern transept and then to face the western façade, above which stood the famous rose window.

'That window is thirty-six feet in diameter,' Daniel said. 'You know, most of the one hundred and seventy-six windows are originals. Quite amazing, when you think about it, that they survived the ravages of humanity intact,' Daniel whispered to Ava who was deep in thought, admiring the magnificent view. 'The windows were dismantled and catalogued during both world wars. They were stored in mines and restored soon after World War II.'

'They're beautiful. The glass is sparkling even though it's dull and cloudy outside,' Ava whispered.

Daniel moved and stood closer to her as she continued to gaze at the magnificent rose window. 'You know, the way this glass was made, to shine as it does with the same luminosity irrespective of the amount of light coming in from outside, is mind-boggling. The process has never been repeated to this day. No glass window in any cathedral in the world has ever been replicated with the same precision, despite the fact that stained glass is easier to produce today than it was hundreds of years ago. Essential materials like sodium and limestone, and the colouring agents used to colour the glass – cobalt, copper and iron nickel – are more readily available today than they were back then. Even the famous blue colour used in most of these windows is difficult to replicate. Astounding really.' Daniel stood transfixed by the rose window.

Ava looked at her uncle. 'How do you know so much about the Nephilim? You must've been studying them for years.'

'Yes. Ever since my trip to the Temple in Abydos. The more I looked, the more ancient evidence presented itself to support the fact that an advanced alien race lived here, long before we were created by them.'

'Haven't you ever wondered what it'd be like if they'd remained here to rule us? Instead of leaving us to fend for ourselves for so long.'

'They never left us. They're still here pulling all the strings. Controlling the financial markets and deciding what technology we do and don't have access to. Working with our governments to hide their existence, increasing our dependence on material things we have no need for. Stunting our spiritual evolution so that we can't reach our full potential as a species. We're far from being left to fend for ourselves, my dear.'

'Talking about pulling strings, who do you think told

them about Dad and what he was protecting? It had to be someone close, right?' Ava said. She glanced at Emily, who was deep in conversation with Peter. Daniel followed her gaze.

'You think it was Emily?' Daniel's voice was laced with astonishment.

'He's spent a lot more time with her than any of us during the past three years. They worked side by side day after day. I'm sure she learned one or two of his secrets. She could be monitoring our every move and relaying it back to them,' Ava whispered to Daniel, and watched as Peter and Emily approached.

'We'll have to return and sightsee some other time,' Peter whispered, checking the time on his phone.

Twelve hours left.

'So which way do we go?' Emily said.

Ava's words were ringing in Daniel's mind. He hesitated for a moment. *There's no way she would ever betray Peter or Marcus.* But he recalled her phone call on the Eurostar. He could feel a knot tighten in his stomach.

'Are you okay?' Emily said, distracting Daniel from his thoughts.

'Yeah, I'm fine,' he said, looking at the labyrinth on the floor in the centre of the cathedral's nave.

'Pilgrims came here to worship and meditate. They travelled around that labyrinth hoping to get closer to God,' he whispered, and pointed at the labyrinth. Its diameter was a little over forty-two feet, with a circular stone in the centre.

'So that's where the pilgrims took their journey, but where are the giants?' Peter said, eager to move ahead.

'The stained-glass window should be over there. We're

looking for the Noah window,' Daniel said, walking to the northern side of the cathedral. Ava and Emily followed behind him, walking side by side.

Emily scanned the cathedral glancing toward the altar, then at the immense ceiling arched high above them. People sat and prayed. Praying for salvation. Praying to their God. A God that Emily could never again think about in simple religious terms, now that God was real. Now that God could be mortal just like everyone else. She wondered if their lives would ever be the same again. Yet on the surface, they looked like all the other tourists visiting the cathedral that day.

Daniel gazed up at the ornate arcade that stretched down either side of the nave. His eyes moved toward the triforium, the level above the arcade, and then upward again toward the clerestory where the cathedral windows were located high above where they stood. Each window depicted different saints and Old Testament prophets.

Daniel stopped and pointed upward. The Noah window glistened above them. It depicted the history of the pre-flood era on Earth. Everyone strained their necks to get a closer look.

'It's difficult to see from here,' Emily said, as she came to a stop beside Peter.

Suddenly the light around them became brighter. The tablet in Daniel's hand displayed a magnified image of the Noah window. 'See, I told you,' he whispered, and smiled. He held the tablet out in front of him and tapped the screen to enlarge a part of the picture. It showed two very tall men talking to two smaller bearded men.

'Here are the giants. This image shows that the Nephilim existed on Earth even before the flood. And the Templars knew about it. Why else would they have put it in their architecture?' Daniel handed the tablet to Ava so that she could get a closer look.

'The giants standing tall.'

'So the labyrinth is where a pilgrim takes a journey and the giants are depicted in the art in the windows. But where's the Ark?' Ava said, her voice brimming with impatience.

Daniel glanced to his right in the direction of the northern transept.

'The reference to the Ark of the Covenant is on a pillar at the northern transept entrance. It's this way,' he said, and pointed toward the altar as he hurried down the aisle, followed by the others. They stayed close to the wall behind the enormous pillars that secluded the aisle from the cathedral's nave, hoping to stay out of sight. Almost halfway down the aisle he turned to his left, pointing to a large brown door.

'It's out here,' Daniel whispered, now walking at a slower, more dignified pace. Daniel pushed hard against the large door and opened it outward. He held it open until Emily, Peter and Ava had followed him outside the cathedral.

'This entranceway is dedicated to the Virgin Mary,' Daniel said. 'Look, Saint Anne, Mary's mother, and Mary herself being crowned.' He pointed to the various stone carvings in the archivolts above the doors. 'The Virgin Mary's seat on Earth,' he said. Even though he had visited the cathedral many times, he never failed to be entranced by the intricate carvings. He often wondered about the secrets of the human race which the Templars had encoded within the cathedral, and how much of the Templars' centuries of illusion and secrecy could be uncovered from within its intricate tapestry.

'Over here,' Ava said to the others.

Daniel was speaking as he rotated. 'Oh good, you've found it. I'd almost forgotten where it was.' Daniel followed Peter as he walked over to Ava. She was looking at an intricate carving on a pillar of a cart transporting a large rectangular object. There was a Latin inscription underneath it.

'"*Hic amititur archa cederis*" - here things take their course, you are to work through the Ark.' Ava translated the inscription.

'I didn't know you could speak Latin?' Daniel looked at his niece in surprise.

'Yeah. I've been studying it for a few years. I'm sure I told you,' Ava said.

I'm sure you didn't, Daniel thought. He frowned before examining the pillar more closely.

'Or, if "*cederis*" is a corruption of the word "*foederis*", it can be translated as "The Ark was yielded from here",' Daniel said.

'So, the Ark isn't here?' Peter said, watching Daniel peer at the inscription.

'"*Hic amititur archa cederis*" is quite an ambiguous statement, in that it does mean "*Hic amititur*" – "Here things take their course". And "*archa cederis*" – "you are to work through the Ark." Some scholars have suggested that the word "*cederis*" is a corruption of the word "*foederis*" and that the Ark was kept here at one time and then moved to another secret location by the Templars. But I've just realised your father didn't send us here to get the Ark,' Daniel said. He turned to face the others, wielding a small archaeologist's hammer. Its head was a tarnished brown colour and its handle had an ancient look about it. 'The clue your father left you? Remember, we're looking for a globe. "'Neath its starry globe",' Daniel added.

'Yeah,' Peter said, frowning at Daniel's hammer.

'Well, here we are. At the northern entrance. Inanna is immortalised all around us.' Daniel pointed to the carvings that adorned the archway. 'The first carving on this pillar here shows the Ark of the Covenant being transported somewhere. And above it, what do you see?'

Peter looked at the carving on the pillar. He could see a cart being wheeled by a group of men with a large rectangular object on top. Then he looked above the Ark. And there it was! Carved into the pillar was a globe. But not just any globe: it was most definitely a starry globe.

'An astrolabe. "Neath its starry globe",' Peter said, and smiled back at Daniel. 'Do you think there's something underneath?' he asked, knowing very well that his uncle was about to convince him to deface part of a world heritage site with his small but effective hammer.

'Yes,' Daniel said with confidence.

'What exactly are you going to do?' Emily said, taking a nervous glance around her in every direction to make sure no one was looking. Luckily the northern transept was empty. It was a cold January day and the many tourists who'd come to see the cathedral were inside the cathedral taking advantage of the warmth.

'The globe carved into the pillar above the Ark is an astrolabe and I'm going to see if there's anything underneath it. The last part of the clue my father left says to look beneath a starry globe. Well, mariners used astrolabes hundreds of years ago to track the stars in the sky. Maps of constellations were carved onto the face of an astrolabe and by moving the dials on the front, they were able to calculate where they were and in what direction they needed to go. Basically they used them to calculate longitude and latitude,' Peter said.

'Kind of like an ancient GPS,' Ava said.

149

'Precisely,' Daniel said. 'I bet the location of the Ark is underneath that globe.' He patted his nephew on the back and handed him the hammer. 'You're tall enough to reach it. And anyway, what's the worst that can happen?'

'I've heard that before,' Emily whispered. Daniel threw her a jokingly perilous look and raised his eyebrows. She had indeed heard him say that before and calamity usually followed.

Peter raised the hammer and hit the globe in the centre.

'Hit it harder than that,' Daniel said, and watched as Peter struck a second, firmer blow to the globe. There was a resounding crack as the globe shattered into pieces, with dust and small fragments scattering to the ground. Peter wiped the dust from his eyes and looked into the opening he'd just created. He could see something gold and shiny buried inside. Striking around the sides of the hole to make it big enough to remove the object, he reached in and pulled it from its hiding place. He took a deep breath and blew away the remaining dust from its surface.

As he held it he noticed that the gold-coloured, ornately decorated object felt heavy and the front of it looked very familiar to him. Something he had loved to play with as a child and which had led him to his current field of work in astrophysics.

'It's a golden astrolabe,' Peter said, examining it in more detail.

He rubbed his fingers along the two long thin golden dials stretched across the top of the two discs. The dials were immovable, fixed in place. Peter then focused on the discs. The bottom one contained a map of the heavens, on top of which sat a smaller circular disc with the signs of the zodiac engraved into it.

'It's set at a point in time when the sun is in Leo,'

Daniel said. He was standing at Peter's left shoulder.

Peter looked at the symbol for the sun engraved on the disc. He knew that before the astrolabe could be used, the position of the sun in the sky had to be set. And this particular device had been set at a time when the sun rose in the constellation of Leo.

'Why the age of Leo?' Peter said.

'I guess it's another clue for us to figure out. Turn it over and see if there's anything on the other side,' Daniel said.

Peter turned it over. There was a verse engraved in the centre of the disc's back. Peter read it in his head at first then paused for a moment before reading it aloud.

> *'Neath a dark starry night,*
> *Shine a blackened light.*
> *O'er the tablet neath his breast,*
> *Where the ancient Pharaoh took a rest.*
> *The knowledge that you seek*
> *Lies hidden beneath his feet.'*

'Do you know what it means?' Emily said.

Peter and Daniel both repeated the words of the verse in their minds hoping to trigger something that would tell them what they needed to do next. Peter knew that his father's clue would mean something to him, once he had the time to ponder over its construction and ambiguous meanings.

'"Where an ancient Pharaoh took a rest." It must be referring to one of the burial tombs in Egypt,' Peter said, and turned the astrolabe over again. 'Does anything on this look familiar to you, Ava? Do you remember these from when we were younger? Dad used to make them with us,' Peter said.

'Not really. It was probably something you and he did,' Ava said sharply.

Peter turned to his sister, knowing full well she was lying. On their summer holidays they would spend days on end sailing through lakes and rivers in Scotland, Ireland and England. And on more than one occasion their father had helped them to build a mariner's astrolabe to teach them about the stars and how they could be used to figure out latitude and longitude.

But the words he wanted to say next were caught somewhere below his Adam's apple unable to pass to his vocal chords. He looked toward his sister and Emily. Two well-built stocky men dressed in black combat trousers and jackets hovered behind them. One of them was holding a gun to Emily's head.

Daniel grasped Peter's arm.

'No sudden movements, or I will kill her,' the soldier said, and pressed the gun against Emily's head.

Peter stood stock-still staring at the silencer on his enemy's black handgun at his wife's head. Any sense of fear he was experiencing was eclipsed by images of events that had transpired over the past twelve hours.

How the hell did they know we were here? Peter thought.

He glanced at his sister, his uncle and then at his wife. Had one of them betrayed him?

Chapter 27

Deep within the heart of South Africa, the cradle of humanity and home of Mitochondrial Eve, Adam's Calendar is a testament to humanity's past that has defied both time and the elements, since its creation over seventy-five thousand years ago.

Meregel looked out of the helicopter window and watched its shadow fall over the ground below. He was high above the giant ancient stones that stood upright close to the precipice. Their existence shouted to the world the true extent of man's history on Earth, but only a handful of humans had ever listened to the story they begged to tell.

Beyond the stones the bright, yellow arm of a hydraulic excavator was tearing without mercy at the ground below it, removing tonnes of earth from the top of the Transvaal mountain range. Meregel watched his father open the helicopter door and jump to the ground, approximately fifteen feet below. Abaddon had learned from the excavation leader that Gibil had barricaded himself inside the weapons storage room and was refusing to let anyone inside. For this very purpose, Nergal had arranged to have an excavation team on standby. If Gibil was not going to let them in willingly, they were going to do it by force.

Abaddon walked toward the enormous crater. Behind him the black helicopter hovered downward and landed feet from where he stood. His son stepped onto the mountaintop and walked over to him.

The site engineer had instructed the digging to halt. They had found what they were looking for: at the base of the enormous crater was a flat limestone structure.

'We've reached the roof. What should we do next?' the engineer said, his hands on his hips, one leg resting on a mound of earth. He arched his neck in an attempt to look Abaddon in the face.

Abaddon stared into the crater. The nuclear weapons hidden on Earth by Marduk's father were right beneath his feet. Abaddon had the detonators; now all he needed to do was persuade Gibil to arm the weapons, and their plans would be firmly on track.

'Is he still in there?' Meregel said.

'Yes. At first we tried to capture him, but failed, so we cut the power supply to the room. Then we excavated until we reached the limestone block. Some of your men also encountered four of Marduk's soldiers. They'd arrived soon after he locked himself inside. They were captured and are being held over there,' the engineer said, pointing to the large, green tent that served as a makeshift control centre near where the helicopter had landed.

Meregel turned his back on the engineer and faced his father. 'We need Gibil alive,' he said in a low voice.

Abaddon nodded in agreement then addressed the engineer. 'Do whatever you have to do. I want what is in that room, intact and soon. And try not to harm the fool inside. I want him alive for now.'

The engineer signalled to his team to move the drill into position and begin drilling into the limestone block.

'How long will it take you to reach inside?' Abaddon said.

'About forty minutes,' the engineer said.

'Good. Notify me when you are finished,' Abaddon said, as he strode toward the large makeshift control centre.

He had the spheres. The ancient weapons were feet

below him. And soon the Earth would be ruled by the Nephilim, just as it was always destined to be.

Chapter 28

Peter's thoughts were distracted by the sound of one of the guards talking.

'Give it to me,' he said, motioning toward the astrolabe in Peter's hand.

'The moment I give this to you we're all dead,' Peter said.

'If you give it to me now, I have been instructed to let you all live,' the guard said.

'Don't give it to him,' Daniel's voice rippled with defiance.

Peter stared at the astrolabe, weighing up his options. He could try to overpower the bulky guard with the gun, but Peter was sure his wife would be dead before he'd even get a chance to try to take the gun from him.

'I've no choice,' he said to Daniel. 'I can't let any of you die.' Peter looked at the guard and began to raise his hand when suddenly he heard a loud gunshot from behind and a bullet thundered past him. Daniel shielded his head beneath his hands. Peter watched Emily crouch down onto her knees and hold her hands over her ears. A loud thud preceded her captor falling to the ground behind her. Peter breathed a sigh of relief and rushed to help her back to her feet.

Ava pivoted around to face the second guard. She watched him raise his weapon and point it in Daniel's direction.

'No one move!' the guard shouted, before a second shot pierced the air. Daniel watched as the bullet hit the guard with precision, right in his chest. The guard loosened his grip on his weapon and fell backward in tandem with it. A second thud resounded as he collapsed.

Daniel hurried over to Ava. Placing his arm around her, he guided her toward the northern entrance hoping to find some cover. Peter and Emily followed behind. Both guards had been taken down with unparalleled precision by someone hiding in the shadows. Peter scanned the area around them. He had no idea whom the mystery shooter would take aim at next.

'Did you see where the shots came from?' he said.

'I'm not sure. I think they came from behind us,' Daniel said, his voice was lowered to a whisper as he peered out from beneath the archway, trying to figure out who the unknown shooter was. He could see the shrouded silhouette of a giant walking in their direction. He moved back beneath the cover of the northern entrance. 'I guess it was him,' he said, pointing.

Peter turned to face the large wooden door behind them. He pushed hard on it, but it wouldn't budge. It was locked. Daniel rushed to the middle door, but it too was locked. He made his way to the third door. The figure of the giant grew closer until the unknown shooter stood before them.

Peter stepped forward and faced him.

A priest dressed in long, flowing black vestments stared at them as they cowered beneath the archivolts.

Another Nephilim, Peter thought. He stepped hesitantly forward.

'We need to move.' It took only a second for the familiar foreign voice to register with Peter.

'Raziel! Is that you?' Peter said. 'How ...?'

'No. My name is Shoer. Raziel was of my

brotherhood.'

Peter glanced at Shoer's left wrist. He bore the same mark as Raziel: a golden-winged disc sat atop a double-barred cross. Another guardian of his father's secrets.

Shoer scanned the entire area.

'We must leave here. More of them will come now that they know you have unlocked the second secret. Come, we must leave.' Shoer pointed toward a small door at the end of the steps, just feet from the entrance.

'Come! Come,' Shoer insisted, trying to hurry them as he walked toward the door.

Daniel frowned at Peter.

'It's okay. We'd better follow him,' Peter whispered, and hurried alongside Emily down the steps toward the door barely visible in the midst of the grand northern entrance.

Daniel followed, scanning the area around the cathedral as he jogged in an effort to keep up with the others, before he suddenly realised Ava was nowhere to be seen. He looked back over his shoulder. She was at the top of the steps, picking something off the ground near where the guards had fallen.

She hurried to catch up with Daniel. 'I dropped my phone,' she said, and smiled at her uncle.

Daniel smiled back at her and walked with her toward the others.

'More of them will come. They are approaching through the western entrance. I can get you safely to the other side of the cathedral from here, but you need to follow me,' Shoer said.

He opened the wooden door beside the wrought-iron railing just below the northern entrance and ushered everyone inside. A loud bang echoed through the small cramped tunnelled entranceway, which stretched out in front of them, as Shoer closed and locked the door behind them.

It took a couple of moments to adjust to the dull light inside.

'This way,' Shoer said.

The cold damp air sent a chill down Emily's spine. 'Where are we?'

'We are in the crypt. The cathedral is above us,' Shoer said, pointing at the ceiling.

Peter ran his hand along the stone wall. There was just enough space in the corridor for them to walk in single file toward the larger room up ahead.

Inside the larger space, fading frescoes adorned the walls and the ceiling was ornate with low-lit long-hanging lights on either side of the arches that supported the underground structure.

Daniel looked around him. He knew where Shoer had taken them. They had entered the Chapel of Notre-Dame-sous-Terre, and at almost two hundred feet in length, it stretched for quite a distance underneath the main cathedral that towered above. Daniel glanced up at the ceiling. He knew that the entire weight of the cathedral above them was supported by the walls of these old churches that had survived the fire of 1194, and which together now formed the largest crypt in France. *Better keep that information to myself*, Daniel thought.

Peter, Emily and Shoer were only steps ahead.

Daniel glanced at Emily, the seed of doubt Ava had earlier planted about her loyalties was playing on his mind. *Could she really betray Marcus like that*, he thought. He swallowed hard then glanced behind him where Ava was following close to him.

'The well of Saint Fort is up ahead, and then the ambulatory with the seven chapels,' Daniel whispered to Ava.

'You've been here before?' Ava said.

'Yes. Several times,' Daniel said.

'So you know your way around in here?' Ava said, while she reached into her pocket and removed the gun she'd taken from the ground outside. She raised it without a sound and rested the tip of the barrel against the back of Daniel's head.

'Don't move,' she whispered to him.

Feeling the gun against him, he came to an abrupt stop. He could feel a rush of adrenaline as everything suddenly became clear: how the Nephilim had known Marcus was a Grand Master and how they'd known he was protecting a sacred ancient artefact. He now understood why Marcus had gone to Balantrodoch alone. She had beckoned him. His own flesh and blood had betrayed him. All this time she'd been hiding behind a well-constructed veil that had kept her true intentions hidden from those closest to her.

'Why? Why would you do this?' Daniel whispered.

'Why do you think?' Ava said in a loud voice, and pushed the gun closer to his head.

Peter heard his sister's raised voice in the distance behind him, and turned to see where she was. His feet wedged to the floor beneath him. His eyes widened.

'Don't look so surprised!' Ava said. She tightened her grip on the gun. 'All we want is the location of the artefact. Once you hand it over, you'll be released. You have my word.' She paused for a moment and looked at her brother standing at the end of the chapel. 'So tell me, Peter, where does my father want you to go next?'

Chapter 29

Gibil leaned against the limestone wall focusing his attention on every breath he took. The sound of the drilling machine boring through the ceiling above him dulled his senses and made every inch of his body vibrate in harmony with the resonances it created. His enemy had cut the power and his only remaining light source was a torch. Gibil's hands trembled as he held it aloft and looked toward the ceiling. He could see and feel the dust trickle past his face and fall to the floor.

He focused the light beam on the weapons near the wall opposite him. His mind filled with the memories of the last time they'd been used on Earth.

Sodom and Gomorrah.

At the time Gibil's father, Enki, had warned the Nephilim council against using the weapons. He had warned them about the devastation they'd cause. But Enki's son Nergal was persuasive and unyielding in his determination to destroy his own brother Marduk, so he enlisted the help of his uncle Enlil and convinced the Nephilim council to allow them to deploy the weapons to stop Marduk from gaining control of Earth. For generations after their use, destruction and disease followed. The seas on Earth became irradiated. The food chain was spoiled. People and animals mutated and died. Gibil knew well that as it had happened before, it would happen again, if the weapons were relinquished to Abaddon.

His thoughts were interrupted by the change in tone of the excavation equipment as the drill came closer and closer. The grains of sand and the pieces of limestone that fell from the roof multiplied as his enemy started to breech his defences. He had closed off the only entrance to the weapons shelter and had trapped himself inside, and with the power cut, he had no way to contact his brother for help. His enemy had the resources and determination to ensure they'd succeed and it wouldn't be long before they took what they came for.

Gibil scanned the room once again. He held the light in his outstretched hand and pointed it at the workbench opposite him. A shiny round cylinder sparkling in the distance caught his eye. Gibil shuffled to the other side of the room. Larger pieces of limestone fell to the floor around him.

He reached forward and heaved the white cylinder off the workbench and onto the ground. It was two foot long, two foot in diameter and was very heavy for its size. Gibil rubbed the beads of sweat from his forehead. He bent to his knees and moved a large box across the floor, beneath which a circular door with a small grey handle had been concealed. He lifted the metal handle and turned the disc. The door clicked open. Gibil pulled it upward from the floor to reveal a long cylindrical compartment four foot in diameter and which stretched approximately five feet beneath the floor. He lifted the cylinder and placed it into the opening with care.

He looked back at the weapons and then to the ceiling. His enemies were almost through. He knew he was out of time. He secured the circular door over the storage space and returned the box to its original position. He stood up and looked behind him. The limestone fragments hurtling to the floor increased. Suddenly the room was awash with the sunlight that shone through the six-foot-diameter tunnel the drill had formed.

Gibil raised his hand over his forehead, sheltering his eyes from the debris that continued to filter into the room. He looked around his workspace and eyed his gun on the shelf to his right. He stepped backward, grabbed the gun and in a futile effort to thwart his enemy's approach, he pointed it at the hole in the ceiling.

'I will shoot if you dare to enter,' he called to the silhouette standing at the top of the newly burrowed tunnel. His hands were shaking as he tried to ward off the intruder.

'You ignorant fool,' Abaddon yelled, and pointed his weapon at Gibil. He fired one shot.

The bullet shattered the ground in front of Gibil. A sense of panic overwhelmed him. He released his grip on his gun and it fell to the floor.

Abaddon watched in amusement as Gibil got down on all fours and shuffled around on his hands and knees looking for his weapon.

Gibil heard a thud behind him. He turned his head. Abaddon stood glaring at him. In a terrified panic Gibil moved to one corner of the room and huddled his head between his knees.

Abaddon followed him and grabbed him by the arm.

'Get up, you moaning mule! I have suffered enough of your nonsense,' Abaddon said, and pulled Gibil to his feet. 'We have work to do.'

Chapter 30

It was her. It was always her. Sneaking around in shadows and hiding in crevices, Daniel thought. He could feel the cold metal of the gun pressed against his skull.

'What the hell are you doing?' Peter yelled at his sister, and took a step forward.

'Don't come any closer,' Ava said, 'I will kill him.' She looked at Shoer. 'Your weapon – drop it on the ground and kick it to me.'

Shoer looked at Peter and then back at Ava. He could kill her with one shot. But he couldn't guarantee that she would not pull the trigger and kill Daniel, or anyone else, before her own life ended, so he conceded. He dropped his weapon to the ground and kicked it in Ava's direction.

Peter's pulse raced. A nauseating sensation rippled through his abdomen.

'You let them kill our father and kidnap our mother. And for what?' Peter said, staring at his sister.

'You really need to ask?' Ava said. 'My father barely even knew I existed. Most of the time I was just dismissed into your shadow. Peter, Peter, Peter. From the day you took your first breath, that's all he was interested in,' Ava said, and laughed. 'And now that I'm finally about to find out all his secrets,' Ava glanced at the astrolabe in Peter's hand, 'why shouldn't I stand on the shoulders of giants instead of walking in the shadow of a fool? A new era is about to begin. The Nephilim will rise once more and rule the Earth. Nergal has plans for us all. He will establish a new world order. Civilisation on Earth as we know it will be rebuilt. Initially the entire planet will be in chaos, but finally, when the population of humans has dwindled and their numbers are manageable, they will once again take on the slave role they were created to fulfil. Then Earth will be ours to rule as we see fit,' Ava said.

'The Nephilim who remain on Earth who do not support Nergal will rise against you. Neither they nor the humans will give up without a fight. Nergal is, after all, no match for his brother. Marduk has proven this in the past,' Shoer said.

'Perhaps. But Nergal has had centuries to embrace this fact and this time he has thought of everything. He has calculated every possible path our enemy will take to defeat us. There is no action you'll take this evening that he has not planned for you to take. Every scenario has been played out. And each and every time it leads to the same conclusion: the destruction of his brother and the enslavement of the human race. So let's not waste any more time. Just tell me where my father hid his secrets.' Ava's voice was calm and serene.

Peter stared in despair at a contorted version of the sister he once knew. *She's insane*, he thought. He turned his gaze to the astrolabe in his hand, then to Shoer who was standing motionless next to Emily.

'You cannot give up its location, no matter what she says,' Shoer said.

Peter looked toward Emily and then Daniel.

His thoughts were besieged with questions, yet Peter knew only one thing mattered right now. He needed to save what remained of his family. He looked again at the astrolabe and read the verse in his head.

'Neath a dark starry night, Shine a blackened light. O'er the tablet neath his breast, Where the ancient Pharaoh took a rest ...' 'Neath his breast, Where the ancient Pharaoh took a rest. The knowledge that you seek, Lies hidden beneath his feet ...' Is it somewhere an ancient Pharaoh was

laid to rest?

'I need time to figure this out,' Peter said eventually.

'My backup will be here any moment. So you have two minutes,' Ava said in a cutting tone.

Peter turned to face the furthest end of the chapel. His thoughts were jumbled in an erratic panic.

The sun is rising in Leo. My father is trying to give me a location. I just have to think. The sun rising in Leo .... Or perhaps a time. I'm looking for a place that was built when the sun was in Leo. When was the age of Leo? 10000 BC. Focus, Peter! A place where an ancient Pharaoh took a rest. A place built at a time when the sun rose in the constellation of Leo ....

'One minute. Then I start shooting,' Ava said.

Peter ran his index finger along the edge of the small dials.

Why is this edge jagged? It should be smooth and even.

He examined the small dial more closely. The word 'Champhol' was engraved on the circular end of it.

Peter managed a covert smile. *Of course, that has to be it!*

He took a step toward his sister.

'You can have it. It's all yours.' Peter held the astrolabe in his outstretched hand. Shoer moved in front of Peter to prevent him from giving the clue to Ava. Peter glanced at her before Shoer blocked his view. He could see her finger tighten on the trigger.

'No, Shoer! I need you to trust me.' Peter's voice quivered as he spoke. He looked at Shoer. 'They can have this. It's meaningless.' Peter held out the astrolabe in one hand to Shoer. In the other he held the jagged dial he'd taken from the front of the astrolabe and placed it in his jacket pocket so that Shoer could see. Shoer frowned and stepped out of Peter's way.

'I just want this to be over. I need you to promise me that our mother will be returned alive and well and that everyone in this room will remain unhurt,' Peter said.

'Yes. I promise. Now where is it?' Ava said abruptly.

Thoughts ran through Peter's head. *There's no way I can trust her, but I have to do something. I need whatever my father was protecting. I need something to bargain with. Something they will trade for my mother's life.*

'"The knowledge you seek lies hidden beneath his feet ... Where the ancient Pharaoh took a rest." Dad is referring to a place where an ancient Pharaoh's remains are kept. Whatever he was protecting is with Tutankhamun's treasures at the museum in Cairo.'

'How do I know you're telling the truth?' Ava said, steadfastly holding the weapon to her uncle's head.

'Because I never wanted any of this. And the irrational individual who killed my father is still holding my mother hostage,' Peter said in a calm voice. 'I just want my family back. That includes you. You don't have to do this. It's not too late to change your mind.' Peter moved closer to Ava. She pushed her uncle to one side and watched as Daniel faltered forward and fell to the ground. She changed the direction of the gun and pointed it at Peter.

'If you're lying, you're dead,' she said, suddenly feeling overwhelmed. She stepped back toward the northern entrance to the crypt.

Peter heard the sounds of Nergal's men approach. He could see Ava's attention was briefly drawn to the entrance, so he slid the astrolabe into his pocket unnoticed. He looked to his right then glanced at Daniel and the others.

'Down here,' Ava shouted with relief. She was the one who would bring the location of the artefact to Nergal. A sense of accomplishment ebbed through her as the sound of Nergal's men came closer, and for a moment her concentration lapsed.

Peter lunged forward and tried to grab the weapon from his sister. The sound of the bullet discharging from the gun resounded around the crypt. Peter faltered backward, away from Ava, his hands gripping his chest. He felt himself grow fainter as the room grew smaller and an abyss of darkness surrounded him.

Chapter 31

The chains that dragged the weapons from the safety of their shelter rattled high above Gibil's head. He sat on the ground looking into the east at the remaining dolomite stones of the human's first calendar, each weighing up to an impressive five tonnes each.

The calendar had been built, over seventy-five thousand years ago, by the human slaves who worked in the nearby gold mines for the Nephilim, so that they could tell both the winter and summer solstices just by looking at the position of the sun relative to the stones on the ground.

Gibil rubbed his hands together anxiously, then wiped the sweat from his brow. He had been given only one task by his father, Enki: to protect and maintain the weapons. And he had failed. Gibil's thoughts were interrupted by a hand grabbing his arm and pulling him upward. All he could see was Abaddon towering above him.

'I will not do it. Never. Never!' Gibil said as Abaddon heaved him toward one of the weapons safely moved above ground. Gibil fell to his knees and continued to mumble the words, 'Never. Never. Never.'

Abaddon leaned down closer to Gibil. 'Arm the weapons. Or I will kill you.' He glared at Gibil.

'I cannot. I-I forget. I f-forget,' Gibil said.

Abaddon stood upright and took his gun from his waist. He pointed it at Gibil kneeling on the ground with his hands above his head.

'Arm both of the weapons, or I will kill you,' Abaddon said again, his voice becoming louder.

'I cannot. I-I cannot. I p-promised I would not.' Gibil's voice quivered as he replied to Abaddon's demand.

A loud gunshot resonated from Abaddon's weapon. The bullet hit the ground inches from Gibil. Pieces of stone and earth shattered around him. Gibil crawled toward the weapons. He continued to mumble to himself as he stood up beside them. His hands trembled as he placed his palms on the sensors in the centre of one of the weapon's casing.

A small rectangular panel slid open exposing an empty cylindrical chamber three feet from the top of the weapon. This was where he was to place the sphere to initiate the first of three separate, but almost simultaneous, explosions that would ultimately result in the weapon's nuclear material beginning a chain reaction known as nuclear fusion. The energy from this nuclear fusion would be released in what was known to humans as a thermonuclear explosion, causing destruction on an unprecedented scale.

Gibil glanced at the detonators in the metal case. He knew that beneath their casing were two inches of high explosive charges surrounding a one inch in diameter neutron reflector. Beneath the reflector was a spherical vacuum measuring one inch in depth. The vacuum surrounded a two inch-diameter sphere of material the Nephilim had amassed from a star close to their home world, material made up of elements that did not yet exist on the periodic table of elements known to humans. At the very centre of the sphere a small neutron initiator awaited the detonation.

Gibil knew that this process was only the beginning – the primary stage that led to the destructive second explosion of the material contained beneath the detonator. He knew he could not let Abaddon detonate the weapon. He had to think of some way to stop him.

Gibil looked anxiously across the mountain top to the east. The South African landscape sprawled for miles beyond the cliff.

If I could somehow reach the edge, Gibil thought. *At least it would slow them down for a little while and perhaps buy me some time so that I can find a way to contact Marduk. Then you will see the error of your ways. He will not be pleased. Not pleased at all.*

Gibil laughed quietly and glanced at Abaddon. He removed one of the detonators from the case and opened it by twisting the two ends in opposite directions. Taking a small gold pen-like object from his trouser pocket, he pointed it at the detonator. He placed his thumb on the top of the pen and a blue light emitted from the other end.

The detonator was armed.

Gibil now had five minutes to figure out what he needed to do next. He carefully placed the detonator back into the case beside the others. He looked again at Abaddon and then toward his other captors.

Abaddon was busy talking to Meregel. Three guards stood watch near the tent in which Chasid's men were held. Two more were standing close to Gibil and one was at the edge of the mountain top, watching over the cliff.

Gibil closed the lid on the case and secured it. He counted down in his head. One hundred and ninety-two seconds were left before the one detonator he had armed would explode and destroy all the others. Just enough time for him to outmanoeuvre his enemy. If his plan was successful, without the detonators the weapons would be useless. He fidgeted as he planned his next move.

Suddenly Abaddon turned and walked in Gibil's direction. 'Hurry up! I have a tight schedule.'

Gibil lowered his head, not wanting to make eye contact with Abaddon. He held the case firmly against his chest.

'How long will it take?' Abaddon said.

'Not long. Not long,' Gibil said, his eyes firmly fixed on the case.

'Then what are you waiting for?' Abaddon shouted. 'Get to work.'

Gibil moved to the back of the weapon, watching from underneath his brow as Abaddon walked away. When Abaddon entered the control tent, Gibil covertly glanced to his right. The cliff face was about one hundred feet away. He looked to his left. The two armed guards were chatting and laughing with one another.

You will not be smiling soon, Gibil thought. He mustered every ounce of strength in his body and charged in the direction of the guard by the cliff edge. He ran as fast as he could, concentrating on the precipice and his mission to throw the detonators into the abyss of trees below.

'Stop him!' A loud roar came from the guards behind Gibil.

Almost there, Gibil thought as he approached the edge. The guard at the cliff face turned to face Gibil. He reached for his weapon. But it was too late. Gibil ran straight at him. He raised his right arm and swung the case as he charged, hitting him on the side of his head and knocking him to the ground unconscious. Gibil stood over his body. He laughed inside.

I did that, he thought. Adrenaline surged through his veins as he looked over the edge. A bullet sped past his left ear. A warning shot for him to stop. But he was exactly where he wanted to be. Gibil raised his right arm behind him and thrust the case forward. He watched it sail out over the precipice in front of him and, as he fell to his knees, he smiled with relief. Then with a thunderous roar it exploded into pieces.

Gibil heard Abaddon cry out behind him, his voice getting louder as he approached.

'No! You fool!' Abaddon roared at Gibil.

'I seem to have mislaid the detonators,' Gibil said, and pointed toward the plume of smoke.

Abaddon pressed the barrel of his handgun to the centre of Gibil's forehead. He felt Meregel place his hand on his shoulder.

'Father, Nergal did not want any harm to come to his brother. It would not be wise to injure him,' Meregel said quietly, hoping not to enrage his father any further.

Abaddon stood firm. His finger pressed harder against the trigger until the bullet shot out and Gibil fell to the ground. Meregel sighed.

'I have wasted enough time entertaining this fool. I want the entire area searched. Bring me any remnants of the explosion you can salvage. Those weapons will be ready for use one way or another.'

Chapter 32

Ava aimed the gun at Shoer. Every nerve in her body was working on overdrive as she listened to the sound of Nergal's henchmen approach behind her.

In front of her, Daniel and Emily were bent over Peter trying to get him to wake up. The consequences of her actions no longer had any impact on her. She was in way too deep. First her father and now her brother. No one was beyond the sacrifices she was willing to make to help Nergal, and in the process remove herself from her brother's shadow where she'd existed for years.

Suddenly, out of the corner of her eye, Ava saw Shoer move. He had already retrieved his rifle from the ground without her noticing and was pointing it at her. She panicked and pressed hard on the trigger. The bullet hit Shoer in his right thigh. He took a step backward and returned fire in her direction. The bullet grazed her right arm and then embedded itself deep into the chapel wall behind her.

In an instant Shoer discharged a shot at one of the guards approaching through the entrance. He discharged a second. Two of Nergal's henchmen were down, as two others arrived behind Ava, who had lost her nerve and was running for cover. She dropped her gun in an effort to balance herself against the wall as she made her way toward the chapel exit.

'Fall back! Fall back!' the guard shouted to his accomplice as Shoer continued to fire in their direction. The guard grabbed Ava by the arm and pushed her protectively behind him.

Further shots discharged in her direction and shattered part of the wall of the small chapel. Shoer realised Daniel had recovered Ava's gun and was shooting a barrage of bullets at the entrance. But he was too late. The two remaining guards and Ava had already escaped down the small corridor between the chapel and the exit. Shoer glanced at Peter who was being watched over by Emily. 'Protect them,' he said to Daniel. 'I will follow our enemies to the northern entrance and make sure they cannot return to the crypt from there.'

Daniel kneeled beside Emily and took his nephew's pulse. She was frantically searching Peter's chest for the bullet wound. She had searched underneath his jacket; his sweatshirt remained intact, yet he was covered in blood.

'His heart is still beating,' Daniel said.

'And he's breathing. The bullet went straight through his hand. It should have gone into his chest,' Emily said.

Daniel searched the ground around Peter. He eyed a small, shiny deformed copper-coloured bullet on the ground beside him.

'Here's the bullet,' Daniel said. It had been crushed at the tip by an impact with something hard. Daniel smiled at Emily.

'The astrolabe – it's in his jacket pocket. It saved his life,' Daniel said, and watched Peter move as he slowly regained consciousness.

'Are you okay?' Emily said, gently touching Peter's cheek.

He looked around the room, and nodded. 'I'm fine.'

Emily retrieved the astrolabe from his pocket. There was a small indentation in the centre from the impact of the bullet. She handed it to Daniel.

Peter cradled his left hand close to his chest and sat upright. 'Where's Shoer?' he said, noticing he was nowhere to be seen.

'I am here,' Shoer said, re-entering the underground chapel. He extended his hand to Peter and helped him back onto his feet.

'Thanks,' Peter said.

'You are welcome. I have blocked the entrance for now. But she will return with reinforcements.'

'Well, let's hope by the time she realises I gave her the wrong location, we'll be long gone from here.' Peter smiled.

'Clever boy. Chip off the old block,' Daniel said, patting Peter on the back.

'I needed some leverage, so I gave them something to think about for a while. And anyway, they're not going to give my mother back unless I have something to bargain with,' Peter said.

'So you did not tell them the location?' Shoer said.

'No, my father's secrets are safe for now.'

'And the key? What is it for?' Shoer said.

'What key?' Daniel said.

'The dial on the front of the astrolabe was uneven down one side. While I was trying to figure out the clue, I realised it was a key so I removed it and placed it out of sight in my pocket.' Peter removed the key and handed it to Daniel, who inspected it eagerly. 'I also noticed an inscription. The word "Champhol" is engraved on the top. Then it all just made sense. The astrolabe is telling us where to go. And the key is how we're going to get there. The sun rising in Leo on the front of the astrolabe is telling us to go to a place built at a time when the sun rose in the constellation of Leo. A place that was built over twelve thousand years ago,' Peter said, wincing in pain as Emily tightened the tourniquet – made from a piece torn off the bottom of her T-shirt – over the wound in his hand.

'You need to go to a hospital,' she said firmly.

'We need to go to Egypt,' Peter said, 'and if we're ever going to see my mother alive again, we need to get there before they do.'

'Egypt! But isn't that where you've just sent Ava?' Daniel said.

'Well, yes. After reading the clue a few times it suddenly occurred to me that it could, with a little exaggeration and manipulation, refer to two places in Egypt,' Peter said.

'That's true. There are lots of tombs in Egypt. I'm presuming you know which one your father was referring to – which of the ancient Pharaoh's resting places we need to go to?'

'I think so. But it's not a tomb we're looking for: it's the Sphinx at Giza.'

'The sphinx? But there are no pharaohs buried there.'

'No, there're not. But my father wasn't referring to a burial tomb – he was referring to one specific pharaoh: Thutmose IV. We need to go to the Dream Stele, also known as the breastplate. It's between the paws of the sphinx. "Where an ancient pharaoh took a rest."'

'That's it!' Daniel said.

'Are you sure?' Emily said.

'Yes. He's right. Before he became pharaoh, Thutmose was resting beneath the sphinx when he had a prophetic dream. The dream, he said, was a vision. It showed him that if he cleared away the sand around the Sphinx, he'd reveal the remainder of the ancient monument and that he'd become pharaoh. He did just that and the sphinx was revealed in all its glory. Not long afterward he became pharaoh and erected the Dream Stele between the two front paws of the Sphinx to commemorate the event. I think the Stele will lead us to the location Marcus wants us to go to. Exactly how, we'll have to figure out on the way,' Daniel said.

'And my father always told me that the pyramids at Giza were older than people thought. They could even be as old as 10000 BC,' Peter said.

'And how do we get to Egypt? Assuming we do make it out of here alive,' Emily said.

'I think that's what this key is for,' Peter said. 'The last time I came to Chartres with my father, we landed at an airfield not far from here. It was called Aerodrome Champhol.'

'I know this place. It is about ten minutes' drive from the cathedral,' Shoer said.

'I've a feeling my father has left me something at the aerodrome.' Peter smiled, and held the gold-coloured key from the front of the astrolabe in his hand. 'All we need now is to get out of here safely.'

'There is another exit out of the crypt, on the southern side of the cathedral. Fr Angelo's vehicle is parked beside the railings just beyond the steps to the southern entrance. It is small, but it will be adequate for you to travel to the aerodrome in.' Shoer checked that the entrance to the crypt from the northern side was still secure. 'The quickest route from the cathedral is to travel down Rue Des Acacias. But we should hurry. I have barricaded the entrance on the northern transept, but it will not hold them back for long,' Shoer said and turned to Daniel. 'I heard you say earlier that you have been here several times before?'

'Yes,' Daniel said.

'Good. We are in the Chapel of Notre-Dame-sous-Terre. The exit I am referring to is near the southern transept on the other side of the cathedral. From here you must first pass the well of Saint Fort, then continue along the ambulatory, which contains the seven chapels. Just beyond the seventh chapel, the Chapel of Saint Mary Magdalene, there is a stairway that will lead you to a concealed doorway out of the crypt. The entrance has been closed off for excavations for the past few weeks so you should not encounter anyone in that area today. The vehicle is a bright green colour and is parked beside the black railings on the southern side of the cathedral. You cannot miss it. The aerodrome is located approximately one and a half miles in an east-north-easterly direction from the town of Chartres. I will stay here and guard the northern entrance for as long as I can,' Shoer said.

'Isn't there another—' Peter was interrupted by a loud banging noise coming from the entrance to the crypt. Shoer lifted the rifle and rested the handle against his shoulder.

'They are here. You must go and I must fulfil my duty to your father and my creator. The keys to the vehicle are under the driver's seat. If it is my destiny, I will follow you to the aerodrome and accompany you on the remainder of your journey. However, should you need to leave before I arrive,' Shoer paused, 'then you should do so without hesitation.'

Chapter 33

Peter, Emily and Daniel passed through the crypt. Every step Daniel took felt more like a passage through time than a journey through the tunnel space, above which, the enormous weight of the imposing cathedral rested. A space considered sacred long before the Christians and Templars had arrived there.

Daniel stood for a moment beside what looked to be a baptismal font. 'This is the well of Saint Fort,' he said. 'It's over one hundred and ten feet deep. The foundation of the well is deeper than the Eure River which runs almost eighty foot below the crypt floor,' Daniel said, and walked ahead toward a narrow, stone-walled semicircular corridor known as the ambulatory. 'This way,' Daniel whispered, and walked toward the dimly lit semicircular path, scanning the corridor ahead for any sign of Ava and her accomplices.

Peter nestled his wounded hand against his chest. It throbbed with every heartbeat, but he ushered it from his mind as he tried to understand Ava's reasons for betraying their family.

'Does it hurt?' Emily said, laying her hand on his arm, and noting the determined look on his face.

'It's sore. But bearable.' He looked down at her. 'How are you holding up?'

'I'm fine.' She smiled at him.

She looked pale and tired and Peter could see the lie in her eyes. He knew she was scared. And so was he. But nothing was going to stop him. He was going to find a way to outwit his enemy and save what remained of his family.

Peter placed his hand over Emily's. 'How far to the exit?' he asked Daniel.

'It's not far. Shoer said it's in a part of the crypt just beyond the seven chapels. Four ribbed vault chapels and the three barrel vault chapels, partly above and partly below ground, are along the ambulatory just up ahead,' Daniel said, then suddenly stopped walking. He noticed a faint light flickering in the distance beyond the first of the seven small chapels. Followed by an outburst of song.

'What's going on?' Emily said.

'They sometimes hold candlelight vigils—' A muffled noise made Daniel pivot around to look behind Peter and Emily. 'Did you hear that?' he said.

'Yes. It sounded like a gunshot,' Peter said.

Daniel looked in the direction of the light. It was fading and he guessed that the crowd of tourists had begun to move toward the southern entrance to the crypt.

'Quick, move forward and mingle with the tourists. The exit is at the other end of the ambulatory. Find your way through the crowd until you get to the end of the narrow semicircular walkway. I'll give you a signal when we need to move,' Daniel whispered.

The trio moved along the ambulatory. There were grey stone walls on their right with the series of small chapels hidden behind stone archways on their left. They passed each of the chapels until they were almost at the end of the corridor, where they merged unnoticed with the crowd of tourists absorbed in the divine atmosphere of the crypt. Peter glanced behind as they edged their way to the front of the crowd nearest the tourist guide. Peter used his six-feet-four-inch height to good effect, watching for movements beyond the crowd on either side.

He looked back, arching his neck to see around the

corner. A hazy shadow appeared from the northern entrance. Then another and another until finally he could see Ava standing beside one of Nergal's men. Peter instinctively quickened his pace through the crowd to get to Emily. The other tourists were throwing him irritated looks as he pushed forward and grasped her arm. She turned to him.

'We need to slip away,' Peter whispered, and gestured toward their unwanted guests who were gaining on them.

Emily looked at Daniel who nodded in her direction. He'd already seen their pursuers and was preparing to leave the crowd. He pointed ahead to his right. Their exit was only feet away.

'The Chapel of Mary Magdalene,' the male tour guide said, and in response the gathered crowd fell silent. 'This is the last of the seven chapels along the ambulatory,' the guide said, as Peter, Emily and Daniel moved along the edge of the crowd toward the exit.

Daniel walked in front at a fast pace, glancing behind him for any sign their enemy had seen them leave the crowd. 'This must be it,' he said, coming to a stop at a sign hung across the bottom of some stone steps leading to a small doorway.

Danger! Excavation site

No Entry

Peter could hear footsteps and muffled voices in the distance behind them.

Quickly stepping over the chained sign, they climbed the stairway. They shrank back into the darkness and watched Ava and three henchmen pass the entranceway

183

below, before their footsteps stopped without warning. Each held their breath as one of the tall well-built soldiers returned to examine the stairway.

He looked beyond the sign and up the stairs, then reached into his jacket and removed a torch. He was about to turn it on when he heard a voice shout in the distance. 'This way.' He replaced the torch and went to join the others along the corridor leading to the south aisle of the crypt.

The sound of their communications devices faded into the distance as Peter, Emily and Daniel breathed a sigh of relief and turned to the door that would lead them to freedom.

Daniel opened it and peered outside. His heart sank. He didn't know whether it was the sight of the tiny escape vehicle Shoer had left them, or the well-built man standing looking into it that disappointed him more. He closed the door and turned to the others.

'The vehicle has been compromised. One of Nergal's men has found it,' Daniel whispered.

'Is there only one?' Emily said.

Daniel opened the door a little and peered out.

'Yes, only one. But he's a big guy.'

'Do you still have your hammer?' Emily said.

Daniel and Peter stared at her.

'Yes,' Daniel said. 'But he has a gun ... a real big one too!'

'Your university ID card – by any chance is it in that bag of yours?' she said.

'Yes, but—'

'No buts. I have a plan. I need your jacket. And give me your ID card. I'm going to try to distract him. When his back is turned, sneak up and hit him as hard as you can with your hammer. If we can get to the vehicle and get moving before he calls for help, then we've a good chance of getting to the aerodrome.' Emily put on Daniel's jacket. She fixed the ID badge onto the lapel. The jacket was a little oversized, but she hoped the fading light outside would prevent the man from recognising her, if only for a moment, and that he'd presume she worked in the cathedral. She peered out through the small opening in the door and looked to her right. The guard had his back to her and his attention was fixed on the small car.

Emily slid her slender frame through the door and walked toward the car.

'*Monsieur, excuse-moi, s'il vous plait. La cathedral est fermee pour la soiree. Passer. Passer!*' she said, and waved her hands at him. She positioned herself at the rear of the car to ensure he kept his back to Daniel and Peter.

'*Je ne parle pas Francais*,' the guard said, in a most ridiculous French accent.

'*Passer*. Move on!' Emily shouted, and pointed to her ID badge.

The man stared down at her, his hand moving to his gun.

'You move on!' he said in an angry tone. She watched apprehensively as Daniel raised his hand behind the guard and hit him in the head with the small hammer. The guard fell to his knees, dropped his weapon and touched his head to nurse his wound. Daniel pushed him to the side with his foot, then picked up the guard's gun and communications device. The guard writhed in agony on the ground as Peter stepped over him to join Emily and Daniel in the car.

'This car's tiny!' Daniel said, frowning as he searched frantically under the front seat.

'I think you need to hurry,' Emily said, Her eyes widened as she looked out the back window.

'He's getting back up.'

Daniel reached as far back beneath the driver's seat as he could. Finally he felt a key. He grabbed it, inserted it into the ignition and started the engine.

The guard shouted at the top of his voice. 'They're getting away!' He disappeared around the corner toward the western façade at the front of the cathedral.

'That way,' Emily said, and pointed to a small road leading to the right.

Daniel pressed hard on the accelerator but the vehicle moved slowly forward. He glanced in the rear-view mirror. Nergal's henchmen had rushed across the street and into a large black van, its tyres screeching in protest as they skidded on the road.

'Hold on! This is a tight corner!' Daniel shouted, and swerved down the narrow street, driving in the wrong direction down Rue des Acacias onto Rue Saint Eman.

Emily looked down the tiny street. 'We're not going to fit,' she said nervously.

'We'll fit!' Daniel said. His knuckles whitened on the steering wheel. The sound of metal rubbing against stone bellowed out from the left-hand side of the car.

'See! I told you we'd make it,' he said, as the road ahead widened.

'Just about.' Emily looked at the wing mirror hanging mercilessly by its wires.

Peter watched the van inch closer behind them. It looked as if it were gaining ground, but then it came to an abrupt stop, wedged between the walls of the narrow street. Peter grinned with satisfaction as he watched Nergal's ally thump the steering wheel with the frustration.

Out of nowhere a strange despondent voice filled the car.

'We're jammed in a narrow street at the back of the cathedral. They're getting away down Rue Saint Eman.' The black communications device Daniel had taken from the guard outside the cathedral had come to life.

'We'll catch them. We're heading down Rue des Changes. We'll cut them off at Rue de la Pie,' Ava's instructions bellowed from the device. Peter listened to the two-way chatter as his enemies planned their next move.

'Where to now?' Daniel said.

'Peter! Your phone. Use the navigation app to figure out where we need to go,' Emily said.

Peter quickly launched the navigation app. The global positioning satellite identified their location. He focused on the map and assessed which way they needed to go next.

'If we go to the right, we'll run straight into them, so keep left just a little bit further down here. This will take us to a bridge over the River Eure. Pont Bouju. At the other side of the bridge take a sharp left onto Rue de la Foulerie,' Peter said.

Daniel veered to the left as instructed and the car sped ahead over the bridge and onto Rue de la Foulerie.

Peter looked ahead. 'Keep going straight then take a right. No, sorry, go left when I say so,' Peter said.

'Right. Take a left turn when you say so,' Daniel said.

'Now! Turn left, and keep going to the end of this road, then take a left onto Rue d'Ablis. Then you have to do a U-turn and head back up Boulevard de la Courtille.'

'Are you sure you know where we're going?'

'Yes, I'm positive. Now do a U-turn. If we take a less direct route, there's less chance they'll catch up with us. You're going to come to a large junction ahead. Just drive straight through it onto Rue d'Ablis. Then it's straight ahead from there on.' Peter glanced out of the back of the car. The black van was closing on them. 'If you could go a little faster ...'

'The lights are red!' Daniel said.

'Just put your foot down, close your eyes and go straight through. They're gaining on us!' Emily yelled.

Drivers blew their car horns and cars skidded to a halt all around them as Daniel sailed straight through the junction, watching the cars approach him from either side as if in slow motion. Peter watched as people got out of their cars waving their hands and shouting obscenities at them as they sped away. The black van was entrenched in the chaos, as Daniel drove further and further away down the motorway in the direction of the aerodrome.

The Renault Zoe was zipping along at a top speed of eighty-four miles per hour when they reached the roundabout outside the aerodrome. Peter could see the green hangar in the distance. The aerodrome was empty as Daniel stopped the car at the entrance and looked at Peter in the rear-view mirror. 'Which way?' he asked.

Peter was trying to recall where his father had taken him the last time he'd been here. 'That hangar, over there,' he said.

'Are you sure?'

'Yes,' Peter said. 'Look at the top left-hand corner; the golden-winged disc is on the outside of that green hangar. That has to be where we need to go.' The sun had already set, but the lights outside the hangar bay were bright enough for

Peter to make out the symbol his father had already used in the clues he had left him.

Daniel pressed the accelerator and headed toward the hangar.

'What do you think is in there?' Emily said.

'I have a hunch, but I'm not sure,' Peter said. Emily threw him a suspicious glance. He knew how much his wife hated flying and the content of this hangar wasn't going to ease her fears.

'It's a plane, isn't it?' she said.

'Well, we do need to go to Egypt,' Daniel said, 'and the quickest way there is by air.' He pressed gently on the brake, stopping outside the hangar door. He got out of the car and pushed the front seat forward so Emily could get out.

Peter was already walking toward the small door on the right-hand side of the hangar. He unlocked it with the key from the astrolabe and stepped inside. It was dark and cold. Suddenly a loud crack resonated through the empty space and a yellowish glow extended outward from behind him. He and Emily turned in its direction. Daniel was wielding a large bright-yellow glow stick. He raised his eyebrows, smiled and pointed at his satchel.

'I want one of those for my next birthday,' Peter said to Emily.

She smiled at him. *If we ever see your next birthday,* she thought.

'And, I want one of *those* for my next birthday,' Daniel said, and walked past them toward a large silver-and-black-coloured oval-shaped aircraft with the words 'LINEL Corporation' imprinted on its fuselage in gold beneath a winged disc.

Chapter 34

The search team had been looking for the remnants of the detonators for over an hour, but nothing had been found. The dense undergrowth and fading light made it difficult to see. Yet hope lingered at the back of Meregel's mind as he rubbed the beads of sweat from his face. He retraced his steps, one last time, chopping his way through the foliage checking either side of the path he'd created until he reached the area close to the centre of the detonation.

Out of the corner of his eye he noticed a small shiny object up ahead. He rushed toward it and lifted it. It was a remnant of the metal case. He continued to search the area around the object. More pieces of the case were buried in the flotsam of debris scattered across the forest floor. Meregel searched through every part of it, hoping he could find something, anything, that would please his father and get them back on track. He walked to his right and lifted a large piece of the case and examined it closely.

But his efforts were wasted. Gibil had done what he had intended to do. With the detonators destroyed, his father had no way to arm the weapons. Without them, their plans were useless.

Meregel watched the others searching through the debris. Walking toward them across the uneven terrain, he twisted his ankle and became unbalanced. He reached his hands out searching in vain for something to brace his fall and landed hard. He steadied himself onto his knees and started to search the ground around him, clearing undergrowth as he crawled through it.

Meregel took a short sharp breath when he realised he'd stumbled upon one detonator- fully intact.

He lifted it carefully from the ground and pulled himself slowly to his feet. He took a long lingering look up through the forest, toward the Transvaal mountain range that towered above him. Finally, they could forge ahead with their plans.

'I have found what we are looking for. Return to the mountain top. I will follow you up,' Meregel shouted to the others who immediately began their trek back to the mountain top as he had instructed.

Meregel followed behind, placing a call as he walked. It was answered at once.

'Were you able to locate the blueprints I requested?' Meregel asked.

'Yes. I will send them to you now,' the male voice replied. The call ended abruptly.

Holding the detonator carefully, Meregel approached his father. A sense of fulfilment rippled through him as the space between them narrowed.

Abaddon turned to face his son who was holding the detonator in his outstretched hand. 'You have salvaged one detonator and given us a further chance to continue with our plans,' he said, as Meregel handed him the detonator. 'All we need now is someone who can place this in the weapon and activate it.'

Meregel smiled. 'Micah's contact in the Antarctic has sent me the weapon blueprints. I am confident that I can ready them for use,' he said.

A swell of pride rippled through Abaddon's chest. He placed his hand on his son's shoulder. 'This day will be remembered by the Nephilim race forever. You have done me proud.'

Chapter 35

'Handprint authenticated. Please enter your destination,' the English speaking, female voice recognition software demanded. The automated navigation system had come online the instant Peter had placed his hand on the scanner in the centre of the control panel.

He glanced at the coordinates on his phone for the Giza Plateau in Egypt, then entered them into the control panel and waited. There was silence for a moment as the automated systems prepared a flight path.

Peter sat back into the pilot's seat of the jet his father had left for him. The airplane's instrument data was shown on an illuminated digital display spread strategically across the cockpit windscreen. He scanned the entire display familiarising himself with the aircraft's navigation system – altimeter, engine status, air speed indicator, rate of climb indicator, flap position indicator, fuel indicator.

'Flight path calculated. Estimated time to destination … one hour thirty minutes,' the female voice interrupted Peter's thoughts.

One hour thirty minutes, Peter thought. *This thing can really move!*

Looking back into the cabin, he watched Emily secure her seat belt around her waist just as Daniel re-entered the aircraft and pushed hard on the button to close the aircraft door.

'They're outside!' Daniel shouted.

He had gone to find a way to open the hangar doors, but Nergal's men were closing in and he had no option but to return to the aircraft and leave the doors shut. He jumped into the co-pilot's seat beside Peter and fastened the belt around his waist and shoulders. He looked worriedly at his nephew. 'I couldn't find any way to open those doors. Ava and her friends are outside so you'll just have to drive this thing through them and out onto the runway. It's now or never, shorty! You can do it,' Daniel reassured his nephew.

Peter stared through the cockpit windscreen at the large doors.

'Prepare for take-off,' he shouted, and fastened himself into the pilot's seat.

'Command accepted,' the female voice replied instantly.

Peter hadn't been expecting the aircraft to take off automatically. He watched as the hangar doors beside the nose and tail of the airplane lifted. Peter gave Daniel a relieved look as the doors opened fully, but the lights ahead replaced his relief with a tint of trepidation. *That runway is too small for this aircraft to take off.*

Peter glanced at the instrument display. All the data the aircraft sensors had gathered was filtered to the automated systems and the display showed all the information needed to perform a short take-off: aircraft weight, air speed, altitude and the length of the runway – a mere two hundred feet in length. But Marcus had taken all that into account: the jet was fully equipped for a short take-off and landing. Much like the jump jets that take off from aircraft carriers at sea.

'This is going to be a steep take-off,' Peter shouted back into the cabin, then eyed the runway ahead of him again. 'What the hell!' he said. In the distance two black vehicles drove toward the hangar. 'They're blocking our take-off path,' he said.

Out of the blue the female voice of the automated

systems filled the cockpit once again. 'Runway obstruction detected. Obstruction clearance required?'

Daniel and Peter glanced at one another then replied in unison. 'Yes.'

A gentle vibration emanated from beneath the left wing as a small missile fired out along the runway in front of them, hitting one of the vehicles head on and engulfing it in flames. The second vehicle reversed and veered off the end of the runway.

'Obstruction cleared. Commence take-off in five, four, three ...'

'She's really growing on me,' Daniel said.

'Me too,' said Peter, looking back at Emily, who was holding on to the arms of her seat as tight as she could.

' ... One. Take-off initiated,' the female voice announced.

'Here goes. Hold on tight. This is going to be quick and steep,' Peter said as the engines roared behind him.

They were pushed back hard against their seats as the aircraft sped from the hangar and began its take-off. Peter focused on the instrument display as the aircraft soared along the runway and into the sky. He could see the spires of Chartres Cathedral up ahead, then disappear out of view.

He looked at the altimeter. In a matter of seconds they had reached thirty thousand feet safely, then the aircraft levelled off and continued to fly on autopilot.

Peter smiled at Daniel and breathed a sigh of relief. They would be at the pyramids soon and the solution to the remainder of his father's clue was now foremost on his mind.

Chapter 36

Ava watched the underbelly of the aircraft pass above her as Peter escaped in the jet Marduk had gifted their father. She could feel the heat from the flaming vehicle.

She lifted her phone and made a call. It was answered immediately. 'They've escaped in one of your brother's aircraft. But I have the location of the artefact,' she said.

'Where is it?' Nergal said.

'It's in Cairo. In the museum, with the treasures of Tutankhamun.'

'We have just entered French airspace. I will come and get you and we shall finish our journey together,' Nergal said, and ended the call.

~

Nergal picked up the computer tablet from the table in front of him and stared at the screen. The locations of all Marduk's aircraft were at his fingertips, including the aircraft Peter was travelling in. He touched the dot that had just taken off from France. A small white box appeared on the screen. Nergal changed the aircraft code that identified Marcus DeMolay's aircraft and replaced it with the identification number of his own. He then placed the tablet back onto the table, clasped his hands together at the back of his neck and rested his head back. He smiled, closed his eyes and sighed. His endgame was near.

Chapter 37

The sensors located at different points on the outer hull were providing detailed situational information as they monitored the spherical area around the aircraft. Peter scrutinized the digital display and reviewed the aircraft's status. Like all LINEL corporation aircrafts, the aircraft itself was undetectable by radar and was fully equipped with its own radar detection systems so that everything in its path and beyond could be monitored at all times. The autopilot was functioning normally and the defence systems were online.

Peter unfastened his seat belt, stood up and stretched his legs. This was the first cockpit that could accommodate his upright six-feet-four-inch frame. *This jet was designed for some pretty tall people; the Nephilim of course,* Peter thought, looking at his uncle, who was transfixed by the digital display in front of him.

'Don't touch anything. I'm going to check on Emily,' Peter said.

'Perhaps I should come with you,' Daniel looked at the display on the windscreen. 'You know me and shiny digital touchscreens. One wrong movement and ...'

Peter laughed. 'I know. Technology malfunctions around you for no reason.' He went into the cabin where Emily was sitting with her eyes shut and her hands grasping the arms of the seat.

'We're safe for now,' Peter whispered, placing his hand on hers.

Emily opened her eyes and looked around.

'Why don't you try to get some sleep? We won't be

over Egyptian airspace for another hour,' Peter said affectionately. He felt exhausted and knew that Emily must feel the same way, but adrenaline and a will to find his father's secrets and bring his killer to justice exceeded any tiredness he was feeling.

'I can't sleep we need to use the time to plan what we are going to do when we get to Egypt. The last part of the clue needs to be figured out. Three sleepy heads are better than none,' Emily said and smiled.

Peter sat beside her and relaxed his shoulders. The cream fabric seats were welcoming and comfortable.

'How's your hand? Does it hurt?' Emily said. She held Peter's wounded hand and removed the tourniquet.

'It's not so bad. It only hurts a little.' Peter stared vacantly ahead of him. 'She must have been planning this for years. How come I missed it? Why didn't I see how much she hated me?' Peter added in a quiet voice.

'We all missed it. Not just you. I've spent more time with Ava than anyone these past two years she's been in London and I never noticed a thing,' Daniel said, as he placed a white tray with three mugs of freshly brewed coffee and some snacks on the table beside Emily and Peter.

'Where did you get that?' Peter said.

Daniel pointed toward the back of the aircraft. 'There's a small nicely furnished and well stocked kitchen down there.' He sat on a chair at the other side of the cabin and swivelled it around to face them. Emily took a sip of coffee and then stood up.

'There has to be a first aid kit here too. I'll take a look. That wound needs to be cleaned and dressed properly,' she said, and ventured toward the back of the cabin where the compact kitchen was located. She found a couple of bottles of water in a small fridge and, after a little searching, a large white box with a green cross on its front in one of the cupboards. She gave Peter and Daniel a bottle of water each and set the first aid kit on the table.

Daniel was staring at the astrolabe while he sipped his coffee.

'What do you think we're going to find?' Emily removed some sterile water sachets, a white plastic tray and some dressings from the first aid box and cleaned Peter's wound.

'It's hard to know. Many people have speculated about Solomon's treasure. One source says it was golden tablets from the Garden of Eden. Other sources say it was the Ark of the Covenant, among other things. But the pillar at the cathedral did depict the Templars moving the Ark somewhere, so obviously at some point they had it in their possession,' Daniel said. 'If it is the Ark, then there is one other possibility we need to consider.'

'And that is?' Peter said.

'There's a theory that there are two Arks.' Daniel stood up to stretch his legs.

'Two Arks!' Peter and Emily said in unison.

'Yes. Now hear me out,' Daniel said, sitting back down. 'Moses met with God on two occasions and on both occasions he returned with a set of stone tablets with the Ten Commandments inscribed on them. Two sets of Ten Commandments.'

'I never knew they were given to Moses twice,' Emily said, looking at Peter. 'Did you?'

'I remember reading about it in a book belonging to my father when I was younger. Moses broke the first set of commandments in a fit of rage at his people's behaviour, after he came down from Mount Sinai. So he returned to the

Mount and received a second set of commandments from God,' Peter said.

'Correct,' Daniel reached for his satchel, 'but what many people don't realise is that for each set of those stone tablets an Ark was built. The first time God commanded Moses to build an Ark, Moses commissioned Bezalel to build the Ark for him. The second time God commanded him to build an Ark, Moses built it himself. Two sets of stone tablets. With two Arks. One of which was stored in King Solomon's Temple. The other was never mentioned again.' Daniel pulled out his computer tablet and turned it on. Emily and Peter watched as the light from the tablet screen shone on Daniel's face. He placed the tablet on the table in front of them.

'Building the Ark of the Covenant is mentioned twice in the Bible,' Daniel said. 'Exodus chapter thirty-seven, verse one: "And Bezalel made also the ark of setim wood: it was two cubits and a half in length, and a cubit and a half in breadth: and the height was of one cubit and a half: and he overlaid it with the purest gold within and without." Then we move to Deuteronomy chapter ten, verses one to three: "At that time the Lord said unto me: Hew thee two tablets of stone like the former, and come up to me into the mount: and thou shalt make an ark of wood, And I will write on the tablets the words that were in them, which thou brokest before; and thou shalt put them in the ark. And I made an ark of setim wood. And when I had hewn two tablets of stone like the former, I went up into the mount, having them in my hands." Two Arks made by two different people,' Daniel said, and relaxed back into the chair.

Chapter 38

Gibil's picture filtered onto the screen in front of Marduk. He closed his eyes. His brother Gibil was a harmless fool with a penchant, much like his father, for intricate engineering. He was not a warrior, nor was he a threat to Abaddon. This in itself was an act of war brought on by the actions of a slinking coward. He could feel an immense uncontrollable rage begin to build inside him. Abaddon had the ancient nuclear weapons and the detonators. His ally and trusted friend Marcus DeMolay had been brutally murdered and Marduk knew deep down that his brother Nergal was lying to him.

These are all connected, Marduk thought.

He opened his eyes slowly.

'Have you confirmed that it was Abaddon who shot Gibil?' Marduk asked Chasid who was waiting on the line for Marduk's reply.

'I have, your Majesty. The remaining workers here have given me a full account of what happened. Abaddon and his son Meregel left this area with the weapons some time ago. Gibil managed to destroy some of the detonators, but we are unsure how many. We are analysing all of our surveillance data,' Chasid said.

'Bring Gibil to Ninharsag at the base before he is beyond her help,' Marduk commanded. He knew that time was of the essence if his brother was to be saved by his chief medical officer and the advanced medical technology he had at his base in the Antarctic.

'Your Majesty, I will do as you request, but what about Nergal and Abaddon? What is to be done with them?'

There was a brief pause before Marduk's reply. He touched the screen to his right. A map of Europe appeared; it zoomed in until a tiny blue dot flickered over the Mediterranean Sea along the north coast of Africa. The transponder signal from Nergal's aircraft was transmitting his location.

'I will deal with my brother. Nergal has committed grave misdeeds in the past and I know well how easily he can manipulate events to cause destruction. He has still not forgiven me for the fact that he was exiled here on Earth by our father after he used the weapons to try to obliterate me. Your priority is to track Abaddon down and regain control of the weapons and the detonators.'

'As you wish, your Majesty.' Chasid ended the call.

Without delay Marduk tapped the screen and made another call. A striking-looking tanned, blonde-haired woman appeared on the screen.

'Good evening, Madam President,' Marduk said.

'Good evening, your Majesty. I wasn't expecting a call from you so soon after our recent meeting,' Katherine Shaw, the President of the United States, said.

'Madam President, events this evening necessitate that I call on you to do something for me. I am sending you a transponder signal from an aircraft travelling in stealth mode toward Cairo. Your conventional radar equipment will not be able to track the aircraft. The only way you can identify it is from this signal. I need you to force it to land by taking out one of its engines,' Marduk said, and watched the president intently, analysing the smallest changes in her demeanour.

It was Shaw's second term in office and like every world leader she was aware of Marduk's covert presence on Earth and the consequences of anyone finding out that most of the world's governments had been interacting with an ancient alien species behind the scenes for centuries. She considered the Nephilim leader's request her voice was serious as she replied. 'Your Majesty, I can't just enter Egyptian airspace and start shooting at an aircraft.'

'I will make arrangements with the Egyptian Government – they will grant you limited access to their airspace. Your aircraft carrier in the Red Sea is minutes away from the Low Earth Orbiter that has now entered Egyptian airspace. I will say this only once, Madam President. I would not be asking you to do this unless it was absolutely necessary. My brother has stolen ancient weapons; the power they can unleash cannot be matched by anything on Earth. We had stored the weapons and the detonators securely at separate locations, known only to a few, but Nergal has found them and he will use them. I am sure I do not have to specify to you the chaos and damage that will ensue if he detonates those weapons or appears on international television declaring our existence and the fact that every leader on Earth has known the truth for centuries. If the human population was to find out the truth, every nation would rebel against its governments,' Marduk said, and paused for a moment to gather his thoughts. 'Nergal has also murdered our trusted friend Marcus DeMolay. He needs to be stopped.'

'I understand.' There was a momentary silence. 'I'll deploy one of our jets immediately. We'll take it down.' She knew Marduk would not ask her to do something of this magnitude without good reason.

'Thank you. Your cooperation is appreciated.' Marduk ended the call and turned to his assistant Zania.

'Get me Abram in the Egyptian Government. He will make arrangements to allow the American fighter jet to enter Egyptian airspace and neutralise my brother.'

'Yes, your Majesty,' Zania said.

Marduk returned his gaze to the dot on the screen. The transponder signal was showing that Nergal's jet was nearing the pyramids in Egypt. Behind him, he could hear Zania end her call. Moments later a second radar signal appeared on the screen, in close pursuit of Nergal's aircraft. The president had delivered on her promise. Nergal's jet would soon be on the ground.

Chapter 39

'Two arks?' Emily said. Her expression reflected her bewilderment.

'Yes,' Daniel said, 'built by two different people, as requested by God through Moses. You see, the Ark was not only a vessel to store the Ten Commandments, it was also used in ancient times as both a weapon and a device through which the Israelites could communicate with God. Its power destroyed the walls of Jericho. And if you study the chapters in the Bible where the Ark is mentioned, you'll see there are several chapters that detail how God told the Israelites when to move forward and when to stop during their exodus from Egypt, by speaking to Moses through the two cherubim on the top of the Ark. It's for this reason the Ark has also been known as the Throne of God.'

Emily frowned and raised her eyebrows at Peter.

'It's possible the Ark is some sort of super conductor harnessing and wielding an unlimited renewable source of energy. Wood is an excellent insulator and gold is known as one of the most powerful electrical conductors. I'd even bet that the technology that powers this aircraft is something similar,' Peter said. He winced as Emily tightened the bandage on his hand.

'Sorry,' she said.

'Well, we can see why Nergal wants the Ark. If it really is a weapon, then I'm sure he'll find a way to use it. But somehow I feel we're not getting the full picture. The Arks have been on the Earth for centuries and Nergal has known this. So why now?' Peter said.

'Perhaps the balance of power is shifting. For millennia

before the human race became technologically advanced the Nephilim ruled us. The Sumerian king lists show when and for how long each king ruled the Earth since they came here thousands of years ago. And because of this, we know that the prediluvian kings reigned for far longer than their post-diluvian counterparts did. In any event, the duration of each kingship was recorded by the Sumerians using a measurement known as a sar. Each sar is equal to one orbit of the Nephilim home planet Nibiru, or three thousand six hundred Earth years. This shows that the extensive lengths of their kingships were as a result of their alien ancestry, which allows them to live for millennia on Earth. But after the flood their reigns became more and more tumultuous until a couple of centuries before the birth of Christ, when almost all of the Nephilim suddenly left Earth and returned, I presume, to their home world.'

'Almost all of them?' Peter said.

'Yes, almost. We know that Nergal is still here. You saw him yourselves yesterday.' Daniel paused briefly. 'Ancient texts also show evidence that some of the others stayed as well, one of them being Nergal's brother Marduk. You see, Nergal and Marduk are both sons of the Nephilim Enki and grandsons of the Nephilim King Anu, and although the line of ascendants to the throne on Nibiru had always been hotly contested by the Nephilim sons of Enki and his brother Enlil, one constant remained: even though Anu's first born son Enki was given the title Lord of the Earth, he would never be king of Nibiru. Enki was Anu's son born to one of his concubines, so the sole right of succession to the throne on Nibiru fell to Anu's second son Enlil because he had a stronger royal bloodline than his brother Enki, and was therefore, next in line to Anu.

'Now this fact didn't bode well with Enki's son Marduk and it was here the trouble started. You see, Enki didn't mind so much that he would never rule Nibiru – he was content here on Earth genetically manipulating humans with his beautiful half-sister Ninharsag. But the same could not be said for both his and Enlil's children, and indeed Enlil himself. And in an attempt to satisfy a growing discontent among their offspring, kingships over lands on the Earth were handed down to Enki's and Enlil's children.

'But after some time unrest between the Nephilim started again after Marduk had developed a unique affinity with the humans and felt he needed to protect them. For this reason he continued to fight with his uncle and his brother to rule the Earth. He even denounced his claim to the throne on Nibiru to marry a human. But eventually Marduk became too big for his boots and the wars between the Nephilim sons grew out of hand, so Enlil was granted permission by the Nephilim council to use nuclear weapons to destroy Marduk's strongholds on Earth and silence him once and for all. In collusion with Marduk's brother Nergal, Enlil's son Ninurta unleashed the nuclear weapons on Marduk's strongholds, destroying the cities of Sodom and Gomorrah and the Nephilim spaceport in the Sinai Peninsula. Marduk's fight for supremacy on Earth ended after the destruction caused by the weapons obliterated the Sumerian civilisation and caused disease and death in its wake. The horror and destruction that followed surprised even Enlil, so he then conceded that the Nephilim should return to Nibiru and leave the Earth to the humans, which they did. But Marduk remained and his presence was noted on Earth until the third or fourth century before Christ. After which he is not mentioned again in any historical records to this day.'

Daniel paused to take a sip of coffee.

'Now, we could presume that Marduk is dead, but a more likely scenario is that he is running the Earth from deep within the shadows of the powerful and wealthy on the planet. We know from experience that Marduk is patient and covert. On the other hand, Nergal is not, as his use of nuclear weapons and his lack of remorse thereafter shows he's willing to risk everything to get what he wants. And that is, I would guess, to rule the Earth.'

'So we could very well be stuck in the middle of an ancient war for ascendancy?' Emily said.

'Most probably,' Daniel said.

Peter checked the time on his phone. 'We'll land in thirty-five minutes.'

'Well, we're sure about the location we've to go to. It's definitely the Sphinx,' Emily said.

'Yes. In the clue Dad specifically states where the ancient Pharaoh took a rest, not where an ancient Pharaoh was laid to rest – this points to the Dream Stele beneath the Sphinx, rather than a tomb,' he said.

Daniel nodded in agreement. 'You know, the Hall of Records is supposed to be located in Giza. Ground-penetrating radar has shown that there's an undiscovered room beneath the Sphinx, in the exact position where the Hall of Records is supposed to be. According to ancient folklore the Hall of Records was supposed to have been sealed in around 10500 BC, during the age of Leo. It's also coincidentally the time when the pyramids are thought by some to have been built. Perhaps this is where Marcus is leading us,' Daniel said.

Emily finished the dressing on Peter's hand by wrapping it with a soft cream bandage. She handed him two painkillers and a bottle of water. 'This should help with the pain. But we need to get that hand seen to as soon as we can,' she said. She looked at Daniel. 'So do you think that the Hall of Records is where the Arks have been hidden?'

'It's as good a guess as any,' Daniel said and reached forward for the astrolabe. '"A blackened light … neath a dark starry night …" What exactly is a black light?' he said.

'Ultraviolet light is black light,' Peter said.

'Where are we going to get a UV light at this altitude?' Emily said, looking around the cabin. 'There may be an ultraviolet light source on the aircraft that we can use.' As she rummaged through the contents of the cupboards, Peter joined her.

The first two cupboards contained cups, saucers, a torch and paper towels. She put the large black torch on the worktop and resumed her search. Much to her relief she found cupboards brimming with lab equipment, presumably stored there by Marcus. 'This is more like it! Petri dishes, filters, notebooks, a torch, black markers,' she said. 'And one LED ultraviolet curing lamp … but it's not portable.'

'Not yet,' Peter said, holding the torch. 'We just have to replace the light-emitting diodes in this torch with some of the ultraviolet ones from the curing lamp.' He unscrewed the face cap and removed the lens and reflector to reveal the light-emitting diodes attached to the head of the light. He removed the bulbs taking care not to damage them and placed them on the worktop in front of him.

Emily put the long, thin rectangular curing lamp on the kitchen worktop. Using a knife, she removed the small screws on either end of the light and removed the glass cover.

Daniel watched them work. 'Do you think they're compatible?' he said.

Peter removed three of the LEDs and compared them to the ones he'd taken from the torch, paying particular attention to the two thin metal prongs at the base of the bulbs.

'I'll need to trim the anode and cathode to make them fit, other than that it'll be fine,' Peter said pointing to the metal prongs.

'Here, I found a toolkit in the drawer.' Emily had a pair of small pliers in her hand.

'Thanks,' Peter said with a smile.

'Why ultraviolet light?' Daniel said.

Peter trimmed the anode and cathode until their length matched the original bulbs from the torch. 'As you know, light is a form of electromagnetic radiation. If you look at the electromagnetic spectrum, or the EM spectrum, you'll see that light falls somewhere in the middle of all possible frequencies of EM radiation. At one end of the spectrum are high energy short waves such as gamma rays and X-rays. And at the other end of the spectrum we have the lower energy long waves such as microwaves and radio waves. Animals such as reptiles, certain birds and even bees can see UV radiation, but without help we can't,' Peter said as he continued to fix the UV LEDs in place. 'The light humans can see has wavelengths of roughly between four hundred and seven hundred nanometres. Starting at the high end, seven hundred nanometres, is red, then orange, yellow, green, blue, indigo and violet.'

'All of the colours of the rainbow,' Daniel said.

'Exactly!' Emily smiled.

'Just beyond violet, beyond four hundred nanometres, what the human eye can see, with some assistance, is ultraviolet light. So I'm guessing that whatever message Dad has left us on the Dream Stele can only be seen with a UV light source,' Peter said, fixing the cover back onto the torch and turning it on. A violet glow emanated from the torch. Peter turned it back off and smiled. 'We should be able to see whatever's on the Dream Stele—'

A loud high-pitched alarm rang from the cockpit and the lights in the cabin switched to emergency lighting. Peter's heart raced as the aircraft's female automated voice resonated around him.

'Hostile aircraft detected. Missile incoming. Defensive

countermeasures deployed.'

Leaving the torch on the worktop, Peter ran to the cockpit. He faltered sideways as the aircraft banked hard to the right to avoid the incoming missile. He jumped into the pilot seat and scanned the display. The radar was showing two missiles tracing through the sky toward the LEO. The aircraft banked hard to the left. The two missiles followed the aircraft. Suddenly everything started to shake violently as one of the missiles was destroyed by a countermeasure only inches from the fuselage.

The other was still in pursuit.

'Warning! Warning! Auto pilot will disengage in five, four, three …'

Peter took hold of the aircraft control stick with both hands and tried to maintain altitude. An instant later the second missile exploded near the left wing. He struggled with the controls. The left engine was damaged. Warning signals rang through the cockpit. The flight instruments showed failures in power, radio signals and hydraulics, but the manual flight control was still in operation.

'We need to land,' Peter shouted to Emily who was frantically trying to fasten herself into a seat.

Daniel swayed from side to side as he joined Peter in the cockpit. 'Can I do anything?' he asked.

'You can pray,' Peter said, as he tried to control the aircraft's descent.

Daniel buckled himself into the co-pilot's seat and looked out to his right. He could see the three pyramids in the distance. He pulled the safety belt across his shoulders, tightened it at his waist and watched the desert below them come ominously closer.

Chapter 40

The pink-toned neoclassical-style building in Tahrir Square had one hundred and seven halls brimming with artefacts from the pharaonic era, but only one room was of interest to Nergal. A room with artefacts the Templars and his brother had been hiding from the entire world for centuries.

Hiding in plain sight, Nergal thought as a wave of excitement and power flowed through him.

The artefact the Templars had used to communicate with his father and brother would soon be his. This and the act of killing the Grand Master, DeMolay, would ensure that his brother would be hot on his heels. Soon Nergal would be in the very place he wanted to be. As the vehicle came to a stop outside the museum, Nergal emerged from his thoughts to watch Micah approach. He reached forward and lowered the window.

'Your Majesty, we have secured the museum. It is now safe for you to go inside. The Tutankhamun treasures are on the second floor,' Micah said, and glanced back at the Cairo Museum.

Nergal smiled at Ava, then glanced at his phone. The transponder signal from DeMolay's aircraft was no longer transmitting. Just as Nergal had planned, his brother had shot it down.

Ava followed Nergal and Micah to the museum entrance, turning around to look at her mother. She felt nothing: no guilt for her father's murder and no guilt for the torment she'd forced her mother to endure. Her feelings of jealously over the years had left her completely devoid of any other emotions.

Inside the museum two security guards in khaki-green uniforms were kneeling on the ground with two of Nergal's men watching over them. The museum had closed a couple of hours ago and the night security guards were the only resistance they were likely to meet. Ava walked by them and on past the extensive collection of artefacts from the New Kingdom – statues, tables and sarcophagi – to the end of the hall where Nergal stood at the bottom of the steps near two enormous statues.

'Soon the humans will build statues like these to commemorate their great ruler and king, Nergal,' Nergal said, looking up at the colossal statues of Amenhotep III and his favourite wife Tiye.

'Yes, they will,' Ava said.

Nergal climbed the steps to Micah waiting on the second floor.

'This is not the place. We have searched the entire floor. It is not here,' Micah said.

'But Peter solved the clue. This is the location he identified before I escaped from them,' Ava said, her voice shaking. 'He said this is the place my father came to use the artefact. I'm sure of it.'

Nergal pushed past Micah and rushed to the section of the museum that housed the artefacts of Tutankhamun. Ava and Micah followed behind him as he came to a stop before the shrine of Anubis.

'No!' Nergal yelled. He had been misled. He glared down at Ava.

'It's obvious my brother has given me the wrong location,' she said. She turned to Micah. 'My uncle stole a communications device from one of our men at Chartres. Can you track it?' she said.

'Yes, all our communications devices can be traced.' On his tablet, Micah immediately found a map showing the locations of Nergal's men around the globe. 'It was Eytan's device that was taken. I'm tracking it now,' he said, watching the software tracing the signal. At first a map of Europe appeared on screen. Then a map of North Africa, accompanied by a set of coordinates.

'Where are they?' Nergal said.

'They are here. In Egypt. The signal is coming from a location not far from the pyramids. It should take us no longer than thirty minutes to reach them,' Micah said.

Chapter 41

Nergal's aircraft sat on the runway at Kruger Airport in South Africa. The tall, slender silhouette of Nergal's pilot emerged from a door beside the cockpit, as the steps stretched out to the ground. She had flown the aircraft to Kruger Airport from Cairo as commanded by Nergal and was awaiting instructions from Abaddon as to where they were to journey to next.

The silence on the runway was broken when a black truck screeched to a halt at the end of the aircraft where Meregel stood. He watched the two guards get out and walk in his direction. 'Secure the weapons in the cargo hold,' Meregel instructed them, gesturing toward the ramp that had just unfolded from the back of the aircraft onto the tarmac.

'Yes, sir,' the shorter of the two said, and returned to the truck.

Abaddon walked over and stood beside his son at the foot of the steps. 'Are the weapons on board?' he said.

Meregel glanced behind his father. The two guards were closing the rear door and securing it. 'Yes,' he said.

'Good. Then we will be on our way.' Abaddon walked up the steps toward the pilot. Meregel followed him.

'Do you have the coordinates, Adira?' Abaddon asked in a quiet voice.

'Yes,' she said and smiled.

'Good. We will take off as soon as you are ready.' Abaddon smiled at her affectionately, and entered the aircraft followed by his son.

They walked the short distance down a tall corridor and emerged into a bright, luxurious oval-shaped cabin.

'At last.' Abaddon sighed and sat on the comfortable cream leather chair behind Nergal's desk. He looked around the generous space that spanned the entire width and half the length of the aircraft. Thick carpet covered the entire floor. On the other side of the cabin a large semi-oval-shaped cream sofa sat behind an oak table. The main wall of the cabin housed a large sixty-inch screen from which Nergal could monitor the progress of his plans.

Abaddon closed his eyes and stretched his legs out in front of him. Everything about this moment enhanced the power he could feel within his grasp. He had the detonators. He had the weapons. All he needed to do now was ensure that they were deployed and detonated as Nergal had planned. Meregel's presence on the sofa across from him, tapping on his tablet, distracted Abaddon from his thoughts and returned him swiftly back to reality.

'I am patching a call through from Nergal,' Meregel said.

Abaddon watched Nergal's image appear on the enormous screen embedded into the cabin wall.

'How are you progressing?' Nergal said. Abaddon analysed Nergal's demeanour. He could tell by his stern look and sharp tone that events in Egypt must not have gone as planned.

'Your brother Gibil was uncooperative and destroyed all but one of the detonators, so I had to shoot him to stop him from thwarting our efforts any further. Otherwise we are on track. We have the blueprints for the weapons. My son will arm one of them. It will be ready to detonate as scheduled,' Abaddon said. 'What about DeMolay's lair and the artefact. Have you reached it yet?' Abaddon said immediately in an effort to divert Nergal's attention from Gibil.

'Not yet. We have had a minor setback,' Nergal said. His gaze shifted to his right and then back in front of him. 'When I have reached my final destination, I will contact you.'

Abaddon paused before he replied. He had learned over the many years he and Nergal had been friends that Nergal's strategic prowess was unequalled by anyone on Earth or beyond. His ability to manipulate and anticipate his enemy's actions and reactions would bring them to victory. DeMolay's distractions in sending him to the wrong location were minute in the grand scheme of things and Nergal's overall strategy would manoeuvre to compensate. Never for one moment did Abaddon doubt this, so he smiled and looked at Nergal. 'It is but a minor stumbling block, your Majesty. Soon we all will be exactly where you intended us to be, and your brother Marduk will be on his knees.'

Chapter 42

The digital display had gone dead and the inside of the cockpit was sporadically illuminated by the flickering emergency lights in the cabin. Peter stretched out his hand to shake Daniel's shoulder.

'Daniel? Daniel, are you okay?' Peter said. His voice was quiet.

His uncle moaned, then mumbled a quiet reply. 'Yeah. I'm fine. I think I hit my head, but other than that I'm okay.' Daniel rubbed his hand along his forehead. It felt stiff where the blood had congealed above his right eyebrow.

It took a few moments for Peter's eyes to adjust to the intermittent darkness. He looked back into the cabin. Emily was slumped over. He removed his safety belt and manoeuvred to where she was seated. Remnants of the first aid kit were scattered on the floor around him. He pushed back her long brown hair from her face and moved her head upward. She was still breathing. He checked to make sure there was no sign of injury, then he gently released her seat belt.

'Is she okay?' Daniel said. He stood behind Peter holding his brown satchel.

Emily opened her eyes and moved her head a little. 'Did we land?' she said.

Peter smiled. 'Yes, we did,' he said and looked up at his uncle. 'She's fine. I'd say she just passed out,' he added, and glanced behind Daniel. There was a huge gaping hole in the side of the aircraft. Part of the cabin and one of the wings were missing.

Daniel retrieved the bottles of water, astrolabe and UV light from the floor. He handed one of the bottles to Emily. 'Take a drink. It'll help you get over the shock,' he said.

'Look!' Peter shouted, pointing in front of him. 'There are lights approaching. Someone's coming. We'd better get out of here.'

Lights moved up and down as the approaching vehicles traversed the sand dunes. Daniel stretched his hand out to Emily and helped her to her feet.

'Are you sure you're able to keep going?' Peter said.

She faced her husband. 'I've just been in an aircraft that was hit by a missile and crashed in the Sahara Desert. If I can do anything to punish the person responsible, then I'll walk to the end of the Earth to do so,' she said, and stood up straight.

'Let's go,' Daniel said in a hushed voice.

The trio hurried through the remnants of the aircraft and escaped through the hole in the fuselage.

'This way,' Peter said, pointing to the pyramids in front of them.

'At least we're in the right spot,' Daniel said, and smiled as he walked across the desert sand that would hopefully lead them to Marcus' secrets, once and for all.

Chapter 43

The subtle evening desert breeze brushed across Peter's face as they stood for a moment to catch their breath at the southern face of the Pyramid of Khafre, the second largest pyramid at Giza. Peter looked up. The sky was a deep dark tapestry adorned with the most beautiful array of stars the eye could behold. *'Neath a dark starry night'*, he thought. Just as his father had planned.

'Which direction is the Sphinx?' Emily whispered.

Daniel looked ahead from their southerly position.

'That way,' he said. He pointed east in the direction of the Sphinx that stood at over two hundred and forty-one feet long and sixty-five feet high, about fifteen hundred feet away from them. To the south-east the trio could see people preparing for the evening light show. Soon the area would be awash with tourists.

We need to get to the Sphinx before more people arrive, Peter thought and nestled his feet into the sand. There was a brief silence as he reached into his trouser pocket for his phone. He looked at the screen as it lit up. 'It's almost quarter past seven. The last time we were here the light show started at eight. We need to get moving,' Peter said.

Daniel and Emily nodded in agreement.

'The causeway that links Khafre's mortuary temple with his valley temple is still partially intact and leads past the Sphinx. If we make a run for it, it should provide us with cover. Most of the activity and security is where the light show is held, to the south-east,' Daniel said. 'I'll go first. You follow my lead.'

'Okay,' Peter and Emily said, and followed closely behind Daniel, moving with care along the eastern face of the Khafre pyramid. Midway they stopped and stooped to their knees. Facing north they were looking toward the Great Pyramid.

'Let's go,' Daniel said, pointing to his right in the direction of the causeway.

The trio hurried over the limestone and alabaster remnants of the mortuary temple in an easterly direction along the causeway that led to a position just south of the Sphinx. Peter could see the top of the Sphinx up ahead as they approached the edge of the causeway where Daniel had come to a stop. They stood close beside him and looked down. Out of nowhere a bright white light shone on the great pyramid.

Emily and Peter cowered to the ground beside Daniel who had already ducked for cover. 'Do you think they saw us?' she whispered.

The light turned to green, then to purple, then yellow, before disappearing.

'It's okay. They're just testing the lights before the show,' Peter said in a relieved tone.

'We should keep moving,' Daniel said, lowering himself to the ground at the back of the enormous statue. They stole along the statue's side making his way to the right front paw before stopping suddenly. He could hear muffled voices on the road beyond the Sphinx. He raised his hand, signalling to Peter and Emily to be silent.

Two stocky men dressed in black patrolled the road on the other side of the Sphinx. Daniel could hear their walkie-talkies' buzz. One of the guards lifted his receiver to his mouth. Peter, Emily and Daniel could hear the voice on the other end notify him that Nergal would be arriving soon. His detour to the Cairo Museum hadn't lasted long. Time was now also battling them as they waited for the guards to leave.

'Do you know what you need to do when we get to the Dream Stele?' Daniel whispered to Peter.

'Yes, I think so. Do you have the torch?' Peter said.

Daniel shuffled through the contents of his satchel and handed it to Peter.

'We should go,' Daniel said, and made his way slowly to the tip of the front paw. The coast was clear. He turned to Peter. 'Now!' Daniel whispered, and led the way toward the Dream Stele between the Sphinx's two front paws. Peter looked up and saw the face of the Sphinx tower above him. Beneath it the rectangular stone stele, with a rounded top, stood at almost eleven feet in height and seven feet in width.

Peter recalled his father's clue. *Neath a dark starry night, shine a blackened light, o'er the tablet neath his breast, where the ancient Pharaoh took a rest, the knowledge that you seek, lies hidden beneath his feet.* He moved tentatively forward and switched on the light, sweeping it over the Dream Stele from left to right. There was nothing. No further clues or markings became visible in the blackened light. He raised his hand higher. Then suddenly footsteps approached from behind. He pivoted around. To his relief he was face to face with Daniel.

'I just had a thought. The winged disc – the symbol of Nephilim royalty,' Daniel said.

'Yeah,' Peter said.

'Well, it's up there. I'm just wondering if that's where you need to shine the light. It's the only symbol on the stele that's in some way connected to anything we've seen today.'

They arched their necks and looked toward the top of the eleven-feet-high stone stele.

'I see it,' Peter said, 'but I'm not tall enough to reach up there.'

'Of course not. But the Nephilim are,' Daniel said. 'How far can you reach?'

On the tips of his toes, Peter stretched his right arm up as far as he could. Daniel stepped back and examined the space between Peter's hand and the winged disc. 'You're about two feet away from it. You should be able to reach it if I hoist you up a little,' he said, and lowered himself onto all fours in front of the stele. 'Be quick,' Daniel said, and prepared to bear the weight of his nephew.

Peter stepped onto Daniel's back and arched his neck upward. He shone the black light along the length of the winged disc. Its centre glowed a bright golden colour as the light passed over it. Peter lowered the light and thought for a moment. *That has to be it.* He placed his palm over the disc. It was protruding a little from the top of the Stele. He pushed hard on the disc and it moved inward. The ground beneath them trembled. Peter lost his balance and landed beside his uncle. He scrambled to his feet, brushing the sand from his clothes.

'Are you okay?' Daniel said, still on his hands and knees.

'I'm fine,' Peter said and extended his hand to help Daniel to his feet.

'We need to go. They're coming.' Emily's whispered voice echoed from behind them. She was pointing to the right front paw of the Sphinx.

The ground had opened up beneath it.

Peter and Daniel rushed over to her.

'It's a corridor leading under the Sphinx,' she said.

They could hear the guard's voices growing louder.

'Quick! Into the tunnel,' Peter said, 'before they find out we're here.'

Chapter 44

'What do you mean, Nergal was not on the aircraft?' Marduk said. He stared at the image of Chasid on the screen.

'The satellite images of the crash site show three humans leaving the aircraft. One female and two male. One of them is DeMolay's son, Peter. We tracked their movements to the front of the Sphinx and then they disappeared. I believe they entered the chamber beneath. The Egyptian authorities are at the aircraft now and have closed off a section behind the pyramids. I have sent a team to retrieve the aircraft and cover up the crash,' Chasid said.

Marduk remained silent.

Why would DeMolay have my brother's aircraft? he thought.

'Your Majesty, there is something else you need to know.' Chasid's voice distracted Marduk from his thoughts. 'When we realised Nergal was not on the jet, we ran our facial recognition software on all the databases on Earth we have access to. We have located your brother. He is also in Cairo. Our satellites picked up images of him at the museum in Tahrir Square this evening. DeMolay's daughter is with him. They left the museum moments ago and are almost at the Sphinx,' Chasid said.

Are Peter DeMolay and Nergal working together to unravel his father's secrets? Have hundreds of years of cooperation been wasted on one futile young man who would give it all away? And for what? Marduk thought. He stood up and rubbed his hand across his chin. One question kept running through his mind.

'Why would DeMolay have Nergal's aircraft unless he

had betrayed his father and is helping my brother?' Marduk said, and looked at the screen. 'What is the serial number of the craft that was shot down?' he said, staring at the image of Chasid as he searched through the information he'd gathered.

'1375993,' Chasid said.

It took only a moment to register with Marduk. He had memorised the full inventory of his advanced aircraft and the serial number Chasid had just called out identified an aircraft he'd gifted Marcus DeMolay three years ago. It was not Nergal's aircraft that had been shot down.

'Zania, display all aircraft and their locations on screen,' Marduk said.

'They're on the screen now,' she said.

Marduk examined the map displayed next to the image of Chasid. It told him that Nergal's aircraft was located not far from the pyramids. The aircraft he'd given Marcus DeMolay was in a hangar in Washington. And his own flying fortress was in his Antarctic base hanger.

Someone close to me is helping Nergal, Marduk thought.

A surge of adrenaline carried an uncontrollable rage through every millimetre of his body. He grabbed his computer tablet from the table and threw it at the on-screen map in front of him. A loud clash of glass and a barrage of bright sparks exploded from the screen.

Marduk composed himself. He turned to Zania.

'This aircraft is not in Antarctica. Why are the transponder signals emitting incorrect locations?' Marduk said in an even, calm tone.

'I am not sure, your Majesty. Somehow the signals are scrambled,' she said.

Marduk turned to a screen integrated into the desk. As he watched the aircraft transponder signals move across the map, he transferred icons from one side of the screen to the other.

'I will tear him and DeMolay limb from limb.' Marduk's raised voice resounded through the cabin.

'Your Majesty, Peter DeMolay is not working with Nergal. His sister, Ava, is the one who has betrayed us. One of our operatives intercepted their communications in France. DeMolay has been on the run since yesterday. Nergal has kidnapped his mother and is holding her hostage. It seems Nergal is looking for whatever his father was protecting.' Though his image was no longer visible on screen, Chasid's voice could be heard through the cabin's speakers.

Marduk called out to Zania.

'Yes, your Majesty,' she said.

'Reboot the transponder array, ping each aircraft and find out how those signals were switched around and by whom.'

'Yes, your Majesty.'

'Chasid, you mentioned you had intercepted communications between Nergal's allies in France.'

'Yes. We did.'

'Send me the frequency they are using. I want to lock in on their signal.'

'I am sending it to you now.'

On the screen Marduk tapped on the small envelope in the bottom left-hand corner and opened the map. Using his thumb and index finger on the map, he zoomed in on the area surrounding the Giza Plateau in Egypt. He analysed the communications devices' positions. He could see three above ground at different positions around the Sphinx and one located beneath it, in the corridor that led to The Hall of Records – DeMolay's secret hiding place.

Marduk looked up from the screen and glanced out the window to his right. *I am missing something. What purpose would the artefact serve Nergal? It is just a communications device,* he thought.

He looked at the world news feeds, which his analysts surveyed daily. Anything of any importance to the Nephilim leader was assessed and brought to his attention.

DeMolay's murder in Balantrodoch was being investigated. A private jet had crashed near the pyramids, but luckily no one was injured. All passengers had survived. The Museum of Egyptian Antiquities in Cairo had been broken into and the two security guards on patrol in the museum for the night had been killed.

Marduk looked toward the end of the cabin, deep in thought.

Abaddon has the weapons and the detonators. Somehow this has to fit in with what Nergal is doing.

'Zania, what would be our ETA if we change course to the pyramids?' Marduk said.

'We can be there in fifteen minutes.'

'Good. Inform the pilot to change course,' he said.

'But, your Majesty, what if someone sees—' Chasid said.

'If someone sees my aircraft land at the pyramids, we will cover it up just like we have always done. The humans will believe whatever we tell them. I need to find out what Nergal is up to. My brother needs to be stopped, and until then, Chasid, you are to double security on the base. No one goes in or out without my say so. And, Chasid?'

'Yes, your Majesty.'

'Find those weapons.'

Chapter 45

'I can't see a thing,' Emily said.

Inside the passageway beneath the Sphinx was pitch black, but from the direction of her voice, Peter could tell that Emily was standing close to his right. He extended his arm and placed it on hers.

'Neither can I,' he said. Remembering his phone, he switched it on and a dull light shone in front of them.

'Where's Daniel?' Emily said.

'I'm over here. Stay where you are. Just give me a minute.' His voice emanated from near the ground, followed by a shuffling noise. Peter pointed the phone in Daniel's direction.

'What are you doing down there?' Emily said.

'He's in his bag again,' Peter said. He could hear his uncle rummaging through the contents of his satchel.

'Wouldn't you think they'd have put some sort of light into this place?' Daniel grunted as he removed his small blue torch and switched it on.

He stood up awkwardly, fixed the brown leather strap around his shoulder and let out a lingering sigh.

'I really feel my age,' he said, and shone the torch ahead of him.

Peter looked at his phone. 'There's no signal in here,' he said, switching it off and returning it to his trouser pocket.

Daniel swept the light down one side of the long corridor and up along the other. They were surrounded by highly polished stone walls and ceiling that glistened as the light reflected off them. Daniel looked back toward the entrance, to where the UV torch had fallen and shattered. Beyond it, the ground was covered with sand. It was a dead end.

He pivoted around and shone the light down the large corridor stretched out before them.

Peter guessed it was about thirty feet in length and at least twenty feet high. At the end of the corridor he got a glimpse of something unusual. 'Shine the light toward the end,' he said, pointing.

'What is it?' Emily said.

'It looks like a door. And given the direction we're facing I think this hallway leads back underneath the Sphinx, in the direction of the pyramids,' Peter said, moving forward.

Daniel and Emily walked close behind him looking for anything that might show them exactly where they were or where they needed to go.

'What is this place?' Emily said, hoping that someone had the answer.

'If I could hazard a guess, I'd say we're in a corridor that leads, most likely, to the ancient Hall of Records. Legend says that an ancient race of people left a Hall of Records somewhere on Earth. And that one day it would be opened and its contents would help to enlighten mankind,' Daniel said. A broad grin covered his face. He stopped for a moment and moved the torch from floor to ceiling. He rubbed his hand against the cold highly polished wall to his left.

'Limestone,' Peter said over his right shoulder.

'Yes. And look at the precision with which these stones have been cut and placed together. These joints are so tight you wouldn't fit a razor blade between them,' Daniel said.

'Just like the pyramids when they were originally built,' Peter said.

'And those stones at Puma Punku – the ones you showed us on the train,' Emily said.

Daniel smiled at her.

'I was listening,' she said.

'These architectural masterpieces have been around us for centuries. We've catalogued and studied them. We've credited our own ancestors with building them. Yet even today we can't repeat their construction using the same resources they had available to them back then. How did we lose all this skill and engineering prowess we claim to have possessed?' Daniel said, as he continued on toward the door. Emily and Peter followed behind. They both knew the events of the past twenty hours were a testament to Daniel's thoughts.

Emily stood behind Daniel and Peter and arched her neck backward to get a full view of the limestone block at the end of the corridor. The side and top edges were framed with a golden border about six inches in width. The block was a perfect square, about twenty feet high and twenty feet wide, with a T-shaped carving in the centre, about nine feet high from top to bottom and six feet wide at its base. A small circular indentation was carved in the centre of the T-shaped doorway.

Daniel scanned the golden rim around the edges. Two carvings had been etched into the polished limestone halfway up each side. A golden-winged disc on one side. And a double-barred cross on the other.

Daniel's eyes moved to the circular indentation. *The circular indentation, the T shape carved into a square stone. Where have I seen this before?* He shone the torch around the entire door and closed his eyes, analysing every image that came into his mind until the memory he was looking for flashed before his eyes.

'I knew it!' Daniel said. 'I've seen this before.'

'You've been here before?' Emily said.

'No. I've definitely never been here before, but I have seen a doorway very similar to this somewhere else. I showed it to you on the train earlier today. Near Lake Titicaca in Peru. Puerta de Hayu Marca – the Gate of the Gods. This doorway has the exact same layout, only it hasn't been eroded or damaged by the elements. It's been kept hidden underground.' Daniel paused. 'These symbols aren't on the Gate in Peru either.' Daniel pointed to the winged disc and the double-barred cross. The symbol of the Nephilim and the Templars.

'If it's a door, then we can open it,' Peter said.

Daniel stood still for a moment trying to recall as much information as he could about the Gate of the Gods in Peru.

'The legend of Puerta de Hayu Marca tells of gods who used the gate to travel between our world and theirs. It's said that in ancient times great heroes from Earth would join their gods and journey through the gate with them to the land of the gods. Once they left they returned to Earth for only short periods of time. The priests who protected the gate spoke of a golden disc inserted into the circular indentation in the centre. That's how the gate was opened,' Daniel said.

'A disc? Like this one?' Peter said, holding up the golden astrolabe.

'Well, yes. Just like that one,' Daniel said. He smiled and took the astrolabe from Peter. He moved the astrolabe toward the circular indentation in the doorway.

'Looks like it's going to be a perfect fit,' Peter said.

Daniel moved his hand closer until the golden disc was inserted in the indentation. The astrolabe sat snugly, but nothing happened. The door remained closed.

'Are you sure that's all you have to do?' Emily said.

'Yes. I don't understand why nothing has happened. The disc is a perfect fit,' Daniel said.

Peter gently pushed the disc further into the indentation. He felt a surge of energy run up his left arm and down through his body. He looked back at the others.

'It just needed a little shove,' he said, stepping back.

They watched the disc disappear into the midst of a blue light. The light filled the corridor as it shone from the circle in the centre of the door and covered the entire limestone block. Daniel moved forward to get a closer look. The limestone block had become transparent, surrounded by a hue of blue light and beyond it they could see a room that was a perfect square, about ten feet long and ten wide.

Peter stretched his hand toward the light, but was stopped by Emily. 'No! It might be dangerous,' she said, concerned that Peter would be injured further.

Peter looked at his wife. 'If I'm ever going to see my mother again, we need to go into that room,' he said.

'Well, there's only one way we're going to find out if it's safe,' Daniel said. He held his breath and walked through the doorway. He turned around and looked back at Emily and Peter on the other side. They watched nervously as he looked to his left and right. He stood for a moment taking in his surroundings.

'He looks a little stunned,' Emily said.

Daniel raised his hand and waved at Peter and Emily to follow him through.

'I guess it's okay.' Emily looked at her husband and smiled.

He placed his hand on her cheek and smiled back. 'We're almost there. I can feel it,' he said, and turned toward the door. He stood close to Emily as they followed Daniel into the blue light.

Daniel was staring at either side of the doorway.

Emily placed her hand on Peter's arm. 'Look,' she said.

Peter turned around. The golden disc was floating in the middle of the doorway.

He scanned the room in every direction. He looked across the ceiling. Then at the floor. With the exception of an angel pointing to an hourglass carved into the wall opposite the doorway, the room was empty.

His heart sank. His father's secrets were nowhere to be seen.

Chapter 46

'The signal is coming from here. Search this entire area. The device and our enemy have to be here somewhere. I want them found,' Micah commanded, and watched as two guards searched the area immediately around the Sphinx. Two others moved further out and began their search near the boundary wall as Micah looked toward the road leading to the pyramid complex. The light from Nergal's vehicle increased in brightness as it came to a stop on the road beside him. The back door of the van opened and Nergal stepped out, followed by Ava. Nergal jumped the wall beside the Sphinx and walked toward him. 'They are not far from us,' Micah said.

Nergal walked along the enormous statue carved millennia ago from a single piece of limestone, and examined the ground around it. 'How this place has changed,' he said.

'You were here when it was built?' Ava said.

'Yes. Thousands of years ago my father designed these pyramids. They were not the crumbling piles of stone they are today. Their glory could be seen for miles around. The polished limestone surface that covered their exterior shone both day and night.' Nergal paused and looked across the Sahara Desert. 'Many thousands of humans lived here and participated in their construction under the control of the Nephilim. The largest of the three pyramids was the control centre – monitoring all space flights to and from Earth. The entire Nephilim fleet was controlled from this area. We could even see the pyramids from our spacecraft as we approached Earth. This place was once a testament to the power of the Nephilim in a time when we ruled Earth and everything on it. And look at it now. A commercialised tourist attraction to satisfy the curiosity of a race who knows no more about their own creation that they feign to know about the construction of this once great place,' Nergal said abruptly.

He examined the sandy area beneath his feet, and followed a trail of footprints toward the front of the Sphinx. He kneeled down beside the front right paw and looked at the area around it.

'There are many secret chambers below the structures in this complex. The entrance to one of them is beneath this limestone block,' he said, and walked toward the Dream Stele. He raised his hand above his head and pushed the disc in the centre. He heard a thud as the limestone block opened, revealing the corridor beneath the Sphinx. He turned to Micah. 'Get DeMolay's mother from the car and bring her here,' Nergal said, and waited as Micah carried out his order.

Nergal watched Sophia move reluctantly, twisting from side to side hoping to loosen Micah's grasp on her arm as they walked toward where he and Ava stood. Suddenly, something in the night sky caught Nergal's attention. He looked up. *Right on time,* he thought, and watched his brother's aircraft move like a chameleon across the night sky.

Finally. Marduk has got my message. Once again he takes centre stage and dances in my intricately choreographed plan.

Chapter 47

'There's nothing here. The room's empty. We've come all this way for nothing,' Peter said, his voice shrouded with frustration.

Suddenly a clapping noise came from the corridor on the other side of the doorway. Beyond the blue hue that surrounded the doorway, Peter could see the outline of three people standing only feet from him: Nergal, Ava and his mother.

Adrenaline flowed through his veins. He instinctively moved toward his mother.

'No!' Daniel cried out, and ran in front of Peter. He grabbed the disc from the centre of the doorway. The limestone block instantly reappeared between Peter and his mother. For a brief moment the room was plunged into darkness, then back into light again.

Peter turned his back on the doorway and glared at his uncle. 'Why did you do that? Give me the disc!' Peter shouted.

'And what? What are you going to do? Look around you, Peter. There's nothing in here. And the moment you step back outside that door with nothing, we're all dead,' Daniel said his voice was firm.

Though Daniel and Emily were standing in front of him, he couldn't hear a word they were saying; all he could see was his mother's face, and all he could think about was his father's dead body and how the individual responsible was feet from where he stood. Peter's emotions swelled inside him as he tried to control his breathing and rubbed his hands through his hair. He stared for a moment at Emily and

Daniel. He knew deep down his uncle had a point. The moment he stepped back outside that doorway, the game was up. 'You're right. I'm sorry.' Peter's voice was a low whisper.

Daniel breathed a sigh of relief and turned to look again at the wall opposite the doorway. He had gained a glimpse of something familiar before Nergal had appeared in the corridor and wanted to be sure before saying anything to the others.

'Do you see something?' Peter said.

'I think there's another clue.' Daniel pointed to the wall in front of him. He'd noticed a faint series of writings running along the sides and top of the wall, where the angel and hourglass were carved. 'There's a message carved into the wall. If you look closely, you'll see. It's around the edges.'

Peter and Emily moved closer to get a better look.

'What language is it? Can you read it?' Peter said.

'It's cuneiform. The ancient Sumerian language. And yes, I can translate it.' Daniel took a moment to read through the ancient writing.

'A passageway ... no ... no, a doorway will open. Your world and mine ... immortality. Passage of time.' Daniel muttered the words as he examined the symbols. He moved further back and looked again at the symbols. 'This part from here to there,' Daniel pointed to the symbols that began on the wall nearest the floor on his left and moved his hand toward the symbol at the top of the wall in the centre, 'reads as "A doorway will open between your world and mine." Then from here to there,' Daniel pointed to the symbols from the top centre of the wall to the floor on his right, 'translates as, "Where immortality lies in the passage of time".'

'"A doorway will open between your world and mine.

238

Where immortality lies in the passage of time",' Peter said, and looked around him. He stepped back and looked at the angel and hourglass carved into the wall.

'Immortality and the passing of time. The angel is the Templar symbol for immortality and the hourglass their symbol for the passing of time,' Peter said, examining the carving in detail. He turned to Daniel and Emily. 'The hourglass – it looks like it can rotate,' he said.

Daniel moved closer to Peter. 'Then that has to be it! I bet that if you turn the hourglass, the sand will begin to shift, triggering some other mechanism that will open a door. I'm guessing whatever Marcus was hiding is behind that wall.'

Peter observed the hourglass. It was shielded behind a glass cover encased with gold around its circumference and had two circular indentations on either side.

'This definitely rotates,' Peter said, eyeing the sand gathered in the lower glass bulb.

'Then turn it and see what happens,' Emily said.

Peter grasped the indentations on the gold rim. He was about to turn it when he was distracted by a beeping sound coming from Daniel's satchel.

'What's that?' Peter said.

'I don't know. Maybe it's my phone,' Daniel said.

'There's no signal in here. Remember, I checked.'

Daniel rummaged through his satchel trying to locate the source of the noise. Finally, he removed the communications device he'd stolen from Nergal's henchman at Chartres Cathedral. A small green icon was flickering on the front of the device in unison with each of the beeps. Daniel handed it to Peter.

'I bet it's him. I bet it's Nergal,' Emily said, and

watched as Peter moved his finger toward the green flashing button.

'Don't answer it yet! Shouldn't we figure out what's in here first? Find out if we have something to bargain with. If there's nothing behind that wall, we need to figure out what to do. If there is something in there, we can't hand it over to him and expect him to just let us go,' Daniel said.

'I agree. But he wants to get in here and if he's going to do that, then he has to agree to my terms first,' Peter said. He looked anxiously at them and then answered the call.

A muffled shuffling sound came from the other end, then the foreign accent resounded around the room. 'Peter DeMolay?' said a man in a deep foreign accent.

Peter's heart skipped a beat.

Chapter 48

Outside the Hall of Records Nergal stared at the limestone block that stood between him and his destiny. He turned to Sophia.

'I need you to tell your son to open this door,' Nergal said.

'Never,' Sophia said.

Nergal grabbed her by the throat and held her aloft in the air. She gasped for breath as he tightened his grip.

'I am the son of your God. You will do as I command. Now tell him to open this door or I will reduce this place to rubble and kill everyone inside here. Do you hear me?' Nergal released his grip and dropped Sophia to the ground. He pushed the button on the communications device in his hand and waited for it to be answered on the other end.

A crackling sound came from the device as it was answered.

'Peter DeMolay!' Nergal said.

'Yes,' Peter said in a strong and defiant tone.

Nergal moved the device toward Sophia.

'Peter?' Her voice was broken and trembling, yet she was relieved to hear his voice.

'Mum, are you okay?' Peter said.

'Yes, darling, I'm fine,' Sophia said, and glanced at Nergal. 'Peter,' she paused for a moment, 'Peter, darling, no matter what happens, do not open that door!'

Nergal snarled at Sophia and grabbed the

communications device from her. He turned his back on her and walked toward the end of the corridor.

'Peter DeMolay, open the door or I will let you listen while I torture your mother to death ... slowly and painfully,' Nergal said.

There was a momentary silence.

'I'll open the door and give you what you want, but only if you let my uncle, mother and wife go. This is between you and me. These are my only terms,' Peter said.

'Peter, you can't!' Sophia shouted.

'Silence!' Nergal yelled at Sophia. He took a deep breath and held the communications device close to his mouth. 'Agreed. I will let your family go. Now open the door.'

He looked at Ava and smiled. 'This is my destiny,' he said, and watched as the limestone block was engulfed by a bluish light and became transparent.

He stared into the room emerging from the light. He had many memories of this place as a child. But never had he presumed that his brother would steep so low as to give any human access to the room in which they were first created. Nergal glared down at Daniel and Emily as they walked slowly through the doorway. Daniel hugged his sister tightly. Sophia smiled at her son over Daniel's shoulder. She watched as Nergal and Ava entered the room.

One of Nergal's men held a communications device in his outstretched hand.

'When you are outside you are to contact your husband with this device and let him know you are safe. You have two minutes.' The tall, blond-haired Nephilim shoved the device into Emily's hand and pointed to the exit from the Sphinx. He then turned to resume his guard at the doorway.

Emily took Sophia's arm affectionately. 'We need to leave,' she whispered.

'We can't leave him there alone. Not with him—'

'Trust me,' Daniel said, 'we have to go.'

Chapter 49

'Chasid requires your presence immediately,' the bulky Nephilim security guard's voice was coming from behind where Maggie sat. She covertly moved the computer mouse and turned on her screen saver.

Since Chasid had returned to the base, security had increased hermetically and everyone's movements were being closely monitored as they used their Radio Frequency Identification chips to move throughout the six levels within the base. Although it was a sign that Nergal's strategy was working, Maggie's window for running the final programme to infiltrate the base's security systems, so they could begin the final part of their plan, was growing increasingly smaller. Chasid's request to see her couldn't have come at a worse moment. Her final update from Andrew to the base's quantum computing and security systems was almost complete.

Maggie got up slowly. She pivoted around, looked up at the young guard and smiled as he stood to one side and ushered her out of her office before him. She approached the lift entrance and glanced at the two guards either side of the shiny grey doors. They remained steadfast, staring straight ahead. She held her wrist in front of the scanner. A high-pitched beep resounded and a green light flashed. The lift doors hissed open and Maggie and the young Nephilim guard stepped inside. He placed his palm over the scanner on the lift wall.

'Level six,' he said in a firm voice. The lift doors closed and carried them down to the sixth floor, over two miles beneath the observatory – the most heavily guarded level on the base.

Her heart pounded as the doors opened onto the sixth floor. She looked out across the enormous room to where Chasid was waiting midway, in front of the vault. To his right two Nephilim guards were standing over a man sitting on a chair.

Maggie stepped out of the lift and glanced behind her. Either side of the lift doors stood two of Marduk's soldiers. Each was armed with a golden staff, which they held in their right hands, and dressed from top to toe in gold and black body armour. Only their pale, stern faces and bald heads were visible.

Maggie scanned the rest of the room as she walked tentatively closer. She eyed the quantum computers situated around the four-thousand-seven-hundred-foot circumference of the room. They were stored securely behind a force field emitting a golden hue and were protected by a further six armed Nephilim guards who stood around the room at equidistant positions from one another ready to obliterate any uninvited guests who entered the sixth floor.

Maggie looked at Chasid then toward his prisoner. She recognised the man sitting on the chair: Andrew, her research assistant. His hands were bound behind his back and his head was hanging close to his chest. She walked over to Chasid and breathed slowly and deeply.

Andrew had been carefully chosen by Ava to join the fight against Marduk. He was one of only a handful of quantum electronics engineers on Earth capable of infiltrating the base's computer technology, which Marduk's chief science officer, Nannar, had designed millennia ago to cater for his leader's activities on Earth and beyond.

After he'd infiltrated the base's network and accessed the tracking systems for Nergal, he'd left a trail that Chasid could track. A trail that would intentionally lead to himself and in the process set off a chain of events that would eventually lead to Marduk's downfall.

'What the hell is going on here?' Maggie said, looking up at Chasid who towered above her. She'd noticed that his usually calm demeanour had somewhat abandoned him and behind his bearded exterior she could tell that a fury had built up inside him.

'He has been relaying information about our activities to our enemies. He has also interfered with our tracking systems,' Chasid said, and took a step toward Maggie. 'Because of this, a friend of mine was killed this evening and one of our greatest enemies has taken possession of weapons they should never have had access to. I need you to speak some sense into him. He needs to tell me everything he knows.'

Maggie felt a sense of relief. Chasid still had no idea that she too was working with Nergal. Andrew had done exactly what he'd promised to do and Chasid still had no idea what Nergal's true intentions were.

Maggie kneeled down in front of Andrew. He had a cut above his eye, his face was bruised and his nose bleeding. He raised his head and looked at her.

'Andrew, is this true?' Maggie said in a soft voice.

'Yes,' he said in a low yet defiant tone.

Maggie stood up and turned to Chasid. 'Did you do this?' she said, pointing to the blood and bruises on Andrew's face.

'You brought him here. Did you not?' Chasid said.

'Yes. And you did the background checks on him yourself.' Maggie raised her voice as she spoke.

'So you knew nothing of the information he was giving to Nergal. You knew nothing about the systems breach we had earlier today. And you know nothing about the nuclear weapons and where they intend to use them.' Chasid's voice was bitter and forceful.

'No, I do not,' she said sternly. 'Who is Nergal anyway?'

'She's telling the truth,' Andrew said. 'She knew nothing about this. Peter DeMolay's sister sent me to do this for her. She emphasised I was to tell no one.' Andrew paused for a moment, then looked at Chasid. 'Ava told me everything. She told me the truth about what you're doing here and how you're going to destroy us all. Your home world will cause destruction on Earth when it arrives back into the solar system. It has done so in the past. We've seen the effects it has had on Earth already. She told us how it's slipping out of its three-thousand-six-hundred-year orbit and will arrive sooner this time than it has ever done before. And you're doing nothing to help us prepare for and survive the catastrophe that will be unleashed on humankind. We should be out there warning the human race! Helping people prepare for what's about to happen. Not hiding it from everyone.'

Chasid looked down at Andrew. 'The only truth that will come to pass is the devastation that will be caused if those weapons are detonated. Now I will ask you once more – where do they intend to use them?'

There was silence. Andrew raised his head. Maggie swallowed hard and waited for his reply.

'I don't know,' Andrew said again, and slowly lowered his head.

'Clean him up and move him to a holding cell on level three. This is not over yet,' Chasid said, and removed a small glass computer tablet from his pocket. He glanced at the screen. 'We should leave now. One way or another I will extract what I need to know from him,' he said, looking sternly at Maggie as they walked to the lift.

Maggie's expression was serious, but inside she was beaming.

And by then we will be in control, she thought, and watched as the lift doors closed and Chasid disappeared out of view.

Chapter 50

Peter stood in front of the hourglass waiting silently to hear that his uncle, mother and wife were safe. A voice crackled out of the device in his hand.

'Peter? Peter, can you hear me?' Peter recognised Daniel's voice instantly.

'Yes, I can. Are you all safe, as agreed?'

'Yes we are,' Daniel said.

Peter sighed with relief and reached forward to place his thumb and middle finger into the indentations in the gold rim. He turned the hourglass, watched by Ava and Nergal who had entered the room moments earlier.

A dull vibration resounded around the room as the sand started to shift through the narrow funnel inside the hourglass and slowly move from one end to the other.

Peter glanced at his sister. Even though she'd done some unforgivable things, he felt that with time he could forgive her. His fraternal need to protect her was still strong.

He stared at the hourglass as he considered the conversation he'd had with the stranger Marduk on the communications device just moments previously.

'Peter DeMolay?' The man's deep foreign accent had filtered through the device.

'Yes,' Peter said. His voice had been forceful.

'We have never met and I doubt you know who I am. My name is Marduk. Your father was a close friend of mine, and your ancestors and I have worked together for generations to protect the truth of my existence. I hope I can trust you to fulfil your father's wishes and help me to continue protecting that truth.'

Peter had felt a lump form in his throat. 'You are one of the Nephilim. You know they killed my father yesterday evening and are hunting me down – how do I know I can trust you? How do I know you're not helping Nergal?'

'I cannot force you to do as I ask, but I can only hope you will. Nergal is my brother and he must be stopped. The communications device in your hand is emitting a transponder signal, which I am sure Nergal can access as well as I can. He knows your location, and I am sure he is on his way to you now. Peter, my brother will not hesitate to annihilate you and your family to fulfil his own desires.'

Peter looked at Daniel and Emily.

'Trust him,' Daniel said in a whisper.

'What do you need me to do?' Peter said.

'When my brother arrives, I need you to keep him in that room until I can apprehend him and bring him to justice. I am not far from the Hall of Records. You can open the door behind the wall with the angel and hourglass carvings. What is in that room is of no consequence to Nergal now that I know what he is looking for. You see, Peter, your father had the ancient communications device given to the Templars after they found it beneath Solomon's Temple in Jerusalem. It was gifted to them in return for their continued assurance that they would not reveal my, nor any other Nephilim's, existence on Earth.' There was a silence for a moment, before Marduk continued. 'If you help me, I give you my assurance that my brother will pay for his actions. But right now I need him alive. He has acquired ancient weapons and I need to find out where and why he intends to use them.'

The thud of the counterweight as it moved behind the wall in front of Peter brought him abruptly back to the present. The details of his conversation with Marduk lingered as he watched the limestone block lift from the ground.

Peter saw Ava out of the corner of his eye. She stood with her hands clasped in front of her watching the space between the ground and limestone block grow larger and larger. Peter moved his gaze to Nergal then back to his sister. Both of them looked at ease, bathed with an assurance they were exactly where they needed to be.

'Your father's death was unfortunate. If he had been more cooperative, it would have saved his life. Unfortunately that was not to be,' Nergal said.

Peter took deep breaths in an effort to contain his emotions. He wanted to punch Nergal hard. He wanted to repay the hurt, but that would risk everything.

'What do you hope to achieve if you get what's behind that door? You won't be able to rule humanity. We'll fight back,' Peter said, looking into the room beyond the opening doorway. He caught a fleeting glimpse of its contents before Nergal spoke again.

'Fight back?' Nergal laughed. 'You humans will be too busy surviving! What is behind this door is merely a stepping stone on my path to true destiny. This is an important albeit minute part of my overall plan to annihilate my brother. You see, at the moment, I am merely trying to get my brother's attention. To get him to focus on the real issue he has been ignoring for the past two thousand years: the fact that *I* should rule the Earth. Not him. What is behind this door is not my end game, by any means. The weapon I plan to use is being transported to its intended destination as we speak.' Nergal took a step closer to Peter. 'And when it is unleashed, history will repeat itself. I will watch from the safety of my brother's orbiting aircraft while humankind is wiped from the face of the Earth by the deluge that will follow when my brother's base is obliterated by a nuclear blast. You see, there is no other way for me to enter my brother's stronghold unless he brings me there himself. Killing one of his most loyal allies, your father, has guaranteed that he will most certainly take me there this evening. He is on his way here now.'

Peter's eyes widened. Marduk was walking into a trap and he had no way to warn him.

'After the flood has reshaped the Earth's landscape and I have gained control of the human infestation my father created and left here to destroy and pillage, I intend to use the other Ark, the one my brother keeps in a vault deep within the ice, to reshape the planet. That is what I really want: to rid the Earth of the uncontrolled infestation left here for millennia. You humans are like a virus to me. You set yourselves up on one part of the planet. You use up all the precious resources around you and then you move elsewhere and do the exact same over and over again until you have soiled and destroyed everything before you. You know, every species that destroys its own environment becomes extinct at some stage. I am just speeding up the process for you.'

Nergal took a step backward.

'I cannot express how much I detest each and every one of you,' he said. He looked back beyond the golden disc.

Micah, who had been keeping watch along the corridor, turned to Nergal. 'It is time, your Majesty,' Micah said.

Ava was standing directly behind Peter. Nergal watched eagerly as she lifted a gun from her waist and pointed it directly at Peter.

'I cannot expect you to appreciate the minutiae of my plan. Your sister has asked that I spare your life, but for the moment you need to be silenced. I have some issues to attend to once my brother arrives,' Nergal said.

'How do you know your brother—?' Peter said.

'How do I know my brother will be here shortly?' Nergal said, with a snide laugh. 'This is nothing more than an intricate game of chess. I move, you react. You move, I countermove. And then you react again and again until you are exactly where I want you to be,' Nergal said, and nodded to Ava.

Peter turned and saw the gun in his sister's hand. He heard the gunshot, and a sharp pain pierced his chest as he stretched his arms toward her in a futile effort to stay upright. In an instant, he lost consciousness and fell forward at his sister's feet.

Thoughts of victory resonated through every bone in Nergal's body as he glared at his brother Marduk now standing behind Micah in the corridor.

Marduk glanced at Peter and tightened his grip on his staff, which stretched from the ground to just beneath his right shoulder. It was encased in gold, approximately three inches in diameter and widened at the tip, from which an energy beam – the power of which was controlled by its possessor – could be released. In a fit of rage, Marduk lifted it from the ground and pointed it at his brother. A sphere of light was released from its top and hit Nergal directly in his chest. The force of light lifted him off the ground and he landed on his back beside Peter.

Marduk's men entered the Hall of Records.

'Seize her!' Marduk said pointing to Ava. 'And get him to the med bay in my aircraft now!' Marduk nodded at Peter. 'As for you,' Marduk stepped closer to Nergal, who'd been dragged to his feet by Marduk's son Nabu and another Nephilim soldier, 'I will deal with you back at the base.'

Nergal looked defiantly at his brother. *The base,* he thought, *exactly where I need to be.*

Chapter 51

Six Nephilim guards armed and dressed in navy uniforms escorted Nergal, Ava and Micah across the hangar bay, toward the lift to the holding cells on the third floor.

At the hangar bay wall nearest the lift, Maggie lingered and watched intently as Nergal passed by. He covertly threw her a knowing glance, then continued to stare at the path in front of him. A wry smile was hidden deep within her eyes. She had successfully integrated Andrew's software into the base's systems. Soon they would have control of everything.

Across the hangar bay Marduk's aircraft was lying idle to the right of the large golden-winged disc engraved in the centre of the floor. A team of medical personnel, including Marduk's chief medical officer, Ninharsag, was attending an individual in one of the advanced medical treatment units created by the Nephilim to manage their every medical need. Maggie had overheard on a couple of occasions that Ninharsag had even brought people back from the dead.

She moved closer to get a better look. She recognised the wounded person immediately.

It was Ava's brother, Peter DeMolay.

Looking around the hangar bay, Maggie eventually eyed Chasid talking to some Nephilim guards. She raised her hand to catch his attention. As he walked toward her, Maggie's mind churned with thoughts of him finding out she'd been working for Nergal before she had time to complete the last part of their plan. Which so far had gone exactly as Nergal had assured them it would. Chasid's face was stern as he approached. She held on firmly to her computer tablet.

'Where's Andrew being held? I thought I might try to

talk some sense into him. Perhaps get him to tell me what he's been doing and why.' Maggie's voice was quiet.

'I do not think there is any need. Now that we have captured Nergal, I am sure that I can extract what I need from him myself,' Chasid said.

'Well, I'd like to go and see him anyway. He was pretty banged up. I'd just like to see if he's okay,' she said, her green eyes pleading with Chasid, who frowned as he thought for a moment.

'He's on level three in cell five. I'll inform the guards to give you five minutes with him, no more.'

Maggie took a slow breath. *That's all the time I need,* she thought.

'Thank you,' she said and nodded toward Peter. 'Is he alive?'

'Yes, barely,' Chasid said, 'but we're hopeful.' He heard Marduk call him in the distance. 'If by some chance Andrew gives you any information, no matter how insignificant you may think it is, let me know immediately,' he said, before walking off to meet Marduk.

Maggie nodded in response and went to the lift. The doors opened with a quiet hiss and she stepped inside, placing her hand on the scanner. 'Level three.' She watched the hangar disappear out of view as the doors closed and the lift descended. She bent down and put her tablet on the floor. She removed a silencer from the pocket of her beige linen jacket, then a hand gun she'd hidden securely in the waistband of her navy trousers. She twisted the silencer onto the gun and returned it to its hiding place beneath her jacket.

She opened a secure wireless connection on her tablet and watched as the signal emitted by the device reached its target. The lift chimed and she stood back up, holding the tablet against her chest, trying to still her nerves. The doors opened and she stepped out into the corridor.

Two guards stood one either side of the lift door. Maggie turned and faced them.

~

Inside the holding cell Andrew sat on a hard elevated surface, approximately seven feet wide and ten long. It was definitely designed for someone a lot larger than him. Suddenly he felt a gentle vibration from the radio frequency identification chip implanted in his wrist. It rippled silently along his left arm. The signal he'd been waiting for had arrived. He jumped to his feet.

He now had precisely one hundred and fifty seconds before the explosives he was carrying detonated.

He rolled up the right sleeve of his dark-green shirt and removed what looked to be a layer of skin, approximately eight inches long and one wide, from beneath his forearm. He walked briskly to the cell door and carefully placed the strip five inches below the lock, exactly where he and Maggie had discussed would be the most appropriate place to detonate the undetectable explosive and force the door open. He hurried to the opposite side of the cell and turned his back to the door.

~

'I'm here to see Andrew,' Maggie said.

'He is in cell five. You have five minutes. If you follow me,' the guard said, and walked toward the end of the corridor. Maggie stalled for a moment as she counted down from ten in her head, then followed slowly behind the guard who was almost at the door to Andrew's cell.

Five, four, three, two, one.

Quickly and quietly, she took her weapon from her waistband and pivoted toward the guard at the lift doors. At the same time the explosive detonated, blasting pieces of debris out onto the corridor and knocking one of the guards unconscious and onto ground. She pointed her weapon at the second guard who was about to take aim at her. She shot him with the precision of a trained assassin. Like the others on the base working for Nergal, she'd received a year of training in preparation for her mission.

She looked into the cell to check if Andrew was okay. 'Nergal is being held in a more secure area on the other side of this level. The guards loyal to him have received our signal and are prepared to attack once he's free,' Maggie told him. 'The final programme has finished integrating into the base's systems. We'll have full control of all systems as long as Marduk doesn't remove the control key before we get to the control room, so we need to act fast,' she said, handing Andrew the tablet.

'Then let's set him free,' Andrew said, and initiated the last part of his programme to release Nergal.

Chapter 52

'I know where it is. I know where it is,' Peter mumbled. He'd been moving in and out of consciousness for the past hour.

Emily leaned in close to him. 'It's okay. Sophia is here with us, she's safe. Nergal and Ava have been taken into custody by the Nephilim. It's all over. We're safe now. Try to get some rest,' Emily whispered, and ran her hand through his hair. She raised her head.

Ninharsag, Marduk's chief medical officer, was standing next to Peter's bed with a small glass computer tablet in her hand. She towered above Emily. She was dressed in a grey tunic and trousers covered by a cobalt-blue coat with a gold edging along its length. Her long silver hair was tied neatly at the back of her neck. Her skin was the palest white Emily had ever seen and her eyes were azure blue. She looked tenderly at Emily.

'It was close, but he is going to survive. I have repaired the damage to his heart caused by the bullet. All he needs now is to rest for a while,' she said. Her foreign accent was the most comforting thing Emily had heard since their nightmare had begun.

'Thank you.' Emily's voice was sincere and quiet.

'You are welcome.' Ninharsag smiled and walked out of the room into the medical bay next door, to tend to a Nephilim she'd referred to earlier as Gibil. As Emily watched Ninharsag through the glass partition, she could see the familiar silhouette of Daniel approach. He was carrying three cups of coffee on a try with some sandwiches. She laughed as he entered the room.

'You'd find freshly brewed coffee in the desert,' Emily

said, and gladly took one of the cups from the tray.

'I sure would,' he said, and turned toward the couch where his sister Sophia was lying fast asleep. He placed the tray on the table beside her taking care not to waken her.

'He's going to be fine,' Emily said. She was holding Peter's hand that'd been wounded by Ava's gunshot in the crypt at Chartres. It was now completely healed.

'How did she do it? How is she healing such catastrophic wounds with such ease?' Daniel whispered, and looked at the monitor behind Peter's bed that showed his vital signs.

Emily took a sip from the coffee cup. 'I'm not sure. Their technology is way beyond anything we've developed, but we're getting there. We're not that far off achieving something similar ourselves. Trials have been carried out on patients with fatal injuries. They call it emergency preservation and resuscitation. The wounded person's blood is replaced with a cooled saline solution that rapidly cools the body. When the body's temperature is lowered to this extent, almost all metabolic reactions have stopped and the cells begin to produce enough energy to stay alive through a process known as anaerobic glycolysis. At lower temperatures this process can keep cells alive for hours, giving surgeons time to repair wounds before the patient is resuscitated.' Emily glanced at Peter then back to Daniel. 'When you spoke to Marduk's son Nabu earlier, did he tell you what Marcus was hiding? What the artefact was?'

'It was one of the Arks of the Covenant. Nabu told me his father had made a secret pact with the Templars after they'd found one of the Arks beneath Solomon's Temple. The second Ark is here and, as we thought, it's a superconductor. It's stored in what Nabu referred to as the ark vault on the sixth floor. Marduk uses it to power this place and much of the Nephilim technology on Earth. The second Ark that Marcus had at the pyramids has been used for centuries to communicate with the Nephilim, both here and on their home world Nibiru. The Nephilim apparently gave the Templars access to some of their advanced knowledge in return for keeping their existence secret,' Daniel said, and sipped his coffee. 'Apparently they have both Arks here now for safekeeping along with whatever else was in the pyramids. It's probably just as well that the agreement with the Templars ends with Peter before he ends up enduring the same fate as Marcus.'

'I agree.' Emily looked down at Peter who had opened his eyes.

He stared blankly up at them, then reached for Emily.

'Hey shorty, seems like you're bulletproof after all,' Daniel said.

Peter pushed hard on his hands and sat himself up. He looked around the room. He could feel the white walls and glass partitions closing in on him. 'Where am I?' he said.

'We're in a secret Nephilim base beneath the east Antarctic ice sheet. This place was built by the Nephilim thousands of years ago. It's Marduk's control centre. He's been hiding out here since he faked his death in the third century before Christ,' Daniel said.

Peter's head was spinning. He fixed his gaze beyond the glass partition to his right. A tall beautiful woman was tending to a wounded person in the room next to him.

The Ark, the weapon. Nergal, Peter thought and pulled himself onto the side of the bed. He grabbed Daniel's arm. 'Help me. I have to get up. I need to speak to Marduk,' Peter said, pulling himself forward.

'Peter, you need to rest. You've just had heart surgery. I know it was performed by an advanced alien surgeon, but all the same. You need to rest,' Emily said sternly as she gently placed her hand on Peter's chest.

'You don't understand. It's here! The weapon is here. Nergal told me before Ava shot me. The nuclear weapon – they're planning to detonate it underneath this base. Nergal plans to flood the Earth just like twelve thousand years ago. He knows exactly where he needs to detonate it. He knew the Ark Dad was guarding was only a communications device – that's why he went after him. He knew that if he attacked Marduk outright, Dad could send a message through the second Ark to their father on Nibiru and warn him. He knew the Arks were never at Chartres. Killing my father was all part of his plan to get Marduk to bring him here and sever the link between the Nephilim and the Templars once and for all. This base is the one place Marduk would never allow his brother access to. Attacking this base and flooding the Earth ... that was his plan all along.'

Chapter 53

A three-dimensional projection of the Antarctic landscape showed an enormous four-hundred-foot-wide cavity appear as the hangar bay doors, to the west of the observatory, opened up to allow Marduk's aircrafts to re-enter the base. The Nephilim operative sitting in front of the projection watched it intently.

'Amelatu, what is our status?' Chasid said.

'Our air traffic control systems are back up and running,' he said.

'Have all our aircraft been notified to return to base?'

'Yes, Commander. All pilots have made contact and are returning as we speak.'

'Nergal's LEO – have you found it yet?'

'No, sir. We do know, however, from satellite images taken over Kruger Airport in South Africa that Abaddon is definitely in possession of Nergal's aircraft and the weapons. The fact that we cannot locate it means they must have disabled the on-board transponder signal.'

'Bring up the satellite surveillance,' Marduk said, as he re-entered the control room and watched as pictures of Abaddon and Meregel entering the aircraft at Kruger Airport filtered on screen.

'These images show the weapons being loaded into the cargo bay. Then shortly before the aircraft took off, the transponder signal went dead and the satellite lost visual contact.' Chasid paused then turned to face Marduk. 'Your Majesty, I have also instructed Nannar to return to the base. If Gibil is not conscious when we find the weapons and they have been armed, we will need someone to disarm them. I have tried to extract what we need from your brother, but he is a stubborn, foolish ... Perhaps if you talk to Nergal. Try to reason with him.'

'The last time I tried to reason with my brother, in circumstances very similar to those we now find ourselves in, it led to the destruction of an entire civilisation. Unfortunately, Chasid, my brother's idea of what should happen on Earth and mine are light years apart. He will never tell me where those weapons are. He would much prefer to target any one of the major cities across the globe and start a war among the humans that we may not be able to control. The only thing I can be sure of is that he most certainly intends to use them, and most likely to try to destroy or in some way incapacitate my activities on Earth,' Marduk said.

'You're right. He does,' Peter said. He was standing between Emily and Daniel. His words turned every head in the control room. 'The weapons are here.'

Marduk pivoted around.

'Mr DeMolay. I am glad to see that you are well. But I assure you those weapons are not on this base,' Marduk said, turning to Chasid for reassurance.

'We have scanned the base for the weapons' signature. They are definitely not here.'

Peter took a step closer to Marduk. 'Before I was shot, Nergal told me he was going to destroy you. That the weapons were right beneath you and that he was going to use them to destroy everything on Earth so that he could reshape the planet's landscape the way he feels it should be. And that he will use the Ark you have in a vault in this base to do so,' Peter said.

Marduk looked intently down at him. 'My brother cannot be trusted. Therefore, neither can you trust anything he says. Most likely this is just another ploy from him to distract me from his true intentions and from finding his accomplice Abaddon and the weapons. Nothing more,' Marduk said.

Daniel cleared his throat. 'Take a look around you. We are surrounded by seventy percent of the Earth's fresh water supply frozen into a massive sheet of ice,' he said. 'You know what will happen if Nergal detonates those weapons here. And I know you know this because you've seen it happen before. You were here twelve thousand years ago when the ice sheets melted, broke apart and fell into the surrounding seas. The Sumerians and many other sources in our ancient literature have catalogued the great flood. They tell of how the waters rose and life was destroyed. And of how our gods, the Nephilim, abandoned us and let almost every human on the planet perish while they watched from the safety of their ships in orbit above Earth.' Daniel felt the adrenaline in his body shifting whatever courage he could muster through his veins. 'Your brother intends to recreate this disaster and he's going to use your aircraft to save those loyal to him. They'll watch, from high above the Earth, while almost everyone below perishes. Including you.' Daniel swallowed hard then took a sheepish step back when he remembered whom he was talking to.

Marduk listened intently, and then turned his gaze to Chasid. 'Is this possible? Could the weapons be anywhere on this base?' he said.

'There is no way those weapons are here,' Chasid said.

'What about just outside it?' Peter said. He was staring at a virtual three-dimensional model of the entire base displayed in front of a control room security operator.

Chasid walked toward Peter.

'Where exactly are we?' Peter said.

'The base is located over twelve thousand feet beneath the ice, in the middle of a subglacial lake. We chose this location because the lake shields the base from human radar and geographical imaging equipment by creating a magnetic anomaly,' Chasid said.

'Lake Vostok,' Emily said.

'Yes. That is what the Russians call it. We have been monitoring their drilling into the ice sheet and their ...' Chasid paused to compose his thoughts. He turned toward Marduk. 'The Vostok research station – there is a possibility they could manoeuvre a weapon underneath the ice from there. Abaddon could use our own technology to adapt the existing drill hole at the station so that it would accommodate the weapon.' Chasid spoke to the operative closest to him. 'Have you scanned the lake outside the base?'

'Yes, Commander. There is no weapons' signature out there either,' he said.

'Then there's a possibility that Abaddon is still at the Vostok Station as we speak, getting the weapon into position,' Peter said.

Chasid turned to another operative sitting near him. Security at the base included satellite and drone surveillance to monitor events above the ice. If Abaddon was nearby, then Chasid would find him. 'Send one of our drones over the Vostok Station. Let us see if that is where our friend Abaddon is,' he said.

The operative used a touch screen panel to send commands to the drone nearest Vostok. There was silence as they watched it move across the ice sheet toward the Russian research station.

'Commander, the current images of the Vostok Station are showing now,' the operative said, and pointed to the screen in front of him.

The drone passed silently over the drilling station. Nothing seemed out of place. The operative sent signals to the drone instructing it to fly higher to get a full aerial view. Chasid focused intently on the images it relayed. The station was the only sign of civilisation amidst the white desert of ice and snow that surrounded it. He could see the research and sleeping facilities and to the left he could see the rusty-brown-coloured drill tower.

'There!' Chasid pointed to an area on the ice behind the research station. 'There it is. Nergal's aircraft.'

Peter leaned forward to get a closer look. All he could see was the white Antarctic ice sheet. 'There's nothing there,' he said.

'Look closer,' Chasid said, and pointed to an area at the back of the Vostok Station. 'It is difficult to make out, but if you look closely enough, you will see an intermittent anomaly generated from the photosensitive material the fuselage is coated in.'

'I thought we had rectified that fault?' Marduk said. He preferred his aircraft to go unnoticed by the humans.

'Yes, your Majesty, we did. On all your aircraft. But not Nergal's. Any time we had availability to maintain his aircraft it never suited him, so it was never done.'

Peter and the others moved in for a closer look. Chasid was right. To the untrained eye, the ice sheet looked no different. But on closer inspection an anomaly could be seen. The ice on which the LEO was sitting was distorted. Similar to watching an object through waves of heat rising in front of it.

'Your Majesty, with your permission I will assemble a team and go to the Vostok Station. However, I would suggest we evacuate the base and move the Ark. For now at least,' Chasid said.

Marduk nodded his head in agreement.

'You're making a mistake,' Peter said.

'Peter, I thank you for your loyalty and your sacrifice to protect our existence, but what is left to be done is between my brother and me. You should return home now. I will send for your mother. She can meet you in the hangar bay,' Marduk said, and motioned to Peter to join him as he walked toward the lift.

'Let's just get out of here. Leave it to them. He knows what he's doing,' Daniel whispered.

Peter stopped beside the lift door. 'If that weapon detonates, we won't have a home to go to,' Peter said. 'Marduk, if I'm right, the Ark is the only renewable, sustainable power source on Earth. It's also the only way for you to communicate with your home world. Everything else on the planet is run by our natural resources and human technology. Nergal said he needs the Ark to rebuild his empire on Earth. Wouldn't it make more sense for you to ignore protocol and guard the Ark right here instead? Don't move it. Nergal has anticipated every move you've already made and he's constantly re-evaluating his actions. He has anticipated every move that has brought us to this precise moment. Believe me when I say your brother is *exactly* where he wants to be. If getting you to bring him here was his intention all along, then he's expecting you to move the Ark from its vault. Do whatever he's *not* expecting you to do.'

Marduk remained silent in thought for a moment. Base protocol was to protect the source the Nephilim could use to power what remained of their ancient technology. And that meant protecting the Ark. But he knew that Nergal had infiltrated their transponder systems and someone within the base had helped him do it.

What if the breech is bigger than that? What if Peter is right and Nergal is exactly where he wants to be? What if his actions over the past number of hours were all part of his elaborate plan to get access to the base and gain control of the Ark, and Earth in the process?

Marduk looked at Chasid. 'Proceed to the Vostok Station and neutralise Abaddon. The weapons must be found before they can detonate them.'

Chasid nodded in response and walked past Peter, Emily and Daniel to the lift that would bring him directly to the observatory on the eastern side of the base. He was talking into a small communications device, assembling a team to assist him. He entered the lift and the doors closed.

'Lock down the Ark vault, close the hangar bay doors and arm yourselves.' Marduk issued his commands to the remaining Nephilim in the control room.

An air of tension and anticipation filtered around the control room as operatives carried out Marduk's commands. Daniel, Emily and Peter stood at the eastern lift. They'd been left in limbo following Marduk's decision to secure the Ark and the base and to go against any predetermined protocol he had in place.

'Increase security around my brother,' Marduk said to a young Nephilim. Suddenly a voice shouted from the lift behind Peter.

'It is too late. He has already been released,' Marduk's son Nabu said. His face was bloodied and he was flanked on either side by four armed Nephilim guards still loyal to Marduk. He approached his father.

'What do you mean "it is too late"?' Marduk said.

'He has already escaped and he is trying to make his way to the Ark vault. I am afraid my uncle Nergal has been planning this for some time. Some of the Nephilim who have been working at the base have joined him. And the two humans –that red head from the observatory and her assistant – they released him and DeMolay's daughter from the holding cells and have infiltrated our security systems. A team of our security officers are holding him at bay on the third floor, for now. Many of my men have been wounded. But they still have not accessed the Ark,' Nabu said.

Marduk remained silent and walked to the centre of the control room. He placed his hand on a scanner next to the main control panel. A small cylindrical crystal rose slowly upward. Marduk reached forward and took it in his left hand. 'Initiate evacuation protocol,' he said.

'Evacuation protocol initiated. All personnel must evacuate. Life support systems will shut down in ninety minutes.' The base's computer systems responded to Marduk's command and initiated a pre-programmed evacuation protocol. Everyone on the base had exactly one hour and thirty minutes to leave before the oxygen supply was depleted.

'Nabu, you and I will remain and try to stop my brother,' said Marduk

'Yes, Father,' Nabu said.

Marduk walked over to Peter and handed him the crystal. 'This controls any remaining technology we have on Earth. You must protect it. Take it and leave the base. Go to the observatory. There you will find the suits and equipment you need to travel to the American South Pole Station. When you reach it, ask for Brandon Shaw. Tell him that I sent you. He will tell you what to do,' Marduk said, and handed the control key to Peter. Without it Nergal would not be able to reverse the evacuation protocol or release the Ark.'

Peter took the small cylindrical object and held it tight. 'I'll protect it. I promise. And when you have dealt with your brother, I'll return it,' Peter said, and joined Nabu at the lift. Nabu placed his hand on the scanner to call the lift back to the control room floor.

Suddenly a bullet skimmed past Marduk's right shoulder. Nabu rushed to his father's side, scanning the control room to see who'd fired a weapon. He counted at least twelve control room operatives who'd armed themselves and had begun to fire their weapons – Nergal's men had already been in position in the control room.

Marduk grabbed Nabu's handgun from his waist and returned fire. 'Move!' Marduk yelled at Peter, and ushered him, Daniel and Emily into the lift.

The sound of gunshots pierced Emily's head as she stood with her back against the lift wall. Those Nephilim still loyal to Marduk moved in front of him, returning fire and keeping Nergal's men on the western side of the control room.

'Go to the observatory with them. Get them out of here!' Marduk said, and pushed Nabu into the lift with the others as the doors were closing.

'But, Father ...' Nabu protested as the doors shut and the lift moved to the observatory floor.

Bullets blasted from either side hitting the walls, the equipment and Marduk's men as the battle for control of the base began. In the distance he could hear the lift on the western side chime before the doors hissed open. He looked across the control room, past the Ark vault shaft. Nergal and more of his men burst forward firing their weapons as they closed in on Marduk. Marduk looked around him. He knew he was outnumbered, but the control key was on its way to safety and no more blood needed to be shed.

'Cease fire!' Marduk shouted, and walked past his men toward Nergal. 'There is no need for any more bloodshed. No one else needs to be harmed, Nergal. I surrender.'

Chapter 54

Fifty miles from the observatory, a group of scientists and engineers had spent decades drilling twelve thousand three hundred and sixty-six feet below the ice, to reach a lake that spanned an area equivalent to that of Lake Ontario in Canada. In the Vostok Research Station the Russians were studying the microbial life that existed in the lake, hoping to catalogue and find new life forms. Yet unbeknown to them, Lake Vostok had been discovered by the Nephilim thousands of years before and had been used as a place to hide one of their secret bases on Earth.

The high velocity snowmobiles hovered silently above the ice as Chasid and his team evaluated their position. He stared at the word 'BOCTOK', Russian for 'Vostok', meaning 'east', on a sign jutting out of the ice sheet. Beyond the drill tower on the right sat the striped buildings that housed the research team's living quarters, Vostok's power station was on the left, and behind the two striped buildings Chasid could see the large red-and-white-striped ball that sat atop the meteorology building.

The photosensitive materials that coated his team's vehicles and their environmental suits had turned a snow-white colour that had made them virtually undetectable in the surrounding landscape, further improving their chances of remaining undetected by Abaddon. Chasid raised his right hand to indicate to the team that they were to remain at the ready while he analysed the station.

'Scan,' he commanded. In response, the sensors positioned at various points throughout his environmental suit scanned the research station and analysed the surrounding area at different wavelengths. An image of the station and drilling platform displayed on his visor.

'Magnify area A3,' Chasid said.

The image became larger and clearer as he zoomed in on the accommodation area. Twelve heat signatures were detected in the main accommodation wing. He could tell by the stature of the individuals that four Nephilim were holding the research station staff hostage. Chasid looked at the image of the drill tower displaying to his left.

'Magnify area C1.'

His visor displayed the images and information his suit had gathered. Infrared and thermal imaging had detected four individuals in the drilling area of the station. All of them were Nephilim. Two outside and two inside. Chasid dismounted his snowmobile and turned to the rest of his team. He lifted his left arm and pushed a green icon on the touch screen on his sleeve to open a secure communications channel.

'The two Nephilim inside the tower are most likely Abaddon and his son, Meregel. If the weapon is in place beneath the base then we need to take Abaddon and Meregel alive. They will most likely remotely detonate the weapon, so we will have a better chance to find the remote trigger that activates the detonator if they are alive. There is one entrance to the tower on the south side, which is protected by two of Nergal's men. You two, take them out.' Chasid pointed to the two guards nearest him. 'The rest of you follow me.'

'Affirmative,' said his team members, dismounting their vehicles and preparing their weapons. As instructed, two members moved stealthily ahead on foot toward the tower entrance. Chasid and the two others took up position at the northern end of the tower and watched as the first two team members moved behind a mound of snow approximately fifteen feet from the entrance. They lay on the ground behind the mound, placed their weapons against their shoulders and rested their chins on their rifle handles, fingers ready on the triggers as they sought their targets through the telescopic sights.

'I have the target in view,' one of the soldiers said.

'Affirmative. Second target attained. Fire in three ... two ... one ...' the other soldier said. They fired at the same time and remained lying in the snow watching through their eyepieces, assessing their enemy. Both of the Nephilim guarding the entrance fell onto the ice. The enemy was neutralised and the entrance was clear.

Chasid moved covertly to the entrance, continually assessing his next move as he neared the drill tower door. The frozen remains of a Vostok scientist, still clutching his iridium satellite phone, lay on the ice beside his feet. Chasid looked back at his men. They all listened intently. 'If the weapons are nowhere in sight, remember, they need to be captured alive. We enter on my mark.'

'Affirmative.'

Chasid placed his hand on the door handle.

'Mark,' he said, pushing the door open and walking quietly inside. He removed his helmet and assessed the area around him.

The space inside the drill tower was cramped and dull. Behind him the rest of his team pressed buttons on their collars, and their helmets and visors folded neatly into their suits at the back of their necks. Their suits returned to their normal steel-grey colour. A musty smell of the kerosene, used to keep the drill hole from freezing over, stuck in their throats and lingered in every crevice around them.

Chasid continued to scan the area. The drilling equipment occupied most of the structure, with little room for movement. He listened intently as he moved cautiously forward toward the drill hole at the back of the building. Suddenly he raised his right hand, indicating to the rest of his men to halt. He heard Meregel's voice up ahead and crouched behind the drilling equipment. He had a bird's eye view; Abaddon and Meregel were standing above the drill hole, the weapon was hoisted above them and one of the Nephilim's construction laser machines was on the ground nearby.

Chasid looked down. At just under six inches in diameter the original drill hole would not have accommodated the weapon, but the hole beneath them was now much larger. *They must have used the laser to enlarge the hole to ensure that the weapon could be placed into the lake,* Chasid thought. He had no doubt that Meregel had already preprogramed the guidance system to bring the weapon exactly where he needed it to be.

'It is in place. Shall we proceed to the final stage of our plan?' Abaddon said, holding a communications device in his right hand.

Chasid tightened his grip on his weapon as he could see that every nuance of Nergal's planning was beginning to fall into place. Nergal had access to everything. The transponder signals. The weapon blueprints. Base security. Everything.

'Yes, send the weapon to its destination and return to the base. I have been freed. We shall see our plans fulfilled together,' Nergal said. His voice echoed through the tower.

Chasid took a brief moment to compose himself. His initial instinct was to break radio silence and warn Marduk that Nergal had escaped. But that would only alert Abaddon to his presence and any chance he had to take them down before they launched the weapon would be lost, so he signalled for his men to move forward and weave silently between the pipes and equipment. Abaddon was standing with his back to the drill hole. He was holding a small, metal box with a red and a green button on the top of it. Meregel was kneeling beneath the weapon making some last minute adjustments.

Chasid signalled to three of his men to take Meregel out. He wanted Abaddon for himself. He snaked silently forward holding his weapon firmly and pointing it at Abaddon. His men followed him through the tight spaces between the pipes.

Meregel suddenly stood up. He'd finished working on the drill hole and had turned toward the entrance. He immediately spotted his adversary; he reached for his weapon and started shooting. One of the soldiers was hit in the shoulder and faltered backward. Meregel lunged forward and grabbed the metal box from his father. He pushed the green button and the weapon dropped into the drill hole and disappeared out of sight. A burst of flames shot from the hole in the ice.

'No!' Chasid yelled, as he fired his weapon at Meregel, hitting him in his abdomen.

Abaddon watched as his son moved slowly backward holding his hands against the wound. He moved forward to help him, but was stopped by the barrel of Chasid's weapon pressed against his face. He could do nothing as Meregel fell to the ground beside him.

'I guess you have finally caught up with me,' Abaddon said. He glanced at the hole leading to the lake beneath the ice, then dropped his weapon and raised his hands in the air. Success was etched in his smile as he held Chasid's glare.

'Guard him. If he moves, shoot him,' Chasid said, and walked over to the drill hole.

The flames from the weapon's propulsion system had burned out the kerosene that had been keeping the hole from freezing over. Water from the lake below had begun to fill the drill hole and at minus forty-one degrees it would not be long before the hole would be completely frozen over.

Chasid had failed. He knew that somewhere, just over one and a half miles beneath the surface of the ice in the subglacial lake, the nuclear weapon was sitting awaiting a command to begin its detonation sequence, and any attempt to reach it through the hole was lost. He turned to Abaddon. The smell of kerosene and smoke stuck in his throat.

'Where is the detonator?' Chasid said.

Abaddon laughed. He was kneeling beside his son who was gasping for air. 'Never!'

Chasid turned to the guards standing watch over the prisoners. 'Do not take your eyes off him for one moment. I will return shortly,' he said and walked toward the exit.

'Your communications will not work out there. We are winning. Nergal has taken the base. Join us, Chasid. Our new leader, Nergal, will welcome a formidable warrior such as yourself with open arms,' Abaddon shouted.

Chasid, who had come to a standstill in the midst of the maze of pipes, felt an unsettling tightness in his chest. The musty oxygen-depleted air in the drilling station was adding to his frustrations, which were stunting his thought processes. He stared at the control panel on the arm of his suit. Abaddon was right. Communications with the base were down. Chasid put on his helmet and walked out of the drill tower. He looked out across the white landscape in the direction of the base. Nergal was forging ahead. The weapon was in place and the base was under attack.

Chasid noticed the sunlight bounce off the reflective surface of a small object on the ground near him. The light was coming from beside the Russian scientist's body. Chasid bent down to prise the iridium satellite phone from the Russian's hand. He knew that communications with the base had been severed, most likely because Marduk had initiated the evacuation protocol to limit the amount of time Nergal had to carry out his plans and gain control of the Ark. And without the Ark, Nergal would perish just like everyone else on the planet unless he had some way to sustain the ancient technology he needed to rebuild his empire. It left Chasid with a small window of time in which he could find the weapon and disarm it.

He turned the extreme weather satellite phone on and extended the antennae straight up toward the sky. He monitored the small screen waiting for the phone to register on the network as he hurried toward his snowmobile camouflaged on the ice. Much to his relief the green LED indicator on the phone flashed and the words 'Registered on the iridium network' appeared on screen.

Chasid immediately interfaced his suit's communications device with the satellite phone. He sat on the vehicle and powered it up. The sound of an open communications line through the iridium network sailed through his helmet. He dialled a number and secured the satellite phone to his utility belt. He looked behind him momentarily at the drill tower then pushed hard on the throttle. *Perhaps all is not lost after all*, he thought as a distant beep resounded through his helmet and his call was answered.

Chapter 55

Micah pointed his weapon uneasily at Marduk. He swallowed hard before yelling at him. 'On your knees!'

Marduk stood resolute and defied Micah's demand.

Micah looked anxiously around him. At least fifteen operatives and security personnel in the control room were being held at gunpoint by Nergal's men, as Nergal himself approached Micah and Marduk, followed closely by Andrew and Ava.

'Hello, brother. It is good to see you again,' Nergal said in a jovial voice.

Marduk took a step forward and lowered his head slightly to look directly into his brother's eyes. 'Whatever it is you are hoping to achieve, I am afraid you will fail,' he said.

Nergal looked around the control room and smiled. With the exception of the control key being removed and the evacuation protocol being initiated, everything was going exactly as he had planned. He had already devised a strategy to counteract his brother's attempts to thwart him, so he returned his gaze to Marduk and said in a calm and defiant tone. 'All those years you kept me on the sidelines. Never completely trusting me. Never allowing me to be part of what you have been building here on Earth. Shutting me out of your sacred base. Only permitting me a mere futile existence on the fringes of your world. Making me watch while you built your Earthly empire and empowered a race of slaves our father created to serve us!' Nergal's voice rose as he ended the sentence. 'And yet I must admit, you have made me what I am. You have enabled me to be exactly where I anticipated my actions would bring me. You have helped me more than anyone to make my plans a reality. I am here because I want to be here. So I must thank you, most sincerely.'

'The humans will never bow before you. You will never rule the Earth,' Marduk said.

'I do not mean for all of them to bow before me, brother. Just those that survive and their descendants will suffice.' Nergal reached into his pocket and removed a small black thin rectangular device – the detonator trigger. He shifted it between his fingers. 'When the weapon is activated, you and all those who remain loyal to you, will have a front row seat. Whereas I, and those loyal to me, will watch from the safety of your aircraft in orbit as the seas rise and the Earth's landscape is wiped clean. Then we shall reshape the Earth and rebuild the human population to serve me as the slaves they were destined to be. With the exception of my few loyal human followers,' Nergal smiled at Ava, 'each and every one of them will feel the wrath of my hatred for the species our father created.' He walked over to Andrew, seated in front of the base's main control panel.

'I see you have removed the control key.' Nergal turned to face his brother. 'Return it and reactivate the systems on the base,' Nergal said.

Marduk stayed steadfast.

'Return the control key!' Nergal yelled, arching his neck forward.

'I do not have it and you cannot stop the evacuation protocol or remove the Ark without it, so you may as well give up,' Marduk said sternly.

'He gave it to the humans,' said a tall grey-haired Nephilim behind Nergal. 'They are taking it out of the base as we speak.'

Nergal clenched his fists and turned to Andrew. 'What

systems have you gained access to?'

'Only secondary systems. Lifts, air traffic control and the security cameras are still online. Communications within the base are down, but our short range communicators will still work—'

'Can you tell me where the humans are?' Nergal said.

Andrew typed on the touch screen keyboard. 'Yes, they're in the eastern lift. It's almost at the observatory. Do you want me to stop it?'

'No,' Nergal said sharply, and turned to Micah. 'Do we have anyone in the observatory?' he said.

'Yes, Ninurta is there. He has already evacuated everyone so it is empty.'

'Good. Ask him to retrieve the control key and bring it to me. Then dispose of everyone in that lift. They are of no more use to us now,' Nergal looked at Marduk. 'I will be out of your hair soon, brother. Once I have the control key, I will have the Ark and we can be on our way.'

Chapter 56

'He is bleeding. At least let me tend to his wounds,' Abaddon said, glaring at the two Nephilim guards holding him captive in the drill tower.

'When Chasid comes back—'

'Chasid is not coming back. He has gone back to the base and is leaving like everyone else. Go and take a look outside yourself if you do not believe me. You will see that he is no longer here. He has gone back to the base and will leave with the aircraft that will soon be evacuating the Earth. He has left you here to die,' Abaddon said harshly, knowing full well that the aircraft leaving the base were occupied by Nergal's followers. He looked down at his son.

Meregel stared back and held tight to the weapon concealed beneath his jacket. He knew he was too weak to combat the two guards himself; he hoped his father could distract them long enough to reach for the weapon and overcome them.

'Go and take a look. See where Chasid has gone and report back to me immediately,' said the older of the two guards.

'But, sir. We were told—'

'That is an order. Now go!'

Abaddon remained on his knees. He moved his head cautiously to his left and eyed the guard as he made his way through the intertwined piping of the drill tower before disappearing from view. There was silence as they waited for his return. One minute passed. Then another and another.

Each sixty seconds felt like an eternity to the remaining

guard. Hearing a noise in the distance near the entrance, he looked momentarily behind, lowering his guard and aiming his weapon away from Abaddon.

Abaddon grabbed the gun from his son and rose quickly and quietly. When the guard turned back around, he was greeted by the sight of the barrel of Abaddon's handgun pointed directly at him. 'Give me your weapon and get onto your knees,' Abaddon said. He took the rifle from the guard who immediately dropped to the floor. 'Put your hands on top of your head where I can see them,' Abaddon said, and scanned around them. To his right he eyed a set of cable ties. He put the guard's rifle on the ground beside his son, then grabbed one of the ties.

'Sit down and put your feet out in front of you, and keep your hands on your head,' Abaddon said. He held out the cable tie. 'Now tie your feet together.'

The Nephilim eyed Abaddon cautiously. He leaned forward to take the tie from him, but suddenly changed direction and wrapped his arms tight around Abaddon's legs. He pulled as hard as he could. Abaddon lost his balance and fell backward, losing the handgun as he crashed to the floor. The guard lunged for his rifle, but he was too late.

Meregel had dragged himself to his feet and thrust his rifle handle into the guard's face, knocking him unconscious. Abaddon scrambled to his feet and rushed over to his son who was wavering over the guard, trying to use the rifle as a crutch.

'You should leave me,' Meregel said quietly. 'Save yourself and see our plans fulfilled.'

Abaddon held his son's arm. 'Nergal's aircraft is outside. There is still time to get you to his med bay and heal your wounds,' Abaddon said, and placed his son's arm around his neck and held him upright.

Suddenly Abaddon could hear the entrance door open again. The second guard was returning. Abaddon aimed the rifle at the entrance and holding on tightly to Meregel they navigated the pipes toward the returning guard. He knew the element of surprise was on his side. He scanned the area ahead and moved behind a large cylinder in the centre of the drill tower. He lowered Meregel to the ground, took up an offensive position and waited for the guard to pass.

The young Nephilim walked slowly through the machinery toward the back of the drill tower. He saw Abaddon's reflection in the large shiny pipework to his left. Immediately he raised his weapon, but he was too late. Abaddon had already stepped forward and pulled the trigger. The young guard released his grip on his rifle and fell backward.

Meregel sat on the ground leaning against the pipes; his eyes were closed, his breathing shallow and his complexion pallid. Abaddon bent to his knees and placed one arm around the back of his son's neck and the other underneath his knees and lifted him off the ground. Meregel's body remained limp and lifeless as his father rushed to the drill tower entrance and out onto the ice.

The freezing cold pierced Abaddon as he braced the Antarctic wilderness, walking steadily past the drill tower and on toward the research station. Beside the station he could see the distortion on the distant ice where Nergal's LEO had landed when he'd arrived with the weapons.

Inside the LEO Nergal's pilot, Adira, was sitting in the cockpit watching the results of some last minute aircraft systems checks display on the cockpit window. Security, engines, hull integrity, sensors all were functioning within normal parameters. She gazed momentarily to her left, then tried to get a better look across the icy landscape. In the distance she could see Abaddon struggling toward the aircraft carrying Meregel.

Adira jumped up and ran to the cabin door. She slammed her hand on the sensor and watched as the cabin door opened and the aircraft steps descended to the ice.

'Power up the med bay. We are losing him,' Abaddon shouted.

Adira rushed to the back of the aircraft and opened the door to the medical unit. She hit the power switch and the device came to life. The transparent door covering the top of the ten-foot-long cylindrical-shaped unit folded back neatly along its length. She moved to the control panel at the top of the device then looked behind her. Abaddon had reached the cabin and was staggering toward her. He entered the room and placed Meregel on the soft white bed beneath the transparent cover. Adira immediately programmed the unit to assess Meregel's injuries. The cover closed over him and a white light scanned him from top to toe. Adira analysed the information the medical unit was displaying on the glass cover over his body.

'What happened?' she said.

'Chasid,' Abaddon said. He had no need to say anything further. Chasid had been the commander of Enki's army for thousands of years and had helped his leader to many victories on both Earth and their home world. His reputation as a formidable warrior preceded him.

'His pulse is weak and his blood pressure low. There is a small, but life threatening, tear in his abdominal aorta. He has lost a lot of blood and requires a transfusion. It will begin immediately,' Adira said. 'He will be fine,' she added. She could tell by the look in Abaddon's eyes that he'd already set his mind on revenge. 'Go and do what you need to do. Chasid should pay for what he has done.'

Abaddon ran his hand affectionately along her silvery-grey shoulder-length hair and smiled.

'I need to return to the base,' he said.

'I will take us there now.'

'No, I will suit up, take one of their vehicles and go there alone. You must wait for me here. Communications on the base are down. Marduk has obviously removed the control key and has blocked our signals from working within and around the base. I will have no way to communicate with you so if I am not back in one hour, you must leave and take our son and the remaining Nephilim in the Vostok Station with you.' Abaddon went into the cabin.

The med bay had begun to heal Meregel's wounds, so Adira followed Abaddon. 'When we entered the research station earlier, I noticed that one of the humans had an iridium satellite phone,' she said, and opened a small concealed panel on the cabin wall, from which she removed two communications devices. She sat behind Nergal's desk and touched the screen in front of her to bring it to life. 'If I am correct, that particular communications system has sixty-six satellites in orbit, one of which I am about to hack into. We can then adjust our own communications devices to work on the human frequency and use these to stay in touch.' Adira moved several icons across the screen. Abaddon moved closer and stood behind his wife. 'Their frequency range is within what the humans refer to as the L band spectrum.' She watched the screen intently. 'Yes, here it is – at one thousand, six hundred and sixteen megahertz.'

She turned to her husband who had zipped himself into a grey environmental suit. She placed the communications device into the pocket on the sleeve of the suit. 'I have sent a wireless command to your suit. It will now use this frequency so you can contact me if needed—'

She was interrupted by a voice from the aircraft's

speakers. 'Come in, Chasid,' the male voice said.

'It is good to hear from you, Nannar. Did you locate the weapon blueprints I requested?' Chasid said.

'Yes I did, but the satellite uplink you are using is slow and is not meant for large data packages, so I have requested a signal change. General Cullen is working on it now. I will contact you again shortly,' Nannar said, and the channel went dead.

'It looks like they are going to disarm the weapon,' she said.

'Not if I get to them first.'

Chapter 57

The sound of gunshots was still ringing in Nabu's head as the lift moved through the hangar bay floor. His initial instinct was to find a way into the hangar bay and join the battle, but he needed to get the control key and the humans to safety. Without it, Nergal's plan to access the vault would hopefully take longer than the eighty minutes of oxygen now left within the base.

Peter looked queasy as the lift came to a stop. Nabu stepped out into the dimly lit hallway that stretched out in a westerly direction beyond the open doors. It was silent and, with the exception of the two Nephilim guards lying on the floor outside the lift, it looked empty. Nabu held his weapon in front of him as he stooped down to check them for a pulse. There was no sign of life; both guards had been fatally wounded. He picked up the weapon nearest him, secured it to his waist and scanned the corridor again. He could see the entrance to the polar gear room next to the exit door straight ahead of him, but the two corridors that led to the conference room on the north side and the accommodation wing on the south of the observatory were out of his line of sight. But he knew they needed to suit up before they could exit the observatory and safely navigate from there to the South Pole Station, so he moved slowly forward.

Without the environmental suits to protect them, no one could survive any long-distance journey across the ice. The complete lack of moisture in the air, the average minus forty-two degrees centigrade temperatures, the lack of oxygen because of the high elevation, the average wind speed that could rise to as high as twenty-seven miles per second and the high ionisation in the air made the polar desert one of the most hostile places on Earth. Normally it could take anything up to one month for a human to acclimatise to its atmosphere, but the suits would compensate for these changes immediately and allow Peter, Daniel and Emily to get away safely.

'My sister's still down there somewhere. We have to go and get her,' Daniel said as he followed Nabu.

'She is on the medical floor. Ninharsag will keep her safe,' Nabu said. 'We need to find something to jam the lift door open. It is the only access to the observatory from the base, as the lift on the western side leads only to the hangar bay. If we jam the doors open, then it will stop them from using it.'

'What about this?' Emily said handing Nabu a long metal coat stand.

'It is perfect. Thank you,' Nabu said. He took the large metal pole from Emily and jammed it firmly between the two lift doors.

'The suits we need are in that room down there beside the exit door,' Nabu said, pointing toward the large black door at the other end of the hallway.

'You can take the control key and bring it to the South Pole Station. We're not going anywhere without my mother,' Peter said firmly, the control key in his outstretched hand.

'As I said—' Nabu was interrupted by the sound of muffled voices filtering down the hallway from the northern corridor. He raised his weapon and listened intently.

'... down here.' The stranger's voice was instantly recognisable: Ninurta, Nergal and Marduk's cousin and one of Nergal's greatest allies was approaching fast.

'Quick! That way. Hide in there,' Nabu whispered, and gestured to the black door closest to them.

'Stop where you are and we will let you live!' Ninurta

shouted from the shadows of the corridor.

Daniel stopped dead.

'Keep going!' Nabu shouted and fired a warning shot in his enemy's direction.

Ninurta moved into view, fired his gun at Nabu and ducked across to the corridor on the southern side. The sound of the discharged weapon travelled up the corridor as the bullet shot toward Nabu, hitting his forearm. He stumbled heavily against the wall, dropping his gun on the ground as he tried to steady himself. He looked at the others. 'Keep going. Barricade yourselves inside the room. Hurry!' Nabu shouted to Peter, Daniel and Emily who were almost at the door.

Nabu retrieved the second weapon from his waist and held it level in front of him. A second shot blasted from the shadows of the corridor ahead and skimmed past Daniel, narrowly missing his head.

'We're not going to make it,' Peter said over the sound of gunshots exchanged intermittently with Nabu and their enemy. 'There's too many of them.' He pushed hard on the door handle. It was locked. He glanced back in the direction of the lift. 'The door's locked, we should go back,' he shouted. He took a step toward the lift, but was stalled by a bullet from Ninurta's gun. A warning for him to stay exactly where he was. Peter moved back into the cover of the doorway and grabbed Emily's hand.

He looked in the direction of the exit.

Through the small, square glass panel in the centre of the black exit door he could see another rifle-wielding Nephilim approach from outside. Nabu was returning fire from the cover of the observatory communications room doorway, stalling Ninurta's approach. They'd nowhere to take cover, and with Ninurta and his men taking up positions at the entrances to the northern and southern corridors, they couldn't move forward. Peter glanced again at the exit door. It had opened and a rush of cold air preceded the stranger who was fast approaching them.

There was nowhere to run. They were trapped.

Chapter 58

The expansive hangar bay was bustling with activity as the final parts of Nergal's line of attack were forging ahead. The Nephilim who'd returned at Chasid's request were being rounded up as they exited their aircraft. None had believed the base could be infiltrated so easily; the element of surprise had worked in Nergal's favour.

On the western side, a lone aircraft was under gunfire, which had erupted when its occupants had refused to come out peacefully. Inside the aircraft, Marduk's chief science officer, Nannar, watched the computer screen on the main control panel and rechecked the frequencies General Cullen had sent him. He touched the icon in the centre of the screen and read the words that flashed up.

`Data upload in progress`

He rubbed his hand along his long grey beard, then picked up a tiny, thin transparent disc. Measuring approximately half an inch in diameter, it was a prototype communications device he'd been developing. He positioned it on the tip of his index finger, pushed his shoulder-length grey hair to one side and pressed the device firmly in place behind his ear.

Nannar knew that the tentative approach of the forces outside his aircraft and the skilled precision with which they were shooting, taking care not to injure the science officer, were a testament to Nergal's commands to take him alive. He had designed, with the help of Nergal's father Enki, almost all of the ancient technology the Nephilim had left on Earth. And more recently he had helped Marduk restore it to its former glory. In Nergal's new world order there most certainly would be a place for him, whether he wanted it or not.

Nannar looked past his science officers, who were sporadically returning fire in the hope of holding Nergal's men at bay, and out into the hangar bay. In the distance he could see Nergal's forces recruiting those who would work against Marduk. Those who would not were being held separately on the south-eastern side of the hangar bay awaiting their fate.

Nannar glanced again at the control panel.

`Upload successful`

He breathed a sigh of relief and walked over to place his hand on one of the young Nephilim soldier's shoulders. 'Let us concede defeat for now. Lower your weapons,' he said in a quiet whisper.

The young soldier – dressed in the science officer's uniform of beige khakis, a brown T-shirt with a golden stripe down each side, and a cream jacket with a golden-winged disc embroidered onto the top left-hand side – turned and faced his superior. 'But, sir,' he said.

'When they ask you, say that you will join with Nergal. We have lost this battle. But the war is far from over and an ally on Nergal's side would prove a valuable asset. Tell the others,' Nannar said, and he stepped past the young science officer. He raised his hands in the air and walked out of the cargo hold at the back of his aircraft, commanding his other officers to lower their weapons as he approached their enemy.

Two of Nergal's men rushed forward, grabbed Nannar by the arms and guided him toward the lift. Nannar glanced behind. The young science officer had done exactly as Nannar had instructed and offered, like many others, to join Nergal.

'We have him.' The soldier to his right spoke into his

communications device. Nannar could hear a muffled reply. He was handed over to two Nephilim standing at the lift doors.

'Take him to Nergal in the control room,' said the soldier and released his grip on Nannar's arm. 'His Majesty is waiting for him.'

~

On the other side of the hangar bay, Maggie gazed at her tablet. Now that every LEO in the hangar bay was ready to be piloted by one of Nergal's men, his forces were to begin evacuating the base immediately. Maggie lifted the communications device to her mouth. 'Can you open the hangar bay doors?' she said.

'I'm on it,' Andrew said.

Maggie watched the enormous doors in the ceiling. A red light flashed either side, followed by a loud hissing sound as the doors glided open. She felt a chill run down her spine as the arctic air filtered in from outside and turned the air inside the hangar bay remarkably cooler.

She looked again at her tablet. *Forty minutes twenty-eight seconds left*, she thought. She lifted her communications device and answered a call.

'Have our aircraft begun to evacuate yet?' Ava's voice filtered through the device.

Maggie could see the first aircraft moving into position beneath the hangar bay doors before the shrill noise of the engine filled the bay and the aircraft flew out of sight.

'Yes,' Maggie said, 'they're leaving as we speak. I've also instructed all aircraft to maintain an orbit in the exosphere five hundred miles out, and to await further instructions.'

'Then everything is going exactly as planned. I will join

you shortly,' Ava said, and ended the call.

Chapter 59

'We're trapped,' Peter shouted to Nabu. He, Emily and Daniel had taken cover in the polar gear room doorway close to the exit door that had just blasted open.

The Nephilim was approaching in their direction fast from outside. The sunlight was shining directly down the corridor obstructing Peter's view. He squinted as he took a better look. The stranger was dressed in a grey, skin-tight suit, his helmet visor covering his face. But Peter could see steely blue eyes firmly focused ahead as the Nephilim lifted a rifle against his shoulder. Peter put his arm protectively around Emily as the Nephilim searched for his mark through the telescopic sight on his weapon. He took aim at Nabu then suddenly altered his target and instead aimed at Ninurta's henchman who'd peered out from beyond the shadows in the northern corridor.

Then Peter realised.

The Nephilim was Chasid. He had returned from Vostok.

Chasid pushed his finger hard on the trigger. The bullet hit Ninurta's man in the centre of his forehead. He chased ahead and took cover in a doorway further down the corridor, searching for his next target. He fired again. Another of Ninurta's men fell as they returned fire at Chasid.

Peter peered down the corridor. Three more of Ninurta's men were approaching from the northern side, shooting a barrage of bullets as they crossed the hallway to where Ninurta was taking cover. He noticed a gun on the ground near where he was standing. He lunged back toward the lift and landed on the floor near Nabu. He grasped the gun firmly with both hands, wriggled to Nabu's side and returned fire, giving Chasid the opportunity to remove a small spherical hand grenade from his waistband while their enemy hid in the protection of the observatory's northern corridor.

'Take cover!' Chasid yelled.

Emily and Daniel cowered to the ground in the doorway as Peter and Nabu took cover near the lift.

Chasid pulled the pin from the grenade and ran. As he passed the northern corridor, he threw it at Ninurta and his men and continued to run toward Nabu and Peter.

'Retreat!' Ninurta shouted. There was an eruption of light and sound as dust and fragments of stone sprayed from either side of the blast, and wall and ceiling rubble blocked the entrance to the northern corridor. It was followed by silence as the gunshots ceased. Ninurta and his men had either ran for cover or were silenced by the blast.

Chasid lowered his weapon and removed the helmet. 'We must hurry,' he said, helping Nabu to his feet. 'Are you badly injured?'

'No, it's just a scratch.'

Emily and Daniel walked in the direction of the others.

'That's more than just a scratch. It needs medical attention,' she said, watching the blood drip from Nabu's fingers.

'There is a medical kit in the polar gear room. This way,' Chasid said, heading for the door nearest the observatory exit.

'Did you find the weapon?' Nabu said.

'Yes, but I was too late. It is already in position beneath the base. We will have to go down there to disarm it,' Chasid said.

'Do you know how to disarm a nuclear weapon?' Peter said, his voice shrouded with worry.

Chasid placed his palm on the scanner outside the polar gear room and unlocked the door. He turned to Peter. 'No. I do not. But I know someone who can, and if that fails, I have the weapon blueprints and we will have to find a way to disarm it ourselves.'

~

Ninurta stood up and brushed the dust and debris from his black khakis and waist-length black jacket. He stared at the rubble at the end of the hallway that had killed his men and blocked him from entering the observatory. He kicked a piece of stone with his black boot and let out a vengeful roar before composing himself and lifting his communications device from his waist.

'Andrew, have the aircraft begun to leave the hangar bay yet?' Ninurta said in a calm quiet tone.

'Yes. They are taking up positions in orbit around the Earth as we speak,' he said.

'I want you to send whatever aircraft is ready to the northern side of the observatory with a team of our men on board. Chasid has rescued the humans and is most likely leaving the observatory with the control key as we speak. I need to stop him.'

'It is on its way,' Andrew said.

Chapter 60

There was an uneasy silence in the control room as Andrew's body fell to the floor.

'Your Majesty—' Micah said.

'His replacement is on his way,' Nergal said. His voice was low and devoid of any emotion as he put his gun away and stared intently at Micah, who remained silent and decided not to articulate any further his protest at Andrew's death. Micah could see that the information Andrew had just relayed to Nergal was spinning around in his head.

Chasid was in the observatory and had rescued the humans. Right now he was most likely planning his next line of attack and Nergal knew that Chasid would not be easily swayed. If he was to succeed, and get the control key back from Peter, he knew he must move quickly.

Nannar was being ushered toward him by two Nephilim soldiers. 'You are right on time, Nannar. My current science officer has just expired. You may take his place,' Nergal said, and gestured to the seat Andrew had been sitting on. 'Your predecessor was too slow and could not keep up. I do hope that you prove to be more resourceful.'

Nannar glanced over at Andrew's body.

'I am your ruler now. Take a seat,' Nergal said in a short sharp whisper.

One of the guards pushed Nannar forward by pressing his weapon sharply against his back. Nannar turned his head slowly to catch a glimpse of the Nephilim who would dare treat him this way. A jab in the back from the tip of a young renegade's weapon was something he would not forget in a hurry. He was the oldest Nephilim living on Earth and a member of the Nephilim High Council, which brought him a certain status among the Nephilim race – one that usually resulted in him being treated with respect and revered by all who knew him.

'Be careful whom you tread on while you ascend on your path to glory, young man. You may be required to rely on their mercy when your pedestal crumbles and you are clamouring to survive as you pass them on your way back down,' he said, and glared down at the young Nephilim who was now wielding his weapon uneasily at Nannar. The soldier took a step back.

'Take no heed of him. He is just a mumbling old fool,' Nergal said.

'A fool nonetheless that you need, otherwise I would be lying beside your former science officer, would I not?' Nannar said.

'You can release the Ark without the control key. Do it. Now!' Nergal said.

'I cannot. You know as I do that the crystal was created by your father. Only he can override it.'

Nergal pursed his lips and pulled his weapon from his waist. He walked over to Marduk and pressed the gun against his head. 'Then switch off the evacuation protocol. I need more time!'

'Do not do it. Let him perish here with the rest of us,' Marduk said defiantly.

Nannar glanced around the control room. He counted fifteen of Marduk's loyal followers who were unarmed and being held at gunpoint by five of Nergal's men at the northern end of the room. Micah was standing at the main control panel opposite Nannar coordinating the evacuation of Nergal's men from the hangar bay.

Nannar glanced at the displayed images of the base. The LEOs were exiting the bay with Nergal's followers on board and the weapon was sitting idle beneath the base awaiting the signal from the trigger. Nergal's plans were certainly steamrolling ahead and this was exactly what Nannar was hoping for. Nergal, for all his strategic prowess, had a tendency to get caught up in a sense of his own self-congratulation, and Nannar knew this could be his downfall.

He turned to Marduk. 'You and I both know the luxury of time is something we all, at one point or other in our lives, require to fulfil our destinies. I am sorry, Marduk, but I must agree to his request. I hope you understand,' Nannar said.

'Stop speaking in riddles, you old fool, and do as I command,' Nergal shouted, and pointed his weapon at Nannar.

Marduk frowned at Nannar's response, but instantly recognised the innuendo it implied, so he remained silent and watched as Nannar sat at the control panel and input the override commands required to stop the evacuation protocol. All the screens in the control room went momentarily blank then returned to life.

Nergal looked on in anticipation as the base's life support systems came back online and the oxygen levels returned to normal.

Nergal smiled. 'Now I will regain the control key.' He walked over to the screen in front of the Ark vault shaft, where a three-dimensional image of the base was displayed. He touched an icon on the screen and blue and green dots appeared throughout the image. Most of them were concentrated on level one in the hangar bay. Nergal looked further down the levels. Three dots were located on the medical floor. Two green, showing the two Nephilim life signatures on the medical floor and one blue. A human – Sophia.

Nergal's smile widened as he looked at Marduk. 'I am sure when Peter DeMolay hears his mother's screams he will give the control key to me. Soon, brother, all this will be mine.'

Chapter 61

The temperature gauge to the left of the exit door flashed a warning.

−41°C.

Beyond the door, a long concrete tunnel stretched out toward the never-ending desert of ice and snow. A place where the coldest ever recorded temperature of minus eighty-nine point two degrees centigrade was recorded.

Peter took long slow breaths, as he watched Daniel making circular movements with his shoulders as he adapted to the skin-tight feel of the environmental suit. Emily was finishing the tourniquet on Nabu's arm, carefully applying enough pressure to stem the bleeding.

Chasid held a thin rectangular computer tablet in front of him.

'As you know, longitude is geometrically undefined here in the South Pole. For this reason all the directions outlined on this model of the base are based on grid north. Do you understand?' Chasid said, and looked at Peter and Daniel.

'Yes,' Peter said.

'No, I don't,' Daniel said, looking questioningly at Peter.

'Because we're in the South Pole, if we were to give directions just like we do back at home, then everywhere would basically be pointing north. So to make things a little easier they use something called grid north, which uses the prime meridian as a northerly reference,' Peter said.

'So basically if were looking toward Greenwich which is at zero degrees longitude, then we're looking north?' Daniel said.

'Exactly,' Chasid said, 'and south would be one hundred and eighty degrees, and so on.'

Daniel nodded and looked at the image of the observatory Chasid was showing on the tablet.

'We are here.' Chasid pointed to the western side of the observatory. 'Through this exit door, in a north-westerly direction, is a maintenance shaft that leads through the ice, down along the side of the base and into the lake. This is the only entrance to the shaft and the lake from the base. You can enter the area beneath the base where the weapon is located from here.'

Chasid handed the tablet to Nabu and took hold of Peter's left arm. He ran his finger across the suit's control panel near his wrist. 'The suit is controlled from here. The display is similar to the one in the aircraft and will display on your visor when you put your helmet on,' he said, and programmed the suit. 'I have entered the coordinates for the weapon's location. It is next to one of the six supporting columns situated at different intervals around the bottom of the base.'

Chasid released his grip on Peter's arm. He started to program Daniel's suit.

'You will have to travel over two miles down the maintenance shaft before you reach the door to the airlock. You must enter the airlock and go to the control panel at the bottom of the ladder. Enter the code that shows up on your visor and the airlock door will automatically close behind you to allow the pressure to equalise before the moon pool opens up. From there you can free fall to the lakebed. The area directly beneath the base is surrounded by a force field.

This means that there is no water in this area, so when you enter it, you can remove your helmet and breathe normally if you wish.' Chasid released his grip on Daniel's arm.

'Airlock, force fields, weapons, moon pool,' Daniel whispered, and looked at Peter, who just smiled in response, knowing his uncle would try anything once, but always preferred to have his feet firmly on the ground if trouble was looming.

'You put on your helmets by pressing the button here on the left,' Chasid said, pointing to the left side of his own suit. Daniel and Peter put on their helmets and watched their visors slide forward from their storage positions in the necks of the suits. 'The suits will form a force field around you to compensate for any change in pressure and will automatically compensate for any external variables such as temperature and oxygen. You will be able to breathe and walk as normal through the lake water so try not to panic. Your communications device is here in the sleeve. I have isolated a channel that should be safe for us to use, so only I can hear what you are saying.'

'Okay,' Daniel shouted.

'You can also speak normally,' Chasid added, and smiled at Daniel. 'The maintenance hatch is one hundred feet from the end of the exit tunnel here on the observatory level. The display on your visor will guide you to it. You can manually enter the code I have pre-programmed to display on your visor when you reach the hatch. The quickest way to the bottom is to place your feet and hands on either side of the ladder and slide down. But first attach the carabineer, the safety clip on the utility belt on your suit, to the metal safety railing on the right-hand side. It will protect you if for any reason you lose your grip and fall. It will also slow your descent before you reach the bottom. Remember, it is over two miles down so do not forget that safety clip. Is there anything you need to ask?' Chasid said, looking from one to the other.

'Are you sure you'll be able to get Gibil back up here in time? And Sophia, just like you promised? It would be an awful shame to get all the way down there just to be blown to pieces by a nuclear device we had no chance of disarming in the first place,' Daniel said. A nervous hesitation lingered in his voice.

'Yes,' Chasid said assuredly.

'And have you stored the control key I gave you somewhere safe?' Peter said.

'Yes, I have,' Chasid said, and pointed to a pouch on his utility belt. He reached forward and opened the exit door. A blast of cold air rushed in.

Peter went over to where Emily was standing near the exit. She placed her hands gently on his arms and looked into his eyes beneath the visor.

'I love you,' Peter whispered

'I love you too,' she said back in a low voice before Daniel arrived beside them.

'Get back here in one piece,' she said to Daniel who smiled and nodded.

'We'll certainly try,' Daniel said.

'Good luck,' Nabu said, and watched as Daniel and Peter ran toward the end of the tunnel.

Chasid shut the door behind them and turned to Emily and Nabu. 'Follow me,' he said quietly, and walked briskly down the corridor to the left of the exit door back in the direction of the observatory communications room. Emily had to jog behind them in an effort to keep up.

'Nergal will not detonate the weapon until he is sure he

can leave the base.' Chasid stopped outside the communications room door. 'The quickest way to disarm the weapon safely is to get Gibil to show us how. He is on the medical floor.'

'We can use the lift on the eastern side of the observatory. We jammed it earlier to prevent Nergal from using it,' Nabu said.

Chasid nodded. He opened the door, stepped inside and walked over to the main control panel and switched it on.

'If Nannar has done what I asked him to do, then we will have access to the base's systems from here and you will be able to monitor our communications,' Chasid said, and pointed to the screen where the base's schematics were displayed.

'We can enter the lift maintenance shaft from the maintenance hatch in the lift ceiling. From there we can descend to the second floor undetected. When I contact you, you are to remove the bar holding the lift doors open and send it to the medical floor. Floor number two.'

Chasid handed Emily a tiny glass cylindrical device measuring just over an inch long and quarter of an inch in diameter.

'This is a radio identification chip. To access the lift you need to place this in front of the scanner. Then choose the floor number.'

Chasid then handed Emily a black handgun with a silencer on the top of the barrel. 'Nergal will continue to look for the control key. We should reach the medical floor within the next five minutes, by which time Peter and Daniel will have entered the lake. This is just in case you need to defend yourself.' Chasid said.

'I'm not sure …' Emily said.

'Just in case. The safety clip is here.' Chasid turned the gun to the side and pointed to a small grey clip near the top of the handgrip. 'This way releases the safety and this way puts it back on. The trigger is here. So you just point and shoot.'

'Safety here, point and shoot. Got it,' she said, and watched Chasid secure his weapon to the belt on his waist then walk with Nabu toward the lift.

Once inside, Chasid reached up and opened the maintenance hatch in the ceiling. He jumped up, grabbed the sides of the opening and pulled himself out onto the lift roof.

'Stay in the communications room and lock the door until you hear from us,' Nabu said. He followed behind Chasid and closed the hatch.

Emily held the gun in both hands as she walked slowly to the communications room, scanning the corridor on either side.

Chasid stood on the maintenance ladder beside the lift. He looked down the length of the shaft. It was an enormous, dimly lit, bottomless pit. He extended his arm out across the shaft. The sensors on the suit analysed the space below him and relayed the data to the small screen on his sleeve. At approximately one point two miles below he would reach the hangar bay on the first floor, after that it would be a further three hundred feet to the lift doors of the medical bay.

Chasid placed his hands and then his feet firmly on the outside of the ladder. He pulled the carabineer connected to his utility belt by a thin metal wire and secured it to the metal rail beside the ladder. Chasid tugged hard on the wire to ensure he was securely attached to the maintenance railing. One wrong move and the long freefall journey to the bottom of the shaft would definitely end in death.

'Are you ready?' Chasid said, and looked up at Nabu.

'Yes,' Nabu said. 'I will be right behind you.'

~

Two miles beneath the observatory, Chasid and Nabu were holding tight onto a ledge in the lift shaft wall above the medical bay door. Chasid released his right hand and removed a small circular device from his belt. He reached below him and placed the device on the lift door. 'I will be opening the door in three. Have your weapon ready,' he said.

'Affirmative,' Nabu said.

'Three ... two ... one.'

Chasid pushed the button on the device. The lift doors opened beneath them. They released their grip on the ledge and swung into the corridor. Chasid removed his weapon from his waist. He scanned the entire corridor that stretched out toward the Ark vault shaft in the centre of the second floor. He motioned to Nabu to move along the corridor. Ninharsag's laboratory was located just behind the shaft on the western side. Chasid presumed she'd be hiding there.

Their weapons were at the ready as they scanned the area for any sign of Nergal's men. Chasid walked slowly and silently behind Nabu. He continually scanned either side of him glancing into each of the treatment rooms through the glass partitions as he passed.

Suddenly Chasid heard movement behind. He turned around, but was stopped by a heavy blunt object hitting him forcefully on the back of his head. He dropped his weapon to the floor as a sharp pain travelled agonisingly from his neck to his forehead. The corridor spun in front of him. As he fell to the ground, he just about recognised the tall silhouette of his attacker before the obscurity of unconsciousness set in.

Chapter 62

'Just focus on finding the weapon and try not to think about it,' Peter said, already regretting saying anything about the massive increase in atmospheric pressure they would encounter deep within the lake and how the technology in the environmental suits would hopefully keep them safe.

Daniel took a couple of deep breaths. He could feel his heart pounding then returned to a normal rhythm. The journey down the maintenance shaft had come to a quick yet subtle end; the metal clip securing him had latched onto the railing close to the maintenance hatch and had extended downward with him, slowing his descent before he'd reached the bottom of the ladder. He loosened his grip on its sides and walked over to Peter.

'Are you sure? I mean, we could be crushed in an instant if these suits fail,' Daniel said.

'The average atmospheric pressure at sea level is about fourteen point seven pounds of force per square inch. I know the pressure in the lake is much higher than that, but Chasid said that the suits will form a force field around us to protect us from the pressure above, so we should be fine,' Peter said.

'"We should be fine"!' That's three hundred and sixty times greater than the average pressure at sea level and you're saying, "We should be fine".'

Peter placed his hands on his uncle's shoulders and pressed his helmet against Daniel's. 'These guys have been running around the universe for thousands of years, much of their time I'm sure was spent in these suits, and they're still alive, so I'm sure they work. I'm going to enter the code and start the sequence to open the airlock so we can enter the lake. Now would be a good time to tell me if you need to back out. I understand if you don't want to enter the hatch.'

What's the worst that could happen? The suits could fail and we'd be crushed. The nuclear weapon could go off and were screwed anyway. I could go back outside and freeze to death. But we could just pull it off and save the planet. Daniel thought for a moment. 'Okay, shorty. Go for it,' he said, and swallowed hard.

Peter smiled and bent down toward the hatch. He entered the code displayed on his visor into the touch screen keypad and watched as the hatch hissed open. Peter looked inside the airlock. It was well illuminated and at least twelve feet high and thirty wide with a dull metal ladder on the wall closest to the entrance. 'I'll go first,' he said, and placed his foot on the first rung of the ladder and set about his descent into the airlock, followed closely by Daniel.

'No doubt this was designed to suit the Nephilim and their long legs,' Daniel said, referring to the extended distance between the rungs of the ladder.

'Just take your time. You're almost at the bottom,' Peter said.

Daniel awkwardly stretched his leg down to the final rung trying to feel it on the sole of his foot before placing his entire weight on the step, then at last he took one more step and could feel the airlock floor beneath his feet.

Peter looked around him. 'There's the control panel,' he said, pointing to the right of the ladder. 'When I enter the code, the airlock will close and the pressure in here will equalise with the pressure in the lake.' He could see the circular outline of the door in the airlock floor. Beneath which, he guessed, was the moon pool where they'd enter the lake once the door had opened and the pressure had equalised.

'We should stand here beside the control panel,' Peter said, pointing to the floor.

'What is a moon pool anyway?' Daniel walked over to his nephew.

'You'll see,' Peter said, and entered the code into the keypad. He could hear a beeping sound followed by the thud of the entrance hatch closing above them.

There was a short silence, broken by the sound of Daniel's voice. 'One, two, three, four ...'

'What are you doing?' Peter said.

'I don't know. I just felt the need to count,' he said, and watched as a small circle appeared in the floor of the airlock and increased in size until a large portion of the floor was replaced with a pool of still, clear light-blue water.

'There's the moon pool,' Peter said. 'The pressure in the room prevents the water from rising and creates what's known as a moon pool.'

'And I guess we're going to have to get into it?' Daniel said in a dubious tone.

'Yeah. The light-blue colour suggests that the area beneath it is well lit, so we'll be able to see where we're going. We can just jump right in,' Peter said, and before Daniel could express his reservations, his nephew leaped forward into the pool and disappeared out of sight.

Daniel moved to the edge of the opening and watched the water ripple from side to side as he tried to see Peter.

'Peter? Peter, are you alright? Did you make it down there in one piece? Peter, answer me.' Daniel peered into the blue abyss for any sign of his nephew.

'Yes, I'm fine. Just jump, the suit will guide you down,' Peter said.

Daniel took a few deep breaths and bent down to his knees. He looked into the water and could see a hazy light in the distance. He turned and shuffled on all fours until his feet were at the edge of the water. He entered the pool feet first, lowering himself down. When he was submerged to his chest, he looked down once more. Then he inhaled long and deep and held his breath as he lowered his head beneath the water.

'You don't need to hold your breath – just take it easy and take some long deep breaths. I'm right beneath you,' Peter said.

Peter's voice resonated inside Daniel's helmet, as he gradually released his grip. Suddenly he felt his entire body spinning around and around; everything went dark and his mind went blank while his body descended to the bottom. His sense of direction was thrown into disarray.

Then he heard Peter's voice again.

'I have you,' Peter said, and grabbed onto Daniel's leg, pulling him down toward him.

Daniel opened his eyes and looked at Peter. 'I think I passed out. Everything seemed to be spinning,' he said. His legs felt heavy.

'It's the force field generated by the suit. It's a little disorientating at first, but you'll adjust to it,' Peter said, then pointed up. 'Look.'

Daniel arched his neck back and looked up.

The outside of the base was a well-lit windowless mammoth structure that seemed to stretch out forever high above them. The six supporting columns, which held the enormous structure in place, extended from beneath the base to the lakebed, where they were embedded deep within it.

'It's enormous,' Daniel said, walking toward the column

nearest them. 'I'd often heard of UFO activity in the Antarctic and rumours of a secret base beneath the ice, but never in my wildest dreams did I ever imagine anything like this.'

'Well, one good thing has come out of all of this.'

'Yeah?'

'We now know for sure the human race has never been alone.'

Chapter 63

Gibil examined the Nephilim lying unconscious on the ground, then looked up at Ninharsag. 'It is Chasid. I think I have killed him. I thought he was one of ...' Gibil glanced at Sophia and Nabu who were on their knees beside Chasid.

Ninharsag bent down on one knee and examined the wound at the back of Chasid's head. 'He is not dead. It is just a mild concussion,' she said, and placed a small, square device on Chasid's head. She stood up.

'Will he be okay?' Sophia said.

'Yes, he will. We should get him into one of the treatment rooms. Help me to lift him onto a bed. Over there,' she said.

Gibil and Nabu placed Chasid's arms around their necks and carried him into the room next to the lift.

'Can you get him back on his feet?' Nabu said.

Ninharsag removed the neck-piece from Chasid's suit and scanned his head for any sign of brain injury. The scan results appeared the instant the scan had competed as a projection on the glass window of the room.

'There is no visible brain trauma. Just as I thought, it is a mild concussion. He will be back on his feet in a moment,' she said to Nabu and removed a small vial from the counter behind her. She opened it and placed it beneath Chasid's nostrils. Sophia watched as Chasid came around. He moved his head from side to side and reached his hands forward in an effort to sit up.

'You should lie down for a moment and get your bearings. You have suffered a mild concussion,' Ninharsag said, and placed her hand on Chasid's chest. He smiled affectionately at her.

'Have you seen Peter, Daniel and Emily?' Sophia asked Nabu her voice soft and quiet.

'Yes,' Chasid said, and sat upright, rubbing the back of his head. 'Emily is in the observatory. She is monitoring our communications. The others are beneath the base,' Chasid said, and turned to Ninharsag. 'Where is Gibil? We need him to tell Peter and Daniel how to disarm the weapon before Nergal has a chance to detonate it. They should have reached it by now.'

'I am here,' Gibil replied.

Chasid smiled at Gibil who was hovering nervously behind him. 'Good, then we should get going.'

'Please don't tell me my brother is anywhere near a nuclear weapon,' Sophia said a cautious undertone could be heard in her voice.

'Yes, he is. Abaddon has succeeded in placing the weapon beneath the base. As we speak, Nergal is trying to retrieve the control key, so that he can bring the Ark to the hangar bay. His plan is to then evacuate any Nephilim loyal to him from the base before he detonates the weapon.'

'There will be no Earth or humans to rule after that weapon goes off. If the ice caps are shifted from their current position, much of Earth will be destroyed. Nergal knows this,' Ninharsag said.

'In fact he is counting on it. That is why he wants the Ark. He will sail in the safety of our aircraft above the Earth until the tides recede. The Ark can power any Nephilim technology that remains on Earth, so Nergal will have what he needs to reshape the planet and rule the remaining Nephilim and humans as he sees fit,' he said.

Nabu moved closer to the treatment room window and scanned the corridor outside.

'That's madness!' Sophia said.

'Yes, it is. And I am afraid the insanity of Nergal's plans has sadly never stopped him before.' Chasid stood up. 'Where are the rest of the medical staff?'

'I told them to leave. They went to the hangar bay before Nergal took control of the lifts. I can only hope that they have escaped.'

'Chasid,' Ninharsag whispered, 'Gibil has not fully recovered from his injuries yet. His short-term memory has been affected so he has no memory of what happened at the weapons storage—'.

'Someone's approaching,' Nabu whispered.

Instinctively Chasid reached to his waist. 'Where is my weapon?' he said.

'It is out there.' Ninharsag pointed to the gun on the corridor floor.

'Please tell me you have some sort of weapon in here?'

'No weapons are allowed on this floor. You know my rules.'

'Now would be a good time to review those rules.' Chasid walked toward the glass partition. He scanned the entire area, not listening to Ninharsag as she vented off behind him.

'You come in here, day after day, with pieces of you hanging off. With pieces of you missing. Some of you on the brink of death and some of you hours after you have experienced death, expecting me to piece you all back together. Most of those injuries are caused by those weapons. So no, there are no weapons allowed in here. This is a

317

medical and research floor, however—' Ninharsag said. She turned to face Chasid who had already left the room, retrieved his weapon and had worked his way toward Gibil, who smiled with relief when Chasid reached his side. 'And then you walk away from me without listening to a word I am saying,' she said, and walked to the wall to her right. She placed her hand on a scanner embedded into the wall and waited as a section, over six feet high and three wide, became transparent. Ninharsag placed her hand into the space and retrieved a long golden staff from inside.

'I do, however, have the staff my brother gifted me. It is more powerful than any weapon you are permitted to use and if you had stayed and listened to me, I might have let you borrow it,' Ninharsag said. She glanced in Sophia's direction, then out onto the corridor.

'Sophia, find somewhere safe and hide. Do not come out no matter what,' she said, and left the room.

The images of the intruders were reflected in the glass in front of Nabu. He could see Nergal's image approaching, followed by two other armed Nephilim.

'It is Nergal. We had better go. I will contact Emily and get her to send the lift to this floor,' Nabu said, and gestured in the direction of the lift. He rushed back into the treatment room where Sophia was hiding.

'I need to get you somewhere safe,' Chasid whispered to Gibil. 'I have sent someone to the weapon and I need you to tell him how to disarm it.'

'Somewhere safe sounds good. What do you propose?' Gibil said, and looked toward the lift to his right. Ninharsag was approaching where they stood holding his father's golden staff. 'Perhaps Ninharsag can help,' Gibil whispered.

'I do not think so. She does not like weapons and will most probably just get in my way.'

'I would not underestimate her. She is quite resourceful.' Gibil nodded in her direction.

Chasid turned to her.

'I will hold him off for as long as I can. You go where you need to go,' she said in a low voice.

Chasid and Gibil made a dash in the direction of the lift behind her. Chasid looked back to see Nergal now standing at the opposite end of the corridor.

'That is one hell of a weapon for someone who detests them,' Chasid whispered to Ninharsag as he ushered Gibil into the room where Sophia and Nabu were waiting for the lift to arrive.

'Indeed it is. However, I am not sure if I can remember how to use it. So I suggest you make your move now before Nergal realises that it may be of no use to me,' she whispered. She held the staff in front of her.

'Emily has confirmed the lift is on its way now,' Nabu said.

'Good, then—' Chasid began.

'I take it you were expecting me?' Nergal shouted.

'Why are you doing this?' Ninharsag said.

Nergal grinned as he walked toward her. 'All I want is the human female. You will not be harmed,' he said.

Chasid and Nabu moved to the treatment room door. Chasid signalled to Sophia and Gibil to remain behind him. He could hear the hum of the lift descending; soon they could make their escape.

Nergal stopped suddenly when he saw the golden staff in Ninharsag's hand. He knew, depending on the setting that Ninharsag had chosen, that one blast from the staff could kill in an instant. It was one of the main reasons Marduk, at

Ninharsag's request, had banned such weapons and only allowed the Nephilim to carry human weapons, the wounds from which were much more easily fixed.

He eyed Sophia standing next to Gibil in the treatment room nearest the lift. His glare moved to Chasid and Nabu who had inched closer to Ninharsag, their weapons drawn.

'I am guessing you still have no idea how to use that,' he said, then gestured in Sophia's direction. 'Seize her!'

The two guards flanking Nergal drew their weapons and advanced on Sophia. Chasid held his weapon level and fired a warning shot past the two Nephilim who instantly returned fire.

Sophia cowered to her knees and covered her head, she was joined by Gibil.

The bullets bounced off the glass in the medical wing and ricocheted in every direction, one missing Nergal by inches. 'Aim away from the glass,' he yelled. 'It is bulletproof, you idiots! Now seize her.'

Ninharsag stepped forward and fired Enki's staff with skilled precision. Spheres of light flew from it as she returned fire killing one of Nergal's soldiers and forcing the other to take cover at the end of the corridor. The continued fire from Chasid and Nabu had forced Nergal's men to take cover in the rooms on either side of the corridor. There was a momentary silence as she walked toward Nergal, who had taken cover in a doorway near the Ark vault shaft. She pointed the staff at his chest. Nergal raised his hands and dropped his weapon to the floor.

This is too easy, Chasid thought and scanned the area around him.

Nabu moved to the lift that had opened behind them as Chasid went over to Sophia.

'Come with me,' he said and helped her to her feet and toward the lift.

As they made their way to safety Sophia glanced back at Nergal. 'Behind you,' she yelled, and released her grip on Chasid's arm. But it was too late.

Micah and a group of Nergal's men had taken a different route to his accomplices. They had moved unnoticed around the circumference of the medical floor and had exited onto the corridor through one of the smaller rooms closer to the Ark vault shaft. He discharged a bullet at Ninharsag, hitting her right arm. She dropped the staff and fell to her knees.

Nergal grabbed the staff and ran to the lift. Sophia in a panic moved back into the treatment room. Chasid tried to follow her, but was forced back toward the lift when a bullet pierced his thigh. Nabu ran to him and helped him into the lift as Gibil returned fire at Micah and his men. Nabu leaned on the lift button and watched as the doors began to close.

'Sophia!' Chasid shouted. She ran toward them, but Nergal was only feet behind her. He grabbed her arm, pulling her back.

Chasid had no other option but to watch as the doors closed and Sophia disappeared out of view.

Chapter 64

'Should we take our helmets off?' Daniel said. They were in the area beneath the base that was surrounded by the force field.

'Perhaps not. I know Chasid said the force field protects this area underneath the bottom of the base from the increased pressure and keeps the water out but just in case, we'll leave them on,' Peter said. He kept what he was really thinking to himself: he was keeping his helmet on in case he needed to leave in a hurry.

'It's bigger than I thought,' Daniel said. He glanced around him in every direction. He was encircled by a huge wall of water that gave off a bluish hue.

'Yeah,' Peter said pensively and examined the tall white weapon next to the supporting column.

'You know, I bet these weapons are the same as the ones they used to destroy Sodom and Gomorrah,' Daniel said.

'Yes, they are.' The unfamiliar foreign accent echoed through Peter and Daniel's helmets. 'I was there when we used them.' A wide cunning grin was etched across the stranger's face as he gloated over the Nephilim's past annihilations on Earth.

After intercepting Nannar's communication, Abaddon had chosen to go to the weapon to stop Chasid from disarming it, instead of to the control room to warn Nergal that Chasid was back on the base. Adira had been monitoring all frequencies and had by some stroke of luck tuned into Chasid's secret communications channel allowing him to hear every word being said, including Daniel and Peter's communication on the way to the weapon.

Peter turned around. Behind Daniel stood the tall figure of a Nephilim, his blue eyes radiating a bloodthirsty gaze in Peter's direction.

Daniel looked at the reflection in his nephew's visor. His eyes widened as Peter shouted, 'Behind you!' and moved forward to grab his arm.

Abaddon lunged at Daniel and raised a dagger high above him. He plunged it into his chest. Daniel fell forward and was thrust further by the force of Abaddon lifting him off his feet and throwing him to one side.

Peter ran away from Abaddon toward the pillar at the furthest end of the base. He could hear each breath he took echo in his helmet. He glanced back. Abaddon was closing in on his prey. He grabbed the back of Peter's suit and thrust him backward, flinging him to the lakebed. Abaddon bent over him, his hands around Peter's neck. Warning signals flashed in Peter's visor alerting him to his decreased oxygen state.

All of a sudden Abaddon's actions were interrupted by a voice.

'Peter? Can you hear me, Peter? We have Gibil.'

Abaddon recognised the voice without delay. 'Peter is dead. And I am coming for you next, Chasid,' he said, and raised his hand high above his head.

Peter watched the dagger in Abaddon's fist move toward him. He grabbed Abaddon's arm with both his hands and tried to stop him. But he was too strong. The dagger edged closer to his chest. Peter looked around for something he could use to defend himself, but there was nothing. Then to his relief, out of the corner of his eye, Peter saw a long grey object travelling toward the back of Abaddon's head. It crashed into his helmet and he watched as Abaddon released his grip, dropped the dagger and moved his hands to his helmet. Peter crawled along the lakebed gasping for air.

Abaddon turned toward his attacker and was once again struck by the object. He looked at Daniel who was preparing to thrust the thin cylinder at him once again and watched as a crack spread across his visor. He could see by the intermittent display that his suit was failing and his oxygen levels were running low. Abaddon reached for the button to remove his helmet, but was thwarted by Daniel who dealt a further crushing blow to his abdomen.

Abaddon faltered backward out beyond the edge of the force field into the water and out of the protection of the vacuum beneath the base. He could feel the crushing force of the lake above him bearing down on him as his suit failed. Unable to move, he watched the warning signals displayed on his visor telling him he was about to be crushed by the pressure. Abaddon laughed as he was forced to his knees. He looked at Daniel. 'I underestimated you,' he said, as his suit's force field gave way and the pressure from the weight of the water above him shattered his body. He shook violently as he fell forward onto the lakebed.

Daniel helped Peter up. 'Are you okay?'

'I'm fine,' Peter said. 'I thought you were dead.'

'I have nine lives, you know,' Daniel said.

Peter heaved a sigh of relief, then saw the congealed blood on Daniel's shoulder. 'You're hurt!'

'Really, I'm fine. The material in the suit is designed to compensate for wear and tear by regenerating and compressing against my skin. See, it's already covered the wound and is applying enough pressure to stall the bleeding. Gibil told me I should be okay.' Daniel dropped the metal cylinder to the ground.

'Where did you get that?'

'Chasid released it from beneath the base. He was watching what was happening from the communications room. It's a maintenance rod from the life support systems.'

Peter placed his hands on his knees and breathed heavily. He glanced out beyond the force field and into the water where Abaddon's body was crushed on the lakebed.

'That was close,' Peter said and patted Daniel on the back.

'Peter, Daniel, we do not have much time. We need to deactivate the weapon. Are you ready?' Chasid said and returned their focus to the weapon.

'Yes.' Peter walked back to the weapon beside the column. 'What do we need to do?'

'There is a maintenance panel on the front of the weapon. Open it by placing your hands over the small sensors located on either side, about halfway down the weapon,' Chasid said. There was a momentary silence followed by the sound of gunshots.

'Chasid, are you there?' Peter said in an anxious tone.

But there was silence. Their communication had gone dead.

Peter looked at Daniel. 'I guess we're on our own.'

Chapter 65

The first round of shots from Ninurta and his henchmen had missed their targets and were embedded in the equipment and the walls. Chasid and Nabu had taken up a defensive position behind the workstations in the centre of the communications room.

'I counted five,' Chasid said.

'I concur,' Nabu said, 'including Ninurta.'

Chasid glanced over at Emily. She was curled up on the ground next to Gibil.

He removed a small sphere from the utility belt on his waist and held it in his outstretched hand signalling to Gibil and Nabu that he was about to throw a photoreceptor stun grenade at the enemy. Chasid could see Gibil talking to Emily then they buried their heads between their knees and covered their ears with their hands as bullets slammed into the walls and equipment of the control room.

'Cover me and when I release the clip, you will have three seconds to protect your eyes and ears or the blast will deafen and blind you,' Chasid said to Nabu, and donned his helmet.

They stood up. Nabu fired shots at Ninurta's men. At the same instant Chasid removed a small ring from the top of the sphere and threw it across the control room and out into the corridor. Nabu counted from the moment Chasid pulled the ring from the device. When he reached three, he pivoted around and shielded his eyes and ears from the blast.

The visor on Chasid's helmet protected him from the blinding and deafening chaos that ensued. He watched as the sphere landed on the corridor beside Ninurta and his men. The fuse inside the device burned down to the magnesium-based explosive in its centre, resulting in a huge explosion of light and sound.

Chasid vaulted the workstation in front of him, and pulling the handgun from his waistband, he ran out into the corridor. His enemies were doubled over on the ground. The bright light from the blast had overloaded their photoreceptors for a short time. They were disoriented and paralysed, but Chasid knew he needed to act fast. He counted five Nephilim on the ground including Ninurta. He moved between them and removed their weapons. When the blinding light and noise had subsided, Nabu followed Chasid out into the corridor.

'Get up!' Chasid yelled, and grabbed Ninurta who clambered to his feet. His eyes were wide, his ears ringing and his vision blurred. Nabu rushed to the others lying stunned on the ground and roused them to their feet.

'We should lock them into the polar gear room,' Nabu said, and pushed Ninurta forward, followed by his men who were still dazed and confused from the blast. Chasid opened the storage room door and gestured to Ninurta to move inside.

'Nergal will win,' Ninurta said, as he walked into the storage room.

Chasid was about to respond, but was distracted by the sound of an incoming communication hail that emanated from the display panel of his suit. Chasid lifted his arm, looked at the screen and smiled as Nabu glared at Ninurta and slammed the storage room door shut before shooting the lock to prevent it from being opened any time soon.

Chasid touched the display panel on his sleeve as he walked with Nabu back into the communications room. He stood beside Gibil and Emily and answered the call, a call he had been expecting from an old friend.

'Chasid, I received your message and sent the frequency to Nannar as you requested. We are now on a secure link using one of our own satellites.' The caller's strong American accent echoed from the phone.

'General Cullen, it is good to hear from you. The iridium communications network was not safe. I knew our enemy would try to use it too, so that is why I requested the signal change. We are still on course to disarm the weapon. Where are you now?' Chasid said.

'We are five minutes out,' the American said.

'Then go to the coordinates I am sending you now and follow the base's ventilation systems to the hangar bay and wait for my signal,' Chasid said.

Chapter 66

We may need an ally on Nergal's side.

From his post at the main control panel near the Ark vault shaft, in the centre of the control room, Yotum watched on as the words Nannar had said to him earlier rustled through his mind. From his vantage point he could feel the air of apprehension building around the remaining Nephilim after Nergal had left for the medical floor. Most of the Nephilim had been evacuated from the base and in a change of plan Nergal decided to create a prison ship. Those who remained loyal to Marduk were on board to await Nergal's final decision on their fate. All the other Nephilim, willing to live in Nergal's new world, had been evacuated and those still in the base holding things together while Nergal finalised his plans were growing increasingly nervous.

'He will leave you behind,' Marduk said. He was staring at Micah who had just re-entered the control room and was busy coordinating Marduk's ships as they entered the exosphere and went into orbit high above the Earth.

'Your attempts to distract or undermine me will not work. I am here to finish my task. Then I will join our new leader and with him create a world where the Nephilim will rule as we should,' Micah said, his gaze fixed on the screen in front of him.

As Marduk and Micah spoke to each other, Nannar covertly brought Yotum's attention to Marduk's staff lying on the floor only feet from him. Nannar nodded in Marduk's direction indicating to Yotum to pass the staff to him. Nergal had already tried to use his brother's staff, but soon realised it had been encoded to Marduk's DNA at Ninharsag's request. Marduk had been unwilling to hand over the weapon to her so she wanted to ensure only he could use it.

Yotum looked at the two guards opposite him and nodded his head. He had earlier sought their alliance and knew they were awaiting his signal to begin the fight against Nergal. Yotum also knew that once Marduk had his staff in his possession, they could take down the five remaining Nephilim loyal to Nergal and their plan to retake the base could forge ahead.

Marduk turned his attention to Micah in an effort to keep him occupied. 'Do you think he will allow you the freedom you have enjoyed for the past two millennia? My brother's idea of leadership is akin to that of a tyrant. He will dictate and you will follow or you will perish,' Marduk said.

With the exception of Yotum and Nannar all eyes in the room were focused on Marduk and Micah. Some of the guards began to twitch nervously as the gravity of their situation dawned on them.

'What is taking so long? Why have we not left with the others?' said the guard nearest the lift.

Micah raised his head and walked toward him.

At the same instant, out of Micah's line of sight, Yotum took a step closer to the staff.

'Pay no attention to anything he says. He is just trying unnerve you. Yes, most of the aircraft have left the base, but his goliath ship awaits us in the hangar bay. We will take the journey to our new world with our new leader, Nergal. When he has secured the Ark, we will leave with him and watch as he wipes the landscape clean,' Micah said, and turned his back on the young Nephilim guard.

'I have suffered your babble for long enough, Micah,' the guard said, and pointed his weapon at Micah's back.

'How dare you ...' Micah said as he grabbed his gun

and swung round only to be greeted by the sight of Marduk raising his hand to catch his staff.

Marduk eyed those loyal to him as they unarmed Nergal's men and took back control of the base. 'Drop your weapon and surrender. Or I will kill you,' Marduk said, and held his staff against Micah's chest.

Chapter 67

'Chasid is proving to be more resourceful than we had anticipated. There was an explosion in the observatory a few moments ago and we have since lost contact with Ninurta. I request permission to go to the observatory and get the control key from him myself,' said one of Nergal's men, standing to attention awaiting Nergal's approval.

Nergal stood beside the control panel in the hangar bay and watched the on-screen image of the weapon lying idle beneath the base.

'That will not be necessary. DeMolay is about to bring me the control key himself,' Nergal said, and eyed the only other place in the base where the control key could be used to open the Ark vault and bring the Ark to the hangar bay. He rotated his ornately decorated dagger in his hand and watched as the precious stone in the handle glistened beneath the hangar bay lights. A sense of pride swelled within him. Soon everything he'd planned to achieve would be within his grasp. Peter DeMolay would do exactly as he had been told to do and bring him the control key in return for his mother.

'Abaddon has still not arrived at the base. Communications are still offline, so take a team and go to the Vostok Research Station and find out why he has been delayed,' Nergal said, and looked across the hangar bay as Ninharsag's voice echoed toward him.

'How dare you touch me!' she yelled at the two Nephilim soldiers ushering her and Sophia across the hangar bay to Nergal.

He returned his dagger to his waist and walked toward them, tipping the golden staff he'd taken from Ninharsag off the floor in unison with each alternative step.

'She is just a woman. You do not need to fear her,' Nergal said in a quiet tone. He lifted the golden staff and pointed it at her. His top lip twitched as he tried to contain his temper.

Ninharsag glared back at Nergal. 'When my brothers hear of what you have done—'

'Your brothers are on the other side of the solar system. You can scream to them if you like, but I do not think they will hear you.' Nergal turned his attention to Sophia. 'I hasten to burden you again, but your son is proving to be somewhat of a nuisance. My brother has foolishly given him something I need.' Nergal nodded to the Nephilim guard standing behind Sophia. The guard placed a chair beside Nergal.

'Has Micah opened the base's public address channel?' Nergal said.

'Yes, your Majesty,' the Nephilim guard said.

'Good. I want to be sure that DeMolay can hear what is happening,' Nergal said, and turned to Sophia. 'You will need to sit. This may take a couple of minutes and I need you to survive as long as you can,' Nergal said. He arched his head forward toward Sophia and removed the dagger from his waist.

'Now sit!'

Chapter 68

The bronze-coloured sphere was suspended in the space behind the opened panel. Peter examined the area around it cautiously then placed his hands on the casing either side of the weapon. He could feel the area around the sphere vibrating. He took a step back and looked up along the length of the weapon.

'I'm guessing the top part contains the guidance system. The bronze sphere is the detonator. There's no visible wires keeping it suspended like it is, but I can feel this section vibrate. It must be some sort of sound, some kind of resonance that's keeping it suspended in mid-air. This panel here beneath the sphere must be the radiation shield. It's keeping me from seeing if the nuclear material is below it. There must be another panel on here somewhere,' Peter said.

'Radiation shield?' Daniel said, and took a step backward.

'Don't worry. The radiation levels being picked up by the sensors on our suits are well within safety ranges. The suits will protect us.' Peter checked the display on his visor once more. 'How can I think when I don't even know if my mother and Emily will make it out of here alive?' he said quietly.

'Emily is with Chasid and Nabu. And Sophia is with Ninharsag. Odds are they're safer than we are right now,' Daniel said, eyeing the nuclear weapon.

Peter examined the area around the detonator. There was nothing: no wires, just the white casing with the detonator suspended in the centre. He knelt down and examined the rest of the weapon. It was seamless: there were no other visible openings anywhere.

'Just stick your hand in and pull the sphere out. It's the detonator – if you remove it, then perhaps the weapon will be disarmed,' Daniel said. He couldn't see any other options.

Peter stood up. 'If you were here on your own, is that what you'd do?'

'Well, yeah.'

Peter gave his uncle a worried look. 'I don't think it's that simple somehow. You know, I'm glad I'm here with you.'

'And so am I.' A familiar voice resounded through their helmets.

Chapter 69

'What is our status?' Marduk said.

Nannar glanced at the huge glass screen that encircled the Ark vault shaft. All of the base's activities were displayed at various points across it. 'Chasid contacted me through an archaic communications channel just before I surrendered to Nergal and apprised me of the situation. I uploaded a programme to the base's computer systems before I was captured, and isolated two communications channels for us to use that Nergal will have no access to. Chasid has also secured a further communications satellite from the Americans,' Nannar said, and continued to move icons to rearrange the base's systems as he spoke to Marduk. 'Chasid has gone to Gibil. They should be disarming the weapon as we speak.'

'I do not think he has reached it yet. The image of the weapon has remained the same. I have been monitoring that screen since Nergal came and took over the control room,' Marduk said.

Nannar smiled at him. 'The surveillance footage of the weapon you see on screen is a replay from earlier today. What Nergal and Micah have been looking at is nothing more than an illusion I uploaded to the computer systems. Your brother became so focused on the control key he did not notice the glitch. When I came in here and stopped the evacuation protocol, I blindsided them. Nergal is in the hangar bay. I will return our security systems back online and make sure that Nergal's illusion is maintained on the screens there. It will buy us some more time before he realises we have taken control down here,' Nannar said.

The control screens went blank for a moment then

returned to life. At once Marduk was drawn to the image of Peter and Daniel at the weapon, then to the security surveillance image of his brother standing over Sophia in the hangar bay.

'What is he doing?' Marduk said.

'He is going to torture her and use her to get the humans to give him the control key. Soon he will have the Ark and you will be wiped off the face of the Earth. The only ones who have been fooled here are you and those who are foolish enough to follow you,' Micah said. He was kneeling in front of Yotum with his hands bound behind his back. A sense of pride at Nergal's willingness to do anything to achieve his goals was evident in his voice as he glared at Nannar and Marduk.

Marduk gave Micah a look of disgust. 'I know my brother's philosophy well. In order to create, sometimes you need to sacrifice, even destroy everything. But I have stood on the precipice of his terror before and have suffered his unrelenting lust for power. And every time he has been defeated, just as he will be today.' Marduk turned his back on Micah and looked once again at the screens.

'What are they doing?' Marduk pointed to the image of Peter and Daniel beneath the base.

Nannar placed his index finger and thumb on the image and spread them apart to enlarge it.

'They are trying to disarm the weapon. I have been monitoring Chasid and Gibil's communications through this.' Nannar removed a small round transparent disc from behind his ear.

'Open a secure channel,' Nannar said.

'Opening secure channel,' said the female voice, followed by a high-pitched beep.

'Chasid?' Marduk said.

'Your Majesty,' Chasid said in a relieved tone.

'It is good to hear your voice, my friend. The two humans – are you sure they know what they are doing?'

'Yes. Your brother Gibil is here with me and is assisting them. They are deactivating the weapon as we speak. And we still have the control key in our possession.'

'Your Majesty …' Chasid hesitated for a moment, '… Nergal has evacuated most of the Nephilim from the base. Only some of those loyal to him remain here until he gains control of the Ark. All those who would not work against you have been imprisoned. Nergal's men are holding them on one of our ships until his new world order is established. We have very few left to fight on our side so I contacted General—'

Chasid's reply was interrupted by the sound of Nergal's voice booming from the base's internal public address system. Marduk tightened his grip on his staff.

~

'Peter DeMolay,' Nergal said, 'I have someone here who wishes to speak to you.'

Nergal lowered the communications device to Sophia. She gripped the sides of her chair and remained silent.

'Speak to your son. Tell him to surrender the control key to me and I will let you live.'

'Go to hell!' she said.

Nergal handed the device to the soldier beside him. 'Make sure he can hear,' Nergal whispered. He nodded to the Nephilim guard behind Sophia who took a firm hold of her shoulders. Nergal lifted his dagger and thrust it into Sophia's thigh. Her screams could be heard throughout the base.

Tears rolled down her cheeks and her hands shook as the pain from her leg rose through her body.

'Peter DeMolay, you have two minutes to bring me the control key,' Nergal said.

'Coward!' Ninharsag yelled at Nergal.

'Be silent. Or you will be next,' Nergal said.

'You would not dare.'

'Do not tempt me; you should know by now no one is beyond my wrath.'

Chapter 70

'Peter, I need you to stay where you are,' Chasid said in a firm voice.

'I have to go and help her. He's hurting her!' Peter yelled back. His voice was frayed with emotion and his mother's screams were ringing in his head as he passed beneath the base and rushed to the airlock ladder.

'Just a few moments more and we will have the weapon disarmed. Then I promise you, I will go to the hangar bay myself and get Sophia back to you alive and in one piece. Peter, your mother can be rescued. If that weapon is detonated, the people who will die as a result cannot.'

'Peter, he's right. My sister is strong and we're almost there. We've come this far. Let's finish this,' Daniel said. Inside he felt a tempest of emotions – fear, anger, frustration, panic – but at the back of his mind hope lingered somewhere in the shadows and he knew that now was not the time to break down. They needed to deactivate the weapon or no one would survive.

Peter made no reply. He stood for a moment staring out beyond the force field then turned back to Daniel. 'Okay, let's do this.' Peter had sensed the pain in Daniel's voice, and he knew this was the right decision. There would be time to deal with Nergal when the weapon was disarmed.

'Peter, you are correct to presume the detonator cannot be removed that easily. There are two sensors at the base of the weapon, on either side. They will open a second panel. It is here that the weapon is deactivated,' Gibil said.

Peter rushed back to the weapon, bent down and placed his hands on the sensors. 'Nothing's happening. It hasn't opened any other panel,' he said, his voice fraught with emotion and impatience.

Gibil looked at the on-screen image of the weapon.

'Peter, the weapon casing is damaged – you will need to force the panel open. Use the flat-headed tool on your utility belt and prise it open,' Gibil said.

'Are you sure that's safe?'

'Yes. Yes, it is safe.'

Emily focused on the image of Peter as he removed the small navy tool from his belt. Without warning her attention was drawn to the sound of Nergal's voice.

'Two minutes are up, Peter. Do I need to remind you that your mother is in pain?'

Emily buried her face in her hands. She couldn't bear to listen. She wiped the tears from her face.

'It's no good, I can't focus,' Peter said, and thumped the weapon. 'I can't do this.'

'Peter,' a familiar voice eased through Peter's helmet, 'I will stop Nergal from hurting your mother. But first you must promise me that you will do everything you can to deactivate that weapon,' Marduk said.

'How? How are you going to stop him?' Peter said.

'I will stop him, Peter, but first I need your reassurance that you will remain where you are and deactivate that weapon.'

Peter took a deep breath. 'I promise, just get her out of there,' he said, and tried once again to prise the panel open.

Marduk turned to Nannar. 'Can you open a communications channel so that Nergal can hear us?'

'Yes,' Nannar said.

'Chasid,' Marduk said.

'Yes, your Majesty,' he said.

'You still have the control key in your possession?'

'Yes I do.'

'Good. Nannar is going to open a communications channel to Nergal. You will inform him that you are on your way to the hangar bay to give him the control key. He does not know yet that we have retaken the control room and this may work to our advantage. We will let my brother think he is standing on the threshold of success – only in the end will he realise that he is on the path to failure.'

Chapter 71

'I had forgotten how uncomfortable battle can be,' Marduk said as he adjusted to the tight, heavy feel of the navy-and-gold-coloured protective battle armour his father had given him when they had last gone to war with his uncle Enlil's forces on Earth.

Nannar smiled at him. 'Perhaps you have put on a few pounds since you wore that last, my young prince. It has been over two thousand years after all.'

Marduk managed a brief laugh and smiled at his trusted friend. He tightened his grip on his staff and stared ahead, composing his thoughts as the lift ascended toward the hangar bay.

'Perhaps ...' he said deep in thought. 'I have become too settled. I have been caught by my brother unaware,' Marduk said.

'Nergal was always going to attack at some point, whether you were prepared or not. What is important now is that we defeat him. What is left of our forces is getting into position, as are the Americans. Do you think your plan will work?' Nannar said.

'Without question it will buy us more time and will force Nergal to place all his cards on the table.'

'But two minutes – is that long enough?'

'It will have to be,' Marduk said. 'You know my father always told me that in one second destinies can be changed forever. But when you have one hundred and twenty seconds to act out your plan, you can control your destiny and mountains can be moved.'

As they ascended to the hangar bay Nannar opened the control panel and stopped the lift just beneath the hangar bay doors. Marduk reached upward and pushed up the maintenance hatch on the lift ceiling. 'Are you ready?' he whispered.

Nannar nodded in response and watched Marduk jump up to the opening and pull himself onto the top of the lift. He reached back inside and grabbed Nannar's arm and effortlessly pulled him out of the lift.

As Marduk stood in silence for a moment and focused on the hangar bay doors in front of him, he felt the gentle vibration of the communications disc located behind his ear, followed by the sound of Chasid's voice.

'Are you in place?'

'Yes,' Marduk said.

'I will be sending you a visual now. Stand by,' Chasid said.

Chapter 72

Chasid kneeled on the lift floor and opened the small white box he had taken from his utility belt. He placed his right index finger into the liquid solution inside and removed the clear lens from its storage place. He held the small object on the tip of his finger and inspected it in detail. The lens was a prototype developed by Nannar to assist the Nephilim as they went about their day-to-day operations. When the digital optical lens was placed on the eye, it provided the wearer with detailed situational information, facial recognition and access to the base's computer networks and other technology, as well as providing infrared and enhanced night vision capability.

He placed his left index finger above his left eye and lifted his eyelid up. He then pulled his lower lid down with the middle finger of his right hand and inserted the lens onto his left eye. He removed the second lens from the liquid solution and inserted it into his right eye. When both lenses were in place, he blinked twice and activated their tiny three-dimensional cameras. A further blink and he activated the digital display. He stood up and removed the control key and his weapon from his utility belt. He placed the weapon on the floor and held the control key. He touched the communications disc hidden behind his ear and opened the secure channel.

'I am entering the hangar bay now,' he said, and left the communications channel open, so that he could be both eyes and ears for those awaiting his signal to attack.

Chasid glanced one last time at the lift display before it chimed and the doors hissed open.

~

The vastness of the scale on which the Nephilim operated on Earth became apparent to General James Cullen as he stared at the breathtaking view across the hangar bay from inside the ventilation shaft. Never before in his life had he witnessed anything like it. He had just travelled over two miles beneath the surface of the Antarctic ice sheet through the base's ventilation shafts and was staring across the expansive space in awe.

He placed the small plastic explosive charges around the ventilation systems grille, then pulled a small computer tablet from his waistband. The small screen displayed a blueprint of the hangar bay floor. Six ventilation shafts were located at different points throughout the bay. One on the north, the west, the south and the eastern sides and two further shafts in the south-east and north-west. Sixty of his most experienced soldiers were divided between each of the shafts waiting for Chasid's command to enter the hangar bay and begin their attack. One by one each of the teams registered their successful placement of the explosive charges and indicated their ready status.

Cullen gazed across the hangar bay once again. Nergal was standing in the centre of the bay staring toward the lift. He followed the path of Nergal's stare: it led to Chasid, who was walking toward Nergal. Chasid came to a stop beside Sophia and handed Nergal the control key.

Nergal snatched it from him and grinned as he walked to the control panel at the edge of the hangar bay and handed the key to a Nephilim operative, who was sitting awaiting his next command.

'Open the vault,' Nergal said. He addressed two guards standing near to Chasid. 'Seize him!' he said. 'He is to be executed with the others in the morning.' Nergal walked toward the large golden-winged disc etched into the floor, the centre of which concealed a ten-foot-diameter circular doorway, which had just begun to open.

Nergal stood above it. A swell of pride engulfed him; his own careful planning and actions had brought him to this moment. He focused on the circular opening in the centre of the doorway as it enlarged until it opened fully. A swell of warm air brushed past Nergal as he listened to the sound of the Ark vault releasing its precious cargo.

Chasid looked around in every direction and blinked to instruct the lenses to begin recording in detail the entire hangar bay and the positions of Nergal's men. He blinked once more and the information from the optical lenses relayed back to Marduk, Nannar and General Cullen.

'Chasid, images are being relayed successfully. We are now awaiting your signal to attack,' Cullen said, and turned to the soldier behind him. 'Notify everyone. Weapons and night vision equipment at the ready. Prepare to enter the hangar bay on my mark,' he whispered.

'Roger that, sir,' the soldier said.

Out of the blue, the young dark-haired soldier behind the general pointed through the ventilation grille across the hangar bay. 'Is that what I think it is?' he said.

Cullen looked in the direction the soldier was pointing. In the distance two objects had been transported from deep within the base to the circular opening in the floor. One was a simple wooden box, about four feet long and two wide and high. The second was a similar size, but covered in gold. Cullen tried to get a closer look. On either end of the gold rectangular box he could see two golden-winged objects seated atop a slab of pure gold. Their wings stretched inward toward each other over and above the golden lid.

The general paused in wonder. *I am actually looking at the Ark of the Covenant.*

This was his signal to get ready. Soon the attack would

begin.

'Stay alert. Be at the ready,' Cullen whispered into his communicator, then removed the pair of clear glasses he had sat atop his head and placed them over his eyes. He scanned the hangar bay in detail using the glasses' X-ray and thermal imaging functions. He was hoping to locate the detonator, but the scans revealed nothing specific. Then Cullen turned on the high frequency millimetre wave scanning function and sent a harmless, undetectable high frequency energy pulse at Nergal and scanned him from head to toe. The high frequency pulse was similar to the signals the Brazilian Tadarida bat emits while it hunts its prey in the dark. The three millimetre wavelengths that the frequency emitted made less dense objects, like clothing, become transparent, but the sensors in Cullen's glasses would be able to detect the energy naturally emitted from more dense objects such as the detonator.

Cullen sat in silence and analysed the images displayed in the glasses. Suddenly he felt a shot of adrenaline rush through him as he eyed a small rectangular object: the detonator trigger was secured to Nergal's belt.

'The detonator is on his belt. On the front left-hand side.' Cullen sent the image to Chasid. He ran through Chasid's plan of attack once more in his head. The golden artefact had appeared in the hangar bay and marked the start of Chasid's initiative to take back control of the base.

Cullen watched Nergal and a team of four Nephilim approach the Ark. The Nephilim soldiers stood on either side of it, bent to their knees and placed their shoulders beneath the golden bars that jutted out from it on all four corners. Nergal smiled. The Ark was his. The weapon was in place. Everything he had spent the last two thousand years dreaming of would soon be a reality.

Nergal signalled to the Nephilim to lift the Ark from the

vault and carry it to Marduk's ship.

'One, two, three, lift,' the Nephilim soldiers said in unison, and heaved the heavy golden Ark up from its resting place as they stood up.

Nergal watched with pride as the Ark rose above the golden platform that had delivered it from the vault. The Nephilim soldiers moved across the golden platform, the weight of the Ark evident in their faces.

Suddenly the entire hangar bay was thrust into darkness as the Ark passed the threshold of the circular platform it had been resting on. Just as Marduk had planned. The signal to commence his attack had come exactly as he said it would.

Chapter 73

The instant the Ark was lifted over the threshold of the golden platform on which it had been resting, Marduk knew the base would be plunged into darkness for one hundred and twenty seconds before the emergency lighting and backup solar-powered systems kicked in. He was betting that Nergal had not anticipated this. This was the weak spot in his plan that Marduk had been searching for.

In the instant that the darkness came, Chasid blinked twice and turned on the thermal imaging and infrared sensors in his eye lenses allowing him to see what was happening in the darkness of the hangar bay. Explosions blasted out high above him, as General Cullen and his team of operatives blew the grilles from the front of the ventilation shafts and entered the hangar bay. The American forces were doing exactly as Marduk had planned: they were rounding up Nergal's loyal followers with ease, using thermal imaging to see the enemy running for cover unequipped and unprepared.

Chasid looked beyond Nergal to the opening lift doors; the familiar silhouettes of Marduk and Nannar appeared from the lift shaft. Even through the darkness Chasid could see a vengeful gaze in Marduk's eyes as he approached Nergal.

In the eighty seconds that had passed since the darkness filled the hangar bay, Nergal's eyes had begun to adjust. He hurried to his right remembering where he'd left Ninharsag's golden staff. He discharged the weapon in every direction trying to bring Chasid's forces to their knees.

Suddenly Nergal sensed someone approaching from behind. He pivoted around and pointed the staff at his enemy. He released a blast of energy from his weapon, but his attempt to immobilise his brother failed. Someone had come between Marduk and Nergal's shot and had taken the hit instead.

Marduk held his staff level in front of him and released a sphere of energy hitting Nergal in the chest. He watched as Nergal spun around in the air before landing with a thud on his back.

At one hundred and twenty seconds the emergency lighting kicked in and the hangar bay was once again illuminated.

Marduk approached his brother, who had dragged himself to his knees. Nergal was holding the detonator in his left hand.

'What is your status, Gibil?' Marduk whispered.

'We need some more time. The weapon casing is damaged and we cannot reach the deactivation switch,' Gibil said.

Marduk moved toward Nergal. 'You need to think about what you are doing,' he said.

'I have, for two thousand long years, so I guess we have reached an impasse, brother. If the Earth cannot be mine, then you will not have it either,' Nergal said, and activated the detonator.

Chapter 74

The second panel on the bottom of the weapon had at last become unstuck. Peter held it in his hand as he stood up.

'Okay, Gibil. What should I do now?' Peter said.

There was no response from Gibil.

Peter frowned and looked at Daniel, then back at the weapon. 'Gibil, are you there?' he said again.

'Yes, yes, Peter, I am here. I have just remembered something. Something that happened earlier. I remember that I had removed the nuclear material from one of the weapons before Abaddon had entered the weapons storage room. I just cannot remember which one,' Gibil said.

Peter glanced at Daniel then without warning their attention was drawn to the weapon. The sphere had begun to emit a bright green light, indicating that the signal to begin its detonation sequence had been received.

'Gibil, what's happening?' he said.

'Peter, the detonator has been armed. You have sixty seconds,' Gibil said.

Peter looked at Daniel. 'Run!' he shouted.

A rush of adrenaline carried them toward the section of the force field closest to them. Peter knew that once the detonator was activated, fractions of a second later the inside of the sphere would reach an optimum density, and a fission chain reaction within the core of the sphere would begin. As the atoms in the core started a process of transmutation, the sphere would begin to expand as energy from the atomic reactions was released.

And that was just the beginning.

Peter edged closer to the force field glancing behind at Daniel. He stopped suddenly and his eyes widened. Behind Daniel he could see the blue flames from the explosion reach out toward them. Their time was up.

The sphere of energy from the explosion expanded and rushed outward in all directions at once, lifting Daniel and Peter off their feet and thrusting them toward the force field. Peter raised his arms high in front of him in an effort to protect himself as the flames sprinted toward him and the high velocity shock waves carried them forward.

A split second later Peter felt his body being dragged backward toward the source of the explosion. It grew hotter and the display on his visor was flashing various warning lights to apprise him of his increasingly dire situation. Then suddenly, everything went blank and Peter was drawn into a dark chasm.

Chapter 75

'No!' Nergal yelled long and hard.

The cataclysmic explosion he had been expecting was replaced by a faint tremor beneath the base. He stared ahead in disbelief as Chasid coordinated an array of Nephilim who were arranging to have the Arks restored to the vault, the injured brought to the medical bay and the remainder of Nergal's men on the base brought into custody.

Nergal struggled as Yotum and another Nephilim guard grabbed him by the arms and dragged him to his feet.

'Put him into the holding cells and this time make sure he cannot get out,' Marduk said.

'Yes, your Majesty,' Yotum said, and pushed Nergal forward.

'Your Majesty, as regards the others – Nergal's allies on board your ships – I uploaded a manual override to all your aircraft at Chasid's request,' Nannar said. 'We now have full control of them. Where would you suggest we send them?'

Marduk thought for a moment and smiled.

'Send them to the Cydonia complex. Some time to think about their indiscretions while they wait to be judged for their actions will serve them well.'

Nannar nodded in agreement. The old Nephilim base on Mars would provide the perfect place for Nergal's followers to appreciate the gravity of what they had done.

Nannar stood in front of the vast aircraft traffic control screen in the hangar bay and watched the locations of Marduk's ships in orbit around Earth. He pushed an icon on screen and hailed the ships. The delicate ping, indicating the open channel, sailed through his head. It was his prelude to a breathtaking symphony, one composed by his own hands. A symphony that would seal their victory over Nergal and return all those who so easily turned against Marduk back to face their fate at his hands. Slowly the commanders of each aircraft appeared on screen, a look of trepidation etched on their faces as Nannar's image greeted them.

'Nergal has been defeated. If you surrender now, it will be taken into account when you are judged for your actions. Those of you who do not will have to face the consequences.'

'Remain at your positions! Nergal is still alive. This is some sort of trick to get us to surrender,' Ava said.

Nannar turned his attention to the bottom of the screen where Ava's image was displayed. She was flanked on her right by Maggie O'Connell. Nannar gave the astrophysicist who had deceived them for so long a stern glance.

'Nergal is in custody and the weapon has been deactivated. If you surrender now, we will be lenient toward you. If you do not, you will spend the remainder of your days aboard that ship adrift in space,' Nannar said.

'We will never surrender to you,' Ava said, and closed her communications channel.

Unexpectedly a familiar female voice hailed through the open channel. 'Nannar?'

'Ereshkigal,' Nannar said, 'it is good to hear your voice.'

'And yours. This is Nergal's prison ship. We have taken control of it and are returning to base.'

'You will be welcomed with open arms.'

'What about the others?' Ereshkigal said.

355

Nannar looked at the images below him. 'Twelve have signalled their surrender. The others will be sent to our old way station in the Cydonia complex on Mars. I am sure some time there will lighten their spirits.'

Chapter 76

Peter raised his hands and waved them in front of him. The display on his visor was filled with flashing warning signals as his environmental suit compensated for the changing environment he had been thrust into. First intense heat followed by an increase in pressure. Then everything went blank again.

Peter took a sharp, long breath and opened his eyes. He could feel a sense of panic and disorientation overcome him. The room spun, but he could hear a familiar muffled voice in the distance. He listened intently trying to focus on what she was saying. The voice became louder and clearer.

It was Emily.

'Are you okay?' she said, and held Peter's hand tight.

'Yeah, I'm fine,' Peter said. 'Where's Daniel?' He sat upright and tried to get out of bed. 'I need to find him … the detonator … the weapon …'

'He's fine. Look, he's in the room next to you.' Emily pointed to the treatment room next door. 'You were really lucky. It was just the detonator that exploded. Gibil had removed the nuclear material from that particular weapon. If they'd placed the detonator in the other weapon, then we'd certainly be dead.'

Peter looked to his right. Daniel was lying on a bed in the adjoining treatment room. He was smiling and chatting to a tall thin Nephilim with shoulder-length grey hair.

'Is that Gibil?'

'That's him,' she said.

'And what about Nergal?'

'He's still alive. He's in a holding cell here on the base until Marduk decides what to do with him. The Nephilim legal system is very complicated, especially when it comes to dealing with royalty. Marduk has to await the decision of the Nephilim Council before Nergal's punishment can be handed down.'

Peter scanned the room then looked at Emily. 'Where's Mum?' Emily smiled back, but he could tell by the look in her eyes that something was wrong.

Daniel limped over to Peter and sat down. What he had to say was never going to be easy. Having lost his own wife suddenly only a few years earlier, he knew the pain that they all would endure would last for an eternity, but over time everyone would become more accustomed to it and it would be easier to bear.

'Sophia's dead,' Daniel said. He knew that Emily wasn't able to say those words. She was fighting back her emotions. The words were too heavy and had stuck in her throat.

Peter looked at his uncle. He could feel an enormous weight bearing down on his chest. 'Then this was all for nothing. She died anyway,' he said, and swallowed hard in an effort to fight back his tears.

Chapter 77

Eleven months later.

Peter walked among the tombstones at Balantrodoch. Everything around him was familiar; his father had brought him here many times. He stopped beside his parents' grave and stood in silence as he recalled his father's final diary entry.

At that sacred place that was yours and mine. Immortality does lie at the passage of time.

Peter took Emily's hand. She smiled at him and placed their joined hands protectively on her growing abdomen.

'I hope he's not going to make an impromptu appearance,' Daniel said, holding tight to his satchel as he came to a stop beside her.

'No. He's a good boy. He won't arrive a minute before he's supposed to,' she said. 'Did you find anything?'

'There're a couple of tombstones with Templar skulls, crossbones and an hourglass over there. The verse Marcus left could refer to any one of them. There's nothing like we saw at the pyramids. There're no secret doors or chambers here,' Daniel said.

As she gazed at the ruins of the old church, Emily hoped to find some sort of closure. Something that would tie up the loose ends. If not for her, then for Peter. But it was late afternoon and the sunlight had begun to fade. They would have to return home soon.

'There's only one tombstone here with both an archangel and an hourglass on it. It's over there. My instinct tells me that Dad may have buried something in that grave.

Perhaps he had something with him when he came here that night. Something he didn't want anyone to find out about,' Peter said, and pointed back toward the church.

'So, do you think we should start digging? We'll be defacing consecrated ground,' Daniel said.

Peter laughed. 'When has that ever stopped you before?'

'Never. I have a shovel in the boot. I'll go get it,' Daniel said, and jogged over to his car.

'He has a shovel in his boot! Doesn't that bother you? Don't you find that just a little unnerving? Why would he have a shovel in his boot?' Emily whispered.

Peter laughed and placed his arm around her. 'He's just well prepared,' he said, and smiled affectionately at his wife as they walked over to the tombstone.

'Where should I start?' Daniel said, wielding a small black twelve-inch folding archaeologist's shovel.

'Try up near the tombstone. Gently does it,' Peter said, and watched his uncle remove the top layer of grass and a small layer of soil from the top left corner near the base of the tombstone. Daniel dug around the area and sifted through the soil to check it for anything unusual. He removed a couple of stones, but there was nothing else. He moved to his right and dug in the top centre of the grave, under the tombstone. The shovel hit against something metal. He stopped for a moment and looked back at Peter and Emily. He could see a small shiny black object hidden in the dirt. With his hands Daniel cleared away the soil from around the object then removed it and wiped it down with a tissue from his trouser pocket.

'It's another cylinder,' Emily said.

'The same as the one Raziel gave you, only smaller,'

Daniel said, handing it to Peter.

'I don't know if I want to open it,' Peter said.

'Your father spoke to you from beyond the grave to tell you where this was. He left the message in his diary in the library for a reason. Of course you're going to open it.' Daniel nudged Peter.

Peter held the cylinder between his palms and pushed at both ends. A green light emanated from a slit in the centre and scanned his eyes.

The top of the cylinder opened to reveal a small golden memory stick, sitting snugly in an indentation in the centre of its white interior. Peter removed it and examined it.

'What do you think is stored on it?' Emily said.

'Let's find out,' Peter said, and removed his phone from his pocket. He inserted the memory stick into the USB outlet in the side and watched the screen light up with an instruction.

`Enter password`

'Try "Peter",' Daniel said.

Peter entered the word into the keyboard on his phone.

`Password incorrect`

'Try "Marduk",' Emily said.

Peter entered the word 'Marduk'. A small egg timer appeared in the centre of the screen and everyone waited in silence as the phone displayed the contents of the device.

A printed document appeared on the screen.

'Queen Puabi – DNA Analysis Results' was printed at the top of the document followed by a series of images showing DNA sequences.

Emily looked at the images. 'Those last sets of DNA

361

sequences are quite like ours. But much, much older,' she said and pointed to the image at the bottom of the document. 'Queen Puabi, do you know who she is?' Emily asked Daniel.

'Well, yes,' he said. 'Puabi's remains were found in a tomb in Iraq during the 1920s. Around the same time as Tutankhamun's tomb was found in Egypt. As far as I can remember, the National History Museum in London did a forensic analysis of her remains. They think she was about forty when she died. It was items in her tomb that suggested she was a queen. Perhaps even a nin. The word "nin" is the Sumerian word for goddess. Or to be more precise a demigod who was the product of the Nephilim's interactions with humans on Earth. It's thought that a new analysis of her DNA would show those genes the Nephilim kept from humanity,' Daniel said.

'So this is a DNA analysis of an ancient mummy that proves the Nephilim exist!' Emily said.

'Yes, and considering the fact they removed any evidence of their existence from the pyramids and increased security in the Antarctic, it's perhaps the only evidence we'll ever have that they truly exist,' Daniel said.

'There's something else,' Peter said, and scanned the other information on the USB. 'There's a message here for you.' Peter frowned at Daniel.

'For me!' Daniel said, his voice tinted with astonishment. 'Let me see it.'

Peter handed his phone to Daniel. The message was in Marcus' handwriting. Daniel read the passage then looked at Peter.

'Did you read it?' Peter was staring at the sky.

'Yeah. But it's—'

'Good. Because now I have to keep a promise and hand it over.'

'Hand it over! Who are you going to give it to?' Daniel said.

'Marduk.' Peter pointed at the sky.

'You can't be serious. This is proof they exist. It may well be the only proof we'll ever have that they exist. Your father meant for you to make this information public. To let people know the truth. That's why he hid it here for you,' Daniel said.

'No, it's not. This is what got him and my mother killed,' Peter said. 'This is how she lured him here. It's how she proved that my father was the Templar Grand Master Nergal was looking for. Marduk told me everything. How he had received information, detailing how a group of ancient alien conspiracy theorists had won a legal appeal to have DNA tests performed on the mummified remains of a Nephilim discovered on Earth, to prove that she had alien genes. So rather than have just any geneticist perform the test, Marduk covertly positioned my father to carry out the research and ensure the results could not prove the Nephilim existed. When my father did this for Marduk, it finally proved to Ava and Nergal that he was one of the keepers of Marduk's secrets. From that moment on, Ava had been watching our father's every move, waiting for him to finalise the DNA analysis so that Nergal could plan the rest. Nergal then had one of his allies at Marduk's base infiltrate their communications systems and send my father an encoded message, allegedly from Marduk, saying he wanted to meet him here to discuss how they could cover up the DNA results. It was all an elaborate lure, so that Nergal could begin his quest to destroy his brother and rule humanity. I guess my father must have sensed that Ava was deceiving him in some way and that's why he left this here so that we

363

could keep the knowledge it contained from getting into the wrong hands. You know, my father always said there is wisdom in keeping secrets, and I guess he's right, in particular those secrets that could lead to chaos and destruction if they're revealed at the wrong time,' Peter said, and watched Marduk approach behind Daniel.

'Thank you for keeping your promise,' Marduk said. He extended his hand to Daniel, who reluctantly handed over the memory stick.

'I know that you would like to enlighten humanity about the truth of their creation and our existence, and I can assure you that time will come soon. The time of the crossing, the time when our home planet is accessible from Earth, is once again drawing near. Soon my father will return and his promise to me to enlighten humanity will be fulfilled. So Daniel O'Brien, I will ask you only to keep the secret of my existence for another couple of years. By then the path to Nibiru will once again be open and humanity will learn the truth.'

Daniel swallowed hard and nodded in agreement. Who was he to argue with a son of God?

Marduk turned to Peter. 'Your sister and the astrophysicist finally surrendered yesterday. She chose to face judgement with my brother when my father returns. Returning to Earth, she said, was not an option for her.'

Peter nodded in response and grieved in silence for the sister he once knew.

'And what about the second weapon. Has that been secured?' Peter said.

'We are close. Abaddon's wife was also captured yesterday. Although she did not have the second weapon in her possession, Chasid will find out where she has hidden it.' Marduk looked back at his aircraft and nodded at the young

Nephilim who had indicated they needed to leave. 'I must take my leave of you, but remember, if you need anything …'

'Well, there is one thing …' Daniel said as he recalled the message Marcus had left him.

Peter glanced in his uncle's direction, knowing full well what was coming next.

'You see there's a message on that memory stick for me and I was wondering …'

'Daniel O'Brien, I know you have already seen and memorised the message, have you not?' Marduk said.

'Well yes,' Daniel said. He watched Marduk walk toward his aircraft, then stop at the bottom of the stairs and turn back to Daniel.

'You know, they were here long before we were. We have searched for traces of their existence, just as you have searched for traces of ours, but we found very little concrete evidence to prove where they travelled to after they left Earth,' Marduk said as he climbed the stairs into his aircraft.

The trio stood and watched as the aircraft door closed and Marduk disappeared out of view.

'He let you keep the aircraft you brought us home in, didn't he?' Daniel said to Peter.

'Yes, he did,' Peter said.

'Can I borrow it? It does fly itself, doesn't it?'

'Not exactly, and anyway where would you go?'

'Didn't you hear what he just said? They were here on Earth before the Nephilim came here.'

'Who?'

'Atlantis. The Atlanteans. The verse on the memory

stick is about Atlantis. The land of youth. And there was a set of coordinates as well. Longitude and latitude.' Daniel rummaged in his satchel.

'We should go,' Emily said. 'It's getting late and it'll be dark soon.'

'Agreed,' Peter said, walking toward the car.

'Maybe after the baby is born we could ...' Daniel said, following them.

'Or maybe never,' Emily said as she got into the car.

Daniel sat into the back seat behind her. 'You can drive,' he said. He held his keys out to Peter, who sat into the driver's seat.

'Thanks,' Peter said, and winked at Emily.

'You know, the verse your father left is part of an ancient Irish folk story over two thousand years old. It's about a king who once lived in Ireland, who watched his son leave with a mysterious golden-haired maiden to a land where there was no death nor old age nor any breach of the law. Marcus and I had often talked about Atlantis. You know evidence does point to its location as being off the west coast of Ireland. And I was right about the Nephilim, was I not?' Daniel said, and threw Peter a knowing glance.

Peter turned the key in the ignition and eyed his uncle in the rear-view mirror.

'We could take a flight after the baby's born. But only to take a look around. If you want to do any digging, you're on your own.' Peter said, and pushed gently on the accelerator as his uncle pulled a notebook and a pen from inside his satchel and wrote down the message Marcus had left him.

The Wisdom of Secrets

For Daniel:

A land of youth,
A land of rest,
A land from sorrow free,
It lies far off in the golden west,
On the verge of the Azure Sea.
In my swift canoe,
Of crystal bright,
That n'er met mortal view,
We shall reach its halls,
'ere the evening falls,
In my strong and swift canoe.

THE END

Made in the USA
Middletown, DE
13 February 2018